FIC   Matthews, Greg.

One true thing

$18.95

DATE			

ONE TRUE THING

ALSO BY GREG MATTHEWS

The Further Adventures of Huckleberry Finn
Heart of the Country
Little Red Rooster
The Gold Flake Hydrant

ONE
TRUE
THING

Greg Matthews

GROVE WEIDENFELD
New York

Published by Grove Weidenfeld
A division of Wheatland Corporation
841 Broadway
New York, NY 10003-4793

Published in Canada by General Publishing Company, Ltd.

Library of Congress Cataloging-in-Publication Data

Matthews, Greg.
   One true thing / Greg Matthews.—1st ed.
      p.   cm.
   ISBN 0-8021-1150-5 (alk. paper)
   I. Title.
PR9619.3.M317054   1989
823—dc20   89-33016
                                            CIP

Manufactured in the United States of America

Printed on acid-free paper

Designed by Irving Perkins Associates

First Edition 1989

1   3   5   7   9   10   8   6   4   2

For Brenda

CONTENTS

PART ONE

A Circle of Cones

1

─────────────

L OWELL CAME LATE to the war. In the unexciting months that followed Hiroshima, he realized he needed something to hold on to, some project to ward off boredom. He'd missed his chance for glory, so he'd have to make his mark some other way. Medals on his chest and his picture on the cover of *Life* would have been wonderful, but in real life you had to be practical. Lowell came from Kansas, where nearly everything was practical.

Confined for months on an island of numbing dreariness, Lowell worried about his future. He did not enjoy gambling, was not overfond of his fellow soldiers, and so spent much of his time alone. Lowell's favored spot for solitude was a small, rocky promontory unsuitable for sunbathing, therefore empty. He sat and gazed at nothing by the hour, wondered what he might devote himself to once out of uniform. He was a serious young man, much given to planning ahead, but despite his cogitations no plan was formed. Every thought seemed to be drained from his head by the limitless Pacific. Confronted by so much emptiness, how could a guy concentrate?

One evening at the mess he picked up a book of matches. On its cover was a cactus and these words: *Blue Sky Motel* —

Tucson, Arizona. Lowell liked the shape and feel of the matchbook, and placed it in his pocket before its owner might return. He left the mess and strolled through camp, fingers idly stroking the Blue Sky Motel's free souvenir, aware that something was taking shape in his head. By the time he reached the motor pool it had emerged, a plan from out of nowhere, inspired yet practical. He knew he would do it.

By early 1946 he was back home, eager to begin work on the great project. Callisto already had one motel, an unappealing collection of cabins called the Traveler's Rest. For years few travelers had reason to pass through that part of the country, so the place had failed to prosper. Then, just before Pearl Harbor, the state ran a brand new concrete highway past the town. Things looked set to boom in Callisto, what with all those cars and trucks humming by, and plans were laid for a second motel, maybe even a third, but the war delayed all that, and the Traveler's Rest scooped what it could from the out-of-state traffic until Lowell Kootz came home.

He borrowed his uncle's car and drove around town. Since there was still only the one crummy motel, he could go ahead and tell Uncle Ray what he wanted. Lowell's parents were dead, so Uncle Ray figured large in his life. Uncle Ray was fond of his nephew; he also had plenty of cash and friends at the bank, so when the grand design was revealed, Uncle Ray's friends at the bank agreed to listen.

From the start, Lowell intended that the Thunderbird be no ordinary motel. Something special was needed to pull tourists off the state highway as they sped past to the national parks and scenic spots of the West, something eye-catching, irresistible. It all came down to a question of shape. What is a building? A building is a box. It can be a long box or a wide one; you can stack several or many on top of each other, but they remain boxes. The new motel, Lowell explained, would be a collection of cones; not just cone cones, but tepee cones. The Thunderbird would consist of twenty concrete tepees, each approximately twice the size of the traditional Indian dwelling to allow plenty of room for the beds and bathroom. They would have windows to prevent claustrophobia, and would be arranged in a circle, at the center of which would stand a twenty-first tepee, much larger than the rest. This would be the office, and Lowell's home.

The bankers were at first made nervous by this radical notion. Concrete tepees? Had anyone ever done that before? Lowell assured them no one had, and therein would lie the Thunderbird's appeal, its charm, its allure. People were always on the lookout for something different, weren't they? You bet they were, and now the car-owning population could come find it in Kansas, right here in Callisto. It would put the town on the map, just think of that, and there'd be postcards for the tourists to mail home, too. The totem pole alone would merit its own card. The eyes of the gentlemen from the bank opened even wider. Totem pole? Lowell showed them a picture from a *National Geographic* article on the northwestern tribes. This was what the place needed, a giant concrete totem pole standing straight and tall, the tallest thing around these parts since the grain silos, tall enough to command the world's attention, with all those ugly little critters stacked one atop the other, all those squared-off bears and wolves and such right on up to the top, halfway to the sky, where the final figure would be the Thunderbird himself, some kind of Indian god, Lowell had deduced. There he'd squat, all beak and wings, eyeing the horizon way beyond town, a lightning rod embedded in his skull.

Still the bankers hesitated, and Lowell wheeled in his biggest gun. The totem pole, all eighty feet of it, would be etched with neon tubes of red and blue, yellow, pink and purple, a pole of candy-colored light unlike anything anywhere in the whole world! Dazed, feeling other than their usual staid selves, the bankers reached for their pens. There was a visionary among them, and they could not deny him.

And so the Thunderbird was born. An architect was hired to transpose Lowell's genius to blueprints, and an engineer who specialized in concrete structures figured out a way to pour hollow concrete cones. The pole would be cast in sections, like massive sewer pipes, and fitted down over a central core of steel to give it strength in case a tornado came through. A local carpenter with an artistic bent was contracted to produce the molds from which would emerge the totem pole's vertical bestiary. Building began. The mayor came down to the site at Twelfth and Locust to initiate the first turning of the earth. The Callisto *Prairie Gazette* made it front-page news. Through the summer the concrete mixers churned and poured, churned and poured their contents into conical wooden molds, forming the tapered shells that Lowell hoped would harbor paying guests before winter.

Every day he was there, consulting, advising, supervising. He fretted as fall approached and work had yet to begin on the raising of the totem pole. It was October before the three sections of long steel pipe that was to be its backbone arrived. The first was sunk thirty feet into the ground, to anchor the pole firmly, then the thing began to rise, each section fitted with its jacket of concrete animal figures before the next was raised, bolted, and welded, and by November it stood tall and gray against taller, grayer skies.

A scaffold was erected about this smokeless chimney, and painters began applying color to the animals, from the bear at its base to the powerfully blunt eagle perched atop the whole, wings spread, talons clenched, as if attempting to haul the entire totem pole up to heaven. As the painters worked their way toward the top, electricians followed in their wake. These men were specialists in neon, and they laced the wolf and deer and fish with tubing until the pole resembled a tree festooned with clinging jungle vines. By Thanksgiving it was done, and the painters moved to safer ground, began to cover the concrete tepees with horses and buffalo and braves and assorted squiggles and zigzags, all rendered in bright pigments unknown to the inhabitants of true tepees. They covered the twenty smaller units, then tackled the office-cum-dwelling of the manager. And finally it was done.

The Thunderbird became front-page news all over again one week before Christmas. The mayor returned and snipped a ribbon; the *Gazette*'s camera flashed. One of the big Topeka papers had sent a photographer, too. Lowell's dream had been made real. He was the newest and youngest manager of anything in town, probably in the whole of Callisto County, and already the most famous. He moved into the big tepee and waited for the world to come to his door.

Come it did. The tepees were filled almost immediately by a stream of traffic from the state highway, directed to Twelfth and Locust by billboards placed at regular intervals for ten miles either side of town. Relatives visiting their kin for the festive season stayed at the Thunderbird rather than on sofas and foldaway cots. Lowell had to turn away many potential customers clear through till New Year's. He really should've built forty tepees, not twenty.

At the end of each day a switch was thrown and the totem pole blazed with unearthly light, a branchless neon tree. The surrounding tepees lost their daytime colors, were bathed in an eerie radiance, a curious luminosity, brilliant and cheerful, yet somehow disturbing. No one could have guessed it would look that way. Lowell quickly learned to like it, but to many it "wasn't natural," and they reserved their approval of the motel for the daylight hours alone. The Thunderbird was still very much a novelty, invested with a great deal of civic pride. It made the town hall (built in 1907) look a hundred years old. Callisto was proud of the motel, and proud of Lowell for having created it. There was just one thing about the young genius they couldn't figure out, and that was the absence of a wife in Tepee 21. The joke around town was that the big tepee was short one squaw.

7

Uncle Ray introduced his nephew to a number of young ladies, but Lowell was shy. His dates reported a reluctance to talk about anything but the Thunderbird, and while the motel was undeniably a fascinating topic, it was hardly romantic. Even the least demanding of the young ladies found themselves disappointed at Lowell's refusal to discuss matters of a more personal nature. They agreed he was just plain boring. And what normal girl would want to live in a pointy house anyway? She'd probably give birth to pointy-headed children in a place like that. So Lowell, after many a candlelit supper at Callisto's best restaurant, was left alone. Uncle Ray was upset by Lowell's monastic ways and told him so. "I'm too busy for stuff like that," said Lowell, and because his smile was winning and his manner sincere, and because the Thunderbird was proving even more successful than anticipated, Uncle Ray didn't push. Given time, the boy would come around.

The truth was that Lowell was more romantic than anyone could have guessed. Far from being uninterested in matrimony, he was waiting for the day he'd see a woman and fall in love on the spot. It would happen that way for sure, would hit him like a thunderbolt and leave him quaking in his shoes, smitten by the merest glimpse of his wife-to-be. He'd see this girl and they'd be married pronto; what's more, they'd be happy forever and have beautiful babies. It was to be total, absolute LOVE. Anything less wasn't worth it. Lowell wanted the whole ball of wax, you bet, and while the motel prospered he waited to see who the magical girl would be. It was kind of exciting to wake up each morning and wonder if today was to be the day he'd meet her. He supposed she'd be a guest, a girl on her own who came into the office to ask for a tepee. She would falter when she saw him, recognizing him as her future husband, and there would be momentary awkwardness as both parties wondered how to proceed now that their paths had finally crossed. Lowell was sure everything would work out fine. He wondered what kind of clothes she would be wearing, and what kind of car would bring her to him—a Buick, an Oldsmobile, a Cadillac maybe? Today might be the day, today and every day. Lowell had never been in love and had never engaged in sexual intercourse. Lowell Kootz had never so much as held hands in the back row of the Bijou.

When the Thunderbird had been operating for a year and had ceased to be a topic of local conversation, interest in Lowell was revived with the death of Uncle Ray and the passing on of his wealth, a modest fortune, to his nephew. Now Lowell was doubly attractive to the young women of Callisto, and mothers renewed their assault upon the bachelor with invitations to every conceivable social occasion attended by their marriageable daughters. Lowell declined them all, and by so doing created the first of a series of rumors that circulated among the community. The gist of these was as follows: Lowell's private parts had been blown off by a Jap bullet; Lowell had contracted an incurable disease from a geisha girl; and perhaps most odious of all, Lowell had discovered, while in the army, that he liked to watch naked young soldiers in the showers. The object of the rumors remained ignorant of them until the woman in charge of the sheet girls at the Thunderbird (Lowell refused to call them maids, thought this an affectation unworthy of Kansas) came to him at the end of a working day and told him all. She knew he didn't deserve such abuse. She also wished to shake him from his complacence; it really was high time he married. She said her piece and left.

Lowell was distressed. There was nothing peculiar about him, so why did people say there was? Hadn't he put Callisto on the map? Wasn't the Thunderbird in all the newest guidebooks as a sight to see in Kansas, ranking alongside the deepest hand-dug well and the world's largest ball of string? It wasn't fair! He especially resented the implication behind the shower story. Lowell had found group showering in the army an ordeal; only his personal fastidiousness had forced him to join the coarse talkers and towel snappers in their tent of steam and laughter. Something had to be done. Lowell liked to be liked, despite his apparent aloofness. It was intolerable that he should become some kind of laughingstock in his own town solely on account of his idealism. Very well, since nobody knew of his quest (he considered it such, though it involved nothing more dramatic than waiting), he could abandon it without appearing a quitter. If he went ahead and got married to some girl, it would seem to folks that he'd at last come to his senses, not thrown an essential part of his private self out the window. The knowledge that he had in fact quit was something Lowell felt he could live with. It didn't take long to make up his mind. His was a public position and could not be jeopardized by whimsical adherence to a notion that hadn't even paid off. He'd waited a year for Miss Right but she hadn't showed. Enough was enough. He had to be practical.

He also had to tell someone, not about the abandoned quest but about his new, realistic approach to matrimony, his straightforward willingness to wed, the opening of his eyes, so to speak. He decided on Mrs. Winchell, who had told him of the unseemly rumors. If anyone deserved to be the first to hear about his change of heart it was her. Leaving the night manager in charge, Lowell climbed into his Plymouth and drove to a house on Figtree. Mrs. Winchell was at the movies with Mr. Winchell, but Carol Winchell was not. Carol had already seen *The Egg and I* the night before with Lonnie, who worked down at the garage. When Lowell learned Carol's mother was not available, he stared at his feet, unable to decide on his next move. He'd had his mind made up on telling Mrs. Winchell.

"You could come in and wait," offered Carol.

Lowell considered this for several seconds, wondering if maybe Carol was marriage material. The porch light was dim and threw most of its feeble wattage over Lowell rather than Carol.

"How old are you?"

"Huh?"

"How old? In years."

"Sixteen."

"Just tell her I stopped by. It's not important or anything. In fact, don't tell her I came. No, wait . . . she'll worry about it. There's nothing wrong, though, nothing that can't keep."

He stared at Carol, at the door with its Christmas wreath. Warm air was streaming past him into the night.

"You want me to tell her or not?"

"Uh . . . not. No. Don't tell her anything."

"Okay."

"Except that I stopped by. You'd tell her that anyway, I guess."

Carol was confused. This visitor was a very strange person. Lowell removed his hat. "Good night."

" 'Night."

The hat was replaced. Lowell turned away and jumped from the porch to the path without bothering to use the steps. Carol closed the door. If she hadn't known it was Lowell Kootz, she might've called the police or something. Her mom worked for the strangest person.

Lowell drove around town. If only Mrs. Winchell had been home. He had to talk to someone. It began to snow, white flurries swirling and scattering around the yellow streetlamps, halos of excitation set all in a row down Sycamore. Lowell pulled over and parked outside Al's Diner, went in, found a booth, sat, and stared at the table.

"Coffee?"

A waitress was standing beside him.

"Yes, please."

Lowell was never abrupt with waitresses or bus drivers or anyone else who had to deal with the public. He had to deal with the public himself, so he knew how nice it was to be treated with courtesy. While he waited for his coffee, Lowell looked around. He'd never been in Al's Diner before. It didn't appear to be very popular; there were only three other customers distributed about the place. Al's was a very quiet diner, and not very clean, but at least it was warm. Lowell wondered which of the customers would be interested in hearing about his decision to marry. Maybe the one cramming the pie in his mouth, or the one gazing into the mirror behind the counter; maybe the sullen one glowering at his cup. No, none of them. They were all men. The waitress was the only woman in the place. Al himself was the only other person present, visible now and then back in the kitchen, his spatula scraping, scraping at the grill back there. But he was a man, too. It would have to be the waitress.

As she approached him with a steaming cup, Lowell studied her. She was young and slim and although not pretty had a friendly, not unintelligent face. She would be his audience. The pie eater detained her en route to Lowell's table, and in the interim, Lowell's plan for this young woman deepened with remarkable swiftness, surprising even him with its audacity. He very nearly swooned over the table as the plan rooted itself in his skull. He would never dislodge it now; he'd have to go through with it, and why not? It was a plan worthy of the mind whose originality was responsible for the Thunderbird Motel, a plan no one else in Callisto could have dreamed up, and it confirmed what Lowell, for all his outward modesty, had always known: that he was a very unusual person. Only an unusual person could take the kind of step Lowell intended taking. The waitress was again heading for his booth. He took a deep breath.

"Will that be all for you?"

The cup and saucer clattered before him and were still. Aromatic wisps of steam set his nostrils twitching. From the corner of his eye Lowell could see the gingham pattern of her apron. His head was level with the girl's abdomen, disturbingly close to it. If he turned sideways he could bury his face in her belly, a thing he realized he wanted very much to do.

"No. Not all."

"What else can I bring you?"

Lowell still had his hat on. To look at her face he would have to tilt his head far back. He removed the hat and looked up. The waitress inspected the crease left around his head by the hat. She thought he was a very nice-looking young man, despite his worried expression. She liked the way he'd taken his hat off, too; that had obviously been for her benefit. Not many customers at Al's were so polite.

"I'd like . . ."

Her pencil hovered above the little pad in her hand.

"I'd like . . . uh . . ."

"Yes?"

"Like . . . to know what time you get off," gabbled Lowell.

"Get off?"

"Yes."

"Me?"

"Yes."

"Twelve."

"I'll be back then. If that's okay."

"Well . . . I don't know. . . ."

"I'm serious. I'm Lowell Kootz."

"I think I heard that name before."

"I run the Thunderbird Motel."

"Oh, now I know. I saw your picture in the paper."

"So is it okay if I come back at twelve?"

The conversation was taking much too long, in Lowell's opinion. Even granted the element of surprise, she should be responding faster than this. He was Lowell Kootz, after all.

"Well, I guess so. . . . Is this a date, or what?"

"Yes, a date." He stood. "I'll be back at twelve."

"Could you make it a little after? I have to help clean up the place."

"Twelve-thirty?"

"I'll be through by then."

"Good." He edged past her. "Well, be seeing you."

Out from Al's and into the night went Lowell. Only when he'd gone did it become apparent to both parties that he had forgotten to pay for his coffee. Lowell was already half a block away and was reluctant to turn back. He hadn't drunk it anyway. The waitress decided to do something she would not have considered before tonight: instead of pouring the coffee back into the pot, the usual policy at Al's, she would throw it into the sink and pay for it from her own pocket, an investment, as it were, in the young man who had swept through the diner and changed her whole outlook in a matter of minutes. Lowell Kootz! This was her first brush with celebrity. How was it possible that he was interested in a nobody like herself? It was like something out of a movie. She wished she'd worn her good coat to work tonight, not the old one with the droopy lining.

Gripping the wheel, steering against the strong gusts attempting to push his Plymouth across the road, Lowell thought about the plan he'd set in motion tonight. So they thought he liked soldiers, did they? Didn't like the way he kept turning down their daughters, eh? He'd lost something this past hour or so, gone and lost a dream. There wouldn't be any chosen one, no great love, no one and only in his life. It was a big loss, but he'd go ahead and compensate for it not by doing what everyone wanted him to, nossir, but by doing what they didn't expect him to. Lowell Kootz and a waitress? He'd love to see their faces when word got around. He would do it to them, do it in spades, and if they didn't like it everyone in Callisto could just go right down to hell.

2

EVEN BEFORE Judith had their son, Lowell knew he'd made a big mistake. Thumbing his nose had been satisfying at the time, but now he was paying for it. Callisto made him eat that thumb and eat it good. Everybody knew he'd done what he did deliberately to make regular folk cluck their tongues and shake their heads; it was clear as a September day. Calculated recklessness was what it was, and no good would come of it.

By the standards of the county Lowell Kootz had been more than well off, primed for respectability and a seat on the council before too long, and look what he'd gone and done with his prospects. Judith Altic was a nice girl, but silver spoons and greasy spoons couldn't be expected to lie down in the same cutlery drawer in a snug fit. It hadn't even been some kind of peculiar love match, not that anyone could see; he'd simply crooked his finger at the girl and she'd followed him to a wedding. Plainly, she was as puzzled as everyone else by Lowell's act, but had shown a brave face even when he took her to the registry office instead of a church. Those hands that had served up hash browns and burgers and pie now had a ring, but only a single band, not the usual tandem of engagement and wedding ring both. Such haste generally meant one thing, but Judith hadn't begun to swell until about ten months later, at about the time Lowell realized he'd done something foolish. He had a wife he didn't want.

It was bad enough having to share his home with someone unlike himself, bad enough to know the town thought him a fool, worse still to have to admit they were right, but then came the child. Nothing could better tighten the injudicious bond between himself and Judith. A door, massive, immovable, closed upon his future. He could not define the limitations imposed on him by this marriage. Having abandoned the ideal for the actual, he found he did not want other women, knew they would prove every bit as irksome as his wife. And he did not want to move elsewhere. Callisto, or at least the Thunderbird, was home, managing the concrete tepees still his passion. No, he simply wanted to be unmarried, to reverse time, unmake his foolish choice, walk into Al's diner and drink his coffee, pay for it, and leave, a free man.

Lowell kept all this to himself. It would have been unmanly to reveal his misery. In Kansas, when you made a decision you lived with it; car, house, job, wife—when you got the one you wanted you figured on being around it for a long, long while. That was the way of things, and if it didn't work out the way you planned, you hunkered down and made the best of it, even if you were Lowell Kootz.

Judith, a virgin when she married, had nothing to compare with her husband's lovemaking. She suspected his first approach should have been sooner than three weeks after the wedding, and was also faintly suspicious of the tally since: surely once a month was less than normal. Then again, she wasn't at all sure she wanted to do it more often than that; it wasn't, after all, very enjoyable, all that weight pressing down on her and that hot breath in her ear. But you had to do it to get babies. In the end that was what marriage was all about—building a family. She hoped she

16

would be happier when there were children about the place.

Both parents wanted a boy, and mutual satisfaction with what was born made their lives a little more congenial. They had accomplished something together, and that meant their marriage was, for the moment, worthwhile. Lowell's contentment dimmed before Judith's, eroded by the baby's never-ending need for cosseting of one kind or another, its insistent squalling, and the never-quite-rid-of stink of babyshit. In no way involved with the day-to-day care of his son, Lowell saw him as an intruder in his life, rather like his wife. Lowell's contribution, apart from siring the boy, was to name him after his departed uncle, and so Callisto was graced with another Ray Kootz. To distinguish him from the dead man, the baby was referred to as Little Ray.

Domestic matters remained in this mode for seven years. Life at the Thunderbird was in no way remarkable, and Lowell's impromptu misalliance gradually was deemed by the community, as well as by the Kootzes, to be pretty much your regular humdrum marriage, not all that different from anyone else's. The motel continued to prosper, and Lowell's family continued to live in the big tepee, despite Judith's pleas for a regular home with a front and back yard and rooms with straight walls. Lowell said he'd do it if the family got any bigger, but it did not, largely because of his marital neglect. Judith could not decide whether he ignored her because his distaste for sex had increased with age or because he really didn't want to move out of his conical brainchild. Either way it was insulting.

Little Ray became Fat Little Ray, Heavy Little Ray, Ten-Ton Ray, and then he was lifted no more, became Shootin'-Up Ray, Watch'm-Grow Ray, and Stringbean Ray, eventually plain old Ray, crewcut, blue-jeaned Ray, just another kid on the block. He went to school, made average grades, was more or less happy. He had never been out of town, saw the rest of the country and world through the distorted lens of Hollywood. This was America, he learned, and way over on the other side of the planet was Russia, a terrible place where the people were all slaves and had nothing to eat and no shoes because the rulers of the country were evil men who intended taking over the entire earth until everyplace was like Russia. That was called Communism, and it was generally accepted that just as his father's generation had gone away to fight Japs and Krauts, Ray would one day have to go and fight Commies. Ray wasn't worried; he'd seen the enemy demolished time after time at the Saturday matinee; American guts was all you needed. Cocooned in a comic book world, wholly convinced of the nation's greatness and invulnerability, Ray led his small existence, undisturbed by whatever reality might lie beyond the flat horizons of Kansas. The Stars and Stripes were upheld by Superman himself; the TV told him so each week, in true-blue black-and-white.

In 1959 the narrow line Lowell had walked for so long, the line separating duty from self-need, led him straight off a cliff. He went into a supermarket to buy groceries, Judith having declared herself unwell that day. Passing by the canned meats, he saw a young woman steering a wire cart, a shopper among dozens also steering wire carts, but this woman was different. Lowell stared at her, attempting to define the difference. It certainly was not external; neither her face nor her dress could be called extraordinary. She was attractive, but not in any remarkable way; why was he compelled to stare? And she noticed. He turned away, hurried his cart with its clumsy castors down the aisle, turned left at the produce section, slammed into another cart pusher, apologized, wheeled on, turned several more corners, and found himself face to face with the woman again, among the cereals this time. They approached each other slowly, carts trundling before them like medieval battle wagons. A youth replenishing the shelves had blocked one half of the aisle; they could not pass each other by, yet neither halted to grant the other passage through the gap. Their wire snouts kissed with a muted clang.

Accustomed to limited sexual attention from her husband, Judith was not at first aware he had deserted her side of the bed for good. It was only when she realized she literally could not remember the last time intercourse had occurred that she began to worry. Lowell was still a young man, and she had kept her figure, so why was he no longer interested in the marital act? She assumed boredom could not be the cause, since boredom was by her definition the result of overindulgence in something—too much of a good thing. That certainly was not the case here, neither the too much nor the good thing. It was not pleasure she missed, never having truly known it, but the habit—the regular, if infrequent, mountings decreed by nature and God to be a necessary part of marriage. Something was wrong. Something unspoken ran around the curved, inward-leaning walls, hovered above the bed, a mystery trapped like risen smoke at the apex of the Kootzes' pointed home.

She asked him outright. He told her no, nothing was wrong, and to prove his point Lowell penetrated her briefly that same night, a miserable experience for them both. Afterward he wept. Her husband wept! It couldn't be money trouble; the Thunderbird was doing well. It had to be a woman. Why else had Ray taken to wearing expensive alligator boots and string ties? More outright questioning was met with fervent denial, followed by more weeping, followed by the confession, which, although expected by then, proved no less a shock to her. Judith sat on the edge of their bed, betrayal chanting its old song in her ears.

Now that the truth was out, she had to know the next-most-important thing: did anyone else know? He assured her the affair was secret. The woman lived in a rented farmhouse outside town, was a painter of calendar scenes who specialized in rusting windmills and dilapidated barns and was also pretty good at clouds. He always parked his car inside her own dilapidated barn for fear of discovery. Afternoon liaisons had been the rule. Judith was appalled. Somehow the notion of Lowell engaging in sexual activity during the daylight hours made it all the more horrible; and whoever heard of a woman making a living from painting calendar pictures? "How much do you pay her?" was her unwise reaction to this train of thought, and it provoked in Lowell a startling response. He stopped apologizing and began to pack a suitcase, his face suddenly gone hard.

Ray's bedroom was a cone at the top of the tepee. The room's diameter was just fifteen feet at floor level, and Ray had to keep his clothes and toys in low chests of drawers, the slope of the walls precluding a closet. His bed lay in the exact center; when he lay down to sleep, the tepee's peak was directly above his navel. Sound traveled upward via the winding staircase with surprising clarity if doors were left open in the rooms below. Ray heard their argument from the beginning, without understanding it. Who was this lady they were yelling about, this Marjorie? He went downstairs to investigate, and his appearance at their bedroom door made his parents pause. With his tousled hair and rumpled pajamas, the boy needed only a teddy bear dangling from his hand to be representative of childhood at its most innocent and appealing. Lowell and Judith were unable to continue in his presence. Ray could see the half-filled suitcase on the bed. "What's that for?" he demanded, and the hastily conjured explanation (the suitcase was being unpacked, not packed—no reason given for its packed state to begin with) not only soothed Ray's confusion, it prompted the rapid emptying of the case by Judith to convince her son the answer was true, and to let her husband know he was not leaving the tepee tonight. Ray returned to his bed. The argument downstairs, robbed of momentum by his intrusion, was postponed.

Morning light brought these resolutions: Lowell would not leave home; he would tell Marjorie (by telephone) their affair was over; he wouldn't do it again. Lowell was relieved to have his waywardness curbed; the sheer sexual enjoyment of it had made him feel guilty; now he could feel comfortable with his unsatisfying love life again. Marjorie left town. She'd completed her artwork in any case and had been wondering how best to break the news of her departure to Lowell, who, for all his country-boy charm, was very old-fashioned; he would not have been happy to be dumped by a woman. Now the problem was solved. With Marjorie gone, tranquillity of an apathetic domestic kind was restored at the Thunderbird.

When Ray was thirteen he saw something bad. The whole country had been on edge for days, waiting to see if the Russkies would pull their missiles out of Cuba. The president sat with his finger poised over the big red button everyone knew he kept in a special drawer in his Oval Office desk. He was running out of patience with that big fat Commie Khrushchev. It was all anyone could talk about, and it was hard to sleep at night, waiting for the rumble of the bombers across the sky, the thunder of ICBMs dragging their tails of flame into the stratosphere. Several people in town had begun digging fallout shelters. It was the most exciting time Ray could recall, and one brisk evening, the crisis still unresolved, he left the tepee to go visit his friend Bernie Swenson and discuss the end of the world. But halfway there, on Eighteenth Street, he was delayed.

At first all he noticed was the car, parked like dozens of others beneath the elms that shaded them through summer and pasted them with leaves at summer's end. It was a brand new Lincoln, shining white, just like the one Lowell had bought himself last month. Two white Lincolns in a town the size of Callisto had grown to would not have been so very unusual, but Ray knew almost as soon as he saw it that this white Lincoln was his dad's. What was it doing parked on Eighteenth Street? He crossed over to take a look at the license plate, to make sure it really was Lowell's car. When he was halfway across, but still behind the Lincoln, a match flared briefly inside. So it wasn't his dad's car after all; Lowell didn't smoke. Ray went on over anyway, since the Lincoln lay in the direction of Bernie's house. In passing, he glanced at the plate. His dad's. Ray stopped dead on the sidewalk. Someone had stolen Lowell's Lincoln, had parked it here, and was casually smoking a cigarette before driving away into the night. He had to get a cop before the car was lost forever. But then he heard the voices within, and one of them was Lowell's.

The curbside window was cranked down a few inches to let the cigarette smoke out, and the conversation came to Ray as if spoken in the same room as himself, a conversation between Lowell and a woman. Ray squatted by the back wheel in case they should look over their shoulders and see him standing there. He was appalled at his willingness to eavesdrop, doubly appalled that Lowell had given him cause.

"You have to be firm," said the woman. "You're not firm, you get walked all over. Firmness is what counts, the only thing. You have to be firm."

"I know."

"Some people can't be reasoned with, not face to face with logic. They just don't respond. Firmness is all they respond to, am I right?"

They were talking about the missile crisis, that much was clear to Ray, and relief swept through him.

"Right," said Lowell.

"You're agreeing with me?" The woman sounded querulous, like the head of a debating team grown impatient with the opposition, but what argument could there possibly be over the missile crisis? There was only one way to handle the Russians, and Kennedy was doing it. Why was his dad so slow to answer?

"I already said so."

"Good. I'm glad you agree."

"Would you mind laying off just a little. I'm not in the mood."

"You're going to have to get in the mood. You won't be firm if you're not in the mood. You'll get nowhere that way. I'm only saying this because I want it to work out, you know that."

"I know."

A pause, during which Ray felt a numbness creep through his cramped legs. Another, more insidious numbness invaded his thoughts. Lowell said nothing for the longest while. The woman's cigarette spun in a red arc from the window and fizzled against damp leaves. Less than half had been smoked.

"So when are you going to do it?"

"When I'm ready."

"There's nothing to stop you doing it tonight. Just go ahead and tell her."

"When I'm ready, I said."

"And when'll that be?"

"Dammit, Ellen . . . !"

"Just tell her, and quit putting it off any more."

"I will. It's not as easy as you think."

"I'm not saying it's easy. I'm just saying go do it. It won't be any easier next week or next month or next year. Be firm with her. Be firm with yourself. I'm not waiting forever, Lowell."

"No one's asking you to."

"You can take me home now."

The ignition key was engaged. Lowell's Lincoln pulled smoothly away from the curb, leaving its tracks in the pulped leaves. A shower of drops loosened by wind fell from the defoliated boughs above Ray's head, pattered across his hair and shoulders, a tiny squall, his alone. He prayed for bombs, for missiles, a storm of incandescent fire to erase Callisto. Ray wanted wrath by the megaton to incinerate the white Lincoln, reduce the traitor behind the wheel to hot ash. The taillights already were passing from sight, turning the corner onto Bixby Street, twin coals in the dark. Ray stood and allowed blood free passage to his legs again. His lower body hummed and tingled with returning sensation, and his head pulsed with a redness that somehow was cool. Bernie Swenson's house was not visited that night.

Long after the Cuban missile crisis had passed from the headlines, Ray waited for an explanation of the Eighteenth Street incident, some clue to the motive behind his father's betrayal. He watched his parents. They seemed to get along. Where were the fights that would have given Lowell a reason to do what he did? Ray thought his mom was a pretty nice person, and not fat or ugly or anything, so why did his dad go behind her back to fool around that way? And what had become of Lowell's promise to cigarette-smoking Ellen? There was no evidence that Judith had ever been informed of his two-timing. It was a mystery. Ray became suspicious of every female guest at the Thunderbird; any one of them might be seducing his father, stealing him away. Or was Lowell the seducer? Ray didn't know enough about men and women to understand how the whole thing worked. He knew what went where, and why, thanks to a book solemnly presented to him on his thirteenth birthday, but the emotional bonds between adults of the opposite sex remained unfathomable. Why weren't they nice to each other? Why was it necessary to have secrets? When would the truth come out and bring the tepee down around their ears? It was intolerable, this waiting for enlightenment. Why had his dad gone and jeopardized Ray's world? It was just the shittiest thing, almost impossible to forgive—unless the incident had been a case of temporary insanity. That must be it. Judith didn't know about Ellen because Lowell had broken his promise to Ellen because Lowell didn't like her any more (Ellen, that is), and so he didn't have to keep his promise to spill the beans to Judith, and he wasn't seeing Ellen any more either, now that his temporary insanity had passed, and that was another good reason not to tell Judith anything, because what she didn't know could never hurt her. It was all in the past! Dad was sane again, and could be forgiven.

Elated, Ray walked around the motel's circular parking lot, looking at the sedans and coupes and convertibles, the station wagons and pickups. To examine their plates was always rewarding. He wondered if he would ever see those distant states. It wouldn't matter if he didn't; he'd stay right here and run the good old T-bird like his father did. Or maybe not. Maybe he'd work in the new chemical fertilizer plant. No, that'd stink. He'd work in the munitions plant instead, fifteen miles outside of town. They made good money out there, danger money, because the whole place could blow sky high any minute and take half the goddamn county with it. Come to think of it, he'd definitely take over the motel and continue the family business. It was the least he could do for his terrific dad. The old man had gone and dragged his tail in the mud for a little while, but now everything was okay again.

Having granted absolution, Ray was filled with majesty, with power, felt he could sweep away these clustered autos to a parking lot on the moon's far side with a wave of his hand. They were lumps of metal, irrelevancies, in no way comparable with or connected to the gustings of emotion that spun him from one vehicle to the next around a perimeter of license plates and rear bumpers, spun him finally to the base of the neon totem pole at the center of everything. It rose above him, tubes buzzing with polychromatic flagrancy, candy cane offerings to voltaic gods. This was his home. This was where he belonged, himself and his dad, big chief and chief-to-be.

At fifteen Ray was asked what he wanted to be when he grew up. "I wanna run the T-bird," he said. Lowell didn't know if this was a good thing. The motel gave him a pretty fair living, but the challenge had been in the building of it, not the everyday renting of rooms ever since. Where was the challenge to Ray? Any bozo with average intelligence could run an established business that saw few fluctuations in trade. He had to admit he was a little disappointed at the boy's response. He supposed it was intended to be a compliment of the chip-off-the-old-block kind, but really he would've been better pleased if Ray had said he wanted to go to college and become a doctor or lawyer or scientist. Lowell's own scholastic record had been distinctly average; he wanted more for and from his son. The idea behind the American dream was to get richer, generation by generation, wasn't it? By not wanting to be a professional man, Ray abdicated his role in the dream, wanted simply to stand still while his father wished him onward and upward. Lowell decided to wait another year before tackling the subject of Ray's future again.

But the plan was not to be. On a crisp night in September Lowell's white Lincoln left the road at sixty miles an hour and began plowing through a field of unharvested corn. The stalks were dry and the Lincoln's grille mowed them down with exhilarating ease, produced a staccato snapping and crackling that kept Lowell's foot planted firmly on the accelerator. He was very drunk, loved the detour his car had made, and decided to harvest the crop there and then. The Lincoln smashed a meandering path through the stands of corn, its path dictated by Lowell's minimal control of the wheel. It spun in circles, it laid a chain of figure eights, it slewed sideways into the tightest loops and crossed its own flattened path many times. Lowell howled with happiness and excitation. His passenger, equally drunk, howled along with him, and the moon, full and round as an uncut cheese, skittered crazily across the sky. Swerving in pursuit of unmolested corn, Lowell spotted a clump remaining impudently upright. His Lincoln chased bucking headlights toward it. Down went the clashing stand in an instant, and the Lincoln launched itself across a drainage ditch of considerable width and depth. It was airborne for the briefest of moments, then hit the far wall of sloping earth. Lowell was impaled on the steering column, breath and life expunged before he was even aware there were no more cornstalks dancing before him. His passenger sped on through the windshield, where most of her face remained; she died seconds later, ears filled with the sound of the Lincoln's horn, stuck at full blast by Lowell's crushed ribs.

It was hard to live down, Ray found. No one wants his father to die drunk, especially when accompanied by a strange woman. It wasn't even the Ellen of two years back; her name was Hazel Prewitt and she worked at the five-and-dime over in Butane. But if Ray was embarrassed, Judith was mortified. Through the days preceding her husband's burial she shed not one tear in public, remained at all times calm, polite, very much in control of herself. She did not clip from the Callisto *Prairie Gazette* the article giving the details of the accident, since this included the other woman's name. After the funeral she collected every item of Lowell's clothing and sent it down to the Salvation Army thrift store. Not a shoelace or cufflink remained. She then turned the tepee upside down in an effort to locate the secret diary she knew he kept, the one recording his affairs with sluts like Hazel Prewitt. Judith knew it would be crammed with names, possibly even with comments; nothing was too bizarre, too perverted for Lowell Kootz. The diary remained stubbornly hidden.

Her hatred's intensity was frightening, even to Judith. Once-wronged, she had been lenient, but twice-wronged and beyond, she found that her ability to forgive lay dormant, frozen. She moved about the place like a robot, mobile yet inflexible, capable of fulfilling her simple duties without comprehending why she continued to do so; shouldn't she be weeping and gnashing her teeth instead? She ignored her son, saw in his face the lineaments of his disgraced father.

When Ray's school grades plummeted in the aftermath of Lowell's death, Judith ignored this also. From being among the top percentile of his class, Ray sagged to the lower end of the scale, with the appearance of being content to do so. What need of straight As when all he'd have to do at the T-bird was collect the cash and pass out keys? He still wanted to be manager. His dad had made the Kootzes look like fools, and Ray had difficulty finding forgiveness within himself this time around. In Kansas you didn't give second chances. Lowell's name would not be mentioned again, but the motel, his brainchild, was a whole different animal. Ray was perfectly willing to step into those empty alligator boots and keep the dream rolling right along.

Because his future was taken care of, Ray began separating himself from the few friends he'd made at Callisto High. He regarded them as no more than kids; most of them didn't even know what they intended doing with their lives, the dopes. Even Bernie Swenson, who had not been among the many who kidded Ray about his father's bimbo, was avoided for a while. Then loneliness set in and Ray began repairing bridges, but he still would not crack his books the way he used to. Ray was marking time, intended doing so for the next few years until he could quit school and enter the real world. It suited him to be that way, and Judith seemed not to care less if he had a D average. Like the sheet girls, he was just part of the regular human landscape around the place.

3

CHANGES CAME to the Thunderbird. Its business was conducted in the usual way, but in the big tepee a subtle game was played between mother and son. The rules were simple: You ignore me and I'll ignore you; first one to crave affection or acknowledgment from the other loses. Ray was aware of the game (and artful in its pursuit) for quite some time before he asked himself why it was being played at all. His mom had never been very affectionate toward him, it was true, but he wasn't aware of ever having felt the lack, had simply accepted the little that was offered and considered it adequate, the norm for all families. His dad hadn't been all that palsy-walsy with him either, but he'd never questioned that; guys didn't make a big deal out of knowing each other after all. He'd always assumed that Judith observed the distance between the two males and followed suit, taking instruction from them. That was what Ray thought before Lowell mowed the cornfield, but now he wasn't so sure. Things between himself and Judith had definitely changed, and he wondered if it was a natural extension of the coolness she'd always shown, or a deliberate attempt to make him feel bad. But what had he done to deserve it? Nothing, that's what, and if she was pissed at him about something she could damn well tell him, or else he'd keep on playing the game for as long as she wanted; it made no difference to him. He was Ray Kootz, son and heir of the man who built the Thunderbird. He had only to wait to get what was coming to him, and young as he was he had plenty of time for the waiting, a whole bunch of time. All those other geeks at school had to worry about their grades, had to worry about how their parents would react when they saw those Cs and Ds, but not Ray, nossir; Ray was sitting pretty.

Judith, formerly a reasonable cook, now relinquished all pretense at interest in the culinary arts, instead stocked her refrigerator with TV dinners. Ray approved, although he sometimes demanded money for a burger downtown, just for variety. His friends envied him his problem-free existence, wished their moms were as distant as Ray's, their dads conveniently dead. Ray let it be known he didn't give a shit about anything. His old lady went and bought him a car when he was old enough for a license, only secondhand but it ran okay, and she picked up the tab for the registration and insurance without even being asked. Ray didn't have to work after school at the supermarket or mow lawns to get gas money, just had to go ask for it. Ray Kootz had it made.

But there was a darker side to his life of ease and nonaccomplishment. Girls didn't like him, and this was a powerful deterrent to the happiness that should have been his. He considered himself reasonable-looking, with no more than the average seventeen-year-old's facial fungus, and the car was a big plus, but despite his wheels he couldn't score. He seriously thought he must have bad breath, gargled mouthwash by the gallon, noted no change in his chaste condition, and so assaulted his armpits with a battery of unguents and sprays. Still no change. He combed his hair forward in the English style and let it grow till he could barely see through the bangs hanging in his eyes. Nothing. Ray couldn't figure it out, and became resentful of females for their indifference. The stupid bitches didn't know what they were missing. The burden of his virginity slowed him down, dragged at his gangling frame, pushed a thorn deep into his pride.

One by one his buddies let fall the big news that their girl finally went all the way last night. Ray suspected some of them were lying, but their claims could neither be proved nor disproved, and when the number of ex-virgins of his acquaintance began to outnumber the cherries, he made his decision and told a lie. His willing partner, he said, had been one of the sheet girls at the Thunderbird. They'd done it in the back seat of his Ford, out by the river, no big deal. No one called his bluff. Now Ray was truly one of the boys, had joined the club, the pussy club, and now was allowed, if not obliged, to talk loudly and disparagingly of women, in particular their physical shortcomings. No girl could enter Pancho's Pizza without running the gauntlet of remarks from Kootz and Company. Sue Ann Mobley had no tits; Betty Schlotnik (*Slot*nik, ha, ha!) had legs as bowed as a cowboy's; Angie Taylor had a butt like two pit bulls in a sack, a real dog, ha, ha! And every comment, every verbal crudity ate at Ray's insides, confirmed his worthlessness and undesirability, stacked his resentment high as a Kansas grain elevator. He would've given fifty bucks to have Sue Ann Mobley talk to him across a cafeteria table; a hundred bucks if only Betty would hold his sweating hand; a thousand bucks, a whole grand, if Angie's lumpy butt could be lowered onto his lap, just to sit there, just sit there for chrissakes, not even wriggle around to give him a hard-on or anything. But these girls and girls of greater and lesser attractiveness gave Ray nothing.

It could not go on. He had to get laid. It was ridiculous that he hadn't yet succeeded in the nooky department, hadn't even gotten to first base, let alone all the way. Things had to change, and fast. He considered hiring the services of a prostitute but didn't know if one could be found in Callisto, certainly couldn't ask around now that it was known he had a steady fuck at the T-bird.

The answer came to him in math. While the rest of the class wrestled with equations, Ray allowed his gaze idly to roam the room, and eventually he fastened upon Ellie Quist, generally recognized as the homeliest girl in school. Her plainness was difficult to qualify; she had no enormous nose or horrific squint, no projecting teeth or matchstick legs; instead, she lacked all emphasis, all presence. Ellie Quist was negligible, no more noticeable than the desk she sat behind, and her nondescript appearance was augmented by a nature so reclusive, so withdrawn as virtually to be absent. Ellie never said anything unless directly addressed, and this did not often happen. Teachers were made impatient by the tininess of her voice ("Speak up, Ellie, so we know what you think") and students by the blandness of her replies ("Gee, I don't know, I guess . . .") and the dumb way she went red, then white if questioned a second time. There had once been a joke that circulated around the school: the only date anyone had ever asked Ellie for was the day and month. It was a feeble joke, lacking the viciousness true slander must have; like Ellie, it was unmemorable, and so fell into disuse. Ellie's dullness might have been forgiven had she been a banker's daughter, but Barney Quist rode the back of a big yellow garbage truck. Ellie must surely be desperate for a boyfriend, reasoned Ray, and began planning his stratagem with a deliberateness that would have surprised and gratified his teachers.

It had to be kept secret, of course. He didn't want to be seen in public with her. Ellie fortunately had no social life, always walked straight home after school. Ray left his Ford in the parking lot and followed her on foot. When they reached Fifteenth Street, he caught up.

"Hey, Ellie!"

She spun around, startled. Ray halted beside her.

"Going home, huh?" was his chosen gambit, rehearsed a number of times in front of a mirror the night before. He knew it was pathetic, but it didn't matter; the girl was only

Ellie Quist. "I'm heading that way, too. Mind if I walk along?"

Ellie shook her head, the briefest of movements, and they proceeded. Ray knew silence would kill this thing stone dead before it ever came alive, so he talked nonstop about the various inconsequentialities that occupy the average student. Ellie occasionally nodded, kept her books clutched tightly across her chest, wore a fixed smile to convey gratitude for Ray's attention. The nearer they drew to Ellie's home on Fourth Street, the more Ray's prattling increased in volume, speed, and triviality, until finally he came to the point. "Listen . . . uh . . . you wanna go see a movie with me tonight?" He knew all the theaters would be nearly empty on a Tuesday; on a Friday or Saturday night they'd be packed with witnesses.

"I don't know. I'd have to ask my dad."

"Sure, okay. Listen, you do that, ask him, and I'll . . . uh . . . give you a call around six-thirty, okay?"

"Okay."

"Well, see ya."

That was mid-September. By early October she allowed his tongue inside her mouth, by October's end his hand inside her bra. In the first week of November he requested a hand job, and by Thanksgiving received one. Ray was working his way toward a Christmas present. Progress had been pretty quick, considering. He assumed Ellie was made cooperative by her desperation for a steady guy. She didn't object when he took her to places no one their own age frequented, saw nothing suspicious in his refusal to introduce her to his friends. Maybe she thought he wanted her company for himself alone, didn't want to share their precious moments together with anyone else. It was crazy, but it might be true. Anything at all could be swimming around inside Ellie's head. Ray was not curious enough to ask, thought raising the subject of Ellie's inner feelings might be a wrong move. Things were going along just fine the way they were. She didn't approach him in the corridors at Callisto High, required neither hand holding nor note passing, seemed not even to need momentary glances. Her connivance in keeping their status as a couple secret was absolute, and Ray was grateful in a grudging kind of way. He played his patient game and kept a Trojan in his pocket.

At the end of an evening spent in Ellie's company Ray could never remember anything she'd said, not that he was interested in retaining any of their conversation, but it was spooky the way her words drifted by him like soap bubbles, popped, became soundless nothings. All he could truly recall was a dumb story about her father, how he hated the new plastic garbage cans, loved the old galvanized metal ones because he could kick and dent them if he thought the owner's house looked too big, too rich, the crazy old fuck. Ray had never met either of Ellie's parents. Ellie always told them she was studying with a girlfriend to cover time spent with Ray. The deception was her own idea. Ray guessed it was because she was ashamed of her mom and dad, which was convenient, but he didn't ask. He spoke as little as possible on their dates nowadays. Talking was a waste of breath. Ellie hardly ever responded, would just nod her head in agreement, whatever he said. Once, apparently trying to make more of an impression on him, she had waited till he gave his opinion on the home team's chances (not that he gave a shit if they won or lost, but he occasionally had to raise a topic of one kind or another to crack the silence), let a moment pass, then nodded her head slowly, wisely. "I think so, too," she said. It was dismal work dating Ellie Quist, but it had to be done.

Ray's Christmas stocking was not filled as anticipated, but for his birthday early in March she at last relented, bullied by accusations of lovelessness. The gift was presented, as had been the gropings that preceded it, in the back seat of Ray's Ford. When it was over he drove her home. His one regret was that he could not brag about losing his cherry, that milestone having been entered in the public record fully ten months before. He'd been seeing Ellie once a week for half a year, a lengthy investment for the few seconds of release at its end. Now he could get rid of her.

In April his mother told him she'd received a phone call while he was out with his friends, a call from a girl; she'd asked for Ray. It could only have been Ellie, and he instantly readied an explanation, but Judith asked for no details. The way she left him alone and minded her own business was very weird, in Ray's opinion. It was kind of disturbing to know his own mother couldn't care less what he did as long as he kept himself out of her hair, but the absence of parental love and concern was a small price to pay for freedom of movement and a total removal of accountability. It was an okay way of life, and now that he was no longer a cherry he could use the confidence gained from his conquest to go get himself a real girlfriend, one who looked less like Ellie Quist and more like Ann-Margret. He had no intention of returning the call. Give Ellie enough silence and she'd get the message.

There were no more phonings to the Thunderbird, but one afternoon Ray found her waiting beside his car in the school parking lot. He was furious but did his best not to show it; there were students passing by, and he wanted them to think this was just a casual encounter. He wasn't going to be seen letting her get into the car with him, though. "Back of the Donut Hole, fifteen minutes," he said, and drove away, circled several blocks to give her time to make the rendezvous, then picked her up and headed for some privacy.

They left Callisto behind, went several miles along a county road, and eventually parked beside a stand of trees along a dirt track. Ray's anger had cooled, but he wanted this to be over with fast. What the fuck did she expect him to do, take her to the prom or something? Ellie sat with her hands in her lap, not looking at him, exasperatingly passive.

"So?" said Ray, to get things moving.

"I have to go away."

"Huh?"

That was another way of saying a girl needed an abortion, wasn't it? Had the rubber split?

"I have to go away next week."

"Next week?"

They only did it a little while back. You couldn't get a rabbit test this soon, could you?

"My dad died."

"Huh?"

"He fell off the back of the garbage truck. A car ran over his head."

"Jesus . . ." said Ray, dizzy with relief.

"My mom says we have to go live in Montana."

"Yeah?"

"Her sister lives up there. In Billings."

"Uh-huh."

Bernie Swenson had been up to Montana with his dad one time. He said it was Kansas with lumps.

"So you're leaving next week already?"

"She's not even waiting for the house to get sold. A real estate agent's going to do it."

"What kinda commission do those guys get? Ten percent? Fifteen?"

"I don't know."

"It's too bad. Why'd he fall off?"

"I don't know."

"Was the rail slippery, or was he drunk, or what?"

"Nobody said."

"That's real tough," offered Ray, then added, "I'm sorry."

This was the word Ellie seemingly had been waiting for. She began to cry, a restrained, hiccuping sound. Ray's Ford had a bench-style front seat, not buckets, so he had no excuse not to slide over and put an arm around her shoulder. Annoyingly, this weakened her further, and she leaned her head against his chest. He could feel her sobbings clear

36

through to his spine. He wanted her to quit, to raise her head, dry her eyes, and ask to be driven home. Instead, she cried all the harder, even grabbed his free hand and squeezed it. Ray fumed quietly and waited for her to exhaust her tears. When this didn't happen, he surprised himself by allowing sympathy to smooth the edges of his irritation. He squeezed her hand in return, even dropped his chin a little and kissed the top of her head. Her crying came jerkily to a stop; her face lifted, presented itself. Ray had gone and opened this can of worms, so now he'd have to eat it. He went ahead resignedly, then found it distracted him, made him feel tender, as if he really did have something to offer this pallid girl, something that it benefitted him to give. It was a disquieting sensation, and he pushed it away; in kissing Ellie he was doing her a favor, that's all. He closed his eyes, felt their mouths sliding over each other like newborns searching for a nonexistent nipple.

Then he wanted to do it, fuck her in the back seat like before. There was no traffic along here, no one to interrupt them, and it was exciting to think of doing it in broad daylight. He twisted himself around, scooped her against him, felt a reciprocal thrusting from Ellie, and knew it could be accomplished without resistance.

On their way back to town Ray felt great. It had been better than the first time, less awkward, with no reluctance at all on Ellie's part. It was almost a shame she was going away, but if she stayed she'd only want to keep on being his girl, probably even want public recognition if they started screwing on a regular basis, and that was out of the question, impossible. With a little luck and planning and smooth talk he could maybe get a few more fucks out of her before she went. He looked across at her unremarkable profile. Nope, not the girl for him. She turned and smiled a wan smile, probably grateful for the sympathetic way he'd handled her crying and all, maybe grateful for the fuck she got, it was hard to say with a person like Ellie.

"Where can I drop you off?"

"I don't care."

Her lack of assertion irritated him all over again, and the faint mellowing toward her that had flickered inside him was gone. A few more fucks, that's all he wanted; what else could she possibly offer him anyway?

"Fourth and Albertson okay?"

She nodded, but Ray was looking away, missed it.

"Huh?"

"Yes."

"How about I pick you up tomorrow night. We could go someplace."

"My mom wants me to stay in. She's been crying all the time."

"Can't you sneak out?"

"I don't know. I don't think so."

"Well, look, the least you can do is try. She got you on a chain or something? You can sneak out if you want. She's not your boss. Do it when she's asleep."

"I don't know. . . ."

"Jesus, will you listen to yourself! 'I don't know, I don't know. . . .' You don't wanna let her run your life just on account of she's feeling bad about your old man."

Ellie hunched her shoulders, stared at her lap. Ray didn't like the peevish expression on her face.

"Listen, you go ahead and leave town without seeing me any more, you go right ahead, see if I care. Just please yourself, okay? Jesus . . ."

"It's just that she wants me there."

"So what? Sneak out like I said. Aaah, forget it, just forget it."

"I do want to see you again."

"Sure, sure. Forget it, okay? Do what Momma wants."

They saw each other twice more, had intercourse three times before Ellie departed for Montana. She cried the last time. Ray was glad she at least waited till after the sex. He patted her shoulder, resisted an urge to turn on the radio. It began to rain, a light drumming on the Ford's roof, a sound Ray always enjoyed. If only Ellie would quit he could listen to the rain and find some music and just sit there and feel good.

"Will you write me? I'll send my new address."

"Okay."

"I'll send it as soon as we find a place, and you can write to my aunt's place before that. We'll be there till we get somewhere of our own. I'll write that down right now. Have you got any paper and a pencil?"

"Fresh out. Don't worry about it, just send me the address when you get there."

"I know my aunt's address by heart."

"I haven't got any goddamn paper. Send it later."

"Could you remember it if I told you?"

"Okay, sure, fire away."

The names, the numbers, all vanished as quickly as they were spoken. Ray deliberately let the sound of the rain drown them in his ears. He thought it'd be great to live in a place with a tin roof. You could really appreciate rain in a place like that. It was the kind of notion he never shared with other guys for fear they'd think him stupid or child-ish.

"I really like that sound."

"What sound?"

"The rain. What other sound is there? Do you hear any other sound right now?"

"I don't know what you mean."

"Who cares."

The drumming became a rumbling as the rainfall strengthened. Ray calmed himself, the better to enjoy it. He wished himself alone. Ellie's presence was incredibly irksome now that their jeans were pulled up, the back seat vacated.

"Can you remember the address?"

"Huh?"

"Can you say it back to me?"

"I'll remember it, don't worry."

"You aren't just saying you'll write and then not do it."

"No."

"You could come see me on vacation."

"Uh-huh."

"You could sleep on the sofa or something. Mom'd let you if I told her ahead of time."

"Does she know about me?"

"No. I won't tell, not unless you want me to."

"Well, I don't. It's none of her business. Don't ever tell her anything, get me?"

Ellie's silence was taken for acquiescence. Ray had the opportunity to enjoy the rain for several uninterrupted minutes. He almost drifted away on the sound.

"Ray?"

"What."

"I'd rather go somewhere else. With you."

"What?"

"Instead of Montana. I don't even like her, my mom. I never have, even before Daddy died. I don't want to live with her any more. It's gonna be awful, I know it."

"No it won't. You'll be okay."

"I won't, I won't, I know it."

"Well, you're just gonna have to like it."

"You won't go away with me?"

"Are you kidding? And do what, exactly? We're in school, for chrissakes. Don't talk so dumb. That really gets me, you know? I'm taking you home."

He reached for the ignition key.

When the first letter came, he tore it up unopened, as he did the second and third. Eventually she called person to person.

"Ray?"

"Yeah."

"Did you get my letters?"

"Yeah."

A silence followed. Ray squirmed, hoping Judith wasn't overhearing any of this.

"What do you think?" asked Ellie.

"About what?"

"About the letters."

"I don't think anything about them," he blurted, hating her for reminding him about those stupid dumb letters. Even the crabbed handwriting on the envelopes had irritated him, begged for erasure, despoilment. "I don't think anything about them and I wish you'd quit writing me, okay? Just quit it!"

Ellie spent a long time digesting this.

"Ray?"

"What."

"I don't think you love me."

"That's right."

There. It was out; the plain truth. She had to know sometime.

"And you don't care about the letters I wrote?"

"I'm sorry, I mean there's no point in even talking about it. Listen, I have to go now."

He waited for permission. That's what it was, he admitted it—permission. From Ellie Quist!

"I said I have to go now."

"Okay."

" 'Bye."

The disconnection came at last, exploded in his impatient ear, made him think of rocket stages separating, one falling away to burn up on re-entry, the other to thrust higher, higher, away from the earth and its women. He hung up. So long and fuck off, baby. Sweat began cooling along his spine.

4

HE FAILED to graduate, didn't attend the proceedings at Callisto High. Ray thought anyone with a cap and gown was a creep. He excluded his buddy Bernie from this category; Bernie had only participated in the ceremony because his old man wanted a picture of him being glad-handed by the principal. Bernie said later the whole thing made him want to barf.

Despite his noninvolvement with graduation day, it was a turning point in Ray's life anyway. When he came down to breakfast next morning he found Judith drinking coffee, the remains of breakfast before her. Ray's side of the table was empty.

"Where's mine?"

"Someplace downtown, I expect."

"Huh?"

"The Cherry Tree does a good breakfast."

"What's happening . . .?"

"Nothing, not in my kitchen. You want breakfast, go buy it."

"Okay, I will. I need five bucks."

"Earn it."

"Huh?"

"Huh? Huh? Huh? Earn it. Look in the want ads."

Ray stared at his mother. Was she crazy?

"I'm not carrying you any more. Go out there and get a job."

"I wanna work here."

"Here?"

"Here, at the T-bird."

"Doing what, making the beds?"

"Management. I'll be in management."

"When I drop dead, then you'll be in management. Meantime, the Thunderbird can't use you. Get yourself a job, Mr. Flunkout."

He was outraged. Why hadn't she warned him this was to be the way of things if he didn't graduate? How come she sprang it on him the way she did? Look at the smile she was trying to keep off her face! His mom was enjoying this, loved seeing him squirm. What a fucking bitch! He felt like crying, could feel the tears itching for release.

"No more breakfast on the table," said Judith. "No more gas money. No burger money either, and I'll expect a little rent from you once you're employed."

"This is bullshit."

"It's called incentive, Raymond. You know about the ant and the grasshopper? Well, my little grasshopper, you can just hop off and work for a living like the rest of us. I mean it."

And she did, Ray could tell. She must really hate him to do this. It was spite and bitchiness because she didn't have a husband and because Lowell had fucked other women. All at once Ray understood and approved of his father's strayings. He bet Judith had been as bitchy to Lowell as she was being to him.

"I'm not staying here."

"Fine."

"I'm moving out."

"Don't use the good suitcases. They're mine."

For five days he held out, was fed by his friends, allowed

to sleep on their sofas and in their garages. He hated it. He'd have to do what Judith wanted and get a job, but he wouldn't bother with all those little boxes in the back pages of the newspaper. The personal touch, that's what he'd use. Who did he know who hired guys? Only Bernie's old man. Rudy Swenson had a landscape gardening business. Bernie worked for him every summer, had often encouraged Ray to join him. Today Ray would consent to do so.

Bernie was happy to have a buddy work alongside him till September, when he'd start college. It was obvious Ray's old lady had gone psycho, pulling a stunt like that. Once Rudy was fully apprised of the situation he offered Ray a back room down at the store, rent free. He'd be a kind of night watchman. There was a camp bed and coffee maker, even a shower stall. The romance of independence was somehow lessened when hedged in by bags of loam and stacks of paving stone, but rent free was rent free, and so he moved his stuff to Swenson's Superior Landscaping. Rudy told him: "No parties. You got a girl, you get her out by seven A.M. except on the weekend, but no parties ever, okay? And keep the place clean." Ray doubted he'd ever bring a girl there. The camp bed was narrow and uninviting, even for a solitary occupant; with a girl he'd have to make out on sacks of Redi-Gro, and only a slut would consent to do that. Ray wanted a nice girl to go steady with. "You bet, Mr. Swenson."

As the summer progressed, it became clear to Bernie and Ray that neither of them was going to get laid. They went everywhere together, to discos, to 3.2 beer joints, to the parties that usually followed. They talked with plenty of girls, even felt a few, but sex, the accomplished act, evaded them.

"Hey, Ray, you still humping that sheet girl at the T-bird?"

"Nah. I wouldn't fuck anyone that worked for my mom."

News of strange lifestyles to the west intrigued them. "In California you can get fucked anytime," said Bernie, "especially in San Francisco. Girls there fuck any guy with long hair. They're practically obligated to do it. They've got this philosophy of free love, so all you gotta do is ask for a fuck and it's yours, so long as you look okay."

They quit visiting the barber. Their ears and necks remained white while their backs tanned down to the beltline in a dozen different Callisto yards. Bernie always figured they'd one day lay down some new turf for a sex maniac who'd invite them inside for an orgy, but it never happened. They dug fishponds and terraced lawns and planted shrubbery, but their lengthening locks and lean brown torsos were admired by not one customer. It was discouraging. They planned on taking Ray's car to the coast before the fall, just to see if the stories about hippie heaven were true. It was hard to picture themselves in bell-bottomed pants and headbands, but if that's what it took, they'd do it. "Carry a flower and they'll eat your dick" was Bernie's succinct prediction. "Hey, maybe they'll really go for us on account of we're from the sunflower state!" But Ray doubted that Kansas would signify exotic allure to anyone.

Two weeks before Bernie's scheduled departure for college they packed a bag each for the big trip to Frisco. Ray's Ford had engine trouble, so Bernie's pickup, a revamped forties Dodge with exhaust pipes that rose on either side of the cabin like a Mack truck's, was to be their chariot on the great nooky quest. They drove to the Interstate and skimmed west across the featureless miles of Kansas, waited for the peaks of Colorado to thrust themselves above that ruler-straight horizon. They drank beer while they drove and threw the empty cans behind them into the truckbed, soon had a fine accumulation clinking and clanking back there. The radio was played full blast, its music spilling out the open windows to scatter notes and hooklines along the highway. Bernie's pickup snorted like a stallion scenting mares, blew prairie winds through high-standing nostrils of chrome, strained westward with its eager riders.

The state line crossed, the mountains at last beneath their chassis, they stopped for more beer outside Denver in the early evening. A summer storm was building ahead, and by the time the fresh carton of brew was installed beside the gearshift the windshield's Kansas dust was being peppered and patterned by Colorado rain. Bernie set the wipers in motion and they rolled on. Now the rain came pelting down, solid sheets of it. Bernie turned on the lights and slowed to fifty. Lightning forked among the peaks; thunder came ambling in its wake, seeming to tumble down the mountains in a landslide of sound. Hunched over the wheel, swearing at the eighteen-wheelers hurtling past on level stretches, Bernie failed to notice the hitchhiker until Ray pointed.

The roadside figure with the uplifted thumb was identifiably female despite the rainsoaked Stetson and loose poncho. Bernie braked so hard the pickup's rear wheels slewed sideways before he could steer across to the shoulder and stop thirty yards beyond her. She started running, flapped toward them like a loose tarpaulin. "She goes in the middle," said Bernie. Ray got out, the girl got in, and Ray followed.

"Thanks," said their passenger, hatbrim shedding rain.

"Don't mention it," said Ray.

Bernie stayed silent for a long moment. He knew you had to establish an enigmatic persona from the start when you met a girl, otherwise you'd blab your guts just to fill in the silences, and girls never screwed motormouths. He'd let Ray be the talker to offset his own cool. The clutch was released and the pickup gathered speed.

"Where you headed?" Bernie finally asked.

"California."

"Us too," said Ray.

"San Francisco?" The girl's face was expectant. She had a great many freckles and her front teeth were crossed.

"Los Angeles," said Bernie.

Ray pondered this. Did Bernie think everyone in the

country was going to San Francisco, therefore they should go somewhere else? Bernie hated to be predictable. Maybe they were still going to Frisco but Bernie didn't want to say so straight out, probably because if the girl turned out to be a pain they could get rid of her easier, not going where she was, or at least not appearing to. Ray had to admit it was fast thinking. He'd take his cues from Bernie for the time being, until he figured out if Bernie was interested in the girl or not. Ray didn't know if he was interested in her himself; she wasn't exactly beautiful or anything. But if Bernie showed interest, Ray wasn't going to let him walk away with the prize, even one as heavily freckled as this. He didn't like the way Bernie always put on an act when they talked to girls, but it wasn't the kind of thing you complained to your buddy about. If the girl had any smarts she'd see what a phony Bernie was and concentrate on himself. Before Bernie could give them both aliases ("Never tell 'em who you really are and they can't track you down for paternity money when the baby comes"), Ray told the girl their names and asked for hers.

"Sarah."

"Where you from?" said Bernie.

"New York."

"Yeah?"

"Where are you guys from?"

"Kansas," said Ray, before Bernie could claim they were from Mars. Bernie thought that kind of shit was clever.

"Jeez, no wonder you want to be in L.A. I just crossed Kansas and I thought I'd die of boredom. I mean, there's nothing there, right?"

The boys considered the insult. Sarah was right, but it hurt to admit it. It was insensitive of her, to say the least. They decided they didn't like her after all. Each knew what the other was thinking. Strange how corny old Kansas could make you bristle at remarks like that, unite you somehow.

"Hey, slow down! That's my sister's car!"

Sarah was pointing. A car, its shape lost in the gloom of dusk but for its flashing hazard lights, was parked on the shoulder half a mile ahead. Ray wondered how Sarah was able to recognize it at this distance, in these conditions; and what was she doing hitching if her sister was traveling on this same stretch of road?

"Slow down! She's in trouble! Blink your lights."

Bernie did it, hoping the sister would be better-looking and sweeter-natured. He pulled up behind the car, a beat-up Fairlane.

"Wait here while I check it out," said Sarah, climbing across Ray's lap to reach the door. She was outside and dashing to the car before they could argue. It was still raining heavily; let her get wet instead of them. Sarah had disappeared inside the Fairlane. Again, both boys knew what the other was thinking. "Fuck it," said Bernie, and reached for the gearshift, but Sarah was already on her way back to the pickup. Ray rolled his window down as she mounted the running board. Her hatbrim jabbed him in the eye as she thrust her head inside.

"Come and take a look at her!"

"What's wrong?"

"I don't know. Come and see, please."

Bernie killed the engine. They got out and went to the car. Inside were two young men. The one behind the wheel carried a .45 pistol. "Keys still in the dash?" he asked, stepping out. The boys stared at his gun. "I said, are the fucking keys still in the dash?"

"Uh . . . yeah," said Bernie.

"Okay, we're trading. Get inside."

The other young man was out of the car now, running to the pickup with Sarah. Ray and Bernie got in the Fairlane's back seat. The one with the gun said, "Listen, we have to do this." He waited, apparently expecting forgiveness, and when none was granted he said, "Fuck you," got out and slammed the door. The Dodge's motor was running and he sprinted to join his friends. Bernie's pickup pulled around the car and was driven away. The transfer had taken less than a minute.

"What a bunch of creeps," breathed Bernie.

"Yeah . . ."

"Dopeheads I bet."

"Yeah, I bet the cops are after them. They're in too big of a hurry. I bet this car's hot."

Bernie hauled himself across to the front seat and turned the Fairlane's ignition key. The motor coughed once and was silent.

"Jesus, what a bunch of fucking creeps."

"I didn't like her the minute she got in. There was something not right about her, you know?"

"Yeah, I felt it, too. You don't expect girls to do stuff like this, though."

"No."

"Shit! They got the beer! We didn't even open one goddamn can. Fuck!"

Rain hammered mockingly on the roof. Ray thought briefly of Ellie Quist and wondered why. "We've been screwed," he said.

"The highway patrol always investigates cars parked along the Interstate. They'll be along anytime and radio ahead to pick those fuckers up."

They waited for the highway patrol, clothes steaming lightly. Trucks howling by rocked the car with the wind of their passing.

"Shitty springs."

"Shitty car."

An hour passed. The highway patrol had not come, the rain had not gone. No motorist stopped to offer help.

"They're getting further away, Bernie."

"So what am I supposed to do about it?"

"Maybe we should wave down a car and get taken to where there's a phone."

"You want to stand outside in this shit? Nobody'd stop

49

anyway. Who the fuck would stop for someone in a rain-storm?"

"Us. We did."

"Apart from us, who'd do it? Nobody, so forget it."

"I feel like an idiot just sitting here. We should be doing something."

"Okay, go ahead, catch pneumonia."

A disgruntled silence filled the car for another half hour. Traffic began to lessen, but the rain did not.

"I'm tired. It's all that driving."

"Yeah, me too."

Surprisingly, they slept. The Fairlane's hazard lights continued to blink. Ray and Bernie slept on through the storm's end, continued sleeping until spotlights dazzled them awake. Red and blue flashes scythed across the seats and roof.

"YOU IN THE CAR! COME OUT RIGHT NOW!"

The voice was megaphone metallic, shockingly loud.

"Huh? Ray . . . ?"

"OUT OF THE CAR! NOW! GET OUT OF THE CAR RIGHT NOW!"

"Jesus, we better do it."

They exited the Fairlane slowly. Two state troopers were aiming pistols at them over the opened doors of their cruiser.

"FLAT ON THE GROUND! FACE DOWN!"

"It's not our car!" bawled Bernie.

"FACE DOWN ON THE GROUND! RIGHT NOW!"

Ray and Bernie adopted the position they had until now associated with pushups in Phys. Ed. They knew, as they breathed the odor of rainwashed highway, that explaining their situation was going to be difficult.

Their return to Callisto by bus three days after their departure for the coast was a humiliation. The story that circulated around town gave unwarranted emphasis to the presence of a girl, played down to an absurd degree her friends with the gun. Ray and Bernie had been outsmarted by a bunch of hippies in a way that shamed all Kansans. Their public disgrace was compounded by personal discomfort; both boys had borrowed the comb of an amiable drunk while being held by the Colorado troopers, and within days of their return home discovered themselves infested with head lice. Both had their heads shaved to the scalp. They could have used a specially medicated shampoo but opted for the close crop; it was their badge of penance.

August sunlight made the gesture impractical, and when their heads began turning pink they bought Stetsons; under hats like these they could walk tall again. Bernie's was black, the exact model worn by the girl in the poncho. Ray chose an ambiguous gray. It was good to be rid of all that useless hair. The guys that stole Bernie's pickup had long hair, and the troopers would've believed their story a whole lot faster had they been crewcut or ducktailed. Long hair was sissified. "We looked like a couple of faggots," said Bernie, "real pantywaists." Any man not shorn to tonsorial rectitude was a pantywaist, and the town suddenly seemed overrun by this new and threatening tribe, at least among the young. "Look at that goddamn pantywaist over there. Jesus, I bet he squats to pee." They abandoned their sneakers and wore heavy western boots to stamp the message home: We are Men, real Men. But while he lay awake for hours on his spartan camp bed, Ray was troubled by a puzzling sense of guilt. The plain fact was, he liked Bernie more than he liked any other human being, certainly more than he'd ever liked any girl. He even liked the way Bernie looked. Was he, beneath all the sneering, himself a pantywaist? He had to get a girlfriend and reassure himself. A buddy came first, but you had to keep a girl in the near background to let people know which way the wind blew, sexwise.

Then Bernie went away to college. Without his one real friend, Ray became morose. He did his work, but without

Bernie it wasn't fun any more, was merely a job. He quit visiting the usual haunts, instead brought a six-pack back to Swenson's Superior Landscaping to consume alone of an evening. It occurred to Ray that he was waiting, just marking time; a part of his life had ended without his noticing, and another was about to begin. No wonder his familiar surroundings, reminders of the old life, were so irritating. But waiting for what? The answer came two days later in a letter forwarded from the Thunderbird; Ray was to report to the Selective Service Board in one week.

It had been a couple of months since he last spoke to his mother, and his mood urged him to make amends. He drove across town to the motel after work and visited with Judith at the reception desk. Conversation during the first few minutes was so sparse the arrival and signing in of guests was not considered an interruption. These people stared at the fuzz-headed youth with the cowboy hat on his knee and couldn't decide if he was local color gone slightly awry or a convict on parole. Judith was aware of their curiosity and discomfort, wondered if the son she thought she knew had somehow become someone else while her back was turned. If that was so, she couldn't see it herself. Ray was an ordinary male, the same useless creature he'd always been. It was just the baldness that made folks stare. She hadn't seen the skullscape of his cranium in such detail since he was six months old.

"Got my draft notice."

"I thought that's what it was. How do you feel about going in the army?"

Ray shrugged. He wasn't worried; Vietnam seemed a million miles away from Callisto. He remembered being told a long time ago he'd one day have to go kill Commies. That time had finally rolled around. Contemplation of army life made him think not of death or glory, but of women and the sex appeal of a uniform. If he had to go, he had to go, and when he went he'd try to fuck himself to death before bullets came anywhere near his ass. Every week the TV news flung images of destruction at its audience. All of it washed over Ray like a commercial, barely disturbed his eye and brain. Vietnam was all about some bunch of slanty-eyed reds that wouldn't do what Uncle Sam wanted them to, so they had to get taught a lesson; that was all he knew. The thought of being inducted didn't bother him, but knowing that Bernie would be exempted from service while he was at college did. He and Bernie could've had good times together in the army, and it looked like Ray would soon be headed for the war zone on his lonesome to take part in the great gook-and-pussy hunt.

"You should've stayed in school."

Ray watched her face. Was she gloating again, letting him know how bad he'd gone and fucked up his life? Somehow it didn't matter if she was. Judith was old and dried out, but Ray was young and strong. Not that these qualities had got him what he wanted recently, or ever. Why was that? He knew he deserved better than what he'd had so far. His life to date lacked direction, that was it. Maybe the army held the key. Maybe something inside him would be unlocked and everything made clear. Desperate for a label to pin himself to, Ray grabbed the one marked SOLDIER. He needed solid ground beneath his feet, and soon.

He presented himself on the appointed day at the Selective Service office downtown, declared himself fighting fit, ready to kill for his country. After filling in several forms, Ray was given a physical examination. He held himself erect as never before, inflated his lungs to their fullest, thrust his chin forward contentiously, while denying any trace of syphilis or insanity in the family. He displayed his testicles and anus, stood on tiptoe, had his mouth probed with pick and mirror, his heartbeat monitored by stethoscope.

"Nervous?" asked the doctor.

"Nah," said Ray.

The doctor listened some more.

"Ever felt your heart skip a beat, kind of flutter?"

"Nope."

"Just wait over there, please."

"Sure."

The doctor went away. Ray waited with other examinees, the bench hard beneath his shorts. The doctor returned with an associate, who listened to Ray's heart for a full minute before unplugging his ears and making a note on Ray's form.

"Okay, Mr. Kootz, I'm afraid it's bad news. You've got heart murmur. It's nothing fatal, probably nothing you have to worry about so long as you don't subject yourself to undue strain, but we can't risk using you. Better have it checked out with your family doctor. I'm sorry."

Ray stared at him. He wore his hair parted low, just above the ear, then pasted sideways and up across a sizable bald spot. Could a man who combed his hair in such a dishonest fashion be trusted to know what he was talking about? Ray felt the floor shift beneath his perfectly sprung arches. Something had gone very wrong here. How could he possibly have a bum heart? He was only eighteen fucking years old!

"You can put your clothes back on, Mr. Kootz. We won't be troubling you again. Thanks for coming in so promptly."

The erstwhile draftee dressed slowly, dazedly, took himself out onto the street, directed himself by instinct to a bar, and there ordered a beer. The unthinkable had happened. Just when his foot was planted on a true and righteous path the signpost turned and pointed another way, pointed nowhere. A 4-F flunkout! Heart murmur? What the fuck was it murmuring about? The heart of Ray Kootz should shout, holler, bay at the goddamn moon, not murmur. How would he ever live this down? What was he going to do with his life now that soldiering was out? And what kind of pantywaist would he turn into if he had to avoid stress for the sake of his heart? Did that include fucking? Goddamn that doctor!

5

WORD EVENTUALLY CAME to Judith of her son's failure to meet the standards of the draft. One of the sheet girls had a boyfriend whose buddy had been examined that same day. She waited, expecting Ray would come to her for comfort, but he didn't show. Ashamed, thought Judith; he's ashamed. It struck her that she was not. If anything, she was relieved. According to the TV, Vietnam was a quagmire where machinery and manpower were squandered in pursuit of indefinite and unachievable goals. She didn't want Ray there. He was not the son she wanted, but like it or not was the son she had. There wouldn't be another. The diagnosis that had exempted him from combat was, in Judith's opinion, wrong. Ray couldn't possibly have a bad heart, not at his age. It was a lucky thing not all doctors were smart men. Now her boy could continue to grow, maybe even become a man someday. She could wait.

In November a robber walked into the Thunderbird. Judith was behind the reception desk. It had been a slow night and she was watching the late show on her Zenith sixteen-inch. She hadn't yet decided if the movie was supposed to be a comedy when a man with a gun came through the door and told her he wanted all the money.

"No," said Judith.

"All the money," he said again. He was small, wore a heavy mackinaw coat and shoes inadequate for the cold outside, a pair of broken-down sneakers that made Judith feel sorry for him; but she wasn't going to hand over any cash just because of the sneakers, any more than she intended giving him what he wanted on account of the gun. The barrel was shaking, so she knew he was nervous.

"No. You get out of here right now."

"I just want the money, then I'll go. I don't wanna hurt no one."

"I understand that, but I'm not going to give you any money, so you can just go."

Her lack of fear surprised Judith. If the robber had been larger, more threatening, maybe she would have felt different, but the little man with the trembling gun was obviously no professional, was probably just down on his luck, desperately needed a few dollars for life's necessities. But she still wouldn't give him the day's takings. Hard luck was no excuse for pointing a gun at somebody.

"Go away," she said, but he continued to stand there, kept aiming the gun, and now Judith felt anger stir inside her. She waved her hand at him, a shooing motion, the kind used to shift a reluctant dog, and its suddenness made the little man flinch. The bullet creased Judith's neck and drilled the calendar hanging behind her, put a hole right through the middle kitten. Accustomed to deafening gunshots from the TV, she thought this one sounded feeble, no louder than a boy's cap pistol, but the side of her neck felt sore so the gun was real enough. He'd gone and shot her. . . .

"Get oooouuut!"

He ran. She wasn't even sure he'd meant to pull the trigger. Judith hurried to the door and pulled it open. The gunman was still running, his shadow lengthened by auroral light from the totem pole until he disappeared behind Tepee 15, the one closest to Twelfth Street, where he probably had a getaway vehicle parked. Judith knew it would be a rustbucket. She went back inside, fingers clamped across the side of her neck, and called the police.

After that incident she thought about nothing but guns. She was a newspaper reader, never missed the network news; she knew something had gone wrong with the country following Kennedy's assassination; after Dallas, nothing had been the same. There were crazy people out there, faces in the crowd one minute, front page news the next. Anyone could die at any time. Urban America began arming itself. That hunting rifle on the garage shelf, the twelve-gauge way back in the closet, these were no longer enough. A wise citizen invested in a handgun, something you could pick up fast to shoot the maniac bursting through the window, the drug addict smashing down your door.

Judith went to Frank's Gun Shop and bought a .38, then joined the gun club, where she quickly learned to squeeze off what male members called "a damn good score, considering." They knew she took her shooting practice seriously when she suggested replacing the regular targets with human silhouettes. The club's board agreed, and the old-fashioned bullseye went the way of the finned auto and the Davy Crockett cap. She kept her Smith and Wesson in a greased leather holster fitted beneath the front desk, could draw and fire in seconds. The idea was culled from a western on the late show.

Ray drank himself out of a job. Rudy fired him only after a number of warnings. Ray couldn't blame him. Every morning for the past week Rudy had found him deeply hung over, still dressed and stinking of yesterday among crushed beer cans, and the little work he was able to do wasn't worth jackshit. He stowed his few possessions in the back of his Ford and took them to a cheap furnished apartment over a garage on Twenty-second Street, where he could be as unwashed as he pleased until his accumulated savings ran out. The apartment came with a black-and-white TV, which, when pounded, grudgingly disgorged two channels into the living room. He watched whatever came through its slowly rolling eye. No diploma, no uniform, and now no job. Was there ever a bigger flunkout?

He kept right on drinking, crushed his six-pack soldiers and flung them against the walls. Ray didn't want visitors, had told no one his new address, and so was startled one night to hear his doorbell ring. He opened up warily.

"Hello, Ray."

"Uh . . . hi."

He stepped aside to let his mother by. Judith stared at the pigsty her son lived in, resisted the urge to throw the package under her arm at his lazy, foolish head.

"Siddown," suggested Ray.

She did, on the very edge of a sofa last cleaned sometime in the fifties, she was sure. Ray sat on the sofa's sagging arm. Both knew he wouldn't feel comfortable sitting any closer to Judith. She placed the package beside her.

"This place is awful."

"How'd you know I was here?"

"You rented from Lonnie Hickman."

"Right. He owns the garage under here. So?"

"Lonnie's married to a lady called Carol. Her maiden name was Winchell. Her mother used to work at the Thunderbird."

"Oh yeah, Mrs. Winchell, I remember her. Didn't she die or something?"

"About ten years ago, but Carol and I kept in touch."

"Okay, so now what?"

"You don't have any manners at all, do you?"

Ray examined his knees.

"You want some coffee?"

"If you have a clean cup."

Ray washed a couple, rinsed the pot, brewed, and served.

"I lost my job."

"I know. Mr. Swenson rang me to say the state police found Bernie's pickup in Utah. It was tipped over down in some little dry wash, just junk now, they said."

"That's too bad. Bernie really loved that truck. Did they get the guys that took it?"

"No. There are some very nasty people out there, Ray."

"You're telling me."

"One of them shot me."

"Huh?"

"He tried to rob the motel, but I wouldn't let him. He shot me right here."

She showed him the scar.

"Jeez, Mom . . . I didn't know. I'm sorry."

"It's superficial as can be, nothing but a little nick, but I've got protection now. Anyone walks in and tries that again, I've got a little surprise waiting for them under the desk."

"Hey, neat, Mom. Blow the fu—. . . sucker away."

"And not just during working hours, Ray. I've got protection all the time."

Her jacket was lifted coyly aside; snuggled in her armpit was a holster and gun.

"The man at the gun shop said this was illegal, Ray. Strictly speaking, it's a concealed weapon if I wear it around town, not just at the gun club, but I wear it everywhere anyway. Isn't it cute the way it fits? And comfortable, too. I don't even know it's there." She stroked the exposed strip of pearl along the butt. "This one's an automatic. The one at the Thunderbird's a revolver. Do you know the difference?"

"Yeah. Can I see it?"

"Of course you can. The safety catch is on, so keep it that way, please."

He handled the little Browning admiringly while Judith watched his reaction.

"They said at the gun shop it's a woman's gun. My thirty-

59

eight's not all that big either." She tapped the package beside her. "But this one's man-size."

"What one?"

"In here. Why don't you open it up?"

He did. The gun fairly leapt into his hand, reassuringly heavy after the dinky automatic. He was sitting beside Judith now, hefting the pistol's weight, smiling.

"Ruger Blackhawk," she told him. "It's a good gun, Ray. Plenty of stopping power. Do you like it?"

He aimed at various objects around the room.

"Yeah!"

Judith had never heard such enthusiasm compressed into a syllable.

"It'll be waiting for you at the gun club when you get yourself another job."

"Huh?"

"It's something to work toward. Everyone needs to work toward something, don't you think?"

"I guess."

His face, so recently agile with excitement, now was its usual sullen mask. He watched with dismay as the Blackhawk was returned to its box.

"There's a holster goes with it," said Judith.

"Shoulder or hip?"

"I'll leave that up to you. You get yourself a job and hold on to it, Ray, that's all I ask. You do that for me and quit this drinking you've got started on, and the gun's yours. It cost plenty, so it's worth having. This coffee is just awful. Why didn't you stay with Maxwell House like you had at home?"

She left soon after, hoping her heavy-caliber seed had been well and truly planted. Give him a gun, make him a man. The army wouldn't, so Judith had to, and this way he didn't even have to risk dying for it. Maybe Ray's troubles stemmed from the lack of manly influence around the place since Lowell died. And she'd been hard on the boy, she saw that now, ignoring him most of the time, resenting his very maleness, resenting her son. What on earth had been wrong with her? Maybe the slug that nicked her neck had let some of the steam out, mellowed her. She wanted to be Ray's mom again.

This time he pumped gas at the Texaco station downtown, dreaming of movie-star blondes who'd pull up in Corvettes or Cadillacs and invite him to fill them up. Only the gun kept him at it. He wanted that heavy Blackhawk for his own, could feel it in his hand still, his finger caressing the trigger. He would've liked to blow the head off at least one customer per day, some fuckhead who sneered at him through the windshield while Ray removed a hundred miles' grime. This was all just temporary; being a pump boy during the oncoming winter would be the worst kind of shitwork. He'd quit drinking after Judith's visit; that might or might not be temporary, it was too soon to say; meanwhile, he filled 'em up and wiped 'em down, took their cash and their coldness with a face as free of malice as the sky was free of cloud.

At night he thought of his conical room at the tip of the T-bird's big tepee, sometimes wished himself there again. But he couldn't bring a girl there, not to fuck. He hadn't brought any girls to his apartment either, but he might get lucky, you never knew. He tidied the place in readiness, took his putrid underwear down to the Big Suds Laundromat, and watched his shorts fling themselves in circles. All just temporary.

The gun was waiting as promised, a beautiful piece of steel and walnut. He got the shoulder holster. The paperwork had all been arranged by Judith. The gun was his. He took it home and paraded around his four small rooms with the shades drawn. The holster hugging his ribs gave him lopsided strength. Ray felt lean and mean and dangerous, a hired gun on the late show, pacing his room in baggy pants and suspenders, counting the hours before the big hit. He felt great. What a wonderful thing a gun was!

What a great mom he had! What other mom would've done this? He felt a new kind of warmth, thinking of her. It was obvious she wanted to be friends. Maybe she was lonely at the T-bird all by herself, surrounded by strangers, a new bunch every night. The big tepee was very big. There was room there for him if he wanted. The gun was just the ribbon on a greater gift. Did he want it, that proffered hand? Ray drew his Blackhawk, aimed at the gunman in the mirror; he needed a half-smoked cigarette dangling from the corner of his mouth to make the picture look right. He tried his Stetson, but that didn't go with the shoulder holster so he took it off. Did he or didn't he want to move back home? He should be wearing a white shirt with elastic armbands and one of those wide neckties like they always wore in old movies.

Mother and son met every week at the Callisto Gun Club, squeezed off their shots side by side, and compared scores. Ray was introduced to other members, but not one was female, so he stayed close to Judith as a way of avoiding them. They were a cross section of the town's social strata, from bank executive to bus driver; their one bond was a mutual love of weaponry, but to Ray the thing that shaped these men into a composite whole was his lack of interest in them all. It soon became known that conversation with the kid who pumped gas for a living would lead precisely nowhere. Woman and boy, the one no longer young, the other unrelievedly morose, were called Granny Oakley and Tonto behind their backs. They came, Judith in her Chevy wagon, Ray in his beat-up Ford, fired a hundred rounds apiece, dumped their empty casings in the bins provided, surrendered their ear protectors, and drove away. The members agreed that Judith, formerly convivial company, had changed completely since her son joined the club. It was very strange. They blamed the boy.

A letter for Ray arrived at the motel and was passed along to him.

Hey Buddy,

Thought I'd write a letter tonight so this is it. You are very honored OK? College is something else. Chix are very hot here, like fucking is on the curriculum. Probably because they're away from home, same as the guys. It's hard to study classes when you can study pussy like you can here. But some of them are very weird too, practically commies the way they talk about Pres. Johnson. This is still girls I'm talking about. Most of the weirdos are guys though, pantywaists some of them to look at but who can say? They talk shit most of the time but let you smoke their dope. That stuff is good good good.

Hey, are you getting any back home? No I'm not talking about dope I'm talking about girls again. My old man says he fired you awhile back, so what are you doing now? Also heard the army grabbed you but then changed their mind because of medical stuff. Are you OK or what? Too bad about my truck but the insurance paid up so who cares. I'll send this to Tepee City and hope it finds you.

> Joe College
> alias you-know-who

Ray hated the letter. He was glad to hear from Bernie but jealous of Bernie's good times, plain old green-eyed jealous. Ray had pretty near forgotten what fucking felt like. If he hadn't flunked out of high school he could've been at college with Bernie, fucking girls and smoking dope, a fun way to live, about as far removed from pumping gas as anything Ray could think of. He'd handed himself a shitty deal, and there seemed no way out unless he went to night school, an option he rejected. Having failed, he wanted to fail completely, absolutely, to wear failure like a medal where everyone could see it. He knew it was dumb to feel that way but couldn't help himself. Somehow, someday, something would come along and change his life completely, and it wouldn't come from night school. Ray wanted flaming chariots to swoop down and carry him away; nothing less would do.

Three days before Christmas a customer got out of his Continental and told Ray to do the windshield again. "It's still dirty. Look at that spot there, and there's another one. Doesn't full service mean full service any more?"

The customer was fat, expensively dressed. Ray thought his porcine face about the ugliest thing he'd seen in a long time. He stared at the man, strangely calm. He should've been angry but was not, felt cocooned inside his greasy all-weather coveralls. The customer's peevishness gusted harmlessly around him like the raw December wind.

"What are you smiling at? Do the windshield. Do what they pay you to do. . . . What are you smiling at?"

"You fat fuck."

The words came from a place deep inside him. He liked the way they dropped from his lips, heavy and confident, fat words for a fat fuck. He wasn't even mad at the man, found him funny, a blustering cartoon character. The man was afraid of him; Ray could see it in his eyes. "Do it . . ." he said, gesturing stiffly at the Continental.

"Nah," said Ray, and dropped his cleaning stick on the customer's highly polished Florsheims.

"Look, all I want is to get it cleaned the way it's supposed to be. You do that and I won't complain to the manager, okay?"

Ray smiled on. The man backed away, turned and entered the station. Ray watched through the window, saw the fat head above a rack of candy bars, mouth opening and shutting. He'd be fired now. So what. He rocked a little in the wind, patted his gauntlets together in front of, then behind himself, front and back, front and back, swinging his arms, waiting for the manager. It seemed to be taking forever. Goodbye, gas pumps. So long, service bell. Now the manager was coming toward him, followed by the fat man.

"Did you do what he says?"

"What'd he say?"

"He says you won't clean his windshield and you cussed at him."

"I called him a fat fuck. Look at him. That's a fat fuck if I ever saw one."

"You're through here, Kootz."

"Thank you. Merry Christmas."

He collected the few dollars owed him, unzipped his coveralls and dumped them, walked away whistling "Jingle Bells."

Judith was surprised when he presented himself at the Thunderbird's reception desk. He placed his Blackhawk and holster before her.

"This is yours now. I lost my job."

"What happened?"

"I was rude to a customer."

"Why?"

"He was rude to me."

"Then you did the right thing." She pushed the gun toward him. "You keep it."

"Okay."

"I've been thinking, Ray."

"Yeah?"

"I've been thinking you should move out of that smelly apartment and come back here."

Ray considered the proposal. He hadn't scored with any girls, hadn't even tried, so what did he need his own place for? The T-bird was always warm and clean. He'd been thinking more and more about his old room, the cone at the tepee's peak.

"How about rent?"

"We'll decide that when we see what the paycheck's like on your next job. The one you'll get after New Year's."

"Okay. Can I use the wagon to pick up my stuff?"

She gave him the keys.

"I'll leave the gun here."

"Fine."

She put it under the counter, alongside her .38.

6

BERNIE CAME HOME for Christmas. They put on their Stetsons and drove for miles in Ray's car, talking and sipping a little beer, then stopped to drain their bladders beside a lonely county road, splashed the frozen gravel with comradely streams.

Tucking his penis away from the cold, Bernie said, "There's this girl I'm crazy about."

"Yeah? At college?"

"Right. She's beautiful, I mean it, really beautiful. Her name's Lori. I'm crazy about her, you know, but it's not working out right. Sometimes I don't think she gives a shit. We dated a few times, then she says she doesn't want to date any more but she won't say why, just says she doesn't want to. I told her okay, if that's the way you want it, okay by me, forget it, but then later on I couldn't get her out of my head, I mean it was real distracting, which is bad, Ray, because my grades aren't exactly terrific right now. So I wrote her a letter, can you believe it? It's the first letter I ever wrote a girl in my life, and I tell her how I feel about everything, straight from the heart, then I wait to get a reaction, but there's nothing doing, and I ask myself if I should maybe call her up or not, and I thought no, I won't do that, that'd be feeble, right? Then it's almost Christmas break and I'm wondering what to do. It's been three days since I mailed the letter and still nothing.

"Then something happens. I'm walking across campus and I see this Kentucky Fried Chicken box on the ground right next to a trash basket, and this is the weirdest thing, I feel like I've got to pick it up and put it in the basket. Any other time I would've walked right on by. It's not my trash so why should I care, you know, but not this time, I've got to put it in the basket, so I do, I pick it up and put it in and there's my letter on top of all the other crap in there, all scrunched up but I knew it just from the little bit of writing I could see. I pulled it out and it's mine all right. She must've read it and dumped it. How about that. You don't expect to see a letter you put your soul into end up in a trash basket, right?"

"Right."

"So with one side of my head I'm thinking fuck her, but the other side is thinking how come I had to put the box in the trash like I did? It's spooky, like something made me do it so I'd see what a bitch Lori is, the unfeeling type, so I don't have to waste any more time on her. But what made me pick up the box, huh? I spoke to some guys about it and they came across with all this cosmic stuff about everything being connected, but it sounds like bullshit to me. If everything was connected Lori'd want to fuck me, right? That's what I call connectedness. But it's spooky the way it happened. There was ketchup on the letter too, like she was reading it while she ate a fucking hamburger. That really pissed me off. You don't eat a hamburger while you read an important letter, you just don't, so fuck her, I'm thinking, then about an hour later who do I bump into but Lori, and I ask her did she get my letter and she says yes, it was a wonderful letter and she has to think about it while she's at home over Christmas break."

"Did you ask her if she still had the letter?"

"No."

"You should've, then you'd know if she was lying."

"She might've lost it, dropped it around campus someplace and someone picked it up and threw it in the trash."

"Yeah, could be."

"But you don't really think so."

"I don't know. Maybe. How would I know?"

"It's important, Ray. I almost called you up long distance to ask you what you think, then I figured it'd keep till I got home so I can ask you face to face."

"You'll just have to wait till after the break and see what she does. If she says yeah she'll date you, you'll know she accidentally lost the letter, and if she says she doesn't want to date you, you'll know she's a liar. You'll just have to wait."

Ray felt gratified, delivering this advice; someone thought him smart enough to consult on an important matter. It was no small compliment, and he was pretty sure he'd said the right thing. He hoped Lori would be proved a liar. He didn't want Bernie fucking some beautiful girl while he didn't even have an ugly one.

"I heard there's a missile silo out this way someplace."

"Huh?"

"An underground silo, supposed to be one out this way, that's what one of the guys in my dorm said, just a single missile, one of those big fuckers hid under the ground way out in the middle of nowhere. We could be looking right at it."

There was nothing to see but themselves and the car, miniatures in an immensity of slate-gray sky and snow-powdered grass. The wind tugged at their hatbrims. Ray suddenly felt small. He shouldn't have wished Lori a liar, should be hoping Bernie would be made happy. He'd been a shit to think that selfish stuff a minute ago. But anything he might say now would just sound lame.

"Let's try the gun."

"Okay."

Ray fetched his Blackhawk from the car and they set up empty beer cans across the road. Bernie missed five shots out of six. Ray sent the cans spinning and dancing. "Mighty fine shootin' there, Tex," drawled Bernie. Ray thought he sounded sore. He reloaded and handed the gun over. Bernie didn't even bother aiming at the cans, instead squeezed off all six shots at the horizon. "Eat lead, Kansas." He gave the gun back to Ray and the shell casings were ejected.

"You want to go see a movie tonight?"

"Sure."

They drove home.

In January Ray found work delivering for a dry cleaning company. He drove a big white truck around town with some skill. He did not drink, stayed home through the week to watch TV with Judith. On Friday and Saturday nights he visited some of the old beer haunts but somehow did not enjoy it. Once he persuaded a girl to have intercourse with him after an acquaintance of less than ninety minutes, but he didn't enjoy that very much either, and this disappointment, rather than his overall lack of enthusiasm for the social life, depressed him greatly. He must be sick in the head if a fuck made him miserable. He could not account for it. He saw the girl several times more, but could never enjoy her company for more than the few minutes required for sex. He quit calling her for dates. He'd never given her his own number.

Ray considered writing Bernie a letter, setting his despair down on paper, but could not find the will to pick up a pen; it wouldn't be right to burden his pal with shit like this anyway. He no longer enjoyed his weekly shooting practice with Judith, but made the effort to maintain his high scores and keep her off his back; how could he possibly have explained himself? They spoke as little as they had before he moved out last summer, but the silence was not acrimonious; she appeared to require nothing more than his presence. What had gone wrong? He still did not know in what career he could find satisfaction, found himself drawn in no particular direction, sat with his mother night after night in front of the tube, watched garbage without flinching, shared her bags of potato chips and said nothing.

A week after Ray's nineteenth birthday, Bernie came home in disgrace. Lori Barton wouldn't press charges against him for attempted assault, but the chancellor insisted he leave immediately. He came to Ray for solace on his first evening home and they parked in a windswept supermarket lot to talk.

"It's all bullshit. I didn't try to rape her or anything. Her sweater only got ripped because she backed off so fast. I just wanted to talk to her. Jesus . . . And her roomie comes in right then and swears I'm assaulting her for chrissakes. They were both screaming and crying when campus security got there, and it was this particular fuckhead I had trouble with before about drinking, which this prick in a uniform got me in deep shit about already, so when he came through the door and saw it's me he got this big smile on his face, this kind of 'Gotcha!' smile that made me see right off no one was gonna believe me about Lori, so I hit him just to wipe the smile off his asshole face. Then they went through my room and found the dope, on top of which I had a lousy attendance record, so I'm outa there pronto. The whole thing got blown way out of proportion. That fucking Lori . . . My dad won't talk to me except to call me a moron and my mom looks at me like I just got scraped off her shoe."

"What are you gonna do now?"

"Who the fuck knows. Maybe join the marines."

"You're kidding."

"I'm kicked out of college so the draft can grab me anytime. The marines are better than the regular army. They really get to kick ass. Fuck it, I'd rather go to 'Nam than piss my life away around here."

Like you, was the implication. Ray felt stung, but forgave Bernie moments later when he said, "You're about the only one doesn't think I'm some kind of asshole. Listen, you want to try again for soldier's pay? Maybe that draft board doctor got it wrong and you can join up with me. Did you ever get your heart checked out by someone else?"

"No."

"Why the fuck not? You hear about doctors misdiagnosing stuff every day. Some guy goes to the doctor, says he's got a bad headache that won't go away, and the doc says go take some more aspirin, and next day the guy drops dead from a brain tumor. Happens all the time, believe me. We could be Green Berets, man. Those guys are the ultimate. They get to do all the really tough shit the regular army can't handle. You want to come down to the recruiting office with me tomorrow?"

"Me?"

"You bet. Fuck it, go for the green. You want to?"

"I'll go down there with you, but I don't want to sign up."

"Why not? What's the matter, you really think you've got a bad heart?"

"I don't know. I guess not. Maybe it is and maybe it isn't, but I don't want to join the marines right now."

"Shit, Ray, I don't want to do it if you're not gonna go in with me. Look at it like this: if your heart's not good like they said, you've got a second opinion for free and you'll know for sure one way or the other."

"Nah, I don't want to."

"Jesus, Ray, you chicken or what?"

"Who's chicken? I just don't want to."

"Your mom doesn't want you to, am I right? Mine won't either, but I bet the old man's all for it. He's a vet. You don't have to do what your mom wants just because she's your mom. It's a free country."

"No!"

It struck Ray that Bernie's response to having fucked up his life was to enlist, while Ray's was to sit with his mom watching *Gilligan's Island*. He couldn't figure out which response was dumber.

"Okay, I guess you better drive me home. No, forget it, I'll walk."

The Ford's door slammed. Ray watched Bernie's hunched figure stamping away across the empty parking lot. He felt awful, felt he'd somehow betrayed his friend, betrayed also his own masculinity, his red American blood. Maybe he really was chicken; how could he tell?

Five days passed. Ray phoned the Swenson home but Bernie wasn't there. He phoned several more times through the following week, always when Bernie had "just this minute gone out somewhere." Bernie's folks sounded angry every time. Ray couldn't find the nerve to question them about Bernie's plans for enlistment, always hung up with a meek "Thank you." Eventually he quit phoning. Fuck Bernie. Ray's wish to renew the friendship was supplanted by a desire never to see him again. He even stayed home on weekends to avoid encountering his erstwhile buddy over a beer.

"How come everything's home sweet home all of a sudden?" asked Judith.

"Huh?"

"You never go out any more."

"I like it here."

"You like it?"

"I like it."

"You like this?"

Judith pointed at the crystalline flickerings across the room. Police were exchanging gunfire with bank robbers in a high-speed chase.

"Love it."

"So the Thunderbird is God's own place to you."

"Right."

"Then you better start getting paid to hang around here."

"Paid?"

"Walter's quitting. His wife wants to move to Florida."

Walter was the night manager. Despite her .38, Judith preferred to handle the daylight shift nowadays.

"You want me to take over Walt's job?"

"I'll pay you a dollar an hour over whatever you get for driving that laundry truck."

Ray panicked. Working nights would curtail his social life, but running the T-bird had been his dream just a year ago, and here was the bottom rung of the ladder to what he'd wanted. Did he still want it? What kind of social life did he have anyway? A speeding car ran off the road, broadsided down an incline, turned over, exploded. The cop car in pursuit came to a screaming halt. The cops looked down at the flaming wreck.

"Okay."

He surprised himself. It had been easy. Ray felt great. A sense of worth crept through him, inflated his lungs. Was this how it was all the time once you found the path? How could he ever have wanted to be anything other than night man at the Thunderbird Motel? It had practically fallen into his lap. No, Judith had placed it there. He came as close to truly loving his mother in that moment as he ever had.

"It's time you found your place."

"Yeah."

"This is it, right here."

"I know."

"It's boring. You're maybe too young to be doing this boring job."

"I want it."

"Well, it's a deal."

Judith too was filled with a sense of gratification. Her original plan to shake him from his complacence hadn't worked. Out there in the working world he'd failed, then succeeded at a modest level; given time he might have risen to become truck dispatcher at the laundry. Ray had all the earmarks of ordinariness, had inherited none of Lowell's flair; then again, chances were he was free of Lowell's faults. Lowell had been a big fish in a small pond, knew it and resented it, and had found comfort with other women. Ray, on the other hand, was the kind to steer a straight path through life without ever finding third gear, without suspecting it existed, and would therefore be happy. Running a motel would be just right for Ray. Judith knew her boy's limits. It had been unfair of her to expect him to exceed them, but now everything was set right again, balance restored. His time out in the world would not have been wasted; now he would appreciate the humdrum, the mundane, would be the perfect custodian of Lowell's creation. It was enough.

"That you, Ray?"

"Uh-huh."

"Bernie. Listen, I'm leaving town tomorrow, so what say we get together for a brew?"

"Okay."

"The Penguin, noon. Be there, buddy, 'cause I'm buyin'."

As he replaced the phone Ray remembered that he and Bernie hadn't spoken in over a month, but somehow it wasn't important. He felt like some dumb high school wallflower who'd finally been asked out on a date. He wouldn't let Bernie see that, though.

The Penguin had been their favorite hangout. Bernie already had beers lined up when Ray came in. Bernie's hair, grown long at college, now was shorn to the severest of crewcuts.

"You went and did it."

"I went and did it."

"Marines?"

"Nothin' but. Gonna make me a man, you know? I beat 'em to the hair."

"No shit. How are the folks taking it?"

"Just like I predicted. The old man's still pissed off about what happened up at KU, but he's strutting around telling everyone how I joined up. My mom's just plain pissed off about everything." He lifted his glass. "Here's to the U.S. Marines."

"Gung ho!"

They talked and drank, talked and drank. Some of their high school acquaintances joined them. The girls ran their hands across Bernie's crewcut. Bernie hoped Wendy Stuckey would offer her body as a parting gift, but she left early. The drinking crew worked hard through the afternoon, then began drifting away to find food. Bernie by now was morose with an excess of beer.

"Listen, you can still do it."

"Do what?"

"You know what. C'mon, don't pull my chain."

"Join the marines?"

"You bet join the marines. What the fuck you want to work at a motel for?"

"It'll be mine someday."

"So'll a hernia, but you don't have to have it right now. Live a little, Ray. You're gonna be old at twenty, you keep on going like you are. Go see the fucking world before you bury yourself at the T-bird. Your old lady'll run the place for another twenty years before she lets you take over. You want to be the night man till she drops dead? Hey, I'm sorry, she won't drop dead. I like your mom, she's a nice lady, but look at the facts. So don't join the marines. Do something else, but do something. Callisto's an armpit, not even an important armpit. Go see an armpit with style. Go see New York or L.A. or someplace. You listening?"

"Sure."

"So?"

"So what?"

"So are you gonna go live or stay here and die? That's what Callisto does, kills you by degrees, I mean it."

"Callisto's not so bad."

"Aww shit, Ray. What's the matter with you anyway?"

"Nothing. I'm fine."

"You're turning into a real tightbutt. You won't like hearing this, but it's for your own good, and if your best friend can't tell you, who the fuck can, huh?"

"No one, I guess."

"You guess right, so I'm telling you—quit that job and bum around awhile, that's my going-away advice to you."

"I'll think about it."

"You do that. Now buy me a beer."

Ray returned to the Thunderbird late, very drunk. Judith wouldn't let him hold down the night shift. "I can't let customers see you looking like that and sounding like that, or smelling like that. Take a shower, then go to bed."

"I don't wanna."

"You'll do as I say. Now move."

Ray moved. Later, staring at the pointed ceiling above his head, wishing it would quit spinning that way, he promised himself he would never again allow anyone to tell him what he should or shouldn't do. Too many people thought they knew what was best for Ray Kootz, but Ray knew more than all of them put together.

By the time he woke up it was noon, long past Bernie's scheduled departure. Ray would've liked to be the last one waving goodbye, the way it happened in movies. It left him unsatisfied. He didn't know why he was disappointed to have missed Bernie's farewell; Bernie had said some pretty cruel things to him yesterday, practically called him gutless, and Ray knew that wasn't true at all. He felt his chest, splayed his fingers across the left pectoral; was his heart skipping beats in there? Maybe, and maybe not. Ray wasn't going to find out for sure, because that particular truth might set him free, to join the armed forces, to leave Callisto, to fuck a thousand women, burn a fiery arc across the sky. His heart was definitely skipping, had to be, because doctors are never wrong, not after an expensive education like they have, so there had to be something wrong with his ticker despite the healthy thumpings traveling through his palm; stay home, they said; stay home, stay home, stay home. Ray snatched the hand away from his chest, then went downstairs to face Judith.

7

THE FIRST LESSON was friendliness. Always appear friendly and helpful, despite your mood. Ray found he could summon a smiling face whenever a customer came through the door. Knowing he'd mastered the trick gave him confidence, and he became even more accomplished at signing in. Judith allowed him occasional stints on the day shift, where he fared equally well. Ray was shaping up as managerial material. He kept his hair short and neat, shaved every day, wore shirts and slacks from J. C. Penney. The transformation was, to Judith's eye, miraculous. She was proud of him. He even began talking to other members of the gun club, was invited to a barbecue given by one of them, and there was introduced to Susan Corcoran, a girl eager for marriage. Ray remembered her vaguely from high school.

They began dating. He took her to restaurants and to movies and didn't have to spend very much cash to find out she wanted him. They came close to sexual intimacy several times, but Susan held back. Her parents, like Susan, were churchgoers, and her greatest fear was of having to confess to them she'd become pregnant while unmarried. She made this clear to Ray without offending him. The answer to their back-seat strugglings was obvious, but Ray refused to bite. The thing went with them everywhere; it was becoming burdensome. His dick wanted it, but Ray wondered if marriage was not too high a price to pay. He met her parents several times. Mr. Corcoran owned a sizable printing business in Callisto. Mrs. Corcoran was a professional Christian, very active among like-minded women. Their house was large, obsessively neat but not ostentatious. The Corcorans kept spare rolls of bathroom tissue on the toilet tank, coyly secreted in a wicker basket covered by a gingham doily. Every time he peed in their bathroom, Ray felt an unsettling urge to zip his pants and run.

Agonizing in his conical room, Ray knew a decision was called for. Judith had let him know she thought Susan "a sensible girl, not flighty or trivial." Ray couldn't tell her he wanted Susan's ass in his hands, not her good sense. He couldn't even explain to himself why he wanted her so much; her face was pretty but her body would thicken considerably over the years, he could tell by looking at her mom. Why this gut-wrenching turmoil inside him? He couldn't write to Bernie for advice, not after receiving the latest breezy letter.

Dear Indian
(cause you live in a tepee ha ha)

This life is tough, just how I like it. No pantywaists on Parris Island, nossir. The sergeant licking us into shape is unbelievable, like King Kong but uglier. Yesterday he called Kendrick who bunks next to me a dogsqueeze moron son of a buttfuck whore, which was complimentary believe me. But I like it here, they are a great bunch of guys from all over and can't wait to do what they train us for—get over there and show them we mean business, they better believe it. But I wish you would join up like I did Ray and be here too. It's a whole different world. I feel terrific. So what are you doing these days, anything you wouldn't want your mom to know about yuk yuk?

But seriously I think you should think about that stuff
we talked about just before I left Ray. I worry about you
buddy really.

yrs with an M-16
Pt. Dogface

Bernie would not be impressed by a girl like Susan,
would only laugh at the notion of marriage. Ray was on his
own. He resented Susan for putting him in this fix, resented Judith for her approval of the match, Susan's parents for their Christian civility and those goddamn rolls of
toilet paper. He couldn't postpone things for much longer,
couldn't maintain his please-the-customer smile forever.
Was there an alternative to life with Susan? Ray couldn't
think of one. He told himself his doubts were rearguard
actions designed to stave off the inevitable, unworthy quib-
blings whispered in his ear by the Ray of old. Surely the
new Ray Kootz could face up to responsibility like a man.
Marriage was a challenge, right? Fuck what Bernie Swenson might think. But Ray postponed asking the question
Susan wanted to hear. Instead, he begged her to go on the
pill. Susan refused, but hinted that after three children she
might consider it.

"Even respectable girls take it."

"I just don't think it's necessary, not if we're getting
married soon. What difference could a few months make
anyway?"

"Because I'm going crazy, that's what difference. Even
nice girls don't want to be virgins nowadays, you know? It's
no big sin any more. Things are different now. That's why
they invented the pill, so people could do what nature
intended and not get all guilty because along comes a baby
just when you don't need one. It's no big deal any more.
Suze, honest."

"Well, I know things are different, but I don't see what
difference that makes. We're getting married, and when
we do we can make love knowing we didn't compromise

our holy vows. I don't want to, Ray. Please let's not argue about it."

"Does your doctor go to the same church as you or something?"

"No, he doesn't. He's in a different congregation completely. I don't know what you're saying."

"You think he'll tell your folks if you go on the pill ahead of time?"

"What are you talking about? I'm not going on the pill or getting a diaphragm or any of that awful stuff."

"What are you, a Catholic?"

"Ray, just quit now. You know very well I'm Protestant. I just happen to think love between a man and woman should result in children. You said yourself nature wants us to do that, make love with each other, and nature also wants children to happen because of it, so if there aren't any children it's going against nature, and God invented nature so I won't do it. You'll just have to be patient and show a little bit of respect for what I think. I'm a normal person, Ray. I have the same feelings you do about the physical side, but I'm prepared to wait so we can do it properly, in a bed consecrated by marriage, not in some awful motel."

When she talked that way Susan seemed about fifty years old to Ray. With that look on her face and that steel in her voice he could no more have argued with her than with Judith. He decided he was beating a dead horse on the sex issue; he'd wait, and hope she could be persuaded to jack him off meantime.

Impatience and frustration forced Ray's hand. He asked her to marry him. She made him ask twice; his first effort ("You wanna get married, or what?") had been far too casual for her liking, and she'd given him the big freeze for five solid minutes until he humbly repeated the question in a manner acceptable to her. Driving home from Susan's house that night, chastened yet curiously elated, he congratulated himself on his gumption. He'd gone and bitten the bullet at last, and it only hurt a little bit. A week later, with the wedding date marked in red on two calendars, he wondered if he'd committed the oldest of blunders, sold himself down the marital river, shackled and chained. It bothered him plenty. Susan had just better be one hot chick in bed.

The wedding was set for October. Susan developed a nervous rash on her arms and spent the last weeks of summer wearing long-sleeved blouses; fortunately the wedding dress would extend to her wrists. She prayed for deliverance from the rash; the thought of revealing it on her wedding night made her feel sick. She didn't show her mother or consult a doctor, didn't wish to share her embarrassment with anyone but God. God would fix her. But her symptoms persisted despite hours of prayer, and Susan could not understand why. Then came revelation. The rash was to ensure she did not succumb to temptation and expose her body to Ray before the ceremony was complete, before they became man and wife in the eyes of God. It was so wonderfully simple she had failed to see it. The rash would disappear the moment Ray slipped the wedding ring on her finger and spoke the magic words. She felt faint with relief. But Susan didn't have to wait till October. Miraculously, the rash began to ease from the moment she understood its purpose, and within twenty-four hours was gone completely. She had no doubt the eczematous stricture laid upon her had now been removed by the Lord because it was no longer necessary, Susan having figured out the reason for it as she had. She felt blessed. When Ray accepted Jesus as his savior, her happiness would be complete. The Corcorans all knew Ray could be roped into the church after marital bliss had softened him a little.

As for the intended groom, he performed his duties at the Thunderbird, squeezed off shots at the gun club, watched TV with Judith, and worried as he'd never worried before. Smart move or dumb? Marriage or flight? Every time he climbed behind the wheel of his car (Judith had bought him a new Ford, knowing Susan hated to be seen in the old Ford), Ray felt like burning rubber out of Callisto. But where would he go, what would he do? It was crazy to think that way. He was doing the right thing by staying and marrying Susan, doing the manly thing, facing up to the responsibilities of adulthood.

On a morning in September the owner of the Thunderbird Motel woke up and felt death nearby. Something inside her head told her it was so, a rushing and swelling of cranial tides that seemed to carry her brain this way, then that, until both hemispheres gave the impression of grinding together like primitive millstones, a steady, rhythmic friction deep within the teeming folds. Then the grinding ignited a flashfire of arcing synapses. The walls of Judith's skull swarmed with flame, burned with the intensity of magnesium flares. She knew the blood must be boiling behind her eyes. I have to get out of bed and tell Ray, she thought, and then all thought was subsumed by the ultimate detonation. Blossoming in a moment, it engulfed her senses completely.

Aneurysm was a word unfamiliar to Ray. A blood vessel had ruptured in his mother's brain and she was dead. A doctor assured him it must have been painless, instantaneous. Judith had not quite reached her forty-second birthday, and this fact, as much as the actual death, set Ray brooding along pathways familiar to the bereaved for millennia: Why her? Why now? Why? It made no sense, and the pointlessness of it stoked his resentment at being left alone. Lowell's death had been understandable in its simplicity: irresistible force meets immovable object— splat! But a ruptured blood vessel? A thing you couldn't even see? She hadn't deserved it, not Ray's mom. They'd argued plenty, but she was an okay lady in her way, and he'd come damn near to actually loving her. He'd definitely miss her around the place. Alone with her body in the funeral home, he planted her little Browning automatic in the coffin. Judith would not go unarmed into the after-life.

In the days following the funeral and the reading of the will (he inherited everything, no surprises there) Ray was tempted to reacquaint himself with beer but resisted. The running of Judith's legacy required a clear head, a post-ponement of grief. From talented apprentice he became a master of the smiling public face, amazed everyone with his ability to keep the motel operating. The transition of responsibility from mother to son had been accom-plished with barely a hiccup. It was almost unnatural, some said, for a nineteen-year-old of no particular talent or worth to rise to the occasion so quickly, with such apparent ease.

The Corcorans were especially proud of him. With sole ownership of and liability for a business resting on his young shoulders (shortly to be followed by marriage and a family), it was unthinkable that Ray wouldn't require the strength that comes from true belief to help him escape his days of atheistic darkness. It was just a matter of time before he saw the light. They were only slightly surprised when Ray set the wedding date back by six months; it would have been unseemly to embrace happiness too quickly after so great a loss.

Susan could wait. Ray had quit pestering her since Ju-dith's passing, hadn't so much as suggested she unhook her bra. It was yet another indication of his continuing matura-tion. It made the delay frustrating; a mere boy had pro-posed, but now a real man awaited her at the end of that long, long aisle. The prospect was so delightful Susan dared to ask herself if God had maybe engineered the early death of Ray's mother to make Susan's intended mend his ways. Not killed Judith outright, of course, but just given that distended vessel in her brain a quick prod, hurried things along so that Ray could come into property, grow up fast, and be a better catch all around. First the rash, now this; the Lord was certainly involving Himself in a very direct way with Susan's wedding plans, practically peeking over her shoulder. She kept these thoughts to herself, smiled a secret smile when her mother told her she was looking more radiant with every new day.

Facing things squarely was Ray's new way of doing things. He faced the Thunderbird and found it wanting. The place was more than twenty years old and looked it. Paint was peeling from the tepees, giving them a scabrous appearance, and several of the totem pole's most colorful tubes had sputtered to funereal black. The fixtures and fittings inside the tepees needed replacement, and the curtains and bedspreads, last overhauled in 1959, cried out for contemporary patterns, brighter hues. Ray didn't know much about interior decoration, but he knew what he didn't like; those squiggly black lines linking overlapped squares and triangles of orange and green just had to go. He asked Susan's opinion. Susan thought beige and apricot would go very well together, or maybe beige and pink. Ray didn't think so, but kept it to himself. He'd decide on a new color scheme later; first he needed to know how much it would cost to renovate the place as a whole. A specialist came and spent the day poking around, scribbling in a notebook, then came to Ray with a shocking figure. There was not that much money in the account Judith had left; the T-bird's weatherworn appearance had, in recent years, turned customers away. The Kootzes had come down a little in the world. Something had to be done.

Ray went to his mother's banker to negotiate a loan. The banker said he'd rather not commit funds to something well past its prime, especially in light of Ray's inexperience. There were plenty of new motels in Callisto now, functional boxes honeycombed with clean, cheap rooms. Would Ray like to sell the land the Thunderbird stood on? That would be a profitable move. Ray would not.

He went to Mr. Corcoran and asked if there were any bankers among the flock he prayed with.

"No, but I do know one member of the congregation

happens to have a first cousin in banking. You're getting very businesslike these days, Ray."

"I need a loan to fix the T-bird. Where does this gentleman work, I mean which bank?"

"Well now, you better just hold your horses a day or two, Ray, and see which way the wind blows, if you know what I mean."

"Sure, I get you. Thanks, Mr. Corcoran."

"Call me Darryl, Ray. We're practically related."

"Right, uh, Darryl. Will do."

The message was passed along: Deserving atheist recently bereaved, affianced to Christian girl, needs cash for investment in family business, potential recruit.

And lo, the money came, at very reasonable interest. Ray switched banks and immediately began renovating the Thunderbird. Six hectic weeks later the motel stood as it had on its inaugural day, gaudy testament to Lowell's, and now Ray's, taste. Like his father before him, Ray invited the press. He was even seen on TV that night on the local news. "Well, I thought the place deserved a lick of paint seeing as it's a piece of Callisto history, the first real motel in town and still the best, also a lot cheaper than those other boring places whose names I won't mention, ha, ha, but seriously, the Thunderbird is something we can all be proud of, you know, because it's been around a long time now, and I'm gonna make sure it stays around a whole lot longer. Every town should hang on to its history, is what I'm saying."

The Corcorans invited Ray to attend church with them. He went along; it was the least he could do. Business had picked up considerably since he used the last of the loan to place new signs along the highway on either side of town. SEE THE ONLY ELECTRIC TOTEM POLE IN AMERICA! SLEEP CHEAP IN A PLACE LIKE NO OTHER! Christian cash had made it possible, so to church he went. Introduced to the congregation, he found he was a celebrity.

"I think it's just wonderful what you've done, taking charge like you have and not letting your tragedy get you down the way some folks would've, but not you. I just wanted to tell you, and I'm sure we all feel the same."

"Uh . . . thank you."

"We think you did exactly the right thing, Mr. Kootz, not giving in like that. The Lord provides a way for them that care to go look for it."

"Yeah, I think so too."

"You're a lucky guy, Ray. Mind if I call you Ray? We're kind of informal at the Nazarene. Real lucky to have this girl of yours. She was sought after by plenty, believe me, but you caught the brass ring. Better make that a gold ring, heh, heh. Just a little joke, Ray. But I want to wish you both every happiness, sincerely."

"Thank you."

"Hi! Welcome to our church!"

"Hi. Glad to be here."

He sat through a sermon on fellowship. Jesus was the first Rotarian, apparently. Everyone around Ray wore a faint smile, nodded now and then in agreement with the minister. The woman seated in front of him had ornately styled hair, or was it a wig? Ray wanted to yank it and find out, couldn't concentrate on the holy cordiality washing over him from the pulpit. He realized his fascination with the woman's hair was all that kept him from fidgeting like a naughty boy in Sunday school. Soon the question of wig or hair was not enough; he wanted to sink his teeth into her neck like a vampire and see if the blood that ran out was lamblike. Now Ray smiled along with the rest. Susan saw the look on his face and knew Ray had found his spiritual home. Her father had been right to advise a long, lightweight line, reeled in slowly to land her fish on this golden shore. Here he was. It almost brought tears to her eyes. Her world soon would be complete.

Before he shipped out for Vietnam, Bernie made a quick trip home. He visited Ray at the Thunderbird, crisp and new-looking in his uniform. Ray barely recognized him.

"Susan Corcoran? With blond hair?"

"That's her."

"We used to call her Betty Bible in school."

"I don't remember that."

"Oh, well, maybe it was someone else. So you're really gonna go ahead and do it, huh?"

"Sure," said Ray, aware that he sounded defensive.

"Wife and kids, cat and dog."

"Right."

Bernie looked at the floor and shook his head. Ray hated him for that. Conversation between them faltered and died. Ray told Bernie to be careful over there. Bernie said he would. They both looked at the floor.

"Well, gotta go back and keep the folks company."

"Okay."

It was a short visit.

Thanksgiving turkey with the Corcorans. Christmas ham with the Corcorans. New Year's Eve with the Corcorans. "We like to stay in and give thanks as a family, Ray." He turned twenty as the last of the snow melted. They gave him a party; their gift was a thousand dollars' credit at Callisto's best menswear store. The wedding was just two weeks away. Then one. Ray felt sick about it. He couldn't stand them any more, even Susan. He wished they'd go for a spin in Darryl's Oldsmobile and drive off a bridge. All he wanted was the Thunderbird. How could he get the Corcorans out of his life? Every Sunday he developed a headache that nagged until sleep killed it. Mondays were a relief; six whole days until Sunday again. But next weekend he'd face the biggest headache of all. He couldn't go through with it, just couldn't, not even if they paid him, which they had.

He went to the gun club for the first time in months, shot his dilemma to pieces for a while, scored miserably, and went home to make sure the temporary alternate manager was handling the afternoon shift without burning the place down. Ray's plan was to replace him with Susan after the wedding. Susan's plan was to talk Ray out of running the motel after a year or two, bulldoze it, and erect a specialty store of some kind on the site. Deep in her heart Susan thought the Thunderbird was tacky. Until the time came to make her pitch for change, she would do as Ray wanted and help him sign in guests and pay the sheet girls every week. The new man Ray had hired, Ed Wilkey, would be let go when they returned from their honeymoon in Hawaii, all expenses provided by Darryl and Margaret Corcoran.

Ray stewed in his private hell. He was about to make the biggest mistake of his life. Bernie had been right to express scorn for this dumbest of moves. How could he have let it get started, let alone proceed to the brink of total commitment? He teased himself with thoughts of Russian roulette, even went so far as to slide a single cartridge into the Blackhawk, spin the chamber, and place the barrel against his temple. He couldn't do it. Just the touch of that unmerciful steel brought on one of his king-sized headaches, and today was only Tuesday; by Saturday he'd need a craniotomy. He gobbled aspirin, was tempted to swallow the whole bottle, but did not. Ray Kootz had gone and fucked up his life again, and this time he'd have to live with it.

Three days to go. Ray's thoughts were filled with disturbing images—guillotine blades dropping, prison doors closing, keys being turned and pocketed by hands other than his own. He drove past the church where the ceremony was to take place, the same white edifice he'd sat inside these last Sundays without number. This Saturday he'd be standing, a lone tree waiting to be felled. The Corcorans had invited almost two hundred people to the reception that would follow in the church hall. Would they sue for breach of promise if he backed out now? He just bet they would. The Corcorans would use their influence to bring down the wrath of God; the Thunderbird would disappear, consumed by torrents of celestial fire. Ray wanted to weep at his predicament. Maybe if he steered off the road, broke his legs and a few ribs, would that give him extra time to figure a way out? With his luck, he'd probably break his neck instead. There had to be a way. Assault a cop and get himself arrested? The Corcorans wouldn't want to be associated by marriage with a lawbreaker. But Ray didn't want to spend time in jail, couldn't afford to be fined, and the Corcorans might see it as a challenge to their Samaritan credo, might want to reform him all over again, this time for keeps. The thought of Darryl bailing him out of custody in time for the wedding was not funny. His sin had to be deeper than mere crime, had to be something that would baffle his future in-laws completely.

It was the spare rolls of toilet paper that gave Ray the answer. Modestly ensconced behind their gingham, they offended him on Thursday night as never before. This was to be his last visit with the Corcorans before the big day. The last of the details finally had been worked out weeks ago (Ray's best man, in the absence of his closest friend, would be the gun club member who had brought the bride and groom together in the first place), and it only remained to make this final visit, to pledge himself to events just thirty-six hours away. Everything had been taken care of.

Screaming inside, Ray went upstairs to void his lurching bowels, and there saw the rolls of toilet paper. Their insufferable coyness, their plump bashfulness enraged him. He ripped them from their little basket and stuffed them deep inside the toilet's U-bend, as far back as he possibly could. The hollow end of the second roll's cardboard tube gaped up at him with a submarine O of surprise. Ray felt terrific, hoped he'd screwed their plumbing but good. It was petty revenge for all they were putting him through, but better than nothing. He could never have explained it to anyone. And then came inspiration. The path to freedom lay through the tangled woods of madness, that unchristian place where the cuckoo bird sings at thirteen o'clock. He'd pretend to be nuts! The Corcorans' bathroom was a peach-

and-mauve-tiled prison no longer but the birthplace of Crazy Ray! He'd have to be careful, very careful, or they'd smell a rat. Ray wiggled his nose in a rattish manner, delighted with himself. How to convey lunacy? He stared at the toilet bowl with its sopping plug.

His hosts were mildly absorbed by the weather report when Ray returned downstairs, and did not at first realize that Ray wore no pants; not only that, he wore no shorts; between his shirttail and his socks—nothing. Penis dangling, he sat down on the sofa beside Susan who, turning to bestow a loving smile, immediately became paralyzed with shock. Darryl was the next to be aware that something strange had invaded the living room. Catching sight of bare knees at the periphery of his vision, he slowly turned, stared but made no sound while his brain tried to reconcile what he saw with normalcy.

"Did they have the extended forecast yet?" asked Ray. "I'm a little worried about rain on Saturday. It can be tricky this time of year."

Margaret turned to answer him, saw his semi-nakedness and gasped in wordless horror.

"Ray . . ."

"Yeah, Darryl?"

"Ray . . . your pants . . . Where are your pants, Ray?"

"Oh, I took 'em off. I don't think tan's my color, you know? I've got a gray pair at home. I should've worn them instead."

"Ray . . . Ray, listen to me. What happened . . . ?"

"Uh . . . I think they're at the dry cleaner's, so I wore the tan pair."

"But you're *not* wearing them. What . . . what's the big idea? You've got no pants on, boy!"

"Well, I just don't think they're right for me, I really don't, so they can stay where they are, frankly."

"But where are they? Margaret, Susan, leave the room. Ray, *sit down!*"

91

"I left 'em upstairs, I remember now."

"Cover yourself, for God's sake!"

"I'll get them," volunteered Susan, and dashed for the stairs. Margaret, meanwhile, was headed for the kitchen, tiny sips of air passing across her frozen lips.

"Ray, now Ray, you sit down and listen to what I say. Are you feeling sick, feeling bad in any way?"

"No, sir, I'm just fine, honest." He jabbed a finger at the TV screen. "The extended forecast! It's gonna be okay! Look—a little sunny face behind the cloud but no rain-drops. Saturday's okay!"

"Margaret! Call Dr. Westley!"

The kitchen cupboards clattered open and shut as Margaret searched for the medicinal brandy that had not been there since the Corcorans joined the Nazarene Church.

"Ray, if this is some kind of very sick joke, I'm going to be very disappointed in you. What in God's name made you take your pants off?"

A scream from the bathroom sent Darryl bounding to the upper floor. Susan was backing out of the bathroom as he reached the stairhead. She turned and ran to her room, slamming the door behind her. Darryl edged forward and peeked into the bathroom. Everything seemed in order, but then he saw the evidence of Ray's mental state. Coiled on top of the toilet lid like a lethargic, headless snake lay a monstrous turd. Darryl approached it warily. If there was excrement on the closed lid, what ghastliness might lurk beneath? He took a long-handled back scrubber, inserted it beneath the furry mauve cover (totally ruined, he knew; the shit smell could never be gotten out), and slowly lifted the lid. Considering the bizarre nature of the last few minutes, it seemed only natural to find a pair of folded slacks resting neatly on top of two waterlogged toilet rolls, the surreal tableau garnished by used squares of paper. Stunned, he lowered the lid.

Ray's car keys were still in his slacks. He was sent home in a cab, legs loosely enclosed in a pair of Darryl's weekend corduroys.

"You married?" he asked the cabbie.

"Nah."

"Me neither."

8

IT WAS CLEAR Lowell Kootz's blood ran strong in the veins of his son. The bank sent him a note reminding him in the strongest language of his monthly commitment to the terms of the loan, whatever his "personal circumstances." Ray wasn't worried: profits continued picking up. He wasn't going to fall flat on his face to suit anyone's idea of retribution. He'd fully intended marrying Susan when he took out the loan, hadn't deceived anyone, but things had changed, things inside him, and he was obliged to do what he did or regret not having done it for the rest of his life. To Ray's mind it was settled.

One thing continued to disturb him: he still wanted to marry. He'd moved from the top room after Judith's death, now slept in the place where he was conceived. The bed of his parents was big enough to be lonely in, so commodious it begged for company. Where was the girl who'd fit? Ray had never been in love, not even with Susan, and he knew it. He would've remembered how it felt. He wondered if Judith had ever loved his father. She'd never said. Ray was determined his own kids would witness love between himself and his wife, so they'd recognize it when it came along in their own lives. He thought about it often, this passing on of love. But there were no kids, no wife as yet, and the lack of these things in his home irked Ray in a way he could never have suspected just a year ago. The difference between nineteen and twenty, it seemed, was measured in something other than time. The new Ray wanted love, real love, the kind they sang about in songs.

Dear Ray,

I was going to write you just before we shipped out but didn't. Then I was going to when we got here but didn't. 'Nam is an amazing place, very hot all the time even when it rains. They tell us not to talk about the war in letters. That's why this is a postcard. I saw the temple in the picture. How is married life treating you? Good I hope.

yrs
Bernie

Summer came, and still Ray was without a wife. Ed Wilkey's services as alternate manager had been retained in the wake of the marriage that never was, and he was grateful for the work. Ed was fifty-four. Ed said he had a niece Ray might like to marry, but when he showed a snapshot of the family reunion last Thanksgiving, Ray knew the girl in the picture was not for him. "Maybe she is kind of plain," admitted Ed, "but it's the kind you could overlook if you had a mind to." Ray wanted to overlook nothing, wanted to be smitten, struck dumb by the Big Dart. Managing the Thunderbird was second nature to him now, the sense of accomplishment it gave him lessening with every week that passed. He went out drinking again, not to get drunk but to meet someone. A bar was an unlikely place to meet a wife, but you never knew, and if it turned out he only found someone to take home to bed, well, he could use a little of that, too. But he found neither, because he was bad company in bars.

* * *

Sheet lightning flickered one night in September, and the totem pole seemed to blaze with more than its usual effulgence. A storm was rolling toward Callisto from the west, inking over the stars. On duty behind the reception desk, Ray felt his neck hair lift and fall like seaweed in the humid air. All day he'd felt uncomfortable, irritable. He wanted the rain to come, but it would not. He had nothing to watch outside but the totem pole, its vibrant neon tubing now and then eclipsed by a sky made white with split-second incandescence. He had the deskside TV on, its volume turned down, the better to hear the thunder grinding slowly nearer, thudding, thumping, a mile-high robot that lurched a few crippled steps then fell to its knees, picked itself up and stumbled on.

The late-night news roundup featured soldiers leaping from helicopters, blasting at a foe made invisible by jungle. Ray had rarely seen a live Viet Cong on TV; it seemed their physical essence could best be captured on film when dead; small people, almost skeletal in their puniness, a body count of black-pajamaed manikins. He wondered how many of them Bernie had killed. It was difficult to picture the kid he'd known with his head under a car hood now raking the undergrowth with machine gun fire. How would they be able to talk and laugh again as friends after so decisive an interlude? Assuming Bernie returned. Ray liked to think he would, and that no great harm would have been done to their oscillating friendship. He was saving the story of how he'd bilked from Callisto's Christians a sizable chunk of cash, jilted one of their pious daughters, too, the one Bernie thought he was married to. Ray had considered writing Bernie a letter to set him straight but didn't know where to address it. He could've gotten the information from Rudy Swenson but didn't. Maybe it was laziness, maybe some kind of protest against Bernie's freewheeling ways, Ray couldn't tell. Meantime, the story was on ice. Bernie would love it.

Customers checked in, departed to their tepees, and still

the rain had not arrived. The sky was blanketed by cloud to all points of the horizon. Ray stepped outside, felt the clamminess of an electrically charged summer night fold around him like a wet woolen glove. Sweat ran from the tributaries of his shoulder blades to the ravine of his spine, trickled down to be dammed by his belt. His eyebrows itched with collected moisture. Thunder had not been heard for some time, and lightning glimmered fitfully only at the sky's farthest edge. Drum rolls and spotlights had set the stage; now Ray waited impatiently for performing showers to be ushered on. He stared at the totem pole. The Thunderbird was supposed to be the god of storms, of thunder, lightning, and rain, all three, so where was the rain? The pole buzzed statically, hummed in monotone, maybe summoning the third element of its triad, calling down a torrent of lashing droplets for the man who craved it.

Ray's eye fell from the eagle's spread wings, down past the bear and wolf and deer to the ground. He began walking around the totem pole. It truly was a work of art. Lowell had been some kind of creative type for sure. Ray knew he didn't have anything like it inside himself but didn't resent the lack. Lowell had failed as a family man, and at that particular job Ray was determined not just to succeed but to excel. Then the Thunderbird would be a complete place. What his father had begun, Ray would finish. It was a concept that anchored him in both the past and future. The time he occupied now, the present, was just something he rode from one to the other, a bubble in a slanted spirit level rising from the abyss of yesterday to the high plateau of tomorrow. Riding the bubble was what life was all about.

Reaching the totem pole's far side, he stopped. A small figure was also contemplating the pole, neck craned to take in the topmost form's wings limned in pink and yellow that seemed to encompass half the sky, that uncompromising beak of blue and those hellish red eyes. Ray could not be sure if the totem pole's admirer was male or female; its hair reached its shoulders. It stood less than four feet high, wore jeans and a white T-shirt made mauve-green by the pulsing neon. The upturned eyes dropped and saw him.

"Like the big pole?" said Ray.

"Yeah."

A boy, Ray decided.

"It's sure a sight. You ever see one like it before?"

Girlish tresses swayed as he shook his head.

"You staying here with your folks?"

"Just my mom."

"My name's Ray. What's yours?"

"Milo."

"Pardon me?"

The boy repeated it. They grew milo by the hundreds of acres outside town, row upon row of nodding brown tasseled heads. Ray didn't even know what the stuff was used for when harvested.

"That's a pretty unusual name."

"My mom says it's Irish."

"Are you from Ireland?"

"No, Chicago."

"Oh."

"It's gonna rain."

"Yeah, I think so."

"There was lightning before."

"I saw it. I like it when it rains; how about you?"

"It's okay."

"Should cool things off some."

"But then it'll be more humid."

"Well, yeah. How old are you, Milo?"

"Five and a half."

"Does your mom know you're wandering around out here on your own? That's not a smart thing for a kid to do."

"I felt a drop!"

Ray was annoyed the first drop had hit Milo instead of himself. He felt cheated, but maybe Milo was wrong, had imagined it out of sheer anticipation the way kids do. A drop hit Ray's nose.

"Yeah, here it comes all right."

The first rain wave whispered around them, speckled their faces and arms, and seconds later became a downpour.

"Better get inside, Milo."

"I forget where."

"What number are you? What tepee?"

"I dunno."

"What kind of car does your mom drive?"

"A red one."

"Okay, let's look for it."

Cars were angled around the circular parking lot like minutes marked on a clockface, rear bumpers inward, noses pointed at the tepees. In the totem pole's prismatic glare it was hard to distinguish one color from another, and they passed around the lot's circumference twice before Ray, thoroughly drenched, decided to use his adult powers of deduction rather than trust the boy's suspect talent for auto identification.

"Hey, Milo, what's your last name? We'll look you up in the register."

"The what?"

"The big book with all the names of everyone who's here."

The T-bird used an index card system, not a book, but Ray couldn't be bothered explaining that. He was getting irritated; if this kid with rattailed hair caught pneumonia, his mother might sue.

"There it is!"

A reddish Buick was indicated by Milo. He ran past it and began pounding on the door of Tepee 12. "Mom! Mom!" Ray followed and pressed the buzzer. "Take it easy, Milo." He knew what he'd see when the door opened; some frowzy bitch with booze on her breath, the kind who never knew where her kid was and didn't care. He couldn't recall signing in anyone like that, so Ed must've done it sometime during the afternoon. Ray had a good mind to chew her out on the subject of parental responsibility.

The woman who opened the door was not like that at all. Milo ran into the tepee. "Was he lost?" asked the woman. Ray nodded. "He's never had any sense of direction," she said. Ray liked her face and the sound of her voice. "We got wet," he said, then added, "I'm the owner," in case she might think him some kind of prowler or bum. He sensed she also had an attractive body, but didn't dare lower his eyes, didn't want her to think he was that kind of guy.

"The owner?"

"Of the motel."

"Oh. Well, thank you. He wasn't supposed to be out."

Behind her the TV was turned on by Milo. Ray wanted to be invited inside, but could think of no good reason why this should happen.

"He was looking at the totem pole. I was telling him all about it when the rain came, then he couldn't remember what number he's in."

"I'm sorry you had to get wet."

"That's okay. We needed it."

He shouldn't have said that; now she'd think he was a Kansas hick who gave a damn about crops. Ray could just about distinguish corn from wheat. The woman said nothing. If he stayed more than another few seconds, he'd seem an even bigger fool.

"Well, enjoy your stay."

"Thank you."

Ray made himself turn away before the door was closed. Trudging back through the rain to the office, he felt the profound weight of loss dragging at his limbs. He'd lost her without ever having known her, without coming anywhere near knowing her. It was a ridiculous situation. She didn't even know how he felt, and why the hell should she? He didn't know himself why he felt like this about her. She was no prettier than hundreds of other women he'd seen, and it was irresponsible of her to let her boy get out that way in a strange town. Where was the husband? Had there been a ring on her finger? He hadn't looked, had stared only at her face, which wasn't even all that pretty now that he came to think of it. The whole thing was dumb, just dumb, he told himself as he looked her up in the register.

Holly Ginty was the name of the woman he'd fallen for. Chicago address, just like the kid said. A '66 Buick Electra. One night only. Paid cash. She hadn't even smiled at him when she said thank you for saving her precious Milo from pneumonia and kidnapping. But maybe she'd been tense, worried about the boy. It was possible. Maybe when she closed the door she got mad at herself for not having been friendlier with the nice man who owned the motel. It was possible.

He turned on the deskside TV, wondered if it was the same show playing in Tepee 12. An actor got out of a car, hurried up some imposing steps, and was gunned down by another actor who stepped out from behind a stone pillar. The gunman began to run but was stopped by a bullet from a cop's .38. A crowd gathered around the dying man on the steps. Ray turned it off. He still had water running down his neck from his hair, went and toweled himself dry in time to sign in another guest and exchange comments on the rainstorm. Then he was alone again.

Maybe she'd need to come over and make a phone call to Chicago, let her husband (if there was one) know she was coming home by way of Reno, where she'd gotten herself a quickie divorce. Or the kid would get loose and Ray would have to round him up again. Or Holly and Milo would drive away like a million guests before them, anonymous vehicles disappearing down a highway to the world. And why not? What was so special about these two? A woman already saddled with a child had never entered his dreams of domesticity, but Ray was prepared to embrace instant fatherhood if the guest in Tepee 12 would have him. His need for her shocked him. This was crazy.

Rain hammered at the sloping window before him. Sloping windows caught more dust than vertical panes, had to be washed more often, a problem peculiar to the Thunderbird. Ray hoped the rain was doing some good. Through the runnels of water Tepee 12 could be seen on the parking lot's far side, just to the left of the totem pole. Inside that concrete cone was a witch unaware of her powers, blithely destroying him by her presence. Ray felt ill with longing. Just the craziest, dumbest thing, but he couldn't help it. His predicament had all the simplicity and banal emotion of a pop song, and all the undeniable insistence; like it or not, Ray had to jig his foot to Holly Ginty's tune.

By 1 A.M. the rain had eased to occasional tappings on the window. Milo was right; the humidity was worse, so bad the air conditioning simply created a clamminess that pasted Ray's shirt to his back. The swivel fan beside him did nothing to cool his inner burning, and the thing that galvanized his thoughts showed no sign of letting go. Tepee 12, an unremarkable cone among cones, had assumed the mystic dimensions of a pyramid, its rain-washed sides scrawled with a code for happiness Ray was unable to decipher. What would bring her out? How could he get in? Mother and son were no doubt sleeping soundly. Ray would have been happy just to stand over them in the dark. Ears filled with the fan's electric humming, Ray knew something had to give. To sit and dream and do nothing was torture.

Outside again, he circled the Thunderbird's parking lot a dozen times, obsession slowing his steps every time he passed the '66 Electra's bumper. By 1:58 he knew what he had to do. He returned to the big tepee, took the kitchen's sharpest knife, and returned to the parking lot. One quick look around to make sure no one was looking, then Ray bent and sank the blade into the Buick's left rear tire. Its plumpness sagged, wafted rubbery air past Ray's nostrils. One hole could be quickly patched, so Ray sank the knife home all around the rim, made it unpatchable. The three remaining tires were similarly bladed. There was no feasible way of tackling the spare inside the trunk, and four dead tires out of five would buy Ray precious time. He washed the knife to remove the smell of rubber from it, showered to remove the same smell from himself, then turned on the NO VACANCIES sign outside and went to bed, but even the fitful sleep of a motel owner evaded him. He talked to her till dawn.

"Must've been vandals," he told her next morning. "We had a couple of tires slashed by kids a week or two back."

The Electra squatted on its rims like a wounded buffalo brought to its knees. Milo solemnly examined the flats.

"Great," said Holly Ginty, "just great. Where am I going to find the cash for four new tires?"

"Maybe you could wire your husband, or your family or someone."

"No chance. Jesus. They did this before, these vandals?"

"Couple of weeks back. The police cruise by every now and then, but they can't watch the place all the time. I'm real sorry, Mrs. Ginty."

"Miss. This really screws my schedule."

"They're expecting you home?"

"It's my mother. She worries."

"You can call her long distance from the office. No charge."

"Really? Thanks, I think I better."

Unmarried or divorced. Ray's heart galloped in his chest. He was definitely in love. There was no holding him back now.

"Tell you what I'm going to do, Miss Ginty. I'm going to assume responsibility for this incident. It happened on my property to one of my paying guests, so it's my responsibility. I'm gonna get you four new tires and allow you to stay on past checkout time at no extra cost until the tires are installed. It's the least I can do."

"Oh, you don't have to do that. I couldn't let you."

"Yes you could. Frankly, I think you'll have to. This car's going nowhere without four new ones."

"Well . . . I guess. I don't know what to say, uh, I don't know your name."

"Kootz. Ray Kootz. Call me Ray."

She called him Ray. He took them to the Cherry Tree for breakfast, then called up the Firestone outlet and ordered four tires, was told the kind required by Holly's car were in stock and could be installed immediately. Ray told them to send a man around to the motel tomorrow morning at the earliest, not today under any circumstances.

"Uh, Holly, I'm afraid you're stuck here till tomorrow. I called every tire supplier in town, even phoned over to Butane, but they're all out of the tires you need except one place, but they've only got two left. They said they'll have a shipment in tomorrow, though, and they'll come right over and change 'em for you. Meantime you and Milo can stay on in number twelve, no charge."

"Well, that's just too generous for words. I hate for you to be put out like this, phoning around and arranging things and losing money over something some kid did that wasn't even your fault or anything. I really appreciate what you're doing, Ray."

"Like I said, the responsibility's mine."

The Cherry Tree again for lunch. Milo was bored.

"When are we gonna go?"

"When the new tires are on the car, honey, and that's tomorrow. Hold your burger straight, you're slopping ketchup everyplace, Milo. . . . Okay, now wipe it up. Use a napkin; that's what they're for, not your sleeve! Jesus, Milo . . ."

"Where'd he get his name?"

"That was my ex's idea. He was real proud of being Irish. Well, his great-granddad was Irish a hundred years ago or something. Brian was the kind who gets Irish all of a sudden on St. Patrick's Day and drinks green beer. Green beer, can you imagine it? I couldn't stay married to a guy like that. He would've ended up being a bad influence on my cutie here. Leave it on the side of your plate. Just scrunch it up and leave it. Do you like his hair like that? I think long hair on guys is fine."

"I used to wear mine long, but I kind of have to look neat, you know, dealing with the public."

"I know what you mean. I had a job as a receptionist in this place one time and they were always telling me to look neat, like if I didn't look a hundred percent perfect I'd scare the customers away or something, real extreme. I like to be casual."

"Right. Casual's best."

"Some guys look okay in short hair too, like you."

"Yeah?"

"Don't the girls all tell you that?"

"Sometimes. I'm pretty busy running the T-bird."

"You must be the youngest manager of anything I ever met."

Ray told her about Judith's early death. Holly was sympathetic, said her own mother was in poor health, probably wouldn't last much longer the way things were going. They talked for some time. He learned she'd divorced Brian eighteen months before, was returning from a vacation spent with an old girlfriend in California, and was not looking forward to resuming work as a filing clerk for a big Chicago insurance company. He could tell she was satisfied with not one aspect of her life. It was also obvious she liked him, liked him more by the minute. He suspected it was because he listened closely to everything she said. Ray had read an article in a magazine that said this was what women truly wanted in a man, the ability to listen without interrupting. That and a small butt. Ray's butt was pretty small. Everything was working out fine. His act of vandalism was proving to be the most important thing he'd ever done. Years from now he'd be able to tell Holly how he sabotaged her car and delayed her departure from Callisto. She'd be mad for a couple of minutes, then they'd laugh about it together. She might even be flattered he'd gone to such crazy lengths to keep her near. He'd done it for love, after all, and it was costing him plenty.

"When are we gonna go?"

"When the car's ready, I told you."

"What's up, Milo, you don't like this town?"

"No!"

"Ignore him. He's just being a little turkey."

They went for a walk.

"How about you, Holly, you like our little piece of Kansas?"

"Sure. I never lived in a small town, but I like it. Chicago's way too big, too noisy and dirty, you know?"

"Right, and too much crime."

"Don't I know it. This one time I got mugged in broad daylight by this guy and no one did a thing, didn't try to stop him or anything. It was disgusting what they did. Is it true about small-town people knowing each other and caring for everyone, you know, like a big family?"

"Oh, sure. People can get a little nosy sometimes, but it's a whole different feeling to being in a big city; friendlier."

"That's what I thought. So you're happy here?"

"Pretty much, yeah, I guess so, only I'm kind of busy most of the time, like I said, running the place, but yeah, I'm happy enough. How about you?"

"I'd be happier in California. My girlfriend says move out there, but I don't know. Would I be any happier just on account of sunshine? Why not Florida?"

"Happiness depends on who you're with, not sunshine."

"You're right. You're so damn right it could've been me talking, I mean it. Who you're with. Right. That's the most important thing. Brian and I weren't meant for each other, definitely mismatched in every possible way. That's a hard thing for a woman to admit, that she made a big mistake, but I feel like I can admit it to you. You know, you're real easy to talk to, did anyone ever tell you that?"

"I don't know. Maybe."

"Well you are, believe me."

"Mom, can I have one?"

Milo was pointing at an ice cream parlor. They all had one: Raspberry Ripple for Ray, Blueberry Pecan for Holly, and Chocolate Fudge Peppermint for Milo, who declared it was not as good as the Baskin-Robbins back home. Holly called him a sourpuss and they strolled on.

"So how come you kept your ex's name?"

"My maiden name was Betzelburger."

"Oh."

Ray asked Ed to stand in for him on the night shift, at least until nine. Ed said no. Ray offered him twenty dollars. Ed still said no, he had bowling tonight. Ray offered him fifty. Ed said yes. After giving Holly time to shower and change her clothes, Ray presented himself at Tepee 12, himself showered and changed. Milo opened the door.

"Why are you here?"

"I live here, Milo. It's my motel."

"No it isn't."

He tried to shut the door, but Ray pushed it open again.

"I bought you an ice cream today, Milo. Be nice."

"I didn't like it."

"Tough tit. I'm coming inside, so move it."

Dinner at the Callisto Inn. Ray had been awake now for over twenty-four hours, but didn't feel in the least bit tired; love was a powerful drug. They had wine. Milo had a Coke. It was just a short walk back to the Thunderbird. Ray wished them both pleasant dreams. Holly reciprocated. Milo said nothing. Ray took over from Ed, who went on home to watch *Gunsmoke*. Now came the body's reprisal; before Ed's Chevy was gone from the parking lot Ray's eyelids flickered and dropped, were forced open again long enough to let him tell the world there was NO VACANCY at the Thunderbird despite the early hour, lock the door, and get into bed. I'm in love, he told himself, and fell asleep.

Next morning the tires came. Holly's Electra stood ready to roll.

"Listen, you've been just so generous I can't believe it, really. No one in Chicago would've done this."

"My pleasure."

"I wouldn't have got to know how nice people are in Kansas if someone didn't slash my tires, how about that, fate or something, huh?"

"I guess. So you're on your way."

"Yeah, or my mom'll worry."

"Have a nice trip. Drive carefully."

"If you're ever in Chicago call me up and I'll show you around the windy city."

"Okay. What's the number?"

He had pen and paper handy. She wrote it down.

"There."

"Thanks."

"Milo, in the car, honey."

"So long, Milo."

"C'mon, Mom."

"Gotta go. 'Bye."

" 'Bye."

When they drove off he was not unhappy. The hard part was waiting two days before calling.

"Hi. It's Ray. From Kansas."

"Ray, hi, how are you?"

"Fine."

The conversation meandered for some minutes while Ray gathered nerve.

"Listen, Holly, I have to ask you something."

"Okay."

"This'll probably sound very weird. I mean we hardly know each other."

"Yes?"

"So how would you feel about, uh, getting married. To me. And coming down here to live. How would you feel about that?"

"Jeez, Ray, you don't waste any time. Let me just think about this. You're some kind of crazy guy, Ray."

"Yeah, well, I had to, you know. Are you thinking?"

"I'm thinking, I'm thinking. Let me think for a minute."

Ray studied the wall in front of him, raised and lowered himself on the balls of his feet. The silence on the line roared.

"Ray?"

"Yeah?"

"I'm still thinking."

"Okay."

"This is very sudden, you know?"

"So what? I mean, what's wrong with sudden?"

"Nothing, I guess, if we're sure."

"I'm sure. I'm positive."

"Ray, I'm twenty-four. I think you're a little bit younger than me, aren't you?"

"I'm twenty. What's that got to do with anything?"

"I just thought I should mention it. You don't care if I'm older?"

"No."

"Okay. I'm still thinking. Don't hang up."

"Fine."

He knew then he'd failed. She would've said yes by now if she wanted him. His entire body slumped. The phone almost slipped from his slackened fingers. His very guts seemed to sag. This was how it felt to lose. This was the essence of defeat. The phone began inching away from his ear. The whole thing, this stupid call, had degenerated within seconds from highest hope to deepest embarrassment. Would it be okay to hang up and spare Holly similar prolongation of this awful moment, or just bad manners? His arm was locked.

"Ray?"

"Yuh?"

"Can you come up to Chicago? I think you should meet my mom at least before we do it. See, I didn't introduce her to Brian before we got married, so I think I owe her this one out of politeness. She's not very well right now and it'll make her feel good to be included in things, don't you think?"

"Uh-huh."

"So can you do that, come up here and meet her? Then we can go ahead and get married. We won't be abandoning her or anything—when I move to Kansas, I mean. She's been talking about moving in with her sister's family anyway, so that's okay. So when are you gonna come?"

"Uh, tomorrow."

And he did, and came home with a wife and stepson.

PART TWO

Epiphany in Kansas

9

MILO DID NOT GET ALONG with his baby half-brother. His jealousy was apparent from the start. Every minute Holly spent with Kevin was a minute spent away from Milo, and that was intolerable. He dogged her steps from crib to bathroom to kitchen till she yelled at him to quit, and being yelled at made him cry. Ever since Ray had married his mom, Milo had suffered, and his suffering reached its peak in the months following Kevin's birth. Milo hated the pink squawling lump with an intensity that was almost pleasurable. Ray was too big to dispose of, but tiny Kevin would surely prove easy to kill. Milo knew how he'd do it; with a pillow, like in a movie he saw on TV. You couldn't breathe through a pillow and it didn't leave any marks, which was handy, because Milo didn't want to get caught and sent to the electric chair like the man in the movie, who was stupid enough to try the same method twice, so he deserved to be caught for dumbness. Milo only needed to kill once.

He sometimes poked Kevin with his finger to make him howl. Why should Milo shed all the tears? He begged Holly to take the baby away, but she wouldn't, even yelled at him again. It would have to be the pillow. The plan, Milo's only comfort, was postponed from day to day. He once took a pillow to Kevin's crib, then heard Holly's approaching footsteps and hurried back up to his room. He thought of the incident as a dress rehearsal for the time he would go ahead and really kill the thing that had edged him from his mother's arms. Milo nursed the plan until it became a part of him that waxed and waned in importance but was never quite forgotten.

Until he was two years old Kevin slept in the spare room next to Ray and Holly's big bedroom, then was moved upstairs to share with Milo. Holly said the boys needed to be together more; they just weren't friendly enough, and sharing the conical room at the top of the tepee seemed the best way to instill in them a sense of brotherhood. With a second bed placed beside it, Milo's own was shunted sideways, out from under the apex. When he lay down now the whole room appeared skewed; from this alien perspective it was no longer familiar, no longer his. Milo was outraged by the invasion, and dusted off his plans for murder. It would be a lot easier with Kevin sleeping right beside him, the little shitbutt. But somehow Kevin survived, and by the time he learned to talk properly his half-brother was more or less reconciled to sharing both the room and his life with the interloper.

Following his discharge, Bernie Swenson became a cop. He seldom talked about Vietnam, not even to Ray. His parents died in a twenty-seven-car pileup while vacationing in Oregon, and Bernie sold the landscaping business. He married Pamela Hubbard, a poodle trimmer at the Li'l Pal Pet Boutique, and divorced her three years later. She left town soon after. "Never marry a woman who cuts hair," Bernie told Ray. "They get a Delilah complex and start snipping below the belt. Jesus, what a big mistake to marry that airhead. That's two big mistakes in my life so far, 'Nam and Pam."

Holly didn't like Bernie. "He's a typical macho shit. Brian was like that, so I divorced him. I can't stand that kind. Do me a favor and don't invite him around here any more, okay? You can go drinking with him, boys' night out, I don't care, just don't bring him back here. I'm serious, Ray. It's disgusting the way he treated Pamela. So she wasn't bright, so what? He knew that when he married her, right? It's his own fault things didn't work out, talking down to her all the time like he did."

"She put him down plenty, too."

"Only because he deserved it. He's a shit and you know it, exactly the right personality to be a cop. I don't want him around our boys, influencing them."

"Okay, okay."

Bernie's relegation to part-time buddy didn't upset Ray. His family was his life. Being a husband and father might be kind of square, but it was the root of his contentment. A night of mild drunkenness with Bernie once a month was all the diversion Ray required from the domestic life he'd embraced, a life that had turned out to be surprisingly fulfilling. He'd lucked onto something good. He heard Susan Corcoran had married a doctor and moved away from Callisto. Ray was baffled; why would anyone want to leave this wonderful little town where everything was so simple, so rewarding? Judith should see him now. The Thunderbird was doing fine, and so was its owner. His wife was a little temperamental maybe, but he could handle that, was still in love with her even; but the light that shone brightest through all his days and nights was Kevin.

Fatherhood was a revelation to Ray. He hadn't minded the stench and noise, had refereed the countless squabblings between son and stepson without, he felt, favoring one over the other. But it was Kevin who crept early beneath his skin and stayed there. Blood of his blood, it was understandable. Milo was a smart kid and had his mother's looks, but Kevin had come from seed planted by Ray. Somehow it seemed that Milo was half Holly's but Kevin all his. He never said so to his wife. To her the boys were fruit from different trees, equally precious, ripening steadily.

Even when Milo behaved outrageously, Ray treated him fairly. He spanked him only occasionally, less often in fact than Holly did, and never without justification. Ray congratulated himself on his ability to appear impartial. No one, not even Kevin, knew of his secret bias.

The Thunderbird was being maintained for a ceremonial handing down to his natural son. It was only right. Ray assumed Milo would find some other avenue of employment, encouraged the boy's juvenile whimsy of one day becoming the pilot of a cargo plane. A fat Hercules hung over his bed, fueling the fantasy. It might even happen; cargo pilots had to come from somewhere, but Ray wouldn't be paying for any hundred-dollar-an-hour flying lessons; let Milo join the armed forces and learn. Ray's own dreams of the military life, hopelessly unreal in retrospect, had fortunately come to nothing (all the bullets that had somehow missed Bernie might well have hit Ray), but Milo's airborne hopes should be nurtured until fully fledged, at which time they might wing him to places far from Callisto. Not that Ray disliked Milo and wanted him gone or anything like that; he just didn't want to bind the kid down if he wanted to ramble, that's all.

Whether Milo stayed or went, Kevin was heir-in-waiting. The Thunderbird would be his. To ensure this came to pass, to literally brand the property with Kevin's seal, Ray took advantage of some sewage renovation at the motel to press Kevin's bare hands and feet into wet cement. There they set, beguilingly inadequate auguries of the man to be. Milo howled because the impressions committed to posterity were not his own, and the flux of his resentment, reduced for some time now to an innocuous simmering, waxed hot once again. Ray might fool himself his preference went unnoticed, but to Milo's eye, honed to avenging-angel keenness by years of benign neglect from his stepfather, this latest in a long line of insults was palpable proof he was unloved. There it was, the imprint of his rival, preserved forever. It was too much. Milo just didn't seem to count for anything, and it hurt. He couldn't even find an ally in Holly; she always told him to stop being such a baby and grow up. Even Milo's name was a source of pain. Ray had yet to formally adopt him, seemed in no hurry to do so, and was not badgered on the subject by Holly. The only Ginty in a family of Kootzes, Milo couldn't be sure if he belonged or not; and if he didn't, was that something to be proud or ashamed of? It was all very confusing.

Late in the bicentennial year, Milo made a discovery in the woods. He went there to be alone. Along the riverbank west of town the trees grew unmolested, bordered by fields. They were not tall trees, nor were they thickly clustered, but in Kansas you couldn't be choosy. Milo strolled among them, his idle brooding complemented by the dun-gray trunks around him, the leafless canopy and pallid sky above. His solitary state granted Milo a kind of peace. At home he was diminished by his surroundings, but the cheerlessness of these winter woods could not offend him, welcomed him among their drabness. The jagged shell that seemed always to surround him was here smoothed by the indifference of nature, and for that Milo was grateful in his own grudging fashion.

The dead man was propped against a tree. It was the orange hunting cap that first attracted Milo's eye in that direction. Once he'd identified the bright splash of color he was tempted to change direction and avoid contact with another human, but the cap's stillness and the shape of the man beneath it, curiously slumped, told Milo he needn't worry about having to make stupid conversation.

He approached the corpse with some excitement; this was the first dead person he'd ever seen. It had obviously been suicide, not a hunting accident. The left boot and thermal sock had been removed and set neatly aside. The foot that had triggered the rifle was a startling shade of blue, as were the face and hands. The big toe, instrument of release, was particularly ugly, asymmetric as a potato, the nail badly in need of trimming. The rifle barrel lay on the man's shoulder, kicked there by the recoil, and its butt had found a resting place between his knees. His hands lay palm upward as if in supplication. The bullet had entered his palate, shattered the brainpan, exited at the back of the skull, and buried itself in the cottonwood the suicide had chosen as his last support. Milo judged him to be around fifty. His dentures had split and dropped, now projected absurdly over the lower lip, ludicrously comic, an idiot's grin of broken enamel. Strangely, the eyes had remained open, fixed on a point in the near distance. Had they seen phantasms from the past coming this way, or brightly burning angels?

It was the most wonderful thing, this dead man. Milo stared, absorbing the essence of nonlife radiating from it. Nothing he'd ever seen before thrilled him so. He didn't feel sorry for the corpse with the ugly toe and broken teeth, was not concerned with the troubles that had brought the man to this anonymous bend in the river; instead, Milo exulted in the movement of his own blood, his warmth, the spinning of his brain. The very breath hanging before his face seemed a magical mist. Milo was alive, and the thing at his feet was not. It was some kind of triumph, he was not sure why. He knew this discovery, this revelation was important. A curtain had been lifted aside, Milo granted a free peek at something of significance, but he could not define its parameters. Twelve years old, he reached for perfect understanding, felt its presence around and within him, evanescent, immaculate; yet the more he stared, the less he knew, and this gradual slipping away of the transcendent moment brought him close to panic. The dead man's meaning had in some manner escaped from his body into the tree bole at his back, and from there traveled to every naked bough and branch and twig, to be plucked away and dispersed by the wind. Now the suicidal hunter was of no more consequence than a squashed cat by the roadside, and the gyrations of mind that had flooded Milo mere seconds before were stilled, made calm as oiled water. Whatever his fingertips had brushed was now gone completely, and the deepest part of Milo keened for its passing. Something wonderful had been tantalizingly offered, then whisked away. It wasn't fair. He blamed the dead man. "Fuck you!" Milo screamed, and pushed the corpse's shoulder with his foot. One half of the broken denture fell to the earth. The body sagged sideways to the ground, was now grotesquely askew. It had been easy, but Milo felt very little satisfaction.

Facing the collapsed agent of his transformation became unendurable, and he hurried away, boots crunching through fallen leaves and dead grass. Eventually he came to the river, stared for the longest time at its icy margins, but found no comfort there. Milo was cold to the marrow. Skirting the dead man by hundreds of yards, he left the woods and stamped his way across the frozen clods of a cornfield, kicked at the desiccated stalk ends left behind after the last harvest. When he came to a drainage ditch he followed it east to the nearest road, passing en route the place where his stepfather's father had died in a white Lincoln. Had he known this, Milo would not have cared; he had a peculiar loss of his own to mourn, and he trudged back to Callisto with funereal slowness.

Kevin, knowing no other life, assumed there were good reasons why Milo should be unkind. Milo was older, therefore right in all things, even when his wisdom caused Kevin pain. Milo must have had a reason to make him stand facing the wall till he peed in his pants, and behind the various arm twistings and ear wrenchings must lie some great but unfathomable purpose. Whatever it was, it had to be kept secret from Mommy and Daddy. Milo told him if he ever squealed he'd be kidnapped by men in black coats who would throw him down a mineshaft, which would break every bone in his body and he'd die in horrible agony; so he didn't squeal, ever.

Somehow Milo, who was only half the size of the grownups, seemed to tower over Kevin like a giant. It was puzzling, but apparently it was the natural order of things; he was simply not old enough to understand. Daddy was always nice to him, but niceness didn't count for much when compared with Milo's sinister power. Grownups lived high in the trees, so to speak, but Milo was down on the forest floor with Kevin, a feral king in the tiny world called Thunderbird. Tribute had to be exacted, and Kevin offered all. To disobey would be to invite punishment. His allegiance, fearful yet trusting, was total.

A small boy is not a natural keeper of secrets. Though his lips may be sealed, his body will betray him. Kevin began wetting the bed at age four and drenched his mattress for two years, until Milo suddenly became a different person, no longer interested in subjugation. The new Milo was distant, aloof, and Kevin became drier overnight. Ray and Holly removed the rubber sheet from his bed with trepidation, but the nocturnal torrent was gone for good. It had just been a phase after all. Milo, they assumed, was entering a phase all his own, some typical preteen upheaval, purely genetic in origin. They didn't know he had entered the river woods a furtive bully and emerged a frustrated mystic. Ray and Holly didn't know very much at all regarding their children; they had problems of their own.

Holly became disenchanted with her life. Ray blamed *Cosmopolitan* and *Ms.* for her restlessness; if she hadn't read all those articles about what a woman should expect, she wouldn't have known she was supposed to expect it, never would've missed it, whatever it was. "My own identity," said Holly, but Ray was still in the dark. Why wasn't his wife happy? He didn't run around on her, didn't booze it up or gamble, and he'd never once hit her. What did she have to complain about?

"I'm just not realizing my potential."

"Meaning what, exactly?"

"Meaning I can be more than just some guy's wife that runs a motel."

"You're not just some guy's wife, you're *my* wife, and what's so bad about running a motel? We make out okay, don't we? Nobody's starving or anything. What are you talking about?"

"I'm talking about satisfaction, personal satisfaction."

"You mean sex? What's wrong with our sex life, huh?"

"You're not listening to what I'm saying. Did I say sex? No, I didn't."

"You know what the national average is? Two point four times a week. We do it around four times, so how about that? You can't argue with figures, Holly."

"I'm not arguing about anything, just trying to explain what I mean, if I could be allowed to slip a word into the conversation now and then."

"Go ahead. I'm very interested. No, really, I'm interested. Go ahead."

"I could be doing more with my life."

"Doing more."

"Yes."

"Like what, for example?"

"That's what I have to find out. I've got potential in me, Ray."

"Potential."

"Right, and I need to use it, otherwise it'll just go to waste. I can't waste my potential."

"So what are you gonna do not to waste it?"

"I haven't made up my mind yet. It needs careful thinking."

"Uh-huh."

"And you can't stand in my way."

"Who's standing in your way? Am I standing in your way? You want to use your potential, go ahead and use it for chrissakes, but it better not mean fucking other guys and group fucking in Jacuzzis. I draw the line at that. Everybody's fucking everybody else nowadays and it's sick."

"Will you please try to get your brain above your belt. I haven't even mentioned sex. Why does everything have to be sex with you? I'm talking about college courses, if you must know, so will you quit with the sex sex sex, thank you very much."

"College courses?"

"Yes, college courses, so I can be smarter and learn things and realize my potential as a human being if that's okay with you."

"You never said anything about college courses a minute ago. You said you had to think about it. You hadn't made up your mind, you said, so where do the college courses come from all of a sudden? How am I gonna run this place on my own with you away at college, and you're too old for college anyway. You'd look stupid sitting in class with all those kids. You're too old, Holly."

"I am not too old. Thirty-two isn't old, and in any case I'm talking about college courses through the mail, which I thought you were smart enough to know what I'm talking about but you're not, it looks like."

"Oh. Okay, then. That's fine. That's a good idea, babe."

"The way you talk I think sometimes your head's full of concrete. You never listen."

"Well, I'm sorry. It's a good idea, college through the mail. What kind of stuff are you gonna study up on?"

"That's what I haven't made up my mind about. History, I think."

"History's important. That's a good choice. Go for the history."

"Or maybe philosophy."

"Also good. The meaning of life. Hey, when you get your diploma, let me in on the secret, okay?"

But Holly didn't enroll, instead took up weaving. The spare room had been intended for Milo once he turned thirteen, but the birthday came and went and Milo remained upstairs, sharing with Kevin. The spare room was cleared of junk, a loom installed. It was now the weaving room. Milo swore he'd never forgive his mom, but he swore silently. Milo lately was silence personified.

"Cat got your tongue, Milo?"

"Nnnnh."

Kevin worshiped him. Milo no longer tormented him, and Kevin's gratitude was unstinting. He wanted to show Milo everything—his school project, a beetle he captured, his library book, his cap pistol—but these heartfelt offerings were just crap to Milo.

"Will you get that crap outa here!"

"It's my room too."

"So keep your crap on your side of it, and quit bugging me with crap I don't need, you hear me?"

"Okay."

"And don't be such a wimp, agreeing so fast like that. What the fuck's the matter with you anyway?"

Kevin didn't know, knew only that he'd gone and bugged Milo again. The only time Milo talked to him was when he got shouted at. Their association had been more intimate when Kevin received Indian burns every other day. Obviously, he was failing as a brother, and it made him sad. What had he done wrong?

"Mom, why doesn't Milo like me?"

"He does, honey, only he can't show it. He's always been a turkey like that. Just ignore him."

Ignore Milo? Dumb advice like that made Kevin aware of the deep gulf dividing adults from their offspring. The answer would have to come from the source.

"Why don't you like me?"

"Because you're a little pain-in-the-ass shitforbrains."

"No I'm not."

"Listen, just go far away from me. I'd be very grateful if you'd do that. Try the South Pole."

Failure again. It was disheartening. Kevin examined his face in the mirror, but could find nothing about it that would make Milo hate him. Maybe it was his voice. Milo once told him he had a voice like Tweety. That was it—the voice! He wished it would hurry up and break like Milo's had. Maybe then they could talk together like brothers did on TV. Milo never rested a protective hand on his shoulder the way TV big brothers did, never gave him little lectures and pep talks to help him through life. Weren't big brothers supposed to do stuff like that? Milo wasn't doing what he was supposed to, but Kevin forgave him.

Holly faced a difficult summer. First had come the realization that her talent for weaving was minuscule; then had come the inevitable "I didn't think it'd work out" from Ray, followed by the ultimate blow: Elvis was dead.

"I grew up with him, Ray, and now he's gone."

"I thought you grew up in Chicago."

"Don't be funny. I grew up with him on the radio. He was the first star I ever worshiped. God, I loved that guy. He was everything when I was a kid. Why didn't they look after him better! Someone should go to jail for this. All that talent, wasted. There'll never be another one like Elvis. He truly was the King, Ray. I mean it; there'll never be another Presley, no way."

"Right."

Ray thought Elvis was a fat fuck who should've quit the music business when he joined the army, not plodded on, the songs becoming as bland and irrelevant as the man; and anyone who ate hamburger for breakfast wasn't human.

"I want to go to Memphis, Ray, to pay my respects."

"You what? When?"

"As soon as I can. Tomorrow or the day after, maybe."

"Forget it. Who's gonna mind the place if we go down there? You want us to close down for a week, or what?"

"You stay, I'll go. You can't fool me, Ray. I know you're not a genuine Elvis fan. You haven't got a single Elvis album."

"I used to have one."

"I don't believe it. Anyway, I'm going down there on my own and you can't stop me, so don't even try. This means a lot to me and I don't want you to screw it up like I know you would if you came along."

"Okay, okay, go! Big fucking deal."

The boys went with Ray to the Greyhound depot to see Holly on her way. Ray wouldn't spring for air fare, not for Elvis. If Richard Nixon had died, he would've flown first class to the graveside, just to make sure the fucker was good and dead.

"Kiss Mom goodbye, guys."

Kevin did but Milo wouldn't. "Turkey," she accused him, but he still wouldn't. Ray gave her a hasty kiss on the cheek; he hated public displays of affection. He knew he loved his wife, so why did he have to prove it to the world?

"Have a good time, babe."

"How can I have a good time, Ray? Elvis Presley has died, okay? You tell me how I'm expected to have a good time at a time like this."

"Okay, have a shitty time. Cry and cry, whatever. This whole thing is a dumb idea."

"Not to me, and not to millions of other fans. To us it's important. It's like those Arabs that go to Mecca. Well, we Americans can go to Memphis if we want, am I wrong?"

"Listen, when are you getting back? It isn't gonna be easy running the place on my own."

"I'll be back when I'm back. This is a traumatic time for me and you're spoiling it. Be happy that I'm going, please?"

Milo found he missed his mother not at all. It was something of a revelation. He hoped she'd find somewhere nice to stay down there and not come back for a year or two. Kevin wasn't sure if he missed her or not. Ray was morose, and the boys avoided him. No one wanted to cook, so they sent out for meals. Ray figured this way the kitchen would be kept nice and clean for Holly's return, an event he hoped to celebrate very soon. Sexual frustration was one problem; having no one to share the work with another; but it was her company, the physical presence of his wife he truly missed. Just knowing she was around the place had become one of the fixed points in his emotional life, an essential ingredient for the low-key happiness he'd grown used to. Why was she taking so long? How many times could you file past a fucking coffin? When she got back he'd ask her if it was a bigger than usual model; King Lardass would be a tight fit for a regular bonebox, so maybe they intended burying him in a fur-lined freight car or something. Where the hell was she?

A postcard arrived. On one side was a picture of Elvis, on the other:

> Saving money by not calling long distance. Gracelands beautiful. Whole city in mourning. Love to all.
>
> Holly

"When's she coming home?" asked Kevin.

"Pretty soon. You want pizza or burgers tonight?"

He thought of contacting the Memphis police. Maybe she was dead, had been murdered since she mailed the card, and thrown in a roadside ditch. Or kidnapped, and was right this minute being sexually abused by rednecks. Not knowing was awful. He couldn't sleep any more. Where was his wife!

On the tenth day she returned home. "What a terrible ride. I'll never go by bus again. My back's killing me. Ray, honey, will you rub it for me?"

"Where the hell were you! I've been going nuts!"

"I couldn't just rush down there and rush straight back. Memphis is a lovely place. How many vacations have I had since we got married? I needed a break, so I took one. Don't get mad at me because I went and saw a little bit of the world."

"You should've phoned! Anyone with half a brain would've figured we'd worry if we didn't hear from you."

"I sent a postcard!"

"Six days ago!"

126

"Well, I'm sorry, okay? Why are you bullying me? What kind of a welcome home do you call this? My back's killing me, and all because you wouldn't let me fly there because you're such a tightwad cheapskate! How dare you criticize me for spending all those awful days on the bus you made me take! How dare you . . . !"

Holly ran to the bedroom, sobbing. Ray followed five minutes later and offered a back rub. Fifteen minutes later they engaged in sexual intercourse, and there was no more shouting at the Thunderbird that day. "Mom's home!" announced Kevin. "I know," said Milo. Now they'd have to eat sensibly again.

Three weeks after her return, Holly asked Ray if he'd had any kind of "tickly feeling" lately when he peed. Ray said he had, just for the past day or so. "Me too," said Holly, "so I went to the doctor today and he said it's just a female thing that happens for no reason, but sometimes humidity brings it on if you're not used to it and it was just terrible in Memphis, the humidity, so I think that's probably what happened. Anyway, I got a prescription for it. We both have to take some pills and it'll go away."

"How can I have some female thing if I'm a guy?"

"I don't know. He told me why but it was real complicated and medical, but it's nothing serious, Ray, just one of those things that happens sometimes for no reason at all, apart from the humidity, and when a woman gets it she just naturally passes it on to her husband. It's no big deal, not a disease or anything. We just take the pills and it'll go away."

"Okay."

"And we can't make love for two weeks."

"Say what?"

"So the medicine can work better."

"You're kidding me."

"It's not such a sacrifice, Ray. Two tiny weeks is all."

"Jesus, Holly . . ."

"Well, it's not my fault. I didn't know humidity did things like this. Women have very complicated bodies, and things sometimes go wrong for no reason at all, even in places that aren't humid, and I think you might show a little bit more cooperative attitude about the whole thing instead of being a baby about it. I'm surprised at you sometimes, Ray, I really am."

"Yeah, but two weeks . . . What difference does it make to the medicine if we do it or not? What's the medical justification for it is what I'm saying."

"If you want to argue about it, talk to the doctor."

"Fine. I will."

But he didn't. Having a female complaint made it too embarrassing. They made no love, took the pills, and the nonspecific genital infection Holly had contracted from Wayne Priddy, unemployed barman, during their weeklong liaison at the Down Home Inn, Memphis, went away. Ray soon forgot about the sexual hiatus, but never got used to the gold-framed portrait of the King in a sequined jumpsuit, surrounded by an ethereal glow, that Holly hung in the living room.

"You fat fuck," he said to it at least once a week.

10

ON A NIGHT during the first year of Ronald Reagan's presidency, Bernie Swenson phoned the Thunderbird to report that Milo had been found by a patrolman down at the Gatlin Road graveyard, lying on a tombstone. Ray was stunned.

"You mean dead?"

"No, just lying there, like you'd lie on a sofa. He's down at the station now. You want to come pick him up?"

"Be right down. Thanks, Bernie."

But Holly wanted to go instead. "He's my son. Someone has to stay here and take care of business."

"He needs a goddamn lecture about this weird stuff. You bring him directly home. What kind of weirdness is that, lying on a gravestone? He's on drugs I bet, the little shit! Fuck it, I'm going down there to get him myself."

"No you aren't, not in that mood. You're not calm about things when you're mad at someone, you know you're not. Just let me talk to him first, then I'll bring him home."

"If he's on drugs, you tell Bernie to keep him there overnight and teach him a lesson, put him in a cell without a blanket or something. No, dammit, I'm going down there myself."

"No, Ray."

"Don't tell me no in my own motel!"

"Will you please listen to sense just one time in your life! I'm going down to get him and you're not!"

"Bullshit you are! Gimme those keys. I'm warning you, Holly . . ."

She ran. Ray took a few steps in pursuit, then gave up. Fuck it. Let her bring the little bastard home if she wanted. He'd give Milo a piece of his mind when they got back, and a piece of his hand, too. Holly's idea of discipline would be to ask him if the nasty cold gravestone had given him a chill. That kid needed a whomping, but good.

Bernie was surprised when Holly presented herself at the station.

"Hi. Come to get the miscreant?"

"I'm here for Milo."

"Right. He's in back. Take a seat."

Bernie collected Milo and returned. Milo wore a deep frown but was unmarked. Holly had expected bruising on his face.

"Do I have to sign anything to take him home?"

"Nope. Strictly speaking, the charge is trespassing, but the cemetery gates weren't locked and there's no sign says to keep out, so he can't be prosecuted. He got brought in anyway just in case he's on something, which he isn't, right, Milo?"

"Right."

"So you can go with your mom."

"Right."

"And stay out of cemeteries, okay?"

"I'll wait until my appointed time."

Bernie liked that but didn't laugh in case the kid was mocking him. You couldn't tell with Milo.

"Thanks, Bernie."

Holly hadn't addressed him by name in years, had barely seen him. Even Ray saw less of him than he used to. Bernie had put on weight.

"No charge."

In the car, Holly waited for an explanation. By the time they reached Fifteenth and Westcott her patience was gone.

"Well?"

"I went in there to look at the stars, that's all."

"You went into a graveyard to look at stars? Are you serious?"

"It's a real clear night."

"That's just totally ridiculous."

"I disagree, but I'll fight for your right to hold a differing opinion anytime."

"Milo, listen to me. When we get home, don't talk like that to Ray. He's very upset, so if you start mouthing off with stuff like that, he'll get mad. Are you listening?"

"Yes."

"Be good, okay? Be nice to Ray, because he's very upset about this."

"Okay."

"Were you in a cell back there?"

"No, just a room, a waiting room I guess you'd call it."

"Good. Ray wouldn't like to think of you being in a cell. He'd flip."

"I bet."

"Was it Bernie got you off the hook?"

"Yeah. They wanted me to pee in a bottle for a drug test, but he said I didn't have to. I don't think they're entitled to demand a test unless there's been an accident or something. They were just being assholes."

"That was pretty nice of Bernie, don't you think?"

"I've got nothing against him."

Ray's temper had not improved. Milo's stargazing struck him as the act of a moron.

"You could've lain down in the park or someplace if you had to lay down. Why the goddamn cemetery?"

"That's where I was when I noticed how bright the stars are tonight."

"In the cemetery? What the hell were you doing in there?"

"Walking by it, right by the gate, so I went in and laid down."

"Just went in and laid yourself down on top of someone's grave."

"On a marble slab. White marble."

"And you think that's normal behavior? Do you think that's the kind of thing a normal person would do, huh?"

Milo shrugged. "What's normal?" he said.

"What's normal? Lying on other people's gravestones isn't normal. That's a perverted thing to do, and I don't even believe it about the stars, so you better think up something better, pal." To Holly he said, "Did your ex ever do stuff like this? Where does he get it from?"

"Brian didn't know anything about stars. Venus or Mars or the moon, he didn't know the difference."

"Venus and Mars are planets, Mom, and the moon's a satellite."

"Crap!" said Ray. "That's total crap! Satellites are man-made, which the moon definitely isn't. Are you saying we put the goddamn moon up there?"

"It's a natural satellite."

"It's a natural satellite like I'm a natural blond! Don't try talking down to people when you don't know what you're talking about, because it just makes you look stupid. The moon, for your information, is a small planet with no air on it."

Milo said nothing.

"Right?" demanded Ray.

"If you say so."

"Well I do, I do say so."

"Fine."

"And you can get that look off your face! Your mother makes things easy for you around here. She doesn't see through you like I do, so you can quit thinking you've got it made, understand?"

"Sure."

"Don't say 'Sure,' say 'Yes I understand!' "

"Yes I understand."

"And if I ever find out you're on drugs, I'll come down so hard you'll think you just died."

"I don't do drugs."

"That better be the truth, I'm warning you."

"He doesn't, Ray. He told me."

"What he tells you isn't worth diddly. It's what you find out about kids that matters. I'll be watching you."

He stabbed a finger at Milo, who stared at the finger rather than at Ray's face, the way a dog would. Small things like this made Ray aware he had no idea what went on inside Milo's head, and this made him angry. A Milo with armor plating around his thoughts was a disturbing Milo, a threat somehow.

"Out of my sight," said Ray, and Milo went silently away. "What are you staring at?"

"Nothing," said Holly, and the way she said it let Ray know she meant it. The woman he loved thought he was nothing. All his anger turned belly-up. Together, his wife and stepson had made him feel a fool. He didn't care what Milo thought, but Holly's opinion counted.

Guests arrived at the reception desk. While they were attended to by Holly, Ray stared at the living room wall. Somewhere inside him the threads that held Ray Kootz together were unraveling. Something was going wrong, and it had to do with how everyone in the big tepee felt about everyone else. Ray had thought he knew how everyone felt, but in recent years his certainty had subtly been eroded down to bedrock. There were no specific incidents or revelations, nothing he could grab hold of and examine to figure out the why and the wherefore, nothing concrete. The evidence for his doubts was shadows glimpsed from the corner of his eye, slyly shifting whenever he tried hardest to determine their nature. He couldn't blame Holly, and it certainly wasn't Kevin (just the world's greatest little

133

kid), so Milo must be the one introducing perplexity into his life.

Why did the boy make him feel like an idiot? It wasn't anything he said: Milo avoided conversation whenever possible, was never directly confrontational. It was the look on his face, that's what it was, that superior look he wore to let Ray know he thought him a dork. But why would Milo, who was only an average student, think Ray was dumber than him? It must be because Ray ran a motel. He knew there were plenty of people who considered that kind of work strictly for boring types, the kind who got a thrill out of watching their odometer roll from 99999.9 back to zero.

Maybe he should tell Milo about the time he and Bernie tried to join the Summer of Love in San Francisco but got ripped off when they crossed the state line. No, that little escapade made them look like hayseeds. How about telling Milo of his brilliant stratagem to unload the Corcorans from his shoulders? No again; Ray wasn't too proud of that any more, even if he'd deserved an Oscar for his performance. What if he confessed to Milo he'd slashed his mom's tires and won the time needed to make her fall for him. Nix to that one, too; he hadn't even told Holly yet. His misadventures and maneuverings, the stuff of anecdote, were too far behind him now to bring into the light of this later day. Milo very probably wouldn't even believe them, and even if he did, would despise Ray all the more for trying to win him over by revealing his secret past that way. Ray was disinclined to stand naked before Milo, begging favorable judgment. Milo would have to accept him on his own square terms, as he would have to accept the boy on Milo's terms; unsquare—octagonal, for all Ray knew. Oddly, he believed Milo's claim to be drug-free. The unique aura of disengagement that angered Ray so often was not a product of the narcotic haze enveloping the nation's classrooms. Milo Ginty was not one of America's chemical children; he simply was not like the rest.

* * *

Kevin was torn. He admired Milo, but Ray was nice to him. Whenever he came near either of these two, Kevin felt the heedless tug of planetary gravities. A tiny body in free fall, his path swerved a dozen times a day. Ray's love for him was clear, uncomplex, like Holly's, and Kevin accepted this as a desirable thing, but from Milo there came an intriguing blankness, a nonchalance that had about it none of the studied teenage mannerisms Kevin had seen other guys practice. Next to Milo, his father was a pleasant irrelevance, and Kevin could not figure out why. Milo never attempted to harvest affection from him, nor did he offer any. He hadn't bullied Kevin in years, but intimidation had not been replaced by warmth. Milo seemed not to care one way or the other, and a sense of isolation, surrounded though he was by parental love, made Kevin miserable. The light that came from Ray and Holly, sputtering and inefficient but always there, could not compete with the darkness surrounding Milo. Milo was like a special kind of light bulb Kevin had seen in a comic book; when switched on, this bulb made bright places grow dark. That's what Milo was—a dark light—and Kevin wasn't the only one to notice.

"As mother to son, I'd like a few frank answers."

"About what?"

"About whatever it is that's troubling you."

"Nothing's troubling me."

"So why are you always quiet? Why don't you bring friends home from school?"

"I don't have any."

It was a statement, not a complaint, and the lack of bitterness surprised Holly.

"You don't like anyone at school?"

"I don't like them or not like them, I just don't think they're very interesting."

"No one in the whole school?"

"I guess you could call Nobby interesting."

"Who's Nobby?"

"The janitor. He's real ugly and everyone hates him."

"That's why he's interesting?"

"He hasn't done anything wrong, he's just ugly, so they hate him. The girls laugh at him—the guys, too. He just ignores them, like he's deaf. They're all basically idiots except for Nobby."

"How about the teachers?"

"They don't have anything to do with him."

"I mean how do you feel about the teachers."

Milo shrugged. "They're very ordinary."

"What's wrong with ordinary? We're ordinary. Just about everyone in the whole world is ordinary. You want to run around with kings and princes and movie stars?"

"No."

"Do you think you're not ordinary like the rest of us?"

Another shrug.

"I'd like an answer, Milo."

"Okay, I'm very ordinary."

"You know, I worry about you. You're my firstborn son, and that makes you very important to me. I'm just an ordinary woman, Milo, so I have these very ordinary emotions, like loving my son and being worried about him when he says he doesn't like anyone in the whole school because they're ordinary. Do you like us, Ray and me?"

"Sure."

But he said it too fast for Holly's liking.

"Do you like your brother?"

"Half-brother."

"He's got blood the same as your blood inside him."

"Only four pints."

"So you don't like him."

"I like him."

"You don't show it. You never have shown affection, Milo, even when you were little."

"I'm just undemonstrative."

"Undemonstrative."

"Yes."

"So really you love us all, even if you can't show it."

"Right."

"And you're not unhappy about anything."

"No."

"So why doesn't a nice-looking guy like you have a girl-friend?"

"Beats me."

"Are all the girls too ordinary?"

Milo didn't like the direction the conversation was taking. He'd recently fallen in love at Callisto High. Pattie Lutz had an arm that terminated in two fingers; there was no palm, no thumb, no other fingers but those two, springing straight from the wrist, their tips opposed like calipers. Pattie didn't hide her deformity, was brave enough to wear a length of ribbon tied just above the point where arm became fingers; a bangle would've slipped right off. Milo admired Pattie intensely for her courage, and admiration had turned to love. He'd even gone so far as to ask her for a date, but Pattie told him she wasn't planning on getting interested in boys; Pattie was saving herself for Jesus, intended enrolling at a Bible college in Oklahoma when she graduated. Milo was stunned. People who believed in God came from the psycho ward, in his opinion. He knew Pattie must have suffered because of her arm, but instead of channeling that suffering back into herself to achieve a fuller understanding of life's cruelly puzzling emptiness, or rather, whatever awesome truth lay behind the emptiness (Milo's own ambition), she intended pouring it away down the timeworn funnel of organized religion. He was appalled. How totally unoriginal! All her grief would go to waste. His offer of love had been rejected by someone who intended placing her faith in a celestial Santa Claus. He was insulted but was gentleman enough to blame himself for the mistake; he should've checked her out for Christian tendencies before he made his move. It had happened three weeks ago, was ancient history, but the memory still smarted.

"I'm keeping myself pure for marriage."

"I'm serious about this. If you had any kind of . . . problem, would you come to me about it?"

"Okay."

"I mean . . . if you found out you're not interested in girls at all."

"You mean if I'm gay?"

"I promise I'll understand."

"I'm not gay."

"Well, fine, I didn't think you were, but I want you to know you can come to me anytime. Ray might not be so understanding, you know?"

"I figured."

"I'm glad we had this little chat to clear the air."

"Definitely."

Holly told herself something had been accomplished. Milo wasn't in trouble of any kind. Milo was simply . . . Milo.

Milo continued to be Milo six weeks later. In biology class one afternoon he declined to eviscerate a frog, instead taped two wooden rulers together to form a cross, then attached his amphibian to it with three thumbtacks. He gave it a tiny tissue loincloth and a crown of bent paper clips, then invited inspection from the student body. The squeals and hooting that followed brought a teacher to his side. The blasphemous object and its creator were sent to the principal's office.

"Do you have an explanation for this, Ginty?"

"He's the king of the frogs."

"I think you have a serious problem. This is the product of a very sick mind. What would your parents think about this?"

"They don't do church."

"Mmmm. Your father is Ray Kootz?"

"Stepfather."

"All right, Ginty, get out of here. Go home and remain

there until I decide you can come back and be part of the school again."

"Will do."

Milo left. The principal's wife's cousin was Margaret Corcoran, so the principal knew of Ray Kootz's abominable treatment of the family in the late sixties, and was not surprised he'd reared a perverted boy like Milo. He phoned the Thunderbird. Ray came straight down to the high school and was shown the offending frog.

"He did that?"

"He did. I'd like to know what you think."

"It's supposed to be Jesus, right?"

"That's right, Mr. Kootz. Can you give me any idea why Milo might have done something like this?"

"He's a funny kid, kind of a screwball but okay underneath."

"Are you sure about that?" He waved the frog under Ray's nose. "Doesn't this suggest something is lacking in his outlook, his attitude?"

"Wait a minute. Was the frog dead when he did it? If he did it when the frog was alive, that's serious. I draw the line at torturing animals for fun."

"The frogs are painlessly made brain-dead before the students perform their dissections."

"That's good. I think I must've been away when we did frog surgery, sick or something. I used to go to Callisto myself."

"I know. I even dug out your record. Have you encouraged Milo to perform better than you did, Mr. Kootz? I don't mean to be offensive, but your example isn't what I'd like to see him use for a role model."

"Didn't do all that good, did I."

"No, and I'd hate to see Milo go the same route. You know he's not popular at school. His sociability rating is very poor. What's wrong with your boy, Mr. Kootz?"

Ray didn't much like the question, didn't much like the man who asked it, didn't even like his face; it was way too smug. This man was a fucking dickhead. So Ray hadn't done well in school, so what. He was doing okay, thank you very much, and Milo would do okay, too, whether this prick thought he would or not. This solidarity with his stepson, made potent by sheer novelty, gave Ray's irritation and resentment wings to fly. Milo's blood wasn't Ray's, but he was a Kootz by temperament and association, and by God it was about time Ray went downtown to fill out the papers and adopt the boy, make him a legal Kootz, so they could stand shoulder to shoulder against the army of dickheads who thought they ran the world.

"Say what?"

"I said, what's wrong with your boy?"

"Nothin'. Nothin' wrong with him at all. Fine boy. Proud of him."

Ray couldn't believe this stuff was coming from his mouth. He sounded like a horny-handed farmer praising the broad back of some kid forking pigshit in the yard.

"I don't think I can agree with you, Mr. Kootz. Seriously, he's just not fitting in here. Callisto High has plenty to offer any student willing to cooperate with the system we have. We aren't tyrants, but we do require a minimum of input from our boys and girls, and Milo just isn't making the effort. He doesn't seem to care at all, frankly."

"Don't blame him. Felt the same way myself. Turned out fine anyway."

"Mr. Kootz, I don't think you appreciate what it is I'm saying. Milo has been sent home for this piece of stupidity, and he'll stay there until such time as I see fit to let him back into class. For a start, he'll need to apologize to the biology teacher. She's a churchgoing woman and was very upset by what he did."

"Can't say I blame you. See your point. Talk to him if you like. See what happens."

"I think that'd be best for everyone."

"Well, gotta go. Things to do. Chickens to feed."

Ray quit the game at that point, aware he'd maybe gone too far.

"Thank you for dropping by."

"Right. Okay."

He left. The principal saw now why Milo was the way he was. Ray Kootz was suffering from some kind of personality disorder. That dumb voice he'd put on, what on earth was that supposed to prove? He half hoped Milo would not go humbly to Mrs. Axelrod and beg her pardon. No apology, no return. The school would be better off without the quietly subversive influence of Milo Ginty.

The principal got his wish. Ray encouraged Milo to stay put at home. Milo was startled by their united front, worried about Ray's true motives. Maybe he wanted Milo kicked out of school so he'd have to work for a living, at which time Ray could justifiably ask him to leave the Thunderbird and support himself someplace else. Ray hadn't even wanted Milo to have the spare room two years back, had griped about it while they removed Holly's dust-laden loom and brought his bed down. Ray wanted him out; it was obvious. Milo could foil this plan by apologizing to the teacher, but that option was almost as odious as the thought of working. There had to be another way. Five school days had already passed.

"Callisto Gazette."

"Can I speak to a reporter, please."

"Which reporter did you want?"

"I don't care."

"May I ask what this is in relation to?"

"It's in relation to a hot story you can have exclusively if I can talk to a reporter."

"One moment, please. Transferring you."

"Jay Carter."

"Hi. Are you a reporter?"

It made page three. Milo was quoted as saying he did it to protest the unnecessary deaths inflicted upon frogdom by high schools everywhere. He'd decided a straightforward ridiculing of Christianity would get him nowhere, not in Kansas, so this other, more sympathetic tactic was chosen. "Frogs have been abused for too long. If you want to know what a frog's heart and liver look like, why not look at a picture in a textbook? Why go and kill a new frog every time to find out something they already found out hundreds of years ago? Frogs are much more interesting when they're alive, and not as slimy as you'd think."

For the first time since the Iranian hostage crisis, the editor received not only letters but phone calls. Milo moved to page one, his cause editorialized. The local cable channel became interested, then the Kansas City and Topeka channels sent camera crews just in time to capture students on videotape as they chanted, "Ribbit! Ribbit!" under the principal's window. This wider coverage caused antivivisectionists to prick up their ears, and when anti-abortion groups contrived to find in Milo's protest an act of kinship with their crusade, the national networks turned their attention to Callisto. Milo had a spot on CBS for twenty-three seconds in ninety seconds of coverage, and the Thunderbird itself was seen for five; ABC gave him eighteen seconds in seventy-eight of coverage (the principal had twenty-one, but came across as a bore); NBC squeezed him into their version in just twelve seconds out of twenty, ran it as an amusing filler at the end of the program. *Time* and *Newsweek* gave the story half a column each, featuring pictures of Milo with a cute frog nestled in his hand or perched on his head.

He was invited back to class. Callisto High could take no more. Frog dissection would no longer be practiced in biology. The champion of web-footed innocents walked the corridors again, and cameras were on hand to record his return. "It's good to be back," said Milo. "I don't regret anything. I think it was the right thing to do. You start by justifying killing frogs and you can wind up with concentration camps. We don't do that stuff in America, that's what I was taught."

Ray was proud of him. Kevin and Holly were proud of him. Girls made blatant sexual advances, and offerings of marijuana were slipped into his locker. Milo took everything, was wise enough to know the adulation would pass, and with it all advantage. He accepted, he savored, he used. A little later than most of his contemporaries, he got laid for the first time, even had his dick sucked by Linda Litmeyer beneath the football bleachers. This was perhaps the pinnacle of his fame, as such things were measured in Callisto.

And then, abruptly, it was over. The social impetus granted Milo was deliberately neglected, allowed to slip away. The frog prince, transformed by the media's hasty kiss, simply didn't want to know the people who wanted to know him. They were dumb. He wondered, briefly, if maybe he should apply himself to his books, gain entrance to a college, and there meet individuals like himself, smart people, people who could scent bullshit on the breeze and laugh about it. Mail from organizations concerned for the rights of animals and fetuses continued to arrive at the school and the Thunderbird, but Milo didn't bother opening it any more. His head became congested, overloaded. It was all too much.

One of his new acquaintances invited Milo over to sample some real south-of-the-border tequila with a worm in it. Milo accepted, prepared to endure dull company for the sake of something he'd never had before. They drank their way through it one Saturday afternoon while the friend's mother was out of town with her lover. Both became very drunk, shook the walls with music, smoked the last of Milo's dope, ate hugely, then got even drunker in pursuit of the worm. It eventually tumbled into the friend's glass. He screwed up his eyes and swallowed it down. The worm returned a few breaths later, flying at the crest of a pizza-

and-corn-chip wave that erupted across the sofa. Milo tried to help him clean up the mess, but his friend passed out, so Milo left him there in his own vomit and went outside for some air.

Evening had arrived, and Milo waded into it with enthusiasm, head swirling, feet a million miles away. The streets, usually signposted in numerical order, had today been switched around: Nineteenth was succeeded by Seventeenth without an Eighteenth in between, and the next one was Fifteenth! Where the fuck did Sixteenth go? This couldn't be happening. He knew his mind was wandering considerably as he walked, so he concentrated every step of the way to what he was determined would be Fourteenth. It was, but it took at least half an hour to reach, by Milo's calculation. Not only were streets being rearranged, the distances between them had been trebled.

When full darkness drew down around him, Milo became aware of urgent pleadings from his bladder. There being nowhere else to go, he voided himself in the corner of a parking lot, but long before he could finish, a police car rolled to a stop behind him. There was no denying the evidence still leaving his body in a hissing stream. He could hear the cops laughing behind their windows. Still he pissed, and the siren was allowed to stretch its throat for a few seconds to hurry him along. He finished, he zipped, he turned and was arrested.

Bernie visited him in his cell.

"First drunk we rounded up tonight. You start early, kid."

"Hafta puke."

"Be my guest."

Milo puked into the seatless toilet, flushed, and puked again, his skin grayish-yellow beneath the fluorescent tubes.

"Get my mom."

"No can do. I already phoned your dad. He says to keep

you here, seeing as you broke a law this time, the three-P law: no pissing in public places."

"I'm sick."

"I bet. You know what your old man also told me? He said to wake you up tomorrow morning with a bucket of water in the face, like in the westerns, but don't worry, we won't do it. You'll even get coffee and a donut."

"Get my mom."

"Don't tell me what to do, Milo. I'll get you some aspirin if you want."

"Gemme outa here. I wanna go home."

He leaned over the toilet to puke again, hair standing up in sweat-drenched spikes. Bernie shook his head, not without sympathy.

"If the network news could see you now. Is there a moral here, Milo? The price of fame, something like that?"

"Go 'way. Please go 'way."

Bernie did, and Milo lapsed into deep communion with the porcelain bowl.

11

H E HATED RAY for that bucket of water request. Holly didn't think much of Ray's judgment either, and when Milo came home on Sunday morning, a perceptible frostiness enveloped the big tepee. Kevin knew Milo had been in jail but couldn't see any connection with the filthy looks being traded between his mom and dad. The instincts of the young told him not to ask questions, even of Milo; the landmarks to understanding lay somewhere above his head, and climbing toward them too soon would bring punishment. Presumably, this would come from Milo, the only one ever to have inflicted pain on him. Milo would probably hit him twice as hard as he used to, because he'd been on TV and was important. Kevin knew the difference between famous and not famous. He wished a little of what Milo had would rub off on himself. To be like Milo would be terrific.

"What's it feel like?" he one day gathered the nerve to ask.

"What's what feel like?"

"Being famous."

"I forgot already."

"No you didn't. Tell me."

"You think it's some kind of big deal, huh?"

"I just want to know what it's like, you know, being you. They ask me at school what it's like to be your brother and all."

"And what do you tell 'em?"

"That it's great."

"Well, that's what it's like to be me, pal—just great."

Kevin wasn't convinced but knew better than to push for the truth. Just by observing Milo he might find out what he needed to know. It was important.

School was out for the summer. Now that he'd sampled briefly the delights of sex, Milo wanted more. Who should the lucky girl be? He didn't want anyone from Callisto High, didn't want to date. Milo wanted what other people didn't. Perverseness was his religion, and he needed a grail in which to deposit his offerings. The thought of having sexual relations with an ugly person appealed to him. Ugly people, he reasoned, would have tasted misery and be wiser for it, be more complete simply because of their suffering. He wanted to place his penis inside the body of a fully realized human being, hoped that this act would somehow siphon off a measure of that person's inner knowledge through a process of psychosexual osmosis. He would draw into himself the essence of his partner and appease the thing that squatted, sullenly insatiable, within him. An emptiness would be filled, Milo made whole. It was a wonderful theory, this transmutation by insertion, and he wanted to test it as soon as he could, wanted someone right now, this minute.

He looked everywhere, inspected every female who crossed his path, but pretty or plain, each failed to ring the internal bell Milo was counting on to notify him of the appointed one's presence. On the third day of his quest, a truly ugly person did come to his attention: Junkyard Jenny, Callisto's only bag lady. Jenny was probably sixty years old, her body without identifiable shape beneath her many layers of clothing, and she carried with her a power-

147

ful aroma of sweat and decay, even in winter. If Milo's theory of ugliness = wisdom was true, then Jenny was surely the goddess of eternal verities incarnate. She was wholly undesirable, except to a seeker after truth and ful-fillment. Milo found her on the library steps, seated beside her rusting Wal-Mart shopping cart and its malodorous treasures. He came within two yards of her, then backed off fast as the wind changed direction.

The plain fact was, he'd chickened out. Milo knew it, and guiltily abandoned his plan. The shortcut to enlightenment probably lay down another road entirely. Meanwhile, there remained the need for sexual gratification, even if it meant he'd have to seek out a girl he found attractive, just like any other guy, and would gain no remarkable insight from the experience. Milo resigned himself. Ultimate truth could wait.

The decision made, his aim simplified, he set off again. Having wandered all over town in search of the extraordin-ary and failed, Milo was disinclined to wear out his sneakers looking for someone normal, and his laziness made him aware of a promising target right on his door-step. Nadine Pitts was young and female, all the criteria his new, streamlined plan required. Nadine had been a sheet girl at the Thunderbird a little less than a year. She was married, but Milo had overheard Holly tell Ray the mar-riage was not a success; the husband drank and ran around with other women, had run so far and hard with the latest he hadn't been seen around town in over two months. Milo, now that he studied Nadine, could see no reason for the husband's behavior. Nadine seemed like a very nice person, unexceptional in every way but basically okay. He'd have to broach the subject of intercourse carefully, not startle her or anything; subtlety was called for.

He found her changing the sheets in Tepee 8. Holly made the sheet girls work alone; in a pair they tended to chatter and waste time, especially Dorothy, who escaped

Milo's attentions because of her resemblance to a sprightly, blue-haired woman on TV who promoted denture cream.

"Hi, Nadine."

"Hi, Milo."

"You look pretty today."

"Huh?"

"Did you do your hair different?"

Nadine pushed at her straight, not very long, not very thick, not very clean hair. "I gave it a wash the day before yesterday. Vidal Sassoon."

"It's nice and shiny. What color do you call that, ash blond?"

"I guess," said Nadine, who had never called her hair anything but mousy. It was nice of Milo to compliment her; no one else had in years. Milo was a nice-looking boy, even if he was a little strange around the eyes, and famous, too, and he was taking time out to be nice to her. Nadine appreciated that, she really did.

"Been on the TV again?"

"Nah, that's all over now. You know what that was, Nadine? That was my fleeting moment of fame. It's all downhill from now on."

"Oh, I don't believe that."

"It's true. The backlash has already started. My girlfriend dumped me a few days back. She says I'm too much of a troublemaker. How about that. I think I'm better off without someone who's got that attitude, don't you?"

"I think people should stick together and think the same."

"Right. We weren't suited right from the start. We weren't happy or anything. It's a shame, but there you go. That's life, huh?"

"You can't always get it right first time," said Nadine, who had never got it right in her life, had got it completely wrong when she married.

"That's what I thought all along. It's nice to hear someone with experience of the world say it too. If someone with experience and knowledge of the way things work between people says it, it must be true, that's how I look at it."

Nadine felt a peculiar sensation creeping from her chest up over her neck to her cheeks. She remembered that sensation from way back; she was blushing. Realization made her blush even harder. Milo had made her blush not with his compliment about her hair but by telling her she knew stuff. He'd practically called her smart. No one had ever called her smart before.

"You live and you learn," she said, and in case he noticed her flushed cheeks she added, "God, it's hot in here."

"Lemme help you with that."

As they wrestled dirty sheets into the wheeled laundry basket, their elbows touched, but Milo had engineered the contact so skillfully Nadine thought it was unintentional. It disturbed her that she thought about the elbow bumping at all. Nobody had touched her, even in this casual way, for a long time. Milo had gone and got her all confused. He helped her with the sheets in Tepees 9 and 10, chatting casually about things of no importance. When he judged Nadine would become suspicious or irritated if he hung around any longer, he quit.

"Thanks for talking to me, Nadine. You're real easy to talk to. 'Bye."

" 'Bye."

He waited a day, then repeated the performance, including momentary contact between their bodies, this time their hips. Twice. Milo knew Nadine knew by now what he was doing. He half expected her to freeze up, but she became even friendlier. He congratulated himself and forged ahead.

"Nadine?"

"Uh-huh?"

"I have a special request."

"Like on the radio?"

"No, a personal favor I need to ask you."

"Okay."

"Don't go getting the wrong idea, now."

"Okay."

"Uh, I'd like to visit you so we can talk some more."

"Visit me?"

"Yeah. If my mom sees me talking to you while you work, she'll figure I'm distracting you or something, so I'd prefer it if we could talk off the premises, if you see what I mean."

"Like in the park or something?"

"I was thinking more along the lines of your place."

"My place?"

"If it wouldn't be too inconvenient."

"Well, I don't know. When would you want to come over?"

"Any time that suits you."

Nadine bundled and bundled the same sheet, thinking.

"I guess tonight would be okay. About nine?"

"Sure. What's the address?"

"Thirteen twenty-two Dogwood."

"I'll be there."

He showed up on time, was encouraged by the fact that she'd taken the trouble to wash her hair and apply makeup. Both were nervous at first, but a six-pack of Budweiser made things much easier. They were in bed before eleven.

Milo went there every Monday and Thursday night. It was a simple matter to climb out his window and slide down the tepee's side to the ground. Toward dawn, getting back up was no problem either, not with sneaker soles and a good long running start. He literally ran up the side of his home to reach the window, an exhilarating end to an exhilarating night. Milo was a very happy boy. Nadine wasn't clever, but she was friendly and instructive, and she doted on this strange person whose talk she often could not interpret. They drank beer and made love and slept, then made love again when the alarm buzzer told them it was time for Milo to leave. A half hour's jog-walk-jog brought him back to the Thunderbird at about the time sky could

151

be distinguished from earth. He ate enormous breakfasts on Tuesdays and Fridays, surprised himself by thinking often of Nadine's face and body. Once, in a frenzy of bravado, they closed the door and fucked themselves silly in Tepee 19 while Nadine was supposedly changing the sheets, but when it was over they agreed it had been a dumb thing to do, especially since Dorothy had come in five minutes later to see if Nadine had any extra window cleaner. "Hi, Milo. Helping out?" "Yeah. Summer vacation always gets boring after a while." In future they would confine themselves to the schedule and not risk discovery. They did it twice more at the Thunderbird during working hours anyway. For some reason Nadine found sex in a shower cubicle irresistible. Bathrooms at the T-bird tended to echo, so she took care to clench a hand towel in her teeth as Milo bent over her from behind. It was the greatest summer either of them had known.

Then came capture and interrogation. Milo ran up the tepee's wall as usual at dawn, caught hold of the window frame, pushed it up, and squeezed through. And there sat Holly, waiting for him.

"Hi," said Milo.

"Hi yourself. Where've you been?"

"Jogging. It's the best time, with the sun just coming up and no one else around."

"Why not use the front door?"

"Oh, I didn't want to wake anyone up."

"So you like the early morning."

"Yeah."

"How early do you call early?"

"Pardon me?"

"I've been waiting here since one-thirty."

"Really?"

"Uh-huh, and I'd like to hear some truth from those lying lips."

"Okay, I went out for a long walk around town because I couldn't sleep."

"Pure bull, Milo. Try again."

"No, it's true. I'm an insomniac."

"Don't tell ridiculous lies. Who wrote this?"

She thrust a piece of paper at him. Milo turned on the light and read it. *I ♡ you.*

"How should I know?"

"Because I found it in your other jeans."

"Yeah? Uh, I guess someone's got a crush on me or something."

It could only have been Nadine. Had he worn his other jeans to her place last Monday? He had, and she must've stuffed the note in while his Levi's were lying crumpled on the floor. It must've been in the back pocket, where he wouldn't notice. Why couldn't she have put it in the front pocket where his fingers were always wedged. Shit! And had she seemed offended tonight because he made no mention of it? No, she was affable as always, probably figured he hadn't yet found the note.

"And naturally you don't know who it might be."

"No."

"And naturally you weren't out with her all night."

"No. Just me, by myself, walking."

"Not screwing around?"

"Nope, 'fraid not."

Holly's manner softened a little. "If you're seeing someone, Milo, you can always tell us. We're not prudes. I hope you're being careful. Is she old enough? Is it legal, is what I'm asking you. Milo!"

"Huh?"

"Stop this innocent act and tell me the truth. Who is she?"

"No one. I'm not seeing anyone."

"You're lying."

"Prove it."

She slapped him across the cheek.

"That's for insolence."

She did it again.

"And that's for lying. You're grounded, kid. If I have to nail that window shut, you're staying in at night, get the picture?"

Milo nodded. He was close to tears; Holly had never slapped him before.

"I haven't decided whether to tell Ray about this or not. It'll depend on what you tell me before dinner tonight. That gives you all day to think about it, okay?"

" 'Kay."

She left. Milo undressed and lay on his bed. Now what? He couldn't tell them about Nadine; she'd get fired, he just bet she would, and that wouldn't be right. He'd have to keep his lips shut tight, that's all, no matter what they said or did. Nadine deserved that much. The decision made, he relaxed a little. Holly had taken away the slip of paper with *I ♡ you* on it. Did Nadine actually love him? How much did you have to love someone to stuff notes in their pocket? That was high school stuff, wasn't it? But Nadine, although at least twenty-five, was still pretty much a teenager in some ways. Maybe the note was a big deal to her. Maybe she really did love him. He tried to measure his feelings for her. Did the red line rise to the top of the scale, or did it fall several inches short? The fact that he could not accurately quantify his affection upset him. How was he supposed to know how to react to Nadine's declaration if he didn't know how much he loved her in return? It would've been better if she'd never written the note. Now he'd have to worry about matching what he finally accepted was top-score-ring-the-bell love from Nadine, as well as defending himself against Holly and Ray. It was a big mess all right. He tried not to feel too angry at Nadine for having caused it. Writing the note had been kind of dumb, though, and his annoyance over the whole thing very nearly prevented him from sleeping through till breakfast.

In the afternoon he snuck along to Tepee 3 and told Nadine what had happened. Her face blanched with fear, something Milo hadn't expected. "She'll fire me. . . ."

Nadine had to sit on a stripped bed to recover from the shock. "She'll fire me, I know it."

"Not if I don't tell her anything, which I won't, so don't worry about it. I'll just have to figure out another way of getting to your place."

"No! Don't! Just don't do anything."

"Don't you want me to come around?"

"Please get out of here before she catches us. Please."

"Okay, okay, I'm going, but listen, don't worry about anything, okay?"

"Just go!"

"I'm gone."

Milo steeled himself for the third-degree that would follow dinner like a vile dessert. It didn't happen. He looked sideways at Holly, seeking clues, but she wouldn't look at him, had apparently decided to let him get away with it. He cheered up considerably, but Holly came to him later with a warning.

"I'll be checking your bed every night. You better be in it, kiddo."

"Okay."

"Ray doesn't need to be hassled with this."

"I agree entirely."

"Stop being a smartmouth and listen. Whoever she is, it's got to be legit, understand? I'm not talking marriage, I'm saying bring her around to meet us, give it the regular boy-meets-girl treatment. Is there a problem with her parents?"

"Uh, no, no problem."

"Then you don't need to go sneaking around, am I right?"

"I guess."

"Fine. We'll leave it at that. But I'll be checking your bed, I mean it."

"Right."

A week passed. Milo missed the bed across town. Nadine avoided him at work, and he grew resentful. What kind of chickenhearted behavior was this from a woman who'd committed her love to paper? Didn't she ♡ him any more?

"Why the long face?" Ray asked him. "Why don't you get a summer job? Save a few bucks and get a set of wheels. Seventeen, all those driving lessons, license, the whole works, but no car. What's the matter, you don't want to go park with some girl?"

"What kind of crapheap could I get with summer job wages?"

"You get the job, you make a few bucks, I'll match you dollar for dollar. We'll get you something, but first go find the job. Summer's half gone already."

"Jobs are hard to find."

"Tell me about it after you've looked. Go check out the want ads, don't wait for a goddamn invitation no one's gonna send you. You know your trouble? You're lazy."

"Yeah?"

"Yeah. In a nutshell. So prove me wrong why don't you."

But Milo couldn't be bothered proving anything to Ray. Ray's opinion didn't count, and a car would only get him to Nadine's quicker, to have her slam the door in his face. He'd phoned her twice. "No," she said both times. "No, forget it. Leave me alone," and hung up. He phoned her a third time; her attitude had changed. "Well, okay, come see me Sunday. Use the back alley, okay? I've got neighbors." Now he felt cocky again. She wanted him back! The big scare was over. Afternoon delight was the answer. Why hadn't he thought of it himself? Maybe the nosy neighbors would be in church, not peeking through their windows. Whatever, he'd go around there come Sunday and swan-dive into her bed.

"Why the smirk?" Ray asked. "Did you discover the secret of staying alive without working?"

"Yeah, it's called living with Mom and Dad."

"You know what happened when I goofed off at your age?"

"I think I remember you telling me a few times you didn't graduate and had to do shitty jobs and had a general all-around hard time until you inherited this place."

"I was already working here when my mother died, so don't make it sound like I lucked onto something. And you can forget about inheriting from me, because one, I don't intend dying young like she did, and two, you're not the type to be a good motel manager, so you better plan on finding work in some other field. I'm serious."

"I know it."

It pissed Ray off that Milo never called him Dad. He didn't even call him Ray, somehow manipulated the conversation so he didn't need to address Ray at all. It was demeaning and it was deliberate, Ray was positive. After all these years of looking after the little prick, he still wasn't acknowledged as a true father. There was something wrong with Milo, some element missing. He needed to be taught a lesson, one with longer-lasting effects than his Saturday night in jail for drunkenness. Bernie had even given him a lift home in a cruiser, which Ray hadn't asked him to do. Milo had stepped out of Bernie's black-and-white like it was a Rolls-Royce. It pissed Ray off.

Sunday. Milo walked around to Nadine's early, went to the back door via the alley, just as she'd requested. Had he gone in the front gate he would have seen the pickup parked in the drive and gone no further. The back door was unlocked; he went inside. Nadine wasn't in the kitchen or the living room, so he opened the bedroom door. Donny Pitts was in bed with his wife, and not expecting walk-in visitors. Man and boy gaped at each other. Nadine began moaning in distress.

"Who the fuck are you!"

"Uh, you want to subscribe to the Gazette?"

"What the fuck you think you're doin' in here!"

"Excuse me."

He backed out.

"Hey! You! Get the fuck back here!"

Milo ran, heard the bedsprings twang behind him as Donny leaped out. Milo was gone from the house in seven seconds, off the property in twelve. There was no chance a naked man would follow him outside, so he slowed to a jog, then a walk, heart hammering. Why hadn't she warned him not to come? Maybe the guy (he assumed it was the wandering husband) had just shown up this morning and pinned her to the bed, given her no chance to make a call, but she might at least have locked the back door or something. Now she'd be in deep shit. The guy had looked like the violent type. Would he beat Milo's name out of her? It was likely, and then he'd come storming over to the T-bird with a gun. Should he go home, or lay low? Where did a guy with no real friends lay low?

He walked aimlessly around town, and when the adrenaline had dwindled in his body Milo was struck by the most important fact to arise from his Sunday morning encounter, the thing that had been obscured until now by surprise and fear—he'd lost Nadine for good this time. No more nooky in her big old lumpy bed. No more six-pack sex. Something warm and good had died. It was over. Now his footsteps dragged with genuine regret. He actually felt like crying. No more Nadine. Milo felt awful.

He stayed away from the motel until evening, but it was clear from the dinnertime conversation no one had come around looking for him. At least he had that much to be glad about.

Monday, Nadine did not come to work. She called in, said her husband was back and didn't want her changing sheets for a living any more, and would Holly please send any wages owed her through the mail. Milo heard the story that night. "I wasn't going to let her go just like that. Nadine's been one of the best girls we've ever had, so I went around there with the money myself, and she was black and blue from the neck up. She didn't want to let me in, but I could see her through the screen door. It makes me sick that a

158

man can beat up on his wife and make her quit a perfectly good job for no reason at all. I asked her why but she wouldn't say. She was just so embarrassed and humiliated that I saw her that way. Men like that make me want to vomit. Couldn't we at least ask Bernie to go around there and give him a warning?"

"Domestic dispute," said Ray. "Cops can't do a thing."

"Well, I'm going to ask him anyway."

"The guy'll just beat up on her some more if the cops start putting their noses in. Leave it alone. Bernie can't do a thing. She was probably playing around with some other guy while hubby was away."

"And what if she was? What's that got to do with anything? Everyone knows Donny Pitts is after anything female—when he's sober enough, that is. He's a creep, and it'd serve him right if Nadine did have a boyfriend while he was God knows where all that time, and it still wouldn't justify hitting her, the coward!"

"Hey! Go easy! Maybe he had a reason to be away! Maybe he was looking for work someplace else! He goes out looking for a job and when he comes back he finds out she's been running around with some guy, and if that's the way it happened he's got every right to get mad at her! Okay, smacking her around is bad, but you don't know the facts, Holly; you're just jumping to conclusions like always!"

"If you ever did that to me I'd kill you!"

"If you ever screwed around I'd kill you!"

"Are you struggling to make a point here? Should I hold my breath waiting for the big point you intend making?"

"The point . . . the fucking point is, you don't know what you're talking about! You're just pissed because now you'll have to interview a bunch of dopey women for the job, which I happen to know you hate doing, so don't lay this male-violence bullshit on me, okay? Okay?"

"Can I have some more Jell-O?"

"Keep outa this, Kevin!"

Milo made no contribution to the topic under dispute.

Bruises such as Holly had described must have elicited a full confession. Milo walked in fear for a week. When nothing happened, he began to relax. Nadine hadn't blabbed. What a terrific, gutsy lady, not to give away Milo's name.

Confident again, he began walking along Locust one evening, on his way to a movie downtown. "Take the car, why don't you," Ray had said. "What's a driver's license for if you never use it?" But Milo preferred to walk. He might have driven Holly's car, had it been offered, but never Ray's.

"Hi. Are you Milo Kootz?"

The girl had come out of nowhere to block his path. Milo assumed she'd seen him on TV.

"Milo Ginty. Kootz is my stepfather's name."

"Okay, but you're the kid that lives at the Thunderbird, right?"

"Uh-huh."

"The guy with the frogs, right?"

"I guess so."

She was older than him, but Milo was hoping she'd be some kind of small-town groupie who'd gone through all the local bands and now wanted to start in on media luminaries like himself. If so, he was prepared to consent. A notebook and pen were pushed at him.

"Can I have your autograph?"

"Uh, yeah, I guess."

Expectations flattened, he scrawled his name, vaguely aware as he did so that footsteps were approaching from behind the girl; another fan, maybe? Milo handed the notebook back, looked over the girl's shoulder, and recognized Donny Pitts the instant the girl skipped aside to remove herself from what was to follow. The nature of the setup was cruelly apparent. The fist that rushed for his mouth was hard and vengeful. Milo felt his front teeth leave his gums, felt his lip split open, felt his mouth fill with blood as he dropped. The toecaps of Donny's cowboy boots began battering his ribs. Milo had adopted an instinctive fetal position to protect his balls and head. It wasn't hurting as much as he'd thought it might, but he hoped it wouldn't go on for too long. It annoyed him that Donny Pitts's girlfriend with the notebook hadn't known the difference between a Ginty and a Kootz. That really pissed him off. His teeth lay on his tongue, pressed against the roof of his mouth like pellets of unchewed gum. Don't swallow them, he told himself; they can be sewn right back in nowadays. He wondered if his kidneys were being damaged; those boots were the pointy-toed kind, their owner panting with effort as he slammed them again and again into Milo's back and ribs. The sidewalk scraping his cheek still held a little of the day's warmth.

"Okay, that's enough," said the girl, and Milo was grateful; he would've thanked her if he could. He really liked her for saying that.

"He's got more comin'."

And Milo did get more, but the kicks were weaker now. A dull ache, the first intimation of real pain to enter his awareness, was spreading from his spine around to his chest.

"C'mon, Donny, quit it."

"Okay."

One last kick, then Milo heard footsteps moving away. He felt great relief; the worst was over. He began slowly to uncramp himself, had got as far as his knees when he realized Donny was back. A final kick was driven into his solar plexus, a kick to make all preceding kicks seem gentle. Milo vomited instantly, losing the teeth held in his mouth all through the attack. They flew from his lips in a jet of stinging bile, and Milo hurt too much to care. A bomb had exploded in his guts. Pain was the all, the everything; existence as agony. He fell over again, unable to draw breath. He truly thought he might be dying.

Ray drove him home from the hospital.

"Just came up and did it for no reason at all, huh?"

161

"Uh-huh," Milo managed to squeeze around the wadding in his mouth. His gums and lip were sutured, his two broken ribs bound. It was easy to avoid talking.

"And you never even saw his face?"

Milo shook his head. Why implicate Nadine by naming Donny? It was over and done with, the affair, the tumble, whatever it had been. Why bring it all into the open by involving the police? Donny would have his lady friend to confirm any alibi he chose. It was all over bar the pain. He just wanted to go to bed and sleep for a week, then wake up feeling like a human again. At least Donny hadn't had a gun. He'd got off lightly, considering.

"No point in taking you down to the station to look at Bernie's badass books?"

"Unh-unh."

"This meaningless-violence crap really gets me."

"Nnnnn."

Milo played king for a week, moving around the tepee with exaggerated slowness, watching endless hours of TV, living on soup, cake, and ice cream. Kevin followed him everywhere, eager to assist the wounded warrior. Milo allowed him to fetch cans of Coke, let him inspect the mutilated lip and the gaping sockets behind it. "Wow! Does it still hurt?" A manly nod. "Jeez . . . I told 'em at school what happened and they said you're gonna need false teeth like old people have." A nod. "Gross! Are the stitches coming out next week? Can I watch? Neato!"

Desutured at last, his face its normal size again, Milo was taken by Ray to an orthodontist, who outlined a horrendously expensive plan for restoring Milo's mouth. Ray's family insurance deductible for the year was wiped out instantly, and on the ride home his thoughts were dark. Milo's teeth-to-be would take a big bite from his savings account, and the kid hadn't even thanked him. Where had he got the idea life was a free ride? It was baffling.

A temporary bridge was wired between Milo's canines

while the four missing incisors were being readied. Milo
went on his own to Dr. Zuwecki's for the various moldings
and fittings, Ray being in no mood to witness the precise
method by which his savings were decimated. Dr. Zuwecki
did phone the Thunderbird once to discuss with Ray a
request Milo had made concerning the permanent bridge.
"What request?" Ray was signing in guests and didn't want
to be distracted by anyone else's problems. Couldn't
Zuwecki do what Ray was paying him to do without bothering him with details? "It's regarding the material he prefers. There are several options, as you know." Ray assumed
this meant Milo wanted teeth of movie star whiteness. Or
maybe, since unnaturally white teeth weren't fashionable
any more, Milo wanted the off-white, faintly cream-colored
kind, not because they looked more realistic, Ray bet, but
because they were probably more expensive. It made no
difference; the insurance took over, whatever the cost, once
the deductible had been met. "I just thought I'd better
check with you first, Mr. Kootz." Now there were two more
couples coming through the door; guests were stacking up
in front of the desk faster than Ray could cope. Where the
fuck was Holly? "Uh, yeah, just give him what he wants,
okay?" He hung up. How come Holly was always in the can
when they got a flood of guests? If she didn't get her butt
out here pronto, they'd lose half these bozos to the Ramada
Inn down the road.

Two days before school resumed, Milo was fitted with Dr.
Zuwecki's creation. He came home. He opened his mouth.

"What the fuck are those?" Ray was aghast.

"My new teeth."

"They're fucking gold."

"Yup."

"You don't have front teeth in gold. You have 'em in
white."

"There's no law says you have to. I like 'em in gold."

"It looks stupid. You look like a clown!"

"I think it looks kind of neat."

"Holly! Get in here and look at this! Gold front teeth!"

"Oh, my God. Why did you let him?"

"I didn't fucking let him! He did it himself. And Zuwecki! Where does he get off, giving a kid gold front teeth just because he's stupid enough to ask for them! I'll sue the prick!"

"He phoned you up," said Milo. "I heard him. He said you said it was okay."

"Like hell I did! I never would've okayed anything so stupid-looking! You look like a fucking Mexican!"

"Milo, honey, why did you want them that way?"

"To be different."

"Two thousand bucks! You little shit! You did it deliberately to piss me off, didn't you!"

"No, I just wanted gold teeth."

"Ray, what's done is done."

"Bullshit it's done! I'm going to the insurance office tomorrow and have them confirm we can get proper teeth in white and not have to pay for these fucking abortions. I'll pull the fuckers out myself."

But the insurance company would not confirm. The gold teeth were top quality, would last a lifetime, and Ray had to admit he'd told Dr. Zuwecki to give Milo what he wanted. The teeth would remain in Milo's head, Ray's check in the doctor's account, and Milo Ginty was reconfirmed, once school started, as just the weirdest kid in town.

12

EVERYONE WAS TALKING about the partial eclipse of the sun. It would happen Thursday. Kevin, like many others, had a piece of black cardboard with a pinprick in it through which the sun, its disk impinged upon by the intervening moon, would be cast in microcosm on the sidewalks of Callisto. But on Thursday morning he woke up with a mild fever, and Holly kept him home from school. "Mom, I'll miss the eclipse!" Tears wouldn't change her mind. Kevin was ordered to remain in bed.

As the time of the moon's passage between earth and sun drew near, Kevin left his room, fully dressed, and crept down to Milo's. Milo had told him it was possible to slide down the wall from his window, and Kevin intended proving it. Nothing would keep him from witnessing the partial eclipse, not even Holly. Milo hadn't lied; it was easy work to reach the ground, and Kevin ran away from the Thunderbird before he could be missed. Only when he was a mile away did he remember the pinpricked cardboard left behind on his dresser. "Shit!" The whole object of his escape had been blown.

Furious with himself, he looked at his watch. Three minutes to go. The sky was hazy, so maybe he could break all the rules and stare directly at the sun to see the moon take a Pac Man bite from its rim. That's what he'd do, and if it burned his eyes he deserved it for being such a conehead. He was sweating, whether from excitement or fever he couldn't say, didn't care. "C'mon, sun!"

He waited for the miracle at Ninth and Main, waited and waited, consulting his watch often. Zero hour had passed, yet everything seemed the same. Maybe the moon was blocking even less of the sun than they figured. If he had his cardboard sheet with him he could tell for sure. It was very frustrating.

And then came awareness of the change. Everything had subtly become different. The sky's brightness, already diffuse, had thinned, become lusterless, indirect. Far or near, all things appeared flat and unreal. Kevin held his breath. The diminution of emphasis, although he fully understood the celestial mechanics behind it, was magical in its nuance, its elusiveness. He raised his eyes but could not look at the sun, still shining, apparently undimmed even behind a skein of cloud. The elms down Ninth Street stood like minutely painted scenery, absolutely still, seemingly lit from all directions, their shadows weakened to the merest suggestion. He stepped off the curb and walked across Main. There was no traffic; the moon's transit seemingly had halted all motion, everywhere. Kevin could believe that movement of every kind had ceased clear across town, across all of Kansas, the entire nation. The very planet seemed held in stasis.

Now he stood beneath an elm, and a second miracle beckoned. At his feet lay a pattern of shifting motes, spread like golden coins across the sidewalk, each one spilled from the tree above. Kevin had seen leaf shadows and their attendant patches of light on the ground before, but never in so strange a configuration as this. Every mote, singly or clustered, was a fat crescent, each of uniform size, their horns, like those of a curious herd, all pointing the same way. They danced, they rearranged themselves constantly in the faint breeze stirring the boughs above his

166

head, but always, overlapping or alone, they were crescents, aligned by nature, a swarm of replicated, partially eaten suns, the very thing Kevin would have seen cast by his forgotten cardboard with its trifling pinhole. Here were holes galore, every one created by enfeebled sunlight passing through the endlessly shifting foliage, a million holes, ragged, variegated, yet inexplicably pasting the sidewalk with indistinguishable, myriad crescents. How was it possible?

Lips parted, breath barely stirring his lungs, he stared at the ground while the rest of Callisto stared at the sky, and it seemed that the golden things, mysterious and beautiful as fairy wings, danced only for him—Kevin. Until this suspended moment he had been the son of Ray and Holly, half-brother to Milo, but now, newly initiated, he was finally, completely, himself.

"I don't see how that's possible, Kevin."

Mr. Maynard was the science teacher. Kevin had approached him after class.

"But I saw it."

"Think about it. How could sunlight come down through the leaves and make identical little eclipse shapes on the ground? Through a pinhole, yes, but not through leaves. All the holes, if you can call them holes, would be different. How could different holes all make the same shape and size pattern on the ground? It's just not possible."

"But I saw it."

"I'm not accusing you of lying, Kevin, but by your own admission your mom kept you home yesterday because you had a fever, right? So isn't it just possible you might've imagined or hallucinated the whole thing? Isn't it possible that's what happened?"

"No."

"Not possible at all? Ever?"

"No."

"I can see I'm not going to convince you, but facts are facts, Kevin, especially scientific facts. What you think you saw is about as likely as me tossing a bag of colored confetti in the air and having it all come down and make a picture of the president. It just can't happen."

Maynard saw dimness invade Kevin's eyes. The boy wasn't listening, had rejected sound reasoning in favor of the fantastic. Kids were like that nowadays. He blamed the movies. Kevin would never be a scientist or engineer, maybe because of this very conversation; another brain squandered, diverted from the path of true learning.

Kevin didn't give up. It was too important. He told Holly and Ray. Holly said it served him right for getting out of bed, and Ray sided with science. Kevin went to Milo.

"Little crescents?"

"Thousands of them."

"You weren't doped up?"

"No. I saw them, just like I said."

"Okay, I believe you."

"But how could it happen?"

"Beats me. It's a weird world."

"But you believe me."

"Didn't I just say so?"

"Okay, then."

Kevin believed that Milo believed. The scattering of suns was made officially real and true. He spoke no more about it.

A new restlessness took hold of Holly. This time it was adult education. Psychology was the subject she wanted. "I want to understand people. I think it could be very beneficial for me, Ray. All it takes is one night a week, seven till ten at the new high school. I could really benefit from this, and it's cheap. I've always been interested in psychology, you know I have. Every time a customer comes through the door I try to get inside his head, try to figure out who he really is deep down, just in the few minutes it takes to sign in. Have you noticed the way I study them? It's like I'm trying to understand everything about them. I think I have a natural talent for that kind of psychological insight, but I need guidance, Ray. I need to study it properly so I can really understand. So what do you think?"

"About what?"

"About me signing up for an adult education course. Stop pretending you weren't listening."

"One night a week?"

"At the new high school."

"Okay. You want to do it, do it. I'll mind the store."

"You're a sweetie."

Now in his senior year, Milo had a steady girl. Her name was Sharon Kincheloe, and it was said of her that although she couldn't tell a nickel defense from a quarterback sneak, she'd studied every conceivable play with the football team. Sharon, they said, was a wide receiver with a tight end. In every school there is a girl whose name is affixed to this tedious and unoriginal story of sexual exploits with the team, the backbone for a standard body of high school apocrypha. If such a girl does not exist, one is elected. In Sharon's case the story wasn't true, although she had once dated linebacker Chuck Speer. With a name like that, she told him, he should be a javelin thrower, not a football player. Chuck didn't really approve of girls who made witty remarks; girls were for decoration mainly, and a regular guy eventually had to marry one, at which point she became interior decoration. He wasn't thinking of marriage when he drove Sharon to a lonely spot one summer evening, parked, and produced a blanket from the trunk of his car. Sharon wanted to know if an athletic type was different from other boys, so they attempted intercourse, but Chuck's penis was so small penetration was virtually impossible. Chuck enjoyed himself anyway, apparently unaware of his personal shortcomings, and could not understand why Sharon wouldn't date him again. A quick look around the showers after a game would have revealed a dozen or more reasons. His pride dented, Chuck spread stories about Sharon, and when these fabrications reached the ears of other team members they didn't bother denying what they knew was untrue; nobody gave a shit.

It was her unfounded reputation that drew Milo to Sharon; not the implicit promise of sexual availability but the reputation itself. It placed her beyond the pale, a fine place to be, in the geography of love as defined by Milo. He encouraged her to dress like a whore, tease her hair into a haystack, wear an excess of makeup, and snap gum, anything to set her apart from the squeaky-cleanness of the average girl. Female rock stars were still a year or two away from adopting this selfsame pose, so Sharon, with assistance from Milo, was way ahead of the rest. She was happy enough to be associated with Callisto's main man for weirdness, at least for the time being; deep down she wanted a condo in Malibu, and Milo was unlikely to provide it. What they required from each other was genital gratification and a mutually supportive aura of defiance. Milo and Sharon made love frequently, but quickly, like monkeys.

They had their friends, an exclusive band of urban exiles who regularly ingested a variety of drugs while slowly mustering the courage to leave town and face the big world outside. Neither had the nerve deliberately to flunk out of their finals. Both had enrolled at KU for the fall term. Milo was seriously considering asking Ray for a car to carry him away to college. Ray might think it was worth the price, just to get Milo out of his hair. They rarely spoke, had barely exchanged words since Ray informed Milo exactly how much college fees were going to cut into his profits over the next few years. Would a car prove the last straw? Sharon's mother had already given her a Corvette. Sharon's mother had married into farming in a big way and still reaped a fat harvest from the divorce settlement. In a car culture such as America's, Milo had so far exercised almost unheard-of unconventionality by declining to drive. Sharon sometimes wondered whether seeing Milo at last behind the wheel would somehow diminish him, but every time he opened his mouth to let something funny or cruel drift past those golden teeth she was reassured; Milo's uniqueness came not from any vehicle he might or might not consent to step inside, but from within his narrow head. He was, for now, all she needed in a male.

She asked him once, "What are people like us doing in this hole?"

"Just passing through."

This was not how Ray had imagined family life. He wanted domestic harmony, the quiet pleasures of the brood. While the boys were still young things hadn't been too bad, but now the tepee was filled with overlong silences and sudden eruptions of temper. It was Milo's fault; anyone could see that. Ray had been anticipating this since Milo's fourteenth birthday, when he'd refused to attend his own party, claimed it was dumb and uncool. Ray had taken the presents and smashed them, an act that had produced not the flicker of an eye from Milo.

And now Kevin was aping his half-brother, allowing his eyes to glaze over when Ray spoke, no matter how inoffensive the topic, how friendly and nonconfrontational his manner. He was the old man, automatically an idiot, and he was only thirty-three. Holly was all of thirty-seven, but they didn't treat her that way. It was insulting. The fact that Kevin, his favorite, was behaving like this made Ray miserable. Ray's own childhood had been filled with emotional switchbacks and untimely separations. He'd wanted to give his own son, and Holly's, a solid family life together, something that would see them through to adulthood, and the whole thing seemingly was falling to pieces around him. Even his wife seemed edgy, and it could only be due to her divided loyalties. Holly knew Ray and Milo couldn't get along, yet wouldn't pass judgment in Ray's favor, wouldn't criticize her boy, even when Milo had brought home his slut of a girlfriend and made it obvious he wanted Ray and Holly to be appalled. Ray appreciated her dilemma, and tried not to force her down from the fence she'd sat on for years now. Sometimes he wondered if he left her there because he was afraid to find out which side she'd come down on if prodded hard enough. Was a little happiness around the place too much to ask for? He couldn't wait for Milo to leave Callisto and start college. Maybe then Kevin would quit trying to imitate him and go back to being a good kid again.

The address on the envelope was typewritten; so was the letter inside. Ray didn't like what it said. It couldn't be true. No signature; local postmark. He burned it, but the letter wouldn't go away. On Wednesday evening he drove over to Butane. The Rest E-Z Motel was close to the highway, a nice place, in Ray's professional opinion, even if it lacked the Thunderbird's originality. He parked a long way down the street, walked back and got a room, entered it, and watched TV. Every fifteen minutes or so he went outside and wandered around the parking lot, then returned and watched more TV. By 7:30 they were both there, Holly's Subaru and Bernie's Plymouth. Ray went to the manager's office.

"I've had a little accident, backed into someone's car. Can you give me the room number for Kansas plate CAS 4357?"

The manager checked. "Fifteen. Do much damage?"

"Just a fender bender."

He returned to his room and watched more TV. An hour passed. Ray vomited once and cried twice. When he felt able, he went and knocked on the door marked 15.

"Who is it?"

"Manager," croaked Ray.

Bernie opened up. His chest was bare. He stared at Ray for a long moment. "Better come in."

Holly was in the bathroom. Bernie got her out.

"Oh, Jesus . . ."

"You want a drink, Ray?"

"No, I'm not staying."

"Drink?"

"No," said Holly.

Bernie poured himself one, a Jim Beam. Bernie had always ordered Jim Beam when they drank together in the club favored by off-duty cops. Ray hadn't had a drink with Bernie in almost a year. Holly sat on a chair and put her head in her hands. He felt sorry for her, wanted to hold her but couldn't, not with Bernie there. Ray had thought he'd want to kill them both, but he didn't even want to hit Bernie. His arms hung as though weighted with anvils. He didn't know what to do or say next, had planned no further than presenting himself in their doorway.

"Okay, now what?"

Bernie was daring Ray with his voice, challenging him to start something. Ray thought it was kind of pathetic that Bernie couldn't see how Ray felt, but Bernie had never been the understanding kind. Ray couldn't imagine why he'd ever had Bernie for a friend. An even bigger mystery was why Holly would want to fuck him. It made Ray feel good to see that Bernie had a gut. Ray was still thin— Snakehips, Holly called him—so why did she want to fuck this other guy with the gut and no sensitivity at all? A bigger dick? Could it be that simple? And where did that leave love? When Holly had completed her psychology course, she'd put her name down for art history, every Wednesday, seven till ten at the new high school. When art history finally came to an end, she probably would've joined up for philosophy or economics or learning how to fold little paper animals, anything to keep those Wednesday nights open for Bernie. Ray felt sick all over again.

"You want to talk about this, or what?"

Ray shook his head. What could anyone say that wouldn't sound feeble, like something in a corny soap. They used this stuff in songs: the faithless wife, the best friend who betrays, the lonesome loser, three minutes of plangent heartache, then on to a fast dance number. Holly was looking at him. He couldn't stand to see her face; she looked even sicker than he felt. Even Bernie was beginning to look uncomfortable; he reached for a shirt and put it on, tucked the gut away.

"You two have probably got a whole bunch of stuff to talk over. Say now if you want me to put in my ten cents' worth."

No one took him up on the offer, so Bernie began pulling on his boots. Holly was looking at the floor, her face frozen. Ray seemed close to tears. Bernie had never seen such pathetic expressions. These two deserved each other. He was better off out of it, had been wanting to finish things up for weeks now, and Ray had done it for him. It was too bad it had to happen this way, but that's how things were in the real world. Ray and Holly looked like children, they really did, a couple of squirts caught playing doctor, ashamed of themselves. Bernie could understand why Holly looked that way, but not Ray. Room 15 was so stuffed with puzzling vibrations, Bernie wanted out, right now.

He picked up his jacket. "You know where to find me." It sounded like a come-on but wasn't intended to be; he simply couldn't think what else he might say. Holly didn't look up. Her shoulders seemed very fragile above her slip, and the arms hugging each other were stick thin. Ray was looking at her, ignoring Bernie. They were both crippled by shock, Bernie could tell; he'd seen stuff like this after firefights in 'Nam, only worse. He left, closed the door behind him. Husband and wife reached for the right words, the phrases that would kill the silence hanging between them, but neither could speak the unspeakable.

13

"I WANT you both with me."

"Aww, Mom . . ."

"In the car. Do it."

"Mind if I excuse myself? I've got other business."

"Get in the car, Milo. Kevin, get in and stop whining."

"I don't wanna go swim in the lake."

"I don't care what you want, just do as I say. Your towels are already in the trunk, and your swimsuits. I've made a picnic lunch, now get in there."

"A picnic? Are you kidding?"

"Get in the car!"

"Is Dad coming?"

"No, he isn't. I want to be with my sons, if you don't mind. Would it be too embarrassing to be seen with your mother? I want to go to the lake and lie in the sun and swim and have a picnic, like we used to when you were little. Can I ask that much of you? Is it too much of a big sacrifice to make for your mother?"

"Why isn't Dad coming?"

"He's busy. Get in the car, guys."

"Jesus . . . do we have to?"

"Yes, is the short answer."

"I don't wanna!"

"Please, Kevin . . ."

They drove to the lake and arranged themselves on the beach, its only occupants. This was the stony western shore, less popular than the eastern, with its beach of imported sand, its snack bar and sailboats for hire. The picnic was laid out and nibbled at. Holly and Kevin attempted to swim, but this early in summer the water was still cold. Milo refused to put on his swimsuit. "Gotta go take a leak," he said, and disappeared among the trees to smoke a joint. Kevin went wandering along the shoreline while Holly sat on a blanket and wondered if her second marriage was over.

Ray had barely spoken to her in a week, wouldn't even look at her if he could help it, and wouldn't let her touch him. Maybe the smartest thing she could do was back off and let him get tired of feeling sorry for himself. She knew he still loved her; if he didn't he wouldn't be acting so hurt. It was a shame he'd found out at all. She'd been working herself up to dumping Bernie for some time, might even have used that interrupted evening to suggest they break it off. Ray wouldn't even tell her how he found out.

Margaret Corcoran had written the letter. Margaret never forgave Ray for jilting Susan. Only after the wedding had been canceled, at great cost and massive humiliation for the family, had it become obvious that Ray wasn't mad at all, had simply wanted to rid himself of their lovely daughter. That disgusting business with the nakedness and the toilet had been nothing but a sham. Nothing had gone right for the Corcorans after that. Susan's eventual marriage to the doctor from their congregation had not been a happy one, and had ended in divorce in 1981, after which Susan left the church. Nothing would entice her back into either institution; Susan had lost her faith in both. Margaret blamed these disasters on Ray. She also held him responsible for the death of her husband; Darryl had died from heart failure the year following the divorce. Ray

Kootz had destroyed the Corcorans. Margaret told God, and God agreed with her.

She became obsessed with the Kootzes, began surreptitiously following them around town, Kevin or Ray, Holly or Milo (who would have been offended at being lumped in with the rest), whichever one happened to leave the tepee first. For a month she did this, and her spying did nothing to alleviate her fixation. She didn't know quite what she was looking for, but was sure she would recognize it when it came along. Margaret wanted an opportunity to hurt them, to punish the family of the man who had punished hers. When her daylight shadowings bore no fruit, she began watching by night. Margaret knew darkness was the natural haunt of sin, and the Kootzes were sinners all, even had a garish devil's pole outside their wizard's hat of a home. Margaret would root them out for herself and for God.

On only the second night of the new nocturnal vigil she followed Holly to her routine assignation at the Rest E-Z. Margaret's heart sang a little victory song when she saw Bernie Swenson, a respectable cop (apart from his divorce), enter the room Holly had unlocked a short while before. Margaret kept a close watch for the next six nights without witnessing further marital transgression, then followed Holly again to the motel on the outskirts of Butane. So it was a regular little Wednesday night fling, probably covered by some harmless meeting or other. Ray Kootz obviously didn't know his wife was cheating on him, but Margaret would be only too happy to play the role of informant—anonymously, of course.

Kevin had wandered back, now was idly kicking through the shallows in front of Holly. She watched him, her darling boy, hers and Ray's, and knew as she watched his unselfconscious play that she would do whatever was necessary to make things right, even beg; it was only fair, since she was the one who had done wrong. She would give Ray another week to quit sulking, and then she would beg. Holly gave herself a fifty-fifty chance of avoiding what she knew would be a humbling experience. If she had to do it, she would, but if it could be avoided, so much the better. Making herself feel as awful as Ray wouldn't help any, she was sure. This thing had to be put behind them as quickly as possible, and kept there. And the boys must never know.

"Show me how you can skip a stone!"

"Okay!"

Kevin picked up a flat one, tossed it across the lake's surface. It skipped three times before sinking.

"You can do better than that!"

"Watch this! This one's gonna be terrific!"

He skipped it five times, whooped in self-congratulation. Holly watched him try to better his best effort. He looked and sounded like a little boy again, not like the Kevin he lately seemed bent on becoming: silent, grumpy, sarcastic, a pseudo-chip off Milo's block. There was the true joker in the pack, the wild card—Milo. Maybe Ray was right—Milo was a dark angel sent to destroy them all—but Holly could do nothing but love him, her other boy from that other, far less happy marriage. This one mustn't end as that one had.

Milo wasn't even Brian Ginty's son, but Milo didn't know it, nor did Ray. That little secret was Holly's alone. The father, she was reasonably sure, was a TV repairman who came to fix the jagged lines on their screen while Brian was at work. Holly gave herself to him on the big green sofa Brian loved to commandeer while he watched the ball game, bag of peanuts in one hand, can of beer in the other, the all-time couch potato. The TV repairman had her once, fixed the set, then had her again. He still charged the full price. Milo looked pretty much like him. Holly hadn't even known the repairman's name. Brian never suspected Milo wasn't his, and Holly didn't tell him even after the divorce, in case his child-support payments should stop.

But Kevin was Ray's, no doubt about it, and that's why she had to fix things this time. Holly didn't know why she had this need to fuck men other than her husband every now and then. She didn't even like them, for the most part, but had to have them, just to work off something wild inside her, the part that had never admitted to being married, the part closest to the ground. Maybe now, having been caught, she'd be able to ease off, even quit. She really did want to grow old with Ray beside her.

"Did you see it? Seven times!"

"Great! Now do eight!"

"Are you crazy! Eight?"

"Go on, kid! Show me!"

"You got a deal!"

He threw several more, then his arm grew tired. He flopped into the water and splashed around, showing off. Holly watched him with pride and sadness. If only Milo would straighten out, there was a chance Kevin would, too. Kevin followed Milo like a lovesick girl. He would never clown around like this if Milo was near, would take his cue from whatever Milo did. Where was Milo? He'd had plenty of time to pee and return. He was probably grumbling to himself nearby, registering his protest at being dragged out to the lake by refusing to enjoy it. Good; let Kevin enjoy his absence, so Holly could enjoy Kevin. These beings had come from her womb, these wonderful boys, so dissimilar yet both so much a part of her it hurt to see them unhappy, confused, in conflict with Ray, who she loved also.

Everything had to change, and the change would have to start with herself. She'd go to Ray when they got home, go straight to him and call herself anything he wanted to hear, would admit to absolute wrongdoing, no excuses accepted. She owed him that much, wouldn't wait a week to let him break first, wouldn't even wait a day, didn't even want to wait another minute now that she had accepted reconciliation on Ray's terms, not her own. It made her feel good to know she planned on doing the right thing at last. She should've done it a week ago. Holly wanted to gather her family around her and feed them love. In five minutes she'd tell Kevin to go fetch Milo from wherever he'd hidden himself. Five minutes and then they'd go home.

She hugged her knees and stared across the lake's bright sheen, happily contemplating a new life. Maybe Milo was screwed up because he sensed all wasn't right between herself and Ray. Maybe if the marriage was remade, the boys would change. It wasn't impossible. There was a new beginning ahead for them all. She felt actual tears pricking at her eyes behind her darkest sunglasses. So it's true, she thought; you really can cry for happiness. Holly surrendered to joy till her mascara ran, all without moving a muscle.

Kevin was pulling larger stones from the beach now, heaving them out into the lake as far as he could. They hit the water with a satisfying *ker-splash!* He found they made more noise if they fell from higher up, so he began lobbing them upward as well as outward. It was like watching meteors plummet to earth. Then he found a perfect rock, about eight inches long, three across, smoothly rounded by water, yellowish veins running through its shining grayness. He judged it to be around five pounds, held its compact bulk in his hands, savored the cool film of water lingering across its surface. It felt good just to hold the rock, but it had a purpose to fulfill. He'd throw this beauty high up so it would come down harder and faster than all the rest.

Kevin bent his knees slightly, held the rock between them, then hurled it upward with all his strength. His arms reached for the sun, his spine curved back on itself like a drawn bow, and the stone flew up, up, its path almost vertical, spinning slowly, droplets arcing from its gleaming sides. Now that it was launched, Kevin thought he'd better get out from under it before the stone reached apogee and began descending. He scuttled away, hoping he could turn in time to see the splash, but when he spun around mere seconds later there was no splash to see, no fountaining of displaced water hanging in the air, nothing. The stone must have fallen on the beach, not in the lake. It certainly wasn't still in the air. The sound of his own running feet must have covered the thud of its impact. He'd find it and try again, this time with a little more of the horizontal in its trajectory, a little less of the vertical.

"Mom, did you see where it landed?"

Holly was sitting as before, arms around her knees, looking across the water. She must've seen the rock land; he'd been right in front of her when he threw it. "Mom?" She wasn't even listening, was off in dreamland somewhere, it looked like. Kevin knew how that could happen on a nice warm day; you just slipped away inside your head and didn't see or hear things around you for a while. "Hey, Mom?" He came a little closer and saw the rock, its blunt end standing some three inches from the top of Holly's skull, the rest buried deep in her brain. Yet she seemed not to have noticed, still sat and stared through her shades. Maybe she'd picked it up from where it fell at her feet and placed it on her head to scare him, scare the shit out of him for throwing dangerous things up in the air around other people. It was a stupid thing to have done, he saw that now, was willing to admit it, wanted Holly to take the rock off her head and laugh at the expression on his face. But the rock wasn't on her head, it was in it, had smashed through the pate, was resting on the brainpan itself. The rock was in Holly's head and Holly was dead, sitting up but dead. He'd gone and killed his mom . . . and the enormity of it rose out of the ground and squeezed him till he couldn't breathe, could barely stand.

Holly was dead, totally dead, and he was the one who'd killed her with a rock he never should've thrown in the air, never should've picked up in the first place, never should've come to the lake, never should've been born to do this awful thing, but he had, and now they'd punish him for it, make him pay for the stupid dumb awful thing he did that killed his mom. . . . A thin mewling sound came from Kevin's throat, and his bladder emptied itself unnoticed.

He was petrified, made of sweating stone, so cold his teeth began chattering. Maybe his whole body would shatter from sheer vibration and tumble in pieces, become stones among others on the beach, guiltless, unfeeling, part of the landscape. Kevin couldn't even close his eyes to shut out the sight of his mother, could only stand and absorb into his atoms the fact of her death, feel his responsibility for it stacking up on his shoulders, another ton with every passing second.

When he returned to the beach Milo didn't at first realize his brother was frozen with terror. From a distance it seemed that Kevin was listening closely while Holly spoke to him, probably telling him to go find Milo. The closer he got, the less sure he became. Kevin wasn't moving at all; he looked like a statue, and Holly looked like one too, a seated statue. Then he saw the stone. Like Kevin, he thought it must be a joke, but by the time he stood beside them he knew it was not.

"Jesus . . . What happened . . . ?"

But Kevin couldn't speak. Milo pushed his shoulder, yelled, "What the fuck happened!" Kevin collapsed, as if released from paralysis by the touch of a living human. He adopted a crouching position, arms over his head to protect himself from blows that never came. Milo looked from one body to the other. There was very little blood around the stone embedded in Holly's skull. The way she just sat there, dead, with her shades still on gave him the creeps. How could this have happened? Did someone sneak up behind Holly and murder her? No, that was crazy; it must've been an accident, must've been Kevin.

"Did you do this, huh?"

He sounded like an irate dog owner pushing his pet's nose at a wet patch on the carpet. Kevin's spine, a line of vulnerable knobs beneath the flawless skin of his back, appeared to twitch; his whole body was twitching, but he still could not make a sound. His fingers were splayed across the top of his head like a helmet. "Was it an accident? Were you throwing rocks, you stupid dumb fuck!" A moan came from Kevin, barely audible. "She's dead, you know that? You killed her!" Kevin voided his bowels. Milo stepped back to escape the stench. "Jesus, Kevin . . ."

He had to think, had to consider what Holly's death meant. Kevin still could not move. Liquid feces crept from the edge of his swimsuit. Kevin's incontinence shocked Milo almost as much as had the stone in Holly's head. Kevin clearly was in a state of shock, and Milo would have to snap him out of it. "Kevin, get down to the water and wash yourself off. Kevin! Get in the fucking water! You've got shit all over you! Get in there!" Kevin had to be dragged, still crouching, to the water's edge, where he fell on his side and began weeping. Milo removed his own clothing and pulled Kevin into deeper water, stripped the swimsuit from him, and cleaned it. "Wash yourself, fuck you! Wash the shit off you! What are you, a fucking baby!"

He tossed Kevin's swimsuit onto the beach, then assisted him in cleaning himself off. Kevin's hands came suddenly to life and cluched at Milo with desperate strength, and this ability to again function physically allowed Kevin to cry. Milo wrestled with him in the water, trying to get free of him. The awful sobbing was too close to his ear, too close to his heart, and the fingers clamped around his arms were like a strangler's. "Get the fuck off me and quit bawling! Cut it out, Kevin."

Milo hauled him back to shore, brought his clothing from the blanket where Holly sat, helped him dress, then dressed himself. Kevin was hiccuping forlornly between whimperings, still hadn't spoken a coherent word. "Listen, we've got to get the cops and an ambulance. Are you listening? I'll take the car and go around the other side of the lake to the phone booth. You stay here and don't touch anything. No, get rid of that shit on the ground. You don't want anyone knowing you shat yourself, right? Scoop it up and throw it in the water, far out as you can. Do it!" Kevin did it. "Now wash your hands." Kevin did. "Okay, now wait here till I get back."

"No!"

The first word; another barrier down.

"Wait here, Kevin. Someone has to wait . . ."

"No!"

Milo asked himself if he would want to hang around the body of someone he'd killed.

"Okay, come on."

He got the keys from Holly's bag. This was what he'd always been told he needed a driver's license for—an emergency. Milo drove badly. Kevin sat slumped against the door, shivering again. Milo couldn't spare any time for him, had to concentrate on the road. When the eastern shore was reached, he parked and went to the snack bar's pay phone. He dialed 911, said what he had to say, hung up, and returned to the car. Kevin's eyes were shut tight, his throat gulping as if starved of air.

"They're on their way. We have to wait right here. Listen . . . Are you listening to me, Kevin? You can't handle this. I'm gonna tell them it was me. Are you listening? I was throwing rocks around and one of them hit her. You weren't there. You were someplace else, off in the trees, taking a leak. Have you got that? Open your fucking eyes! Have you got that? Where were you while I was tossing rocks around?"

"Trees . . ."

"Doing what?"

"Leak . . ."

"Taking a leak, that's right, and when you got back our mom was dead and you freaked out, okay? You didn't see it happen because you weren't there. It was me. I did it. You get that? Who did it?"

"Me . . ."

Milo slapped him across the face.

"Who did it?"

"I did. . . ."

Another slap.

"Who did it?"

"You!"

"Correct, and don't you forget it. You tell the cops you did it and I'll cut your fucking ears off and cram 'em down your neck. It was me. It was an accident and I'm responsible, because I was tossing rocks around, right? Right, Kevin?"

"Yes . . ."

Milo scented acquiescence. Kevin was too scared to fight him over this. He wasn't quite sure why he was doing it. Kevin wasn't exactly his favorite person or anything; Milo's favorite person was Milo. Maybe it was sudden compensation for all those years of casual bullying. He'd known the petrified kid beside him since he was small enough to fit into a fruit bowl. They'd shared a bedroom and a mother. Proximity alone seemed reason enough, let alone blood, he guessed. Milo's motives remained unclear, even to himself; he knew only that he had to do this. Kevin wasn't ready for the finger-pointing, the social ostracizing—"There goes the kid that killed his mom!" Milo could spare him that, because Milo was already beyond Callisto's reach, just marking time before leaving town. It was no betrayal of Holly, either; she would've understood. Ray was another matter. Ray would hate him, but it was better that Ray hate someone he already disliked—especially if that someone was far away—than someone he thought was little Mr. Wonderful, someone he had to continue living with. It was the right way to handle this, the right way and the only way, but the plan would be implemented mainly because it was Milo's way. Milo was in charge here, and in a crazy kind of way he liked it.

Holly's car was surrounded by sunlight and the commotion of radios and screaming children. The air smelled of hot dogs and ice cream and suntan oil. Girls in dazzling swimsuits paraded slowly past the windows like exotic fish,

Cokes and fries in hand, mouthing shallow nothings. Milo smiled a lopsided smile and said goodbye to it all.

"How old are you, Kevin?"

"Twelve in November."

"That's old enough to know the difference between the truth and a lie, isn't it."

"Yes."

They were in an interrogation room at the station.

"Did you throw the rock that killed your mom?"

"No."

Bernie looked at the boy across the table. Kevin was a bad liar.

"It was Milo, huh?"

"Yes."

"That's what Milo says, but I tell you what, Kevin—I don't believe either of you."

Kevin produced the smallest of shrugs, his eyes skittering around the room. Holly was in the morgue, Milo in the adjoining room, and Ray outside the door, wanting answers. Bernie thought he knew the answers, but they weren't the ones being given by Holly's sons. At first he'd thought Ray had killed Holly because of the affair, but Ray had been behind the desk at the T-bird all day; he'd checked it out. It had been an accident, like Milo said, but Milo said it much too calmly. Kevin was the one who did it, Bernie could tell; his cop's intuition told him so. What he couldn't figure out was why Milo was covering for Kevin. The role of protective big brother just didn't seem right. Holly had told him quite a bit about her family in their conversations between fucking.

"Call it a hunch, Kevin, but I know it was you."

"Well, it wasn't."

No outrage over wrongful accusation here. The whole thing stank.

"Why does Milo want to take the blame? It wasn't a

186

criminal offense, just an accident. No one's going to be charged with anything."

"I didn't do it."

"Sure you did."

"I want to see a lawyer."

"That's what they say on the tube, right? You don't need one, Kevin. You're only eleven. An accident is an accident. We just need to get the facts straight for the record, not to punish anyone."

Kevin kept his eyes on his lap.

"I want to see my dad."

"In a minute. The swim shorts on the beach, they were yours?"

"Yes."

"You changed into your clothes before you went for help."

"I guess."

"You don't remember if you changed into your clothes first?"

"Right, I changed."

"Then went for help."

"Yes."

"Why?"

"Huh?"

"Why'd you waste time changing into your clothes before going to get help?"

"I dunno . . . Milo said to."

"He did, huh? Did he give any reason for wasting time that way?"

"No."

"No reason at all?"

"He said to be respectable."

"Respectable?"

"And decent."

"Respectable and decent."

"Yes."

"If Milo saw something respectable and decent, he'd take a dump on it, we both know that, Kevin. Why bother getting dressed to go to the other side of the lake where there's a couple hundred people lying around in swimsuits and bikinis? Does that make sense to you? Doesn't make a whole lot of sense to me. You want to take five and think about it, maybe change your story?"

"I want my dad."

"You think he's gonna be mad at you for what you did?"

"I didn't do it."

"Oh, that's right, I forgot. Milo did it."

"I want my dad."

"Okay."

He let Kevin out, caught a glimpse of Ray pacing around outside. He switched rooms by way of a soundproof connecting door; he wasn't ready to face Ray yet. Milo sat at an identical table, staring at its blank surface. Bernie pulled up a chair.

"Well, your little brother cracked, Milo."

"Pardon me?"

"Told the whole story, how he did it, how you covered up for him."

"I'm not covering up for anyone."

"I'd like to know why, I really would. Brotherly love?"

"Kevin didn't say anything. You're bluffing."

Bernie allowed himself a small sigh. There were definitely too many cop shows on the tube.

"Why'd you tell him to get dressed?"

"Who?"

"Kevin. Why make him get dressed before you got in the car?"

"I don't know. I wasn't thinking straight because I just killed my mother, okay? And that's all I'm saying."

"You want a lawyer, I bet."

"I don't need one. It was an accident."

"Then I guess you'll want to see your dad."

"No."

"No?"

"He'll kill me."

"He wouldn't kill Kevin, though."

"That's right. Too bad Kevin didn't do it."

"How come you're so cool, Milo? You killed your own mother today. That's a terrible thing, but you're just as cool as cool. How do you explain that?"

"I'm holding it all back. I'll crack up later."

"That's very psychological, very plausible, even kind of witty. It's also bullshit. A very fine lady died today, and you can just sit there and lie about it?"

"I'm sorry it happened."

"Are you? I'm glad you told me, otherwise I wouldn't have known. You look shook up some, but not sorry. Let me give you a piece of advice, Milo; when they hold the inquest try to squeeze out a few tears, because if you don't they'll think you're a heartless little prick that couldn't give a shit if his mother's dead."

"I'll bear it in mind. Thanks."

Bernie wanted to slap him silly. It was partly because Milo wouldn't cave in and partly because Holly, who Bernie had really liked for a little while there, was dead. He knew Milo hadn't done it, but wanted to hurt him anyway. Someone ought to pay for the loss, and a snide little fuck like Milo deserved to be the one.

"Get out of here."

Milo left the room. Bernie was furious at Holly's ludicrous death, at Milo's intransigence, and at himself for his personal involvement. He wasn't treating this thing like a good cop should, but the chief had told him to handle it because he knew the family and could presumably question the boys with kid gloves. Well, he'd blown it, and had better get his ass outside to do what he could when the family met; there might be fireworks, as Milo predicted.

Ray was with the boys at the waiting room's far end. As Bernie approached, he saw they weren't talking, just standing, their eyes everywhere but on each other.

"Ray, I'm sorry." It was all Bernie could say, but he truly meant it. Ray simply stared at him for a moment. Bernie guessed he was still shattered by the news. "Has Milo told you what happened?"

"A cop told me."

The flatness of Ray's voice should have warned Bernie, but his alertness was cramped by week-old guilt.

"What do you make of it?"

He wanted to know if Ray also thought Milo's story was crap, wanted to hear him say so right here in front of both boys. With Ray's help he might be able to get the truth out of them.

"I want to know how much you paid him," said Ray.

"What?"

"How much did you pay him to do it?"

Ray's voice was quiet, overenunciated, as if he were talking to a backward child. Bernie resented the tone as much as the ridiculous insinuation.

"Hey, come on now, Ray. . . ."

"Just tell me the amount in dollars."

Milo was looking at his stepfather as if Ray was chanting the phone book above the clatter of police typewriters; Kevin, too.

"Look, this has been a shock to you, Ray, I know. . . ."

"You thought you could wipe her out of my life, both of you. You really thought you could do it."

Milo's mouth was open. Bernie had never seen his face so naked, his expression so uncool. He couldn't blame him; Ray had flipped out completely. This was total lunacy.

"I don't expect anyone to believe me. I know better than that. I just want to hear it from your lips, the two of you. It won't go any further than this. I just have to know."

"Ray, you're talking nonsense. It was an accident. Your own boys were there. If you can't believe them . . ."

Ray jerked his head at Milo. "That one's not mine. I wouldn't believe a word he said to me."

190

"Jesus Christ," said Milo. "This is fucking crazy. I'm outa here, okay?"

He didn't wait for Bernie's permission, turned and began walking away. That was when Ray pulled the gun from beneath his jacket and shot at Milo's back. Milo spun and fell. Ray turned the gun on Bernie and fired again, but Bernie chopped at his wrist in time and the bullet entered the floor. Another chop and the gun clattered at their feet. The station was filled with shouting and stampeding footsteps. Milo could feel the floor shake beneath him as Ray and Bernie struggled somewhere behind his head and cops went flying past to join in. He wondered if death was coming, didn't really care if it was. Then he passed out.

14

DISCHARGED from the hospital, Milo couldn't return home in safety. He moved in with Sharon for two days, then her mother told him to leave. He found a friend with a comfortable sofa. Sharon told her mother she would never forgive her; didn't she know who it was she'd given marching orders to? "A boy who killed his mother, that's who, and I don't want you seeing him any more." Mrs. Kincheloe clearly was not impressed by what Sharon saw as Milo's star quality. Fame, whatever its cause, was the only commodity worth pursuing, in Sharon's opinion, and Milo had it in spades. He was a somebody, in Callisto anyway, and the new pink scar tissue below his ribs was stigmata of the highest order. "He almost lost a kidney, Mother." "He deserved to lose more than that. You tell him it's over, and if I find out it's not, I'll take the Corvette away and you can damn well walk." Fearful of losing her car, Sharon met Milo only during the daylight hours, when her absence from home was justified. His wound was still tender, so she fucked him very gently.

A backed-up court log delayed the inquest for several weeks. Late in June it became official; Holly Kootz had met death by misadventure. Ray Kootz, in a separate hearing, was fined two thousand dollars and placed on probation for one year. Milo had refused to press charges against him, and the circumstances were unusual. Bernie didn't tell anyone the second bullet had been intended for him. Ray's Blackhawk was confiscated. He let Milo know he'd canceled all college fees; Milo could go work for a living, as Ray had done at his age. Kevin wasn't saying much about anything to anyone.

Milo had no cash, and without college at summer's end, no future. He'd already left the Thunderbird, so he may as well go ahead and leave Callisto, too. Everything there was finished for him; he'd start over someplace else. Sharon insisted on coming along.

"What about college?"

"Screw college."

"Got any money?"

"I can get some."

"Okay. Tonight we go."

They partied late with their handful of friends, crammed a few bags into the Corvette's minuscule trunk, and drove down Main to the state highway, followed this to Interstate 70, and headed west. Sharon had over a thousand dollars, stolen from her mother. Howling across the plains in the small hours before dawn, Milo realized he'd forgotten to say goodbye to Kevin. Maybe it was just as well; this way Kevin would hold a grudge, and never let Milo off the hook by telling the truth about Holly's death. The lower his opinion of Milo, the better off he'd be. It was pretzel logic, but it worked. He settled back in his bucket seat and let Sharon speed him to the cocaine canyons of L.A.

Recovery was slow. Still unreconciled to Holly's betrayal, Ray had to cope with her death, and on top of that came the galling fact that it had been Milo who killed her. He accepted that Bernie had nothing to do with it, but hated him anyway for having stolen Holly away while she lived. Wife, best friend, stepson—all had failed him. Only Kevin was left. Ray was a lonely man. He ran the place on his own, learned to catnap in his clothes till 2 A.M. He lost twenty pounds, and the sheet girls agreed he looked like a zombie. Ray could have coped better had Kevin given him love, but the boy kept his distance. Ray put his silence down to postponed shock over his mother's death, and abandonment by his half-brother. Ray was glad Milo had done that, left town without saying goodbye; it showed Kevin the true nature of the individual he'd worshiped—selfish, thoughtless, generally inferior. Ray was glad he'd never gotten around to organizing adoption papers; this way the cuckoo was out of the nest for keeps. Once Kevin accepted that Holly was dead and Milo a shit, he'd snap out of his mood and appreciate what a good dad Ray was, and they would talk. It would take a long time, but Ray was in no hurry. True parenthood, unstinting and complete, lay at the end of whatever solitary highways he and Kevin were traveling. Somewhere up ahead lay a crossroads of understanding between father and son.

The revenge Margaret had planned bore wonderful fruit. Everyone knew Ray Kootz was a struggling man, and his whore of a wife had received the ultimate punishment. It was difficult to see Milo Ginty, with his golden grin and porcupine hair, as God's agent, but that must have been how God wanted it, because that's how it happened. Margaret was well satisfied. She told her dear dead Darryl all about it, and he approved. Now she just had to effect a reconciliation between Susan and her ex-husband and return her to Callisto and the church. That was the final goal of her machinations. That was why God had directed her to shadow Holly Kootz to her bed of shame. It was a pity that Bernie Swenson appeared to have come out of the whole affair without blame, but Margaret was sure some kind of ax was poised above his head, to fall at a later date. All sinners were punished, without exception. She sometimes drove by the Thunderbird just to look at the place, amazed that it hadn't fallen into ruin yet. How could so unchristian an enterprise have flourished in the first place? First Ray's father with the floozy, then Ray's own wife, the

194

shoe on the other foot this time, a scarlet shoe that never walked a righteous path. Margaret hoped one day to see the Thunderbird consumed in a pillar of fire.

Living with his father wasn't easy. Milo's name could not be mentioned, nor Holly's. It was as if Ray and Kevin had sprung into existence just last summer, without any kind of family history. Before this present time—nothing. And Ray annoyed him by getting too close, wanting to know if his homework was done, his room tidied, wanting to know where he was every hour spent away from home, practically a prison warden.

He learned to hate dishes. Ray taught him to hate them with the dishwashing ritual. "Bachelors like us have to learn to take care of ourselves, Kevin. It's not unmacho to wash dishes. Any man that prefers to be surrounded by filth instead of washing a few dishes isn't a real man, he's just a lazy slob. We have to be a team. That way we can be like civilized human beings and not like animals. Personal hygiene, that's important, making sure our clothes are clean. Making sure we eat right—that's important, too. We don't eat right, we get sick; we get sick, we die. It's just that simple. I don't mean to lecture, just inform you of certain facts. It's my turn to dry."

Worst of all was Milo's betrayal. He'd covered up for Kevin like a hero, then deserted him. How was Kevin supposed to feel about someone like that? It was just like when he was little and Milo pushed him around, only now Milo was pushing his head around. So far he hadn't told anyone the truth about the day at the lake that had changed his life. Where was the advantage in telling? Milo was already gone, a scapegoat that fled before it could be pelted with stones. Every night spent in the same tepee with his father strengthened the lie, and in its strength lay Kevin's weakness. Every day he did not reveal the truth, his life lost meaning. Reality, as he had always understood it, rested on truth, on that which is incontrovertibly, uncontestably true.

The lie—not even his own, but Milo's—grew bigger with Kevin's silence. He had only to announce, "That's not how it happened!" and the lie would die, but to kill the lie Kevin would have to admit he killed his mother. People would ask why he hadn't told the truth sooner, would despise him for letting Milo shoulder the blame, for causing Milo's wound, for causing Ray's two thousand dollar fine and probation, for not telling the truth. It was too much to ask. He accepted the lie into his life, and his life became unreal. The lie was a hole, and Kevin fell in.

Fortitude and personal hygiene were not enough. Ray began to drink. He wasn't particular what he drank, as long as it wasn't Jim Beam. As a boy, exiled from the Thunderbird and Judith's graces, he'd chugged beer; now it was spirits, real booze. He didn't get falling-down drunk, just nipped at the bottle all day, blurring the edges of his pain. He did it not to forget, but to ease the misery of remembrance. His face was freshly shaved each day, his hair combed, shirt laundered. Ray Kootz could face the world and anything it cared to throw at him, he'd proved that, but he needed a little help, a jigger at a time. He kept it a secret from Kevin, afraid the boy might think him weak. The big tepee was even bigger now, with just the two of them. There were plenty of places to hide liquor, but he kept his supply in the master bedroom, just to be sure. Kevin never went in there. Ray knew he shouldn't drink like this, but it was necessary, and only temporary. When he was fully recovered from the events of last summer he would quit; he promised himself that. Meanwhile he drank, and ate a great many peppermints, the drinker's furtive candy.

Ray's tippling remained moderate for eight months, then something happened to increase his intake, an incident involving Kevin. Ray was taken by surprise; he'd only wanted to give his son a little advice about keeping up with his homework instead of watching TV, something he'd done plenty of times before without getting this kind of response. Kevin turned and screamed at him, "Get away from me! Just leave me alone, willya!" He'd never raised his voice like that before, and Ray didn't know what to do. He guessed he should punish Kevin somehow, but couldn't think what form the punishment might take. His reaction was dulled by drink. His anger at being talked to that way by a twelve-year-old, slow in coming on the heels of the shock, already was being overrun by embarrassment, a kind of cringing acknowledgment that maybe he deserved to be yelled at for making himself a pain in the ass, lecturing the kid like that. Kevin had turned away, dismissed him. The time to respond with punishment, verbal or physical, was already irretrievable seconds behind him. He waited to see if Kevin would yell at him again; if he did, Ray was all set to smack him upside the head, had his right palm flattened and ready, but Kevin said nothing, sat hunched in his armchair (the one Holly used to occupy), frowning intently at *Magnum, p.i.*

Ray could only stare at Kevin's profile, trying to recognize in that nose and chin, rigid with avoidance, the baby boy he'd loved. This was the kid who had proudly invited inspection of his poop in the bowl, his sense of ownership so strong he would allow no one else to flush away his creations. Ray and Holly had laughed about that; Ray had even told Bernie, and Bernie laughed too. Once Kevin was big enough to sit on the toilet, Ray trained him to wipe his ass before he got off, while his cheeks were still spread; prior to this instruction he would get off first, then vainly swab at his fat little backside clamped like two buns around a turdburger. "You've got to get the paper right up there, Kevin, and get all that poop out." Anxious to please, Kevin had next day run naked to the front desk, bent over, pointed his anus at Ray, and asked, "Am I clean?" with an earnestness that set the guests signing in at that moment howling.

That was Kevin then, and this was Kevin now; moody,

sullen, intolerant of his own father's presence. It was unbelievable. Ray had read somewhere that the cells of the human body replenish themselves every seven years. Maybe in the process some part of the individual failed to reproduce itself fully and became lost forever. What else could explain the gulf separating the baby that used to be from the boy before him now? Sometimes Ray wished he'd completed his education. He was stumbling among the ruins of his world, without a clue to whatever was wrong. He'd thought he was pretty sharp as a kid but now felt old and clumsy. It was Kevin who made him feel this way, and it hurt. What had Ray done to deserve it? The boy must be missing his mother, and his feelings could only be expressed in negative displays of temper. Ray couldn't blame him, hoped that time, already counted on to heal Ray's own wounds, would serve Kevin the same way. If it didn't, there'd be some kind of hell to pay, and the thought of that made Ray drink more. He was on a carousel, the sole rider, colored lights dimming, music slowly grinding down to a growl as Ray and his bottle leaned toward outer darkness together.

Bernie came to visit. He came late, so he'd have Ray's attention.

"You look like shit," he said.

"You smell like it," was Ray's retort.

"How long do you plan on keeping this up?"

"What up?"

"The drinking. The chip on the shoulder."

"My drinking is my business. That sounds like a motto or something. Drinking Is My Business."

"You won't believe this, but I worry about you."

"I believe you. I worry about myself."

"So why not quit? Then we can both stop worrying."

"Why don't you go fuck yourself?"

"Look, Ray, what happened, happened. Between Holly and me. It was nothing serious. You know what? I don't think she even liked me, how about that. I'm being honest here."

"Hated the man, loved his prick."

"Listen, mostly we just talked."

"About me, I bet. 'Boy, are we ever fucking Ray over.' "

"You're so far off track you're lost. You want to know something? Pam screwed around on me when we were married. It's true. I never told you this. You know the reason she gave? I never talked to her. Yeah. Look, it's all in the past for both of us. You want to start thinking about Kevin. He grows up with a drunk for an old man, it'll fuck him up. You want to quit before that happens, Ray. How about it?"

"How about you keep your advice to yourself?"

"Every week at the station I see kids in trouble—basket cases, some of them. I'd hate to one day see Kevin down there. If you don't give a shit about yourself, give a shit about your kid."

"Don't tell me about my kid. Have you got a kid? What the hell do you think you can tell me about my kid! Where the fuck are you coming from!"

"Okay, Ray, you don't want to listen, I can't make you, but when it all starts coming down, don't ask yourself why, because I already told you."

"So you told me, so get lost. Thank you and goodbye."

When Bernie had gone, Ray thought seriously for several minutes about giving up alcohol, then decided he wouldn't be able to stomach the look of satisfaction on Bernie's face if he did. Fuck Bernie. Ray would drink himself to death before he let that happen, and as for Kevin, the little shit didn't deserve looking after, sometimes.

Holly had been dead a year. Ray couldn't face that awful date without an excess of drink. He began on Tuesday and kept it up till Saturday, and his blurred sorrow gave rise to introspection, not about his life as a man but about his role in the community; specifically, he thought about the clientele that frequented the Thunderbird on this particular night of the week. At least two-thirds of his guests were fucking someone they weren't married to. Ray signed them in as he had always done, asking no questions, accepting their cash, avoiding their eyes.

Saturday night was the motel's most profitable, and always had been. The men got the rooms while the women waited outside in their cars. Sometimes it was two boys wanting one room with two double beds. Ray wondered about four people having sex in one room: was it done purely for economy, or did they like to watch each other? His own experience was limited. He'd missed out on the sexual revolution; it hadn't hit Callisto till Ray was safely married. Maybe he should've waited. He wasn't so old he couldn't still take part; some of the men hustling women inside the tepees were older than him. He just plain didn't want to. He wanted Holly back. But Holly had been a swinger too, like the others out there. What kind of men were they? What kind of women? Suddenly, he despised them all.

After midnight, when trade had slackened, Ray began to brood. He was pandering to all kinds of evil out there, sexual potpourris that made a mockery of love; shallow couplings, frenzied mountings, adulterous liaisons of the kind he knew too well. And he condoned it by taking money from the cheaters, the one-night-standers, the duplicitous spouses and their partners. The cash right there before him in the till was tainted with the rancid perfume of extramarital intercourse. It stank! He was surrounded by the faithless, by betrayers of love's promise. The T-bird was a circle of concupiscence. Ray's ears, newly opened, seemed to hear a hogwallow grunting that filled the air around the neon phallus of the totem pole. It shouldn't be that way. Lowell had built the place to shelter travelers weary from the road, decent people desirous only of a place to rest themselves before traveling on, and what was his son doing? Ray was running a Saturday night fuck-house! Judith would have scented the odor of carnality as it came through the door, would have told her would-be guests to go home to their husbands and wives, would have refused entry to the legion of fornicators attempting to populate the place. Did Ray do that? He did not, and it ate at him like acid.

By 1:30 he was talking to himself. Kevin was not at home. Ray had no idea what his son did with his leisure hours, no longer bothered to ask. "It's a whorehouse," he muttered. "It's a fuckin' whorehouse. Fuck fuck fuck. Whorehouse." The words fell like stones from a mouth stiffened with alcohol. Ray heard neither the slurring nor the repetition. His role as ringmaster in the sexual circus around him preyed on his mind in a nagging monotone. He convinced himself of his worthlessness, and this granted him superiority over the customers; he bet they wouldn't have the guts to admit they were worthless too. Just scum, all of them. Scum scum scum. Ray liked that word. He rolled it from his tongue many times, like a machine stamping out ashtrays of tin. Something had to be done about the filth out there. Ray had to distance himself from the self-indulgence practiced in his tepees, had to make a statement, a stand for what was right. He couldn't go on living with the guilt he felt over his profitable involvement with all that fucking.

Ray stood up. He felt tall, tall and strong. He left his chair, left the office, went outside where the totem blazed, humming its idiot song. Over there was the place he'd first seen Milo. If he hadn't stepped out to take the air that rainy night, he never would've become aware of Holly's existence, never would've married her or taken into his tepee her freakish boy. So much had hinged on that casual act. The totem pole stood like a monument to the encounter and to the disaster that followed. The pole had been sputtering with electricity that night, buzzing with prescience, but Ray hadn't listened. Now the world would listen to Ray.

The first door he pounded on was number 5. "Go home to your husbands and wives and children! Go home now!" He moved on to 6. "Get out of that bed! Go home! Your families are waiting for you!" Then 7. "Why aren't you at home where you belong! Go home! Get dressed and go home!" By the time he reached Tepee 12, in which Holly and Milo had stayed, many of the guests were opening their doors, intrigued by the commotion. They drifted across to Ray and surrounded him, pajama-clad, partially dressed, barefoot or slippered.

"What's the big panic here?"

"He's got a load on, look at him."

"What's all the noise for?"

"Go home!" Ray shouted. "Go home and be good!"

"Say what?"

"You shouldn't be here! You should be at home, all of you! Don't you want to be with the people you love? Don't you?"

"Somebody call the cops."

"Anybody know who he is?"

Every man there had been signed in by Ray, but not one recognized him; motel managers are seldom memorable figures, and guests do not expect to find their cordial host banging on the door, commanding them to leave. Ray was an anonymous drunk.

"Leave him alone. He'll quiet down and go to sleep."

"Yeah, under your car. Somebody call the cops. There's a pay phone in the office."

"You want cops, you call 'em."

"Someone tell the manager to get them."

"I'll go get him."

"Hold it. See? He's gone quiet. Listen, guy, you want the cops to come take you away? You want to quit all the noise, huh?"

"I want you all to go home where you belong and be with the people you belong with! That's what I want!"

"Listen to that. He's a nut. Get the manager."

"I *am* the manager! I *am* the manager! Go home when I tell you!"

"Hey, Mr. Kootz, what's the problem?"

Mickey Booth, high school senior, older brother of a casual friend of Kevin's ("Yeah. You can bring your girl-friend to my old man's place, he won't give a shit. Eighteen bucks a night, but the TVs are crap."), stood before Ray wearing jeans and an unbuttoned shirt. Ray didn't know Mickey was the brother of his son's friend, had signed him in as just another sex-crazed teenager.

"Go home," he said.

"Sure, Mr. Kootz, tomorrow."

"You all have to go home."

"You know this guy? Is he the manager?"

"Yeah. Hey, Mr. Kootz, you want to go back in the office now?"

"No."

"I really think you better do it, you know, or the cops'll come."

"Get 'em anyway. Guys like that always end up hurting themselves."

"He's okay, aren't you, Mr. Kootz."

"You're all scum."

"That's right, but we don't care, do we, gang?"

The crowd was becoming lighthearted, as crowds do when they realize the thing that angered or frightened them is harmless, pathetic.

"Fuck it. Let him alone. It's his place. Let him shout it down if he wants."

"C'mon, Mr. Kootz, let's go back in the office."

Ray flinched when Mickey placed a hand on his arm.

"I don't know you."

"That's okay. Let's go back in the office, Mr. Kootz."

Mickey was a confident boy, proud of his gift for gab. He knew he could talk anyone into doing anything (witness the

203

girl in Tepee 19, until two hours ago a virgin) and saw Ray as a challenge. He practiced his grin, the one he knew was so engaging. "Let's go, Mr. Kootz."

But Ray wouldn't respond, pushed past Mickey and the rest and made his own way across to the office and locked himself in. Mickey readied the story he would tell his girl, and the rest of school come Monday. The other guests drifted back to their tepees, where some of them, rejuvenated by the excitement of seeing Ray make a fool of himself, made love to their partners again.

Ray's attempt at putting a stop to fornication at the Thunderbird had backfired, and further repercussions followed. To hide his embarrassment when the story circulated the corridors at Callisto High, Kevin was obliged to deny all sympathy for his father; this would, he hoped, deflect accusations of geekdom by familial association. He not only welcomed all disparaging comments directed at Ray, he embroidered them. "Yeah, he's some kind of fuckup all right. I practically have to put the poor old fart to bed at night, he's so far out of it. He's gonna need a liver transplant pretty soon. He better not ask for one of mine, no way." At home he refused to talk to Ray at all.

And there was Margaret Corcoran's reaction to the story. Margaret had for some months suffered terrible back pains. Her doctor prescribed pills, but they did no good; even prayer seemed not to work. Then Margaret heard about Ray's efforts at imposing a moral code at his motel. It was disgraceful that he'd attempted such a worthy task while drunk, but at least it represented a turning point in his way of thinking—and about time, too. Margaret thought very hard about this new development; it served to distract her from her crippling pain. She searched for meaning. What did Ray's act signify?

It came to her in a rush of understanding: the incident was dictated by and representative of an overwhelming confluence of circumstances. Ray Kootz was once again ripe for religion. Not only that, he was once again in need of a wife. Susan was living in sin with a chiropractor in Des Moines (who by some convoluted psychic connection was responsible for her mother's back pain), and it was clear the man had no intention of marrying her. It was also clear Susan could not remarry her ex-husband, as Margaret had once hoped she would; that person had recently married again, removing himself from Margaret's plans. But that was also a part of this new situation that had arisen. Everything fitted together perfectly. The clock would simply be turned back. Susan would come home and marry Ray as they'd intended in 1969. Margaret would forgive Ray his terrible transgressions if he would do this. The man had suffered for his mistake in turning down lovely Susan and marrying the whore from Chicago. It was time to make amends, time for everyone to put their lives back on the rails that led to Christian fulfillment. It was a radical re-thinking of the whole sad story, and Margaret was proud of herself for having seen the light.

She would contact Susan on the weekend, when the phone rates were cheaper, but first she had to reveal to Ray what his troubled mind probably could not see unaided—the inevitability of marriage with Susan, his original choice. More than that, Margaret would reveal the full extent of the threads that bound the Kootzes and Corcorans together: she would tell him about her spying on Holly, admit it was she who had set the implacable wheels of retribution in motion. It was only fair that he knew. He would forgive her, because his suffering this past year would have brought him humility and understanding of God's great plan for us all. And he would quit drinking immediately. Revelation of divine truth would make alcohol unnecessary. She would do it tonight, if her back allowed her access to the wheel of her car. It felt a little better already.

When first she came through the door, Ray failed to recognize her, slid a registration card across the desk and loosened the ballpoint in its holder.

"How are you this evening, Raymond?"

She thought he looked awful. Susan would change that, Susan and the Almighty. His mind was obviously so fuddled by drink he could not remember. There was room here for massive moral rearmament.

"Margaret Corcoran, Raymond."

"Oh."

"I want to talk to you."

"Uh, okay."

"It's very important."

"Uh-huh."

"In private."

"Right. You better come on through."

He took her to the living room, pointed to a chair. The reception bell could be heard from here if guests arrived. What the fuck could old Margaret possibly want?

"This is very important, what I'm about to say." Ray nodded, and she continued. "It isn't easy for me, bringing up things from the past this way." A blank stare from Ray. She pressed on. "But I had to come and reveal to you what has been revealed to me."

"Okay."

Margaret revealed it. Ray absorbed the revelation slowly. When it was fully ingested he thought about his gun, his hard-hitting Blackhawk. The police still had it. There was still Judith's .38 in its greased holster under the desk out front. Should he get it and drill a hole in Margaret's head? No. That way she would truly have finished off his family. He held himself back, trying not to tremble. It scared him, the way he hated her for what she'd done.

"Why did you tell me?"

Margaret explained the Lord's plan for reuniting Susan and Ray.

"Have you talked to Susan about it yet?"

"You were nearer, and I had the other thing to tell you about."

They looked at each other across the room. Elvis looked down at them both. Finally Ray spoke. "Did anyone ever tell you you're crazy?"

"I am not crazy. I know some of the things I've had revealed to me are strange and hard for nonbelievers to accept, so I intend to ignore what you just said. I want things to be nice between us again."

"Mrs. Corcoran, things were never nice between us. I always thought right from the start you were a stupid bitch. Now I think you're even stupider. Get out of here, and don't bother calling Susan. She's probably got enough to worry about without you talking bullshit in her ear. Get out right now."

Margaret stood.

"I'm not hearing any of these words. You'll come around, Raymond."

"No I won't. Forget it. You're a stupid, spiteful, crazy person. Can't you see it?"

"I see what God reveals."

Her chin was high, her face serene.

"Hey, lady, fuck God up the ass, know what I mean?"

Margaret blanched. Ray knew he'd got through. The patronizing look she'd worn on her face since she walked in began to crumble. No stopping Ray now.

"God gets jacked off by angels. That's what makes snow fall. When they give him head, it thunders. That's his balls knocking together. Are you leaving yet? When he bends over to take it butt-style, we get sunny weather. Did you know the sun shines out of God's ass, Mrs. Corcoran?"

Margaret did something she would never have believed herself capable of: she spat at him. "Missed," said Ray, smiling, and seeing him smile, Margaret knew there would be no marriage. Her revelation this afternoon had been false, planted in her mind by whatever demon was tormenting her poor back. Her visit to the Thunderbird had been a waste of time. The filth she'd had to listen to made her stomach turn. How could she possibly have believed her Susan could marry this disgusting drunk? Demons were turning her head around, using Ray Kootz to try to shake her faith. It would never happen, not while there was breath inside her, and when there was not, it would be too late; she would be on her way to her Christian reward. She turned and left, and the smile that had driven her out left Ray's lips in an instant. He felt sick with anger and helplessness. Margaret Corcoran, agent of reprisal. If he could've killed her tonight, knowing he could get away with it, he would have. Ray hated her, could not remember hating with such intensity since he'd pulled the gun on Milo. He wished Margaret a lingering and painful death. It was all he could do.

The phone call to Susan was never made. Margaret's pain increased. Her doctor ordered a steel corset to support her back, and when this failed to alleviate the pain she insisted on surgery. But before she could be booked into the hospital, Margaret met with an accident while crossing Seventh Street late in September. An ice cream van, returning to its depot after one last pass through town before being mothballed until May, struck her as she stepped out from between two cars parked along the curb. She hadn't bothered to look before taking that first step onto the street, and her second step was barely completed when the van hit her. Margaret was killed outright by the impact, transported to the arms of King Jesus by a vendor of King Kone.

PART THREE

Buzz-saw Sunsets

15

Down at the Trailways depot a girl got off the bus. She asked where she might find the Thunderbird Motel and was told she could walk there in around ten minutes; no, better make that fifteen in the June heat. She made it in twelve, entered the office, and set her suitcase down by the desk, stood where the fan could cool her skin.

"Hello," she said to Ray.

"Afternoon," he said.

"Are you Mr. Kootz?"

"Yes I am."

"I'm Autumn. That was my mother's favorite season, autumn, so she called me after it. Everyone calls me Autie."

Ray nodded politely. The girl's smile, already brightly nervous, became wider. "Autie Quist," she said. "My mom was Ellie Quist."

Ray thought he knew that name.

"She used to live here," said the girl. "You used to know her."

"Oh . . . yeah, Ellie Quist, that's right."

"I thought I'd drop by and say hello."

Her smile was still wide. She really was very nervous. Ray could see Ellie in her face now that his memory had been nudged. Ellie's daughter, how about that. He hadn't thought of Ellie in years.

"Well come on back and have some coffee, uh . . ."

"Autumn."

"Autumn, right. Nice name."

"Thank you."

He sat her down, made coffee, sat opposite his guest, his mood made amenable by remembrance of a highly selective nature.

"We used to go to school together, Ellie and me. We even dated for a little while, did she tell you?"

"Yes."

"Good old Ellie. She was a nice girl, I mean it. So how is she?"

"She died last month. She had cancer."

"Awww, no . . . but she was only young."

"Thirty-six."

"Jeez . . . gee, I'm sorry. I really liked Ellie. Everyone did. She was a genuinely nice person. God, thirty-six . . . How's the rest of the family taking it, if it's not a personal question?"

"There's only me."

"Now, that's a real tragedy, it really is. No brothers or sisters, no cousins or grandparents or anything?"

"No, just me."

"How about your dad?"

"I don't know. How about him?"

The smile was back. Ray didn't understand until the smile began to fade. He dropped his eyes to her sneakers, pretty blue ones set side by side. He felt himself shake, made himself look up at her face.

"How old are you?"

"Seventeen last March."

Ray did some hasty arithmetic.

"Are you, uh, mine?"

"Yes."

Ray stared at her sneakers again. This wasn't happening.

"I had nowhere else to go."

"Ellie never got married or anything?"

"Yes, but he went away a long while back."

"One of those guys that can't stick it out, huh?"

"No, she made him go. He was doing things to me when I was little, you know, so when she found out she told him to go or she'd call the police, so he went."

"I'm sorry."

"It's okay. I don't remember very much about it."

Both sipped their coffee. Ray couldn't believe it; he had a daughter.

"So, uh, what are your plans?"

"I don't have any. I couldn't stay up in Montana, that's all."

"How long have you known I'm your dad?"

"She told me around Christmas time. She was real sick by then. I had the phone operator check and see if the motel was still here and if your name had the same number as the Thunderbird."

Ray searched her face for the characteristics of himself. They were there. She was his all right. He remembered now; Ellie Quist had sent him letters he wouldn't read, probably telling him she was pregnant. And he'd told her over the phone he didn't love her, practically told her to fuck off. What a little shit he'd been. He felt like crying. "I'm sorry . . ." he said. Screws and knots inside him were loosening. He'd had a couple of drinks already since lunch; that must be what was giving him the shakes. He had to put his cup down or spill it. His body just wouldn't quit shaking. It was embarrassing to be seen like this. "I'm sorry . . ." he said again.

"I didn't mean to upset you or anything."

"It's okay."

But it was not. Ray's head found his hands, and he cried. She'd only walked through the door five minutes ago, and his life was turned upside down. Ellie was in the ground after a short and shitty life, and their daughter had sprung from nowhere into his. It was way too much. Now that she'd seen him cry, it didn't matter if he cried some more, so he did, unable to decide if his guilt over Ellie was causing the tears or his delight at finding himself the father of a girl; a nice girl, he knew that from her face; a smart girl, and sympathetic, too. Eventually he stopped.

"Did you get married?" she asked.

"Yeah, but she died. We had a boy, Kevin. He's fifteen now. Listen, you better live with us. There's a room you can have. I don't know if that's what you'd like, but if you've got nowhere else to go . . ."

"I'd like to. Thank you."

Then she too began to cry. Ray went over and sat beside her, put his arms around his daughter's thin shoulders.

"It's gonna work out," he assured her.

Minutes after she had unpacked, a boy stood in her doorway, his hair a Medusan tangle of dreadlocks.

"Hello," she said.

"Hi."

"Are you Kevin?"

"Yeah. Are you really called Autumn?"

"You can call me Autie."

"He says you're my half-sister."

"That's right. Big surprise, huh?"

Kevin sauntered into the room. He had a black skate-board under one arm, its surface decorated with a skull in electric orange.

"He said your mom's dead from cancer."

"Yes."

"This used to be Milo's room."

"Who's Milo?"

"My half-brother. Didn't he tell you about Milo?"

"No."

"My mom had Milo before she had me. She was married before."

"Everybody's half and half around here."

"Right, half crazy mainly. You gonna stay?"

"Ray invited me."

Ray had suggested she call him by his name. It was too soon, or maybe too late, to be called Dad.

"I've got the top room. It's like a cone. There hasn't been anyone in here since Milo went away."

"Where did he go?"

"Beats me. He doesn't write or anything."

"Why did he leave?"

"Didn't get along with the old man."

"That's too bad."

"Milo was cool."

"Ray says your mom died too."

"Yeah, an accident. You wanna see my room?"

"Okay."

They went up the stairwell. Kevin's cone was painted black.

"I did it myself. He practically flipped when he saw it."

"Who did?"

"Him. Ray. He doesn't like it."

"It's a pretty neat job."

"I used a roller. You like Megadeth?"

He slid a tape into the player by the unmade bed. Autie had never seen a bed located in the middle of a room before. Music made conversation impossible, so she looked around. A plastic skull leered at her from the dresser, its cranium capped with black candle wax. The floor was littered with shirts, sneakers, and underwear, but the scuffed edges of a chalked pentacle could be seen here and there. The lower reaches of the continuous wall were covered with pictures of wizards, old and bearded, and sorceresses, young and nubile. Quasi-humans crouched in dungeons and dark forests, showing their fangs. Autie knew what this stuff meant.

"Are you into black magic?"

Kevin turned the volume down.

"Huh?"

"Are you into black magic?"

"Are you initiated?"

"No. Initiated into what?"

Kevin's face had a different look to it, a caginess, suspicion leavened with condescension. Autie had thought him nice-looking, but now saw an ugliness of expression that seemed to pass through his skin from the inside. It was only there for an instant, then erased, gone so fast she wondered if she'd truly seen it.

"Nothing. I guess I'm pretty lucky. A cone has got psychic energy stored in it. I soak it up when I'm asleep."

"I thought it was pyramids that had that."

"Yeah, but cones too. You can feel it."

"Who's that?"

She pointed to one of the pictures on the wall, a portrait of a huge-headed man, totally bald, the broad expanse of scalp melding with porcine jowls below ears that gave the impression of being pointed; it was an ungracious wadding of flesh, embedded with two madly staring eyes.

"Aleister Crowley. He was into the mysteries. No one understood him. He's been dead a long time."

"He's ugly."

"On the outside, granted, but inside he was a truth seeker, you know? It takes guts to penetrate the veil. That's what he did. Stuff was revealed to him about the mysteries."

"Uh-huh."

A length of computer printout paper was stuck to the wall like a banner, proclaiming APPRENTICES in dot matrix. "Who are they?" Autie knew it wouldn't be the school team.

"Just a bunch of guys I hang out with."

The look was back. Autie turned away. She wanted to like this boy, her new half-brother. A stack of books drew her to the room's opposite curve. *Ancient Wisdom. Arcania. Cabala. The Warlock. A History of the Black Arts. The Dark Order. Occult Practices.* This stuff hadn't come from a supermarket rack like Stephen King. It had all been thoroughly read, she could tell by the arching of the spines.

"Is that Apprentices as in sorcerer's apprentices?"

"Hey, yeah! How'd you know?"

"It was a Mickey Mouse cartoon."

Kevin lifted his lip defensively, raised his voice a little. "Are you gonna go to school here?"

"One more year. When I graduate I'll go to college."

"Did he say he'd put you through college? He said that to Milo, but it never happened."

Autie smiled at him. He was two years younger than her, was probably trying to make an impression. The real boy might reveal himself later, when she was accepted here. She was not yet sure she wanted to belong. The smell of liquor had been strong on Ray's breath, and Kevin's conical temple of juvenile phantasmagoria made her uncomfortable. She didn't know if she was ready to share a home with a drunk and a skateboarding Satanist, but the alternatives held no appeal at all. For now, at least, she had to fit.

In the big tepee that night three people lay sleepless, thinking about one another, juggling expectations.

Autie Quist got a job, nine to five at Jesse Bob Franklin's 7-Eleven. She insisted on bringing home money until school started. Ray was impressed, wished Kevin had the same attitude. Autie was a delight. She kept her room tidy, cleaned up the rest of the place (excluding Kevin's necromantic cone), even dumped Ray's clinking empties without comment. She was pretty near perfect, and he was proud; there was hope for his family yet.

On Autie's third day at the 7-Eleven Bernie Swenson dropped in for a Coke and noticed the new girl behind the counter. Bernie had finally made detective, no longer wore a uniform, drove an unmarked car.

"Hi," he said. "Don't think I've seen you before."

"I just started working here."

"She's from out of town," put in Jesse Bob from over by the frankfurter rotisserie.

"That right? Where from?"

"Billings, Montana."

"I went up there with my dad a long time ago—not to Billings, though. Nice country. What brings you to Callisto?"

"Came down to see her dad," said Jesse Bob, moving closer.

"Local man?" asked Bernie.

"Yes."

"Only Ray Kootz over at the T-bird," declared Jesse Bob.

Ice clinked against Bernie's teeth. He regurgitated a little of his Coke back into his king-size plastic cup.

"That right? What was your name again?"

"She didn't say, Bernie, but it's Autie Quist. How's that for a name. Short for Autumn."

"Jesse Bob, how about you get me a pretzel to go."

"Haven't got any warmed up right now."

"Well, how about you warm me up one."

"Okay."

The microwave was located at the counter's farthest end. Bernie waited, then said, "I didn't know Ray had a daughter."

"Neither did he until last week. My mom died."

"I'm sorry to hear that. What was her name?"

"Ellie Quist. She went to school here."

Bernie barely remembered her, was staggered to learn that Ray had gotten her pregnant. Ray had never bragged about scoring with Ellie Quist, but if Bernie remembered correctly, Ellie hadn't been the kind to brag about. Still, her daughter seemed like a pretty nice kid—attractive, too. Ray was a dark horse, Autie a fine filly.

Jesse Bob returned with a paper sack.

"Here's your pretzel."

"Thanks."

"Bernie here used to be kind of a special buddy with your dad at school."

"Really?"

"Uh-huh. Used to be Ray and Bernie went everywhere together, right, Bernie?"

"Right. So you're here for keeps, Autie?"

"I hope so. Did you know my mom too?"

"Only a little."

Bernie wondered if the new presence at the Thunderbird would change things there for the better, sincerely hoped she would. He finished his Coke and left. Jesse Bob explained that Bernie was a cop. Autie thought he was a pretty nice guy and wondered why Ray hadn't mentioned him at home.

Since her boss was both talkative and informed, she went ahead and asked Jesse Bob about Milo. He told her the story of the stone that killed Holly Kootz, of the shooting that followed, and Milo's departure from Callisto. He'd assumed she already knew this juicy stuff, and it was gratifying to be the one who filled her in on her own family tree.

"Milo was always peculiar, so everyone expected he'd get mixed up in something crazy sooner or later. He was even on TV one time for killing a frog."

"A frog?"

"Made the prime time TV news—papers, too."

"When was that?"

"Oh, around spring eighty-one, I think. You could go through the back numbers at the Gazette office, just down the street."

Autie did so during her lunch break. There he was, the mysterious Milo, looking not too different from any other kid, seventeen like herself. He'd be twenty-one now. She wondered where he was.

After dinner she asked Ray about her discoveries. He corroborated the bare facts but was not inclined to discuss any of it more fully. She went to Kevin and asked for his version of events, especially the incident with the rock. He wouldn't talk, drove her from his room with a multidecibel blast of Judas Priest, and Autie went to bed that night with a bizarre scenario of life among the Kootzes swirling in her head, its various loose threads flailing, beckoning, inviting further investigation.

In her second week at Jesse Bob's three boys came in and sat on counter stools, then proceeded to stare coldly at Autie.

"Can I help you?" she asked, but they needed no help in scrutinizing her. It was not a sexual staring; their eyes never left her face. One boy wore a black headband, another had a feathered earring dangling almost to his shoulder, and the third wore a T-shirt with THRILL KILL across the chest. They looked about Kevin's age, beardless urban bandits intensely concerned with their effect on her. All wore dreadlocks, even the wispy blond whose hair was much too limp to support his modest clumpings.

"Coke or Pepsi?" she asked. "Sprite or Seven-Up?" No response. "Twinkies? Marshmallow pie? How about a hot dog?" Their eyes became positively squinted as they subjected her to maximum overstare. Autie found their fright tactics funny. Jesse Bob was arranging things out back, so she could play a game with them, as they were playing with her. She knew what name the dark one would have stenciled on the back of his sleeveless denim jacket, with maybe a sword or pentacle. "Can I interest you in a chicken wing? This one was killed upside down over a virgin. Were you guys there?" Their eyes lost concentration, blinked, sought reassurance from one another and could not be regrouped for further intimidation. The one with the earring stood, signaling retreat; together they made for the door, and there it was, emblazoned between narrow shoulder blades—APPRENTICES. "I'll be sure and tell Kevin you came around!" she called after them, but they remained mute all the way past the long front window and out of her sight.

Autie felt she'd won something. Sometimes she felt older

than her years, at least twenty; she supposed it was because she'd seen a good person die slowly and painfully and bravely. You couldn't live through something like that and stay seventeen. Kevin and his friends were interesting but unimportant, fledged with darkly provocative plumage that had yet to carry them far from the nest. She doubted the Apprentices would try to faze her again. Had Kevin told them to do it, or had they simply trooped in to check her out in their own fashion, this half-sister of their blood brother? She wouldn't ask, because it didn't matter.

Bernie and the Apprentices, linked in Autie's mind because all had sat before her at the 7-Eleven, were brought together in fact by a discovery at the Gatlin Road cemetery, the site of Milo's innocent stargazing so long ago. A black cat was found with its throat cut, draped across the headstone of Henry Lovell, Callisto's mayor for many years until his death in 1983. Had the cat been found gracing the headstone of a lesser person, the outcry might not have been so loud. The *Gazette* editorialized at length on the creeping anathema of devil worship among the young, declared it especially insidious when coupled with drugs— the unlucky puss had half a joint in its mouth. Bernie thought Kevin might know something about it, and called around for a chat.

"What do you want?" demanded Ray. Bernie hadn't been inside the Thunderbird's office in two years.

"Like to talk with Kevin. Police business."

"I'll get him. What's he supposed to have done?"

"I don't know if he's done anything yet."

"Come on through."

Kevin, at home for once, was brought down to the living room.

"Hi, Kevin."

"Hi."

"Cut yourself?"

Kevin looked at the bandage around his hand as if realizing for the first time it was there.

"Yeah."

"How?"

"Shaving."

"What are you, a werewolf?"

"I fell over and cut myself. I only said shaving for a joke."

"Killing a cat is no joke."

"What cat?"

"Gatlin Road. A little bit of hoodoo-voodoo in the graveyard. Know anything about it?"

"No."

"How about your pals?"

"What pals?"

"Are you a lonely guy, Kevin? That's a shame. I thought you had a bunch of pals call themselves the Apprentices."

"Oh, yeah; they had nothing to do with it. They don't do stuff like that."

"What kind of stuff do they do?"

"No kind. They don't do anything."

"Mind if I take a look at your hand?"

"You don't have to, Kevin," said Ray. He was worried, hadn't noticed the bandage himself until now.

"No, he doesn't, but if I'm satisfied it's not a cat scratch I'll get off his back pronto."

Kevin looked from his father to Bernie, then began slowly to unwind the bandage. He did it carefully, deliberately, wincing a little as he removed the last of it. Ray held his breath; what if there really were claw marks? Kevin extended his hand for inspection. Its skin had not the slightest graze. Bernie examined it closely to be sure.

"That's a good joke. You're a very funny boy, Kevin."

"Thanks."

He tossed the wadded bandage back and forth, smirking. Bernie figured Kevin had seen him arrive from the upstairs window and had run to the bathroom for a length of bandage to pull this cute trick, the little fuck. He'd been

222

at Gatlin Road all right, but if Bernie visited the other Apprentices, he wouldn't be able to beat three quick phone calls from Kevin; they'd all greet him with bandages and laugh about it afterward.

"Ray, I'd like a word."

They went out to Bernie's car.

"He'll get caught, not today, but sometime."

"Doing what? He hasn't done anything except play a joke."

"Him and that bunch of freaky friends are trouble, for you, for me, for themselves most of all. Get him off this devil shit before it's too late, Ray."

"It's harmless, just a bunch of pictures and books. He doesn't do anything wrong. Have you got any proof he does anything wrong?"

"I know it."

"You know it."

"Right."

"What's that, your cop's nose for crime?"

"Something like that. You better rein that boy in. Last month it was a dog, some kid's pet, opened up like a can of beans down along the riverbank with circle of candles around it. Black dog, black candles. The stupid little shits even left the candles burning. They'll go too far pretty soon. I know it's them."

"You don't know anything. You want it to be Kevin because you've got a grudge against my family."

"This family doesn't need grudges from outside, know what I mean? If I had a grudge I'd have Kevin down at the station right now sweating blood till he 'fessed up. He's in it up to his neck, but I'll hold off till I get proof. That gives you a chance to straighten him out. I'm telling you this because there's someone here now who doesn't deserve to get sucked into any of the bad news that happens around this place. You want to see that new daughter who's a nice kid go the same route as your boys, huh? Clean the shit out of Kevin's head fast, before he passes it on to her. When he takes a fall he'll try and drag whoever he can along with him, because he's not strong enough to fall alone. You think about it."

Bernie drove off. Ray went and had a little drink. Kevin was okay, kind of loopy maybe, but basically okay. Autie seemed to like him, and Ray trusted her judgment. Bernie was just pissed because the dickheads chopping up animals were making the police look dumb, which police were. None of it had anything to do with Kevin. Kevin's greatest offense had been to paint his room black. Ray had come very close to telling him to paint it white again, but decided not to in the end, had gone and had a drink instead. Kevin would get sick of the black room by and by and repaint it without being told; kids were like that. Bernie didn't know shit about Kevin, because Kevin wasn't his kid. Fathers know their sons.

Bernie called in for a Coke at least three times a week. He liked Autie. Ray Kootz didn't deserve someone as un-spoiled as this girl for a daughter. Ray wasn't evil, he just wasn't one of life's achievers, yet having Autie under his sloping roof was a big achievement. Bernie despised people who got something for nothing, hated lottery winners and inheritors of wealth. He sometimes wondered if he shouldn't try marriage again, if only so he could one day be proud of a girl like Autie, someone belonging to him. It wasn't fair that Autie was Ray's. He doubted she'd stay at the Thunderbird for long, not with those two bozos.

Sometimes, as he sipped his Coke and made small talk with Autie, he thought about what it would be like to go home to a girl like her, but it disturbed him the way his picture of opening the front door to be greeted with the cry "Daddy!" was hastily reshot while he sipped, became instead a door opened by a wife—Autie again. It was a very dumb daydream. He was more than twice her age. He didn't allow himself to indulge in sexual fantasies, just imagined talking with her over the breakfast table, maybe

224

watching a little TV together. It was weird. Autie Quist was messing with his head. He should definitely get himself a wife before he said or did something that got him in big trouble.

She was the light of his life, no doubt about it. A long while ago it had been Kevin, but now it was Autie. In less than a month she'd eclipsed the residual glimmerings Ray saw in his boy. He still loved Kevin, but only out of habit, obligation, out of instinct maybe, whatever jungle feelings bound blood to blood. But Autie he loved because she deserved it. She was just the most terrific girl, a shot in the arm, a pick-me-up, the first drink of every day, the one that made everything that followed go smooth and easy. He loved it when she walked in the door after a day at the 7-Eleven. Even his enjoyment of simple things like eating improved, because Autie knew a little about cooking; no more TV dinners. She was nice to Kevin, too, even if the little snot didn't deserve it, and the sound of conversation could be heard in the big tepee for the first time in years.

It was a tiny miracle. Ray was grateful, and to show it he intended doing something to show he cared; Ray was going to quit drinking. Autie would appreciate that. She never mentioned the booze, never shook her head or lectured with her eyes, but Ray knew she didn't approve, which proved how smart she was, because no one with brains approved of booze. That's how Ray knew he was still a smart person himself; he didn't approve of it either, and now was the time to quit, not that he was an alcoholic or anything, but everyone knew drinking was bad for your health, so that's why he'd do it, for his health, and for Autie. Beginning next week he'd cut his intake by half; no, better make that a third seeing as cold turkey remedies were tough, not that reduction by half was exactly cold turkey, but a third would be easier, so why not do it that way, and a couple weeks later he'd reduce it by another third, and a couple weeks after that he wouldn't be drinking at all. It was the least he could do for Autie and for himself. Beginning next week. Ray knew he could do it. A little common sense, a little discipline, an approving look from Autie and he could do it, no sweat. He even looked forward to starting, wanted next week to roll around faster.

Things were going to change at the T-bird, change for the better. Ray was filled with a sense of purpose that had been gone a long time now. He would turn his life around.

But that was before Milo came home.

16

A T FIRST Ray thought he was pushing religious pam-
phlets, wearing that cheap black suit, that black tie
and white shirt, hair pasted back across his head and those
black-framed spectacles; a gung-ho Christian straight out
of Bible college. Then he saw who it was, and the "No thank
you" readying itself in his throat froze there, blocking air
from his lungs.

"Hi, Ray."

No mistaking those teeth.

"What are you doing here?"

"Passing by."

"Well, you can just keep on passing."

Ray wished the quaver in his voice would quit.

"I wondered how you and Kevin were doing."

"We're doing fine."

"Place looks the same."

"Everything's the same."

"How about you? You sick, Ray?"

"No . . . yeah, since about ten seconds ago."

He couldn't get used to Milo in glasses. And a suit. It was
too respectable.

"How about if I came in for coffee. Just for a minute."

Denying Milo entry would look like Ray was afraid of
him, wouldn't it?

"Okay. One cup."

They sat in the living room. Ray regretted having let him in, and so didn't bother with coffee. He was shaking.

"Still got old Elvis on the wall," observed Milo. Ray didn't answer. "In memory of Mom, right?"

"That's right. What have you been doing with yourself?"

"Traveling around."

"Doing what?"

"A little of this, a little of that."

"What kind of this and that?"

"Delivering cars, mainly."

"Say again?"

"Suppose a guy wants his car taken somewhere, like if he's moving from New York to L.A., but he's driving a rental truck with all his furniture and stuff inside and doesn't want to complicate things by hitching his car on behind. What's he do? He goes and hires someone like me to drive the car for him. Or maybe he's too busy to drive, so he takes a plane and lets me spend a few days behind the wheel instead."

"You can make a living doing that?"

"Sure."

"So you're delivering a car to Callisto, or what?"

"Kind of. You want me to make the coffee?"

"And you thought you'd drop by and see how things are. Forget the coffee. We're fresh out."

"That's too bad. Is Kevin around?"

"He's out someplace. I'll tell him you came by."

"That's okay, I can wait."

"No need, I'll give him the message."

"When I deliver a car I take it right to the guy and put the keys in his hand. Same thing with a message. I'll wait. You want me to wait out on the curb, I'll do it."

"He could be anywhere, be home real late."

"Fine by me. How is he?"

"He's okay—doing pretty good, in fact."

"That's good. Anyone else living here besides the two of you?"

"If you're thinking of moving back in, forget it."

"I was just wondering if you got married again."

"No."

"So it's just you and Kevin."

"We get along fine. I don't think I want you to wait."

"You want me to go."

"Correct."

"I'll see him anyway, sometime."

"But not here, not now."

"Okay. You don't look well, Ray."

"I'm fine. I've got work to do."

"Right. Can't keep the customers waiting. They could roll up anytime."

Ray escorted him to the front desk.

"Well, I'll see you around."

"We don't need you."

"Never said you did."

He left. Ray watched through the window to see what kind of car he drove, so he could recognize it if Milo started hanging around. It was a bright-red Firebird, brand new, sleek and shiny. Ray's heart was galloping nowhere in his chest. Why had Milo come back? He'd fucked up Ray's day completely. Ray needed a drink. He got it.

When Autie arrived at 5:30, Ray was very drunk. He hid it as best he could, but she wasn't fooled, and it wasn't just a question of drunkenness; there was something about Ray she'd never seen before, like he was afraid, and trying to hold it back.

"Did anything happen today, Ray?"

"No."

"Are you okay?"

"I'm okay."

"It's just you look so upset. Are you sure nothing happened?"

"Nothing happened! Okay?"

He'd never raised his voice at her before. He sheepishly busied himself restacking the registration cards. Autie went through and started dinner, her face flushed. She'd heard that drunks had drinking cycles that veered from casual day-to-day tippling to all-out liquor marathons that could end in violence. Maybe she should go to the movies tonight and come home late, or not at all; her bedroom door had no lock. Autie told herself she was panicking. Even if he did get stinking drunk, he wouldn't hurt her; she was his daughter, his natural daughter, and he was her true father, not like the awful creep who'd married her mother. Maybe the cycle had come around without requiring anything to trigger it, was just a biological thing. She didn't know enough, would have to visit the library and read up on alcoholism. Her father needed help. It wouldn't come from Kevin, who hadn't been home in two days.

Ray wouldn't eat, or talk. Autie washed up. Ray drank openly now, right there in the kitchen with a bottle in front of him. He hadn't done that before. When the reception bell rang, he levered himself up from the table and went to attend the incoming guests. Autie just bet they could smell the whisky on his breath. Tonight was going to be bad for business. She tried watching TV, but Ray said he wanted peace and quiet, so Autie went to bed. She hated to leave him on his own, but if anything bad happened she'd be able to hear it from upstairs if she left her door open.

That was her plan, but when she entered her room Autie closed the door behind her, then jammed a chair under the handle. She did it without thinking; only when the chair was in place could she step back and consider its implications. One part of her wanted to remove the chair and open the door, but another part did not. The chair remained, but the room, lacking an air conditioner, quickly became stifling. Autie opened her window. A sluggish breeze stirred the curtains but could not penetrate the cloth, so Autie turned out the light and pulled the curtains back, stood bathed for a moment in the totem pole's unearthly colors. Now the cool night air could drift inside the tepee and soothe her with its touch.

She fell asleep and dreamed of nocturnal invaders, stealthy sex burglars, uninvited visitors of earnest manner, peculiar needs, unstoppable strength. The dream flooded her body with the secretions of fear, pumped her awake so suddenly she sat upright before her eyes had completely opened. Someone was at the foot of her bed, not a dream figure, a real person, she was able to grasp that much despite the whirling flux of her thoughts.

"Kevin?"

"Kevin?"

Both spoke at once. It wasn't Kevin standing there, and it wasn't Ray. The door was shut, the chair in place, so this must be one of the Apprentices making a vampirish social call, probably his idea of a big joke. Kevin had told her it was possible to run up the tepee's wall to her window, and had obviously told his friends, too.

"Get out!"

"Excuse me, I thought this might be Kevin's room now."

His face and clothing were lit by the totem pole's nightmarish glow. He did not come any closer than the foot of the bed.

"Get out!"

"Okay. Excuse me, I really thought he might've moved down here. There's no light at all from the top window, but this one was open, so I thought he might be here. I'm sorry. I didn't mean to scare you. I'm not a thief or rapist or anything."

His voice was sincere, but Autie couldn't trust it, reached out and switched on her bedside lamp to kill the neon-lit murkiness in her room. Now she could see him, and he was no Apprentice, not with that suit and slicked-back hair. "I'm sorry," he said again, and this time she saw the flash of gold as he spoke. Jesse Bob had told her about those teeth.

"Are you Milo?"

231

"That's me."

"Jesus . . ."

"No, you were right the first time."

He laughed weakly. Autie could not respond. Her shoulders relaxed a little and her breathing slowed. There he was, in the flesh, the one and only—Milo. The dream that preceded his appearance was already forgotten, yet he seemed its logical extension, had sprung from her head to stand before her, a chimera incarnate in a sixty-dollar suit.

"So," he said, "are you Kevin's girl?"

"No."

"Well, you couldn't be Ray's wife."

"No."

"So who are you?" The smile again. "Not that it's any of my business."

"I'm his daughter."

"Pardon me? Whose daughter?"

"Ray's."

"Oh, really?"

Milo was almost amused. Ray obviously had a girlfriend stashed away at the T-bird, an underage girl who'd been coached to respond with this daughter nonsense when questioned. How long had Ray been getting nooky from jailbait? Didn't anyone ever challenge such a bullshit story? And what did Kevin think about it?

"Where's Kevin?"

"He hasn't come home tonight. Sometimes he stays with his friends."

"Tell him when you see him I'm at the Prairie Moon, Room Twenty-two. I'll be there a couple of days. If he doesn't show up, I'm gone. Okay?"

"Okay."

He put one foot over the window sill, ducked his head, hesitated on the ledge.

"Listen, close this up. I could've been anyone. Open the door if you want cool air." He looked at the door as he said this, noticed for the first time the chair wedged under the lock. "What's that for?" Autie said nothing. "What's the door jammed for?"

"He's kind of drunk tonight."

Milo stepped back inside the room.

"Does he beat you up?"

"No, I just get nervous."

"Who are you really?"

"I told you, his daughter. My mom and Ray weren't married. It happened when they were in school."

"I never heard about it when I was here."

Autie told him about Montana, about Ellie's death. Milo believed it. He was seated on the bed by then.

"So now you're here for good."

"I guess."

"Jesus, what a weird situation."

"Are you going to stay here again?"

"No way."

"Are you going to tell Ray you're here?"

"I already did, this afternoon."

"Oh."

Now she knew why Ray was drunk. She supposed it was understandable; Milo had killed his wife after all.

"I've gotta go. Give Kevin the message, okay?"

"Okay."

"Nice meeting you. What's your name?"

"Autumn."

"Autumn?"

"My mom's favorite season. Everyone calls me Autie."

"Okay. See ya."

He left through the window. She heard him slither down the wall. Then he was gone.

The half-brothers met in Room 22 the following day. After an exchange of reticent banalities, they stared wordlessly at each other. Both had been transformed, Kevin from gawky preteen to mega-hip poseur, Milo from borderline punk to insurance salesman, or so it seemed; only the teeth remained to indicate he was not part of the common herd. Kevin was disappointed; anyone who climbed through windows in the night should look like Dracula, not John Q. Citizen.

"Where d'you go?"

"Everyplace. I drive cars."

"Racing?"

"Nope."

He told Kevin what he'd told Ray. Kevin's face conveyed his lack of interest. Mere minutes before, he'd knocked with trepidation at the door, expecting reunion with someone more than mortal; the acolyte would again touch the hem of the venerated one's robe—and there sat Milo with lace-up shoes and argyll socks. There was even a pair of glasses peeping from the pocket of that whiter-than-white shirt. It was a grievous betrayal of image, an unforgivable backing-down from yesterday's dizzying nonconformity. How could Kevin possibly brag about this guy to the Apprentices? He knew he'd leave here with a fistful of nothing. Now Milo was asking how he was doing at school! Was he for real?

"You look like a user, Kevin."

"Huh?"

"Do you indulge?"

"You mean drugs?"

"Right."

"Hey, who doesn't? So what?"

"Just asking."

He stared at Kevin's T-shirt, on which four androgynous Nazis pouted and sneered.

"Blitzkrieg," said Kevin, noticing his interest. "They're very bizarre, you know?"

"Autie says the old man's a lush."

"Yeah, since you left. He's pathetic."

"You like Autie?"

"She's okay. Kind of straight. I guess you have to be to

work at a Seven-Eleven. Pretty amazing her showing up, huh?"

"Yeah."

"She said you won't be around for long."

"That's right."

He searched Kevin's face for indications of regret. There were none. Milo smiled weakly.

"What's so funny?"

"Nothing. Relax."

"So where did you go, exactly?"

"L.A. Then New Orleans, Miami, New York, back to L.A. All over the block."

"What's L.A. like?"

"Interesting."

"What, the movies, the music, the girls? What's interesting?"

"All of it. Everything is interesting, everywhere."

"How about New Orleans?"

"Humid. Miami's sunny. New York is tall."

Kevin wondered if he was being made fun of. His foot jiggled nervously; his dreadlocks nodded like heavily fruited boughs.

"Why do you look like that if you just drive cars?"

"Like what?"

"Like you sell shoes for a living."

"I like to be anonymous, Kevin. There's all kinds of anonymous. This is the one I picked—square anonymous."

"Yeah, but why?"

"No reason."

Now he was sure Milo was hiding something. No one would willingly choose to look like that, not unless he was brain damaged. What was the big secret? Milo and Kevin already shared a secret, the biggest kind of all, but Milo apparently had another one, and didn't want to share it. Kevin had hoped they could talk like real buddies now that he was older, but Milo seemed somehow to have aged more than three years. The gap between them had widened, not shrunk.

"Back in a minute," said Milo, and shut himself in the bathroom. Kevin quickly went through the cheap suitcase beside the bed, looking for clues to Milo's recent past. Some shirts and underwear, socks, and a tie even more boring than the one around Milo's neck. He looked in the closet and dresser; empty as only a motel closet and dresser can be. He looked under the bed, then under the pillows. The first hid nothing, but beneath the plumpness of the second his fingers found an automatic pistol. Kevin grabbed it, still had it in his hands when Milo came out of the bathroom; the toilet hadn't flushed to give him warning.

"Kind of a snoop aren't you, Kevin?"

"What's it for?"

"Handguns exist for just one reason—to kill people."

"Who do you wanna kill?"

Milo took the pistol from him. "See this gun?"

"Yeah."

"No you don't. There is no gun in this room. Repeat."

"Uh, no gun in this room."

"Very good."

"What kind is it, a Colt?"

"If it existed, it'd be a Beretta, but it doesn't exist."

"Are you gonna kill Ray with it?"

"This is for self-defense only. Got that? Self-defense."

"Sure."

"Just because Ray put a bullet in me doesn't mean I want to put a bullet in him."

"Okay."

"Do you want me to put a bullet in him, Kevin?"

"He's drinking himself to death anyway."

"That takes fifteen, twenty years." Milo put his face close to Kevin's. "You want him to die right now, huh?"

"No . . ."

"That's good. Ray's a dork, but he put food in our mouths. Forget the gun. You never saw it, okay?"

"Okay. Can you get one for me?"

"What the fuck would you want a gun for?"

"Self-defense, like you."

"Got a schoolyard bully hassling you, Kevin? Learn karate. Guns are for big boys."

"Yeah, but why do you carry one?"

"That's my business. You never saw the gun. There is no gun. Got it?"

"Right. Are you, like, in disguise or something, you know, the suit and all?"

"This is me. No disguise."

"Whatever you say. Listen, you want to meet some friends of mine?"

"I don't think so. I just wanted to see you and Ray, and Autie too, it turned out. Just the family."

"These guys are cool. I told them plenty about you."

"You don't know anything about me. How could you tell them what you don't know?"

"Then you tell 'em."

"Forget it. I'm not in a meeting-people mood."

Milo knew it was the Beretta that had made him suddenly acceptable to Kevin. The kid was pathetic, the very label he'd applied to Ray. It was a jolt to see them both this way. Autie Quist was the only one with any kind of handle on reality. He felt he could look at Autie, talk to her, spend time with her without becoming depressed, but maybe that was because she was a girl. Was he feeling horny? No, he was not. He didn't know how he felt. Milo was one step removed from everyone and everything, an observer occupying his own body, living his life in a near-perfect facsimile of normalcy. The reason for this sense of dislocation was not hard to pin down; Milo knew he was soon to die. Maybe it was curiosity that had brought him back to Callisto for a last look at his family, maybe genuine concern, maybe mere sentiment. What else could he do before the end—see Grand Canyon? The lack of courage within himself was disheartening. He sometimes found his whole body trembling, knew it was gut fear, the shivering of the rabbit before the snake; uncontrollable, elemental. Milo's life was drawing to a close because he had done something stupid. It was his own fault. Thinking about it, which he did at length every half hour or so, numbed him. His encounters yesterday with Ray and Autie had awakened him briefly, but the sheer novelty of trading spite with Ray and discovering the human appeal of Autie had not lasted long. His ability to focus properly on Kevin had evaporated within minutes, and Milo had been obliged to retire and snort some cocaine to revive himself, a bad idea, since Kevin had snooped while Milo was gone, and now the little prick admired him because of that useless gun.

"You ever think about our mom, Kevin?"

"Sure."

"What kind of things do you think about her?"

"Just, you know, what she looked like, stuff like that."

"That's all?"

"Sure, what else? What difference? She's dead."

"That's right. She's dead."

He waited for Kevin to acknowledge his role in Holly's death, but Kevin twitched and fidgeted and wouldn't look at him. Milo didn't want tears of remorse, didn't want to hear expressions of gratitude for the coverup that day by the lake; he just wanted to hear the facts stated. If Kevin could do that much, open his mouth and say, "I killed my mom," there was hope for him. But he wouldn't, or couldn't, say it.

"Got any hobbies, Kevin?"

"Music."

"You play, or you listen?"

"I listen."

"Anything else?"

"The mysteries."

"What mysteries?"

Kevin told him, eyes shining, face animated by conviction.

"You really believe that stuff?"

"It's the path to truth."

"Bullshit."

"It's not!"

"Sure it is. When people go to church, that's bullshit tied up in a pink ribbon. This crap you're into, it's bullshit tied up in a black ribbon. All of it's bullshit. You need to wake up, Kevin."

"What the fuck do you know?"

"I know bullshit when I smell it. Your Apprentice pals are a bunch of geeks."

Kevin was outraged, and his opinion of Milo reversed itself again.

"*You're* a geek!"

"You really think you can get Satan on your team by killing animals? That's straight out of the fucking jungle. It's crap. How'd you like to have your guts ripped out because some idiot thinks it'll keep his god happy. Grow up and quit believing in fairy tales."

"I'm talking about the fucking eternal mysteries and how you have to take the left-hand path to get into them, nothing to do with fucking fairy tales!"

"It's a big mystery to me why you have to believe any of this stuff. You're just filling in the empty spaces in your head with bullshit!"

"Raising the dead isn't bullshit! It's going over to the other side and bringing part of it back! It's true!"

"Raising the dead? Are you kidding? Who the fuck do you want to talk to that's dead? Adolf Hitler? Sid Vicious?"

"None of your fucking business!" howled Kevin. The Apprentices were in fact trying to contact Aleister Crowley; failing that, any available imp or demon would do.

"Hey, the one person who's dead that you need to talk to is the one you killed! Get Mom back here and apologize for throwing rocks around, you stupid little fuck! I'll get you a dog to carve up for that! I'll get you a fucking horse! I'll get you a herd of elephants if you'll get down and say what you did, not to the cops, not to Ray, not even to me—just say it to her!"

In attempting to point a finger at Kevin, Milo had unconsciously aimed his Beretta at the boy's face. Kevin truly believed himself threatened, and began to whimper, eyes almost crossed as they focused on the barrel. Milo quickly lowered it. Both were flushed with anger, breathing hard. Kevin broke for the door, clawed it open, turned and yelled, "You're crazy!" then ran, leaving it swung open behind him. A wedge of sunlight fell across the carpet. Kevin had left so fast the air was filled with agitated motes of dust. His sneakers could be heard slapping the concrete in retreat. Hiding the gun behind his thigh, Milo closed the door before any passersby could see inside. It clicked shut, and he slumped against it.

"Not crazy," he said, although staying around this town might be termed just that. He should get in his car and drive, drive anywhere and everywhere and hope they never caught up with him. But of course they would; they always did. He'd heard the stories, all of them true. No one got away. The time and manner of his death were up to them. Milo could only choose the place.

17

HE DROVE half a block past the figure on the sidewalk before recognizing him, braked, spun the wheel and drove back, did an illegal U-turn, and pulled up at the curb beside Milo. It was the glasses that had fooled him for that half block, and the suit and slicked-back hair.

"Hey, Milo."

"Hey, officer."

Bernie took off his shades and squinted up at him.

"Been back long?"

"Yesterday."

"You look different."

"You too. No uniform."

"Plain-clothes detective nowadays. Been around to the T-bird yet?"

"First thing I did."

"How's Ray these days?"

"Fine."

"Uh-huh. Meet your new sister?"

"She's not my sister, not even my half-sister."

"Whatever. Big surprise, huh?"

"Pretty big."

Bernie was getting a crick in his neck. He killed the engine and climbed out, stretched elaborately. "Feels good to get out and decramp," he said, wanting Milo to relax; he didn't want his curiosity to be interpreted as confrontation. Milo's face was thinner than it used to be, almost wasted, and the muscles of his skinny neck stood out like ropes beneath the skin. Bernie looked him up and down.

"You look almost respectable, Milo. You working these days?"

"Looking for it. Any vacancies on the force?"

Bernie gave that more laughter than it deserved. He knew Milo wanted to get away from him, but he wasn't about to let him go so fast; he'd made the effort to appear friendly, and Milo could damn well carry on a conversation in the same vein. Milo's face was sweating from more than the summer heat. Bernie was willing to bet he had dope on him, the suit and tie being a fairly obvious attempt at looking straight. Bernie wasn't falling for it, but neither was he interested in a cheap bust.

"So, is this a flying visit or a homecoming?"

"I'd call it a visit."

Milo shifted his weight from one leg to the other. The pistol wedged in the back of his pants was pressing uncomfortably against his spine.

"Bring home any exciting stories from faraway places?"

"Nope."

"That's a shame. Travel's supposed to broaden the mind."

"I must've got on the wrong bus."

Bernie laughed again, with less effort this time.

"Spoken to your kid brother yet? Excuse me—half-brother."

"Sure."

"Changed some, wouldn't you say?"

"A little."

"Every day's Halloween for that boy. You meet his friends?"

"Heard about them."

242

"Stick around, you'll hear more. Kevin wants to be on the six o'clock news, like you."

"Yeah?"

The police waveband crackled and babbled through the open window. Bernie offered a pack of gum to Milo, was refused with a shake of the head, slowly peeled himself a stick.

"Callisto's changed some, too. Backlash, I guess you'd call it. Took people a little while to realize the place had changed, but when they did they wanted the old Callisto back again, law-abiding, kind of square, just a little old Kansas town, you know? Everyone's very down on drugs and rule breaking now. You thinking of looking up your old buddies at all? There's some of them still around, but getting thinned out fast, moving away. What happened to that girlfriend of yours, what was her name again?"

"Sharon."

"Right. What happened to her? I heard her mother sent a private detective after you both. He ever catch up with you?"

"No, not while I was with her, anyway."

"You broke up?"

"A couple of years back."

"So you don't know where she is now?"

"No. We didn't keep in touch."

"Where was the last place you saw her?"

"Albuquerque," lied Milo.

"I'll tell Mrs. Kincheloe that, and maybe she'll hire another detective to track her down. But she could be anywhere by now, right?"

"Sharon liked to move around."

"I'll tell her anyway, and leave it up to her. What were you guys doing in Albuquerque?"

"Nothing. Passing through. We had a fight and split up. That's the last I ever heard from her."

"That's too bad. Where you staying, Milo?"

"Prairie Moon."

"Not the T-bird?"

"Not classy enough."

Bernie snapped gum for some time, watching Milo try not to squirm with impatience.

"Well, take care of yourself. It's a dangerous world."

"Is that right."

"Yes it is. You tell Kevin I said hi."

Bernie got into his car, started it up, leaned back through the window. "How long did you say you were staying in town?"

"Not long."

"See you around."

He drove off. Milo felt his body shiver with relief. His armpits dripped sweat. He could save Mrs. Kincheloe a lot of money by telling her Sharon was dead, but because her death was linked with his current state of despondence and alarm, he was not inclined to tell anyone. He wondered if Bernie intended having his room at the Prairie Moon searched. His cocaine stash was vulnerable, incriminating; so was the gun he carried. Then again, the safest place for him might be behind bars. Not true. They could reach you anywhere, anywhere at all. He panicked for fifteen seconds, then calmed himself; in daylight he was probably safe. He took several deep breaths and headed for the 7-Eleven.

Autie thought he looked sick when he walked in, sat on a stool, and ordered a Coke. Jesse Bob was already staring at him, sieving his memory; he'd know when he saw the teeth.

"Kevin said he'd call around and see you today."

"He just left."

"How did it go?"

"We had an interesting little chat. He's a regular space cadet."

"Did he tell you about that stuff he believes?"

"All about it."

Jesse Bob was edging closer. Their voices softened to keep the conversation private.

"He'll probably grow out of it," said Autie.

"He better, and fast. You can't get away with disemboweling dogs forever."

"Does he do that? He didn't tell me."

"He told me, and he's proud of it. He's got to quit before he gets caught. He won't listen to me, not after the argument we had. Does he like you a lot? I mean, does he listen to you when you give advice?"

"I've never given him any. I think he likes me okay, though."

"Try and talk some sense into him, would you? I'd hate for him to wind up in juvenile court."

They were almost whispering by the time Jesse Bob pounced. "Aren't you Milo Ginty?"

Milo eyed him for a moment.

"No, I'm his evil twin. Now butt out."

Jesse Bob retreated. Milo drained his cup.

"What time are you through here?"

"Five."

"I'll see you then. We need to talk."

"Okay."

He left. Jesse Bob was annoyed that Autie appeared to know something he didn't.

"That was him, wasn't it."

"Was who?"

"Milo Ginty, your dad's other boy, the stepson."

"Was it? He told me his name was Glenn Ford."

"He what? You didn't believe it, did you? Glenn Ford's a movie star, must be sixty years old by now, easy. He said he was Glenn Ford? That's not possible, Autie. He was playing a joke on you."

"Well how about that. What a nerve, telling me he's a movie star."

"That was Milo Ginty, I know it. Did you see the teeth,

those gold teeth? That was him. Someone must've told him about you and he's checking you out. You better tell your dad, Autie."

"I will, Jesse Bob."

Milo went back to his room for cocaine and left again, revived. His return to Callisto had released a tide of re-membrance and association that carried him from street to street, past houses unremarkable but for their startling familiarity. Utterly unchanged, yet somehow not the same, the town lured him on with its frowzy appeal, every tree and curbstone a signpost to earlier times, when Milo had been someone else. These were the streets he'd pedaled down on his tricycle, growling engine sounds, fat knees pumping. How could that have been him? Where was the link between then and now?

He began to quake with an excess of narcotics and poig-nance. Memory Lane was a narrow alley, its trash made beautiful through tears, and down at the far end, parked across his way, was the long black limousine that would swallow him whole. Milo had come home to set his broken house in order, he saw that now. Things had to be set straight before he died, but he was doing a god-awful job, could barely function part of the time, had already made an enemy of Kevin instead of a friend, hadn't even been able to offer Ray the gift he'd planned on handing over. Atonement was a recondite path; Milo was unsure if he was equipped to follow it, but what else could he do in the time remaining? He drifted from Main to Ninth to Walnut, mourning what was left of his life.

They met at five, and while Milo drove her home, Autie persuaded him to enter the big tepee and try again.

"What's he doing here?" was Ray's response. He was panic-stricken at seeing Milo and Autie together. The fact that they'd somehow met was bad enough, but their physi-cal proximity as they came through the door sent a jolt through his body that almost made his hand reach for the .38 under the desk.

"He wants to talk to you."

"We've got nothing to say."

Autie urged Milo on with her eyes.

"I got you a present, Ray."

"I don't want it."

"Maybe you should take a look at it first. It's right outside."

"I'm not interested."

"Please, Ray," said Autie, "just take a look."

Since it was her asking, Ray obliged and went out. Milo was referring to the car, the shiny new red Firebird.

"What'd you do, steal it?"

"Paid cash for it at the Pontiac lot downtown. It's yours, already registered in your name."

"Why?"

"Because I want you to have it."

"And then what'll you drive?"

"I'll get myself another car."

"With cash."

"Sure."

"Where'd all this cash come from?"

"My job."

"Driving cars around."

"Right."

"Bull. That much? In cash? Where'd the money really come from? What are you, a bank robber?"

"I'm a driver. Jesus . . . You want it or not?"

"No."

"Okay. Fine. Anything else I can get you? A paint job for the place maybe? It's looking kind of tacky."

"I don't want anything except for you to stay away from my family."

"Ray, he wants you to have it."

"I don't care what he wants! You can't wipe out the past with money!"

"Forget it," said Milo, and got inside the car.

"Ray, let him give it to you. Please."

"No way, not from him."

"You can't keep blaming him for something that was an accident."

"I do blame him. I want him out of here."

Milo started the engine and drove off. They watched the Firebird swing around the totem pole and turn onto Locust.

"This is just stupid."

"You're entitled to your opinion, and I'm entitled to mine. How come he knows you?"

Autie told him.

"You keep that window locked from now on. Has he talked to Kevin yet?"

"Yes, today."

"Shit!"

"You can't keep him away."

"You bet I can. He's not welcome here, and I don't want you or Kevin having anything to do with him. He's poison. You think he got all that money legally? No way. He's in some kind of racket. You stay away from him, you hear me?"

"But he's only trying to be friendly. He bought you a car."

"With criminal money! I can smell it. He's bad news and I don't want you hanging around him. It's for your own good."

Autie thought otherwise but stayed silent. She fixed dinner. When Kevin wandered in, Ray demanded to know the extent of his conversation with Milo. "He just talked about a whole bunch of nothing, school and stuff. I was only there five minutes." Ray liked that answer, but gave Kevin a lecture on future avoidance of Milo anyway. For reasons differing greatly from his father's, Kevin was willing to oblige. The smallest of small voices occasionally intruded among his thoughts to goad him; maybe Milo was right, and everything Kevin believed in, the arcane dabbling he

248

built his life around, was crap. After dinner he refused to discuss with Autie his visit to Milo's room.

"He's worried about you, Kevin."

"I don't give a shit. Let him worry, the geek."

It was clear to Autie she was Milo's only champion, and like any believer, she wanted to replenish her faith at the source. At ten o'clock she opened her window and slid down the wall, walked a block to the nearest pay phone, dialed the Prairie Moon, and asked for Room 22. Milo said yes, she could come around. She was there fifteen minutes later.

"Ray know you came?"

"No. I sneaked out." She saw his suitcase on the bed. "Are you leaving?"

"Working my way towards it."

"I wish you wouldn't. He just needs time to come around. Both of them do."

"I don't have that kind of time. Take a seat."

"If I told him how you got the money, he'd probably be friendlier."

"I already told him how I got it."

"He doesn't believe you?"

"Do you?"

"I don't know. It's a lot of money. Ray said a car like that costs plenty."

"It's only a Pontiac, not a goddamn Porsche."

"But you said if he accepted it you'd go buy yourself another car, just like that. Two cars, both cash. It's a lot of money whichever way you look at it, Milo."

It was the first time she'd used his name. As names will, it altered subtly the ambience in Room 22. Milo decided he could relax a little with this girl who was so concerned with reconciling her new and splintered family.

"How about you? You believe me? Be honest."

"I don't see how you could make that much just by driving other people's cars."

"So how do you think I got it?"

"By doing something illegal."

"Well, it hurts me to admit it, but you're right. I work on the wrong side of the law. Now you know."

Autie didn't look away from his face.

"What do you do, exactly?"

"Coke mule. You know what that is? A mule picks up a shipment and carries it here, carries it there, runs it to rinky-dink towns you'd think they never even heard of coke, but they have, Autie. They use the stuff everywhere, and the mule is the delivery man."

"To Callisto too?"

"Not my territory."

"Then why are you here now?"

"Because I don't do that work any more. I quit. I'm out of the business, totally and forever."

"That's good." She smiled, and the smile met Milo's hardness head-on and shattered it. He'd been trying, in his forlorn locker-room fashion, to impress her with his outlaw image, but she'd only wanted to hear that it was all behind him. So it was, but the situation arising from his change of heart was more difficult to speak of. Not only did he not know where to begin, he was surprised to find he wanted to begin at all. To tell what he knew, to explain his plight, would accomplish nothing, alter nothing. There was no reason for her to be involved. He'd been as honest with her as was practicable; to open further the door on his flawed past and truncated future would be pointless, would probably upset a sympathetic type like Autie, and he didn't want to cause her pain. His own pain would have to be met with whatever courage he could muster, a fast-dwindling commodity, he knew, kept operational only by lines of coke. He ingested the resolution to face his death, snorted strength, and his intake was escalating daily. Milo figured his stash would last just five days more. If they hadn't killed him by then, he was in big trouble.

"Sure it's good," he said. "Crime does not pay, right?"

Autie shrugged. "Wrong. Crime pays very well. Crime is a good job with terrific wages but no retirement plan, and drug crime is where the real fat money is, the biggest bucks outside of Wall Street. Guys like me are the littlest cogs in a machine big as Manhattan."

His finger was jabbing the air below her nose. Autie kept watching Milo's eyes. She wasn't smiling now.

"Everybody wants cocaine. May the bird of paradise fly up your nose. No messy needles, no cigarette lighters under bent spoons, just line it up and snort it, then you're ready to party. You feel good, the way you should feel all the time, and pretty soon you need to feel that good all the time if you want, only you've got to pay, and when you can't, when the money's gone and you feel bad because you spent every dime and your nose is crying for coke, you climb on the carrousel again, only this time from the inside, where the deals get made, where the stuff comes from, and you push it to people like it was pushed to you. But don't worry, it's not hard work because people want it, you only need to let them know you're open for business and they come, all of them, everybody, in a Ford or a Learjet, it's all the same, they've just got to have it to keep on feeling good, and you feel good too because you're making a bunch of money and snorting a little of your stock to keep ahead, to keep riding the wave, and you ride it all the way to the bank."

Sweat ran into his eyes. His hand fell. He seemed almost to collapse as the last of the words left him. The shirt hung from his shoulders like a windless sail, its armpits drenched. Milo breathed rapidly for a short while, stared at the hand that lay palm upward in his lap, as if divining in its overlapping creases the inevitable confluence of fate. Autie didn't move. Milo required help, but she was not sure what kind. His mouth was slack, unpleasant to look at.

"Are you okay?"

"Yeah. Excuse me."

He went into the bathroom, closed the door. Autie heard

water running. It ran for a long time, then Milo returned, his face washed, hair slicked back, his manner rejuvenated. "Have to change my shirt," he said, and stripped off with his back to her. Autie saw briefly the ugly scar above his hip, the scar Ray had given him, then it was curtained by the new shirt Milo put on.

"I need some fresh air. Feel like taking a walk?"

"Okay."

Milo put on his jacket.

"You won't need that. It's real warm outside."

"I catch cold easy."

He went to the bed, took something from beneath a pillow, and put it under his belt at the back. He was not facing Autie when he did this, but she knew it could only be one thing.

"Is that a gun?"

"Yeah, it is."

"Why do you carry it around?"

"Protection."

"From what?"

"The forces of evil that stalk our fair land," he said, and gave a whinnying laugh.

Autie was not happy as they left the motel and began walking. The night air throbbed with atonal insect raspings and the rhythmic humming of traffic along the state highway.

"Where are you going when you leave here?"

"Hadn't thought about it."

"But you definitely won't be staying."

"I can't."

"Why?"

"There are reasons, believe me."

"I do believe you. I just wonder what the reasons are."

But Milo wouldn't say.

"I'm going to stay," announced Autie. "I like it here."

"It's a free country."

"Ray and Kevin need someone to help them."

"I agree."

"Don't you want to help them, too?"

"I tried. You saw what happened with Ray."

"How about Kevin?"

"He won't listen, so screw him."

"I think you're just mad at them because things didn't work out the way you wanted. If you stuck with it, I bet they'd come around in the end."

"It'd be 1990 by then."

"No it wouldn't. Maybe they need time to get used to you again."

"I haven't got time to spare."

"Why haven't you?"

"Excuse me if I sound impolite, but that's my business."

"Fine."

"I'm not mad at you. Don't think that."

"I know."

"I just don't have the time."

"Sure, I understand."

Milo had to crank out a laugh at that. Autie understood nothing. Sometimes Milo didn't understand it himself, the moves that had sent him streaking for shelter in Callisto like a fox run to earth. The chain of events was obvious enough, but his motive, originally so clear, had been muddled by narcotics as much as by emotion; he suspected he would never work out the percentages. He had done what he had done, then tried to undo it, and had failed. So now he would die. Simple.

"The Quist family wasn't a very big success," said Autie. "Maybe with a little work the Kootzes could be."

"My name's Ginty."

"So what! Why don't you want to help? You say you've quit pushing drugs, but you don't want to do anything to make up for what you did. Drugs are bad, so you should do something good to make up for it. You don't have to be Mother Teresa, just help your dad and brother a little bit."

"He's not my dad, and I don't get the connection anyway."

"You don't want to."

"Look, all a mule does is transport the stuff to wherever they want it. I didn't ram it up anyone's nose. I didn't kill anyone."

"Oh, you . . . chickenshit!"

Autie began walking fast. Milo hesitated, then caught up.

"Wait a minute! You don't know what you're talking about."

"Don't I?"

"I can't do anything here. I can't do anything anywhere."

"Why! Just tell me why!"

"Because . . ."

They both stopped. Autie glared at him. "Well?"

"Because they're gonna kill me anytime now."

"What?"

"They're looking for me, and when they find me, I'm dead."

"Who's looking for you?"

"The people I used to work for," he said, and leaned wearily against a chain-link fence, as if this admission had drained the last of his strength.

"Why do they want to kill you?"

Autie didn't believe it; he was just looking for dramatic excuses. She was very disappointed in him.

"I took some of their coke, okay? That's why."

"Why did you do that? That's dumb."

"I gave it back. I only had it forty-eight hours."

"Then why do they want to kill you?"

"Because I took it in the first place. It doesn't make any difference if I gave it back. They're not ordinary people."

"How much did you take?"

"About eight million bucks' worth, street value."

Milo couldn't keep a note of pride from his voice. Autie

was appalled. "That much? Why? It's so stupid to do a thing like that."

"I felt bad about something that happened."

"What thing?"

"That's my business," he said stiffly.

"Oh, Milo . . ."

"Go on, call me an idiot. I am an idiot."

"Isn't there anything you can do? What makes you think they can find you?"

"They've got contacts everyplace. Believe me, it's just a matter of time. Don't look at me like I'm giving up. Facts are facts. Telling myself I won't be dead isn't brave, it's dumb. They'll get me."

"Go to the police."

"They've got so many cops in their pocket I wouldn't know who to trust."

"Go talk to Bernie Swenson. He's a cop right here in town. He'll listen."

"I know Swenson. He'll bring charges against me for possession and criminal association and Christ knows what. Forget it."

"If you tell the FBI and say you'll be a witness for the state or something they'll give you a new identity and set you up someplace with a new life. I saw a movie about it."

"Witness relocation isn't foolproof. They'd find out sooner or later. I personally heard about one guy up in New York did that, ratted to the feds, and they gave him a new identity in Arizona, but he was gunned down six months later anyhow. They find out, always."

"Then go to another country."

"It wouldn't matter if I went to fucking Mars! It doesn't work that way in the real world!"

"You don't know that!"

"I fucking do! You don't know shit!"

Autie still didn't think Milo's life was threatened. He'd given back what he took, so killing him would prove nothing. Milo was exaggerating, but she didn't doubt he truly believed his fears. Maybe they were drug-induced; that would explain plenty.

"Do you take any stuff yourself?"

"I snort a line every now and then."

"Oh."

"You think I've got so much snow in my head I'm seeing spooks, right?"

"No."

"Yes you do. They're on their way. Believe it."

"You want to keep walking?"

"Sure. It's a nice night for it. Walking is healthy. I'll die a healthy man, so let's walk."

They walked.

"Are you shortsighted or longsighted?"

"Huh?"

"Sometimes you wear glasses and sometimes you don't."

Milo took the glasses from his shirt pocket and placed them on Autie's nose. Instead of subjecting her to instant visual distortion, the lenses changed the appearance of nothing.

"Display frames," said Milo. "I boosted them from an optometrist's."

"A disguise?"

"Sure." He lifted them from her face, placed them on his own. "Little did people know that Milo Ginty, mild-mannered fuckup, was in fact"—he whipped the glasses off—"Goldfang, underworld crime boss, whose name struck fear in the hearts of honest men."

Autie laughed, figuring humor to be a sign that Milo was returning from whatever realm of paranoia his coke habit had taken him to.

They walked on, eventually reaching Main Street. This being Friday night, both lanes were jammed with teenagers and their vehicles performing the ritual promenade of chrome and steel, radios blaring through open windows, screams of bogus joy and needless alarm punctuating the roar of gunned engines and shrilling of tortured rubber at the lights. Milo, the nondriving nonconformist, had never taken part when he lived here, and Autie was much too self-possessed for herd activities. They strolled the length of Main, observing the clamor and movement. Participants taking time out along the curb sat on their fenders and hoods with six-packs, talking at the top of their voices. It was inevitable that they notice someone as out of place as Milo.

"Hey, get the monkey suit!"

The cry was contagious.

"Monkey suit! Hey, monkey suit!"

Two boys capered like chimpanzees around Milo's knees while their girlfriends laughed. Milo and Autie attempted to sidestep, but were not allowed. Gibbering happily, the boys pawed their legs. "Stop it!" said Autie when one of them gave an unsimian pinch to her thigh, and that was enough for Milo. He pulled out the Beretta, cocked it and jammed the barrel against the boy's ear. "No more monkeyshines," he said. The second boy scuttled backward, and Milo's target froze. One of the girlfriends let out a thin squeal when she saw the gun.

"Say you're sorry," said Milo.

"I'm sorry."

"Tell me you're a stupid monkey fuck."

"I'm a stupid monkey fuck."

"Absolutely right. Have a banana."

He uncocked the gun and returned it to his belt. "Bye-bye," he said, and steered Autie away by the elbow.

"You shouldn't have done that. They'll tell the police."

"Nah, they'd be too embarrassed."

"Was it loaded?"

"What good's an unloaded gun?"

"I wish you wouldn't carry it."

"When they come for me, I'll need it. Maybe I can take a few with me."

257

Useless to pursue the matter, thought Autie, and they walked to the end of Main, turned and started back. A police cruiser was headed along Main toward them, siren off, flashers on. Milo barely had time to place his gun beneath a parked car and walk on before they were arrested.

18

"PLACE CHANGED MUCH, do you think?"
"Not much."

Milo had been kept waiting over an hour before Bernie talked to him. He hadn't seen Autie since they were brought to the station. He'd seen the two monkeys and their girlfriends being ushered into another room.

"Where's the gun?"

"There isn't one."

"Those guys are lying?"

"Right."

"Making it all up because they don't like the shape of your nose."

"I couldn't explain their motives. They're probably stoned."

"How about you, Milo, are you stoned?"

"I was just walking along the street with Autie and they started in on us."

"For no reason."

"No reason at all."

"How long have you been back in town?"

"About thirty-six hours."

"And already you're in trouble. That's fast work."

"Am I in trouble? I haven't done anything."

"You don't look good, Milo. Are you sick? You're sweating."

"Your air conditioning doesn't work."

"Feels cool enough to me. So, no gun."

"No gun."

Bernie took Milo's Beretta from his desk drawer and examined it. "Found this one myself, just a little way down the block from where they picked you up—under a Toyota, as a matter of fact."

"It's not mine."

"Just coincidence, you think?"

"I don't have an opinion."

"Would you like to hear mine?"

"Sure."

"You're in deep shit, right up to your ears. Where'd you get a weapon like this?"

"I didn't get it. It isn't mine."

"So if we dusted it for prints we wouldn't find yours."

"Correct."

Milo had had the presence of mind to wipe the Beretta on his shirttail before dumping it. He'd been tucking his shirt back into his pants when the cruiser stopped.

"Would we find anything as interesting as this if we searched your room at the Prairie Moon?"

"I don't think so. You're free to look."

"I might just do that. I already called them up today to check if you were there like you said, and guess what, you're registered as Alvin Gross. They didn't know who the hell I was talking about till I said you had gold teeth, then they remembered. So what's the story, Alvin?"

"I did it for a joke."

"On who?"

"On no one. On the way they don't give a shit who you are when you register. One time I signed into a place as Attila T. Hun. I had to keep from cracking up when they called me Mr. Hun. 'Enjoy your stay with us, Mr. Hun.' It's ridiculous."

"Can't see the humor in it myself."

260

"That's how it is with humor."

"Milo, what the fuck are you doing here?"

"Autie and I were brought in by a cop."

"I mean in Callisto. Don't get smart."

"Excuse me. I'm in Callisto because I wanted to make peace with Ray, bury the hatchet."

"You want to be friends again."

"I do, he doesn't."

"And you think strolling around with his daughter, who I happen to know he thinks is the angel on top of the Christmas tree, is going to make him like you?"

"I don't care what he likes or doesn't like."

"You said you wanted to be friends again."

"I said that's why I came here. Now I know it's not gonna happen. I tried, but it didn't work. I even tried giving him a present. He wouldn't take it."

"He's a very bitter man."

"Like a lemon."

"Because he thinks you killed his wife."

"Right."

"Which you didn't actually do."

"Yes I did."

"You're sure it wasn't someone else?"

"It's history."

Bernie turned the gun over and over. Milo needn't have bothered erasing his prints.

"You know what I'm going to do with this? I'm going to wait for someone to claim it, and when no one does, I'll get it for myself at the next police auction. This is one terrific gun. I'd even go so far as to call it beautiful. Seven-hundred-dollar price tag, fifteen-shot clip; that's firepower. Makes my trusty piece look like Buffalo Bill's. I like this gun. Finders keepers, hey, Milo?"

"Sure."

The gun was returned to the drawer. "Wait here," said Bernie, and left. He returned a short while later.

"You're in luck. Those guys had fifteen-year-old girlfriends and beer in their pickup. I asked them if they were sure they wanted to press charges against you, and they thought about it and said no, then they left. You can go, too."

"Okay." Milo stood.

"How long are you going to hang around town, Milo?"

"I don't know."

"Think hard. I'm willing to bet by the time Monday rolls around you'll realize it's a waste of time staying here. I'm betting you'll be gone."

"You could be right."

"I hope so. Being wrong screws up my whole day. One more thing. You keep away from that girl. She's had enough tragedy in her life without you adding more. She backed up your no-gun bullshit, so you've got your hooks in her a little way already. You quit now, you hear me, Milo?"

"Yes."

"There's the door."

But Milo didn't move. He wanted to tell Bernie everything, wanted to fling himself on Bernie's lap and weep angry tears, tell how the big boys were going to beat him up and kill him dead. The temptation was overwhelming. Milo was paralyzed.

"Get outa here!"

The proud half of Milo took control and directed him toward the door, but the half that wanted to confess made him do so by walking backwards. Bernie thought he was being mocked. Only his eagerness to own the beautiful gun kept him from slamming Milo back down in the chair and really working him over. Milo was twitching when he reached the front desk, where Autie stood waiting. By the time they were out on the sidewalk, his whole body was shivering.

"Are you okay?"

"Yeah."

He'd even wanted to tell Bernie it was Kevin who killed their mom; that's how badly he wanted to unburden himself. He knew he must be in terrible shape to even think about doing that. His shape would be improved by the bag of white powder in his room.

"If you see a cab, grab it."

Autie touched him on the shoulder, but his shivering was a humiliation, and he shook her off.

It was almost 1 A.M. when they returned to the Prairie Moon. Milo went straight to the bathroom. This time he didn't bother running the water. When he came out, Autie asked if she could try some.

"What for?"

"So I can feel the same way you do."

"You don't want to feel like me."

"But maybe I could understand better."

"You're not getting any. End of argument."

"Is it really that bad?"

"It's that good."

"Then why can't I try one little bit?"

"Because I don't know if you've got what it takes to have one little bit without having another little bit later on, and another little bit after that. So you can't have any. I'm sorry. Look, coke is like a beautiful body, all your fantasies in one beautiful-to-look-at body, but then the body falls over and splits open, and inside there's nothing but shit and maggots, so you have another little bit to sew the body back together, and just when you think it's beautiful enough to make love to, it falls over again and splits open just like before, and there's the same old maggots squirming. You don't want that, honest, Autie. Don't ask me again, please."

The phone rang. He picked it up.

"Milo?"

"Yeah."

"Bernie Swenson. Ray just called, says his daughter's missing. Get her back to the T-bird right now."

"I hear you."

He hung up.

"I have to take you home. Ray called the cops."

"I don't want to."

"Well, I'm sorry, but I can't let Swenson climb on my back twice in one night. He's pissed enough at me already."

"Can't I just call Ray and let him know I'm okay?"

"You know it wouldn't be enough. Let's go."

On the drive across town Milo was struck by a thought. "Does Ray still have guns around the place?"

"He's got one under the reception desk in case he gets robbed."

"I know it. How about his Blackhawk, the one he shot me with?"

"Kevin said the police still have it."

"Bernie probably nabbed that one, too. That guy is something else. I need a gun. I can't just go buy one. You have to have proof you've lived in Kansas for the last thirty days before they'll sell you one. I can't do that."

"I won't steal it for you."

"I wasn't going to ask you. I'll ask Ray."

"You know he won't."

"He might. I need one."

They parked by the big tepee and went inside. Ray was signing in some late arrivals. Milo took advantage of this to walk right by and enter the living room with Autie close behind. Ray joined them there a few minutes later. Milo half expected him to have the .38 in his hand, aimed at Milo's heart.

"I told you you're not welcome here. Autie, get upstairs."

"Milo wants to talk to you about something."

"I'm not interested. Upstairs!"

"No!"

The word hit Ray like a slap in the face. He ignored it by turning to Milo. "Okay, what's the big topic of interest?"

"I need to borrow your gun."

"You what?"

"The .38 you keep out there. Someone's after me."

"For stealing money, I bet."

"For stealing dope. Eight million bucks' worth."

"Say again?"

Milo told him what he'd already told Autie.

"Bullshit," said Ray. "You're full of shit. Go buy your own gun if you think someone's after you. Frankly, I hope they get you. Dope running is disgusting. You're a criminal and a moral degenerate to do something like that. I hope they get you good, whoever they are. I should've known you'd turn out like this. Jesus . . ."

"So I can't have the gun."

"No you can't. Go tell the cops. It's not my problem."

"They can't do anything."

"Then I guess you're in shit city."

"That's my guess, too."

"This dope you run, you take it too?"

"Yes."

"You're an addict?"

"That's maybe not the right word for a coke user. It's not like heroin addiction."

"But you take it all the time, a regular thing."

"Right."

"Then I don't care. Anyone that gets hooked on dope, they're beyond sympathy. You've got no one to blame but yourself."

"I agree, but I still need the gun. How about a trade— the car for the .38. You wouldn't take it as a gift, so how about as a trade?"

"Dope money bought that car. I wouldn't even sit in it."

"Then I'm a dead man," said Milo, smiling.

"I guess you are."

Autie had sat silently through this. "Help him!" she demanded, and Ray got mad.

"You keep out of this! This is between him and me!"

"He's asking you for help."

"And I'm telling him no!" To Milo he reiterated, "No! No way! Now get out."

His voice cracked. He needed a drink. A triple scotch

would help him assimilate Milo's story. Milo looked half dead already, his hair stiff with dried sweat, skin pallid as porcelain, still with that spooky little smile perched on his face; it just wouldn't go away. Only a doper would smile as he predicted his own death. It was macabre, too far removed from normalcy. Ray wanted no part of it.

"Get out," he rasped. "Autie, go to bed."

"Aren't you going to do anything?"

"He deserves what he gets. I don't believe it anyway, hit men and eight million dollars' worth of dope. It's bullshit. He wants to pawn the gun for more dope, that's all."

"I don't need cash for coke, Ray. I've got plenty."

"Good. Go get high and enjoy yourself, but not around here, not in my place."

Milo stood. "Okay." He went to the office, escorted by Ray, who wanted to be sure Milo didn't grab the .38 in passing and run. Milo waved his fingers at the gun butt peeping from its holster. "Bye-bye, little gun. You could've kept me alive. Bye-bye."

Autie had followed them out. "Where do you think you're going?" said Ray.

Autie looked at Milo. Milo said, "Stay here. Forget it."

"You bet she's staying here."

Autie simply turned and went back inside. Ray knew it was because Milo told her to, not himself. It burned him the way she'd sided with Milo from the start. Where did she get off, turning her back on Ray like that? She needed a good talking-to, and when Milo was gone she'd get one, right after Ray had that triple scotch.

"So long, Ray."

"Yeah."

Milo got into the Firebird. Ray watched as it was driven away, exhaust pipes burbling throatily, its rakish profile low and mean; Milo's death barge. Good riddance.

He made himself a drink, tipped it into his mouth immediately to calm himself, then it was time to lay down the law to Autie Quist. When he was halfway up the stairs he remembered how it was that she'd already snuck out of the tepee once that night. He'd gone and sent her upstairs to an open window and a fast escape. It was no surprise to find her room empty. She'd even packed a suitcase. He closed the window, went downstairs again, and made another drink, a quadruple. Milo had poisoned Kevin a long time ago, now he was turning Autie's head, and he appeared to do it without even trying. What was there about Milo that drew people into his wake, to be left floundering when he moved on?

Should Ray call Bernie again and humble himself in pursuit of Autie, or should he just get drunk and forget the ungrateful little bitch? She had to be a bitch or she wouldn't have gone running after Milo that way. Bitches weren't worth the trouble. Women in general weren't worth the trouble. Look at his own wife; he'd loved her honest and true, and what did it get him? Betrayal and heartache. They were all bitches in heat, and it was the Milos of this world who stole them away and had them and murdered them, leaving decent men like Ray stranded and alone. He hadn't even looked at another woman since Holly's death. That should change. He should get himself a new wife and start a new family. He was still young enough. It never would've worked with Autie; she'd tried grafting herself onto the Kootzes too late, and the first wind that came along had dislodged her. Kevin had already fallen far from the tree and sprouted, a twisted creeper of his own design. It was definitely time to start over.

He knew it was her before he opened the door. She had a suitcase, and his stomach dropped as she set it on the floor.

"What's that for?"

"I don't want to stay there any more."

"You can't stay here."

"Why can't I?"

"Christ . . . Pretty soon I'm dead, that's why."

"Not if we go away. They can't look everywhere."

"Yes they can. Autie, please go home."

"It's not my home. I don't have a home."

Milo was exhausted. Autie Quist loved him, or thought she did, and her love blanketed common sense and logic, smothered them in pretty pink. She loved him, therefore everything would be okay. He couldn't be bothered arguing, not tonight.

The bed was a double, with plenty of room. When Autie finished in the bathroom and slid in beside Milo, he was asleep. She was very happy, because things were going her way. She hadn't known she loved Milo until an hour ago, when he was asking for Ray's gun; that's when it became clear. He didn't love her in return, not yet, but that was no problem; he just needed time to see how right she was for him, time together; proximity would breed attachment, and given further time—love. She would take him far away and bind his wounds, nurse his soul toward redemption. The faceless people wanting his blood would never catch up. Milo just needed encouragement to see beyond his immediate fear, needed a friend to help him pull a disappearing trick. Autie could make it happen.

In the morning she put an arm around Milo, but when he woke up he slipped free without comment. Autie had to admit he looked awful. Getting him away from his enemies would be the first task, then would come something tougher—getting him off cocaine. He was already in the bathroom, snorting a new line, hadn't even bothered closing the door. He sounded like someone with a bad cold. Autie knew she was the cure for what ailed him.

They breakfasted at Denny's. She tried several times to open a conversation, but Milo made it clear he wanted silence. It seemed he was deliberately being rude to give her a taste of what she was in for if she stuck around. Autie saw this as thoughtfulness on his part, letting her know the road ahead was rocky, but he could quit now, because she was smart enough to know it already. Autie Quist was no kid. Milo could be as sullen as he pleased; it made no difference to her plans. She'd never experienced this kind of certainty when she moved into the big tepee, never felt herself drawn to Ray and Kevin this way, or anyone else. Autie knew love when she found it.

"Are we going to leave town today?"

She waited for him to curl his lip and say, "We?" but he didn't. This was progress of a kind.

"Not till I talk to Kevin again. It's no good talking to Ray. He'll never listen, not if I stay around forever. Kevin I might get through to. What's he generally do on a Saturday, hang out with his friends?"

"I guess so, but I don't know where. He likes to keep everything a big secret."

"Yesterday I yelled at him. I shouldn't have done that. This time I'll keep it calm, try to make him see what I'm talking about. Why are you smiling?"

"I'm not. I think it's a good idea. If we drive around town, maybe we'll spot him. I've seen him skateboarding a few times along Main."

"When I've talked to him, I'm outa here."

Autie panicked. "With me?"

"No."

"But I want to come."

"They'd bump you off, too, so there wouldn't be any witnesses. See that guy down at the end of the counter? For all I know, he's one of them, just tailing me and waiting for a safe hit."

Autie knew he wasn't serious, but said nothing; to argue would only make him more determined to leave without her. This was going to be harder than she thought. Still, she had as much time as it took to locate Kevin in which to change Milo's mind.

One obvious possibility had to be eliminated before the search began. Milo dialed and waited, coughed a few times.

"Thunderbird Motel," said Ray.

"Is Kevin there?" asked Milo, a full octave above his usual register.

"No. Who's calling?"

"A friend."

"Is it Michael? Michael, where's Kevin? Tell him I want him home. I want him home now or his ass is gonna get kicked, you hear me? And tell your buddies to tell him."

"Okay," piped Milo, and hung up. Michael presumably was one of the Apprentices. "Not home," he said to Autie outside the booth.

They began looking, driving slowly around town. The streets today held no message for Milo, were simply places where Kevin was not. He turned the air conditioning up full blast but sweated anyway. Twice before noon they returned to the Prairie Moon for cocaine, then drove some more.

"Why don't you carry it with you?"

"And get busted by some cop who pulls me over for running a stop sign?"

"Don't run any stop signs."

"I never carry a personal supply in a car. When I deliver a load it's stashed behind the panels, out of sight. I can drive with that setup but not with coke in my pocket. If it's somewhere handy enough for me to use, it's handy enough for a cop to find."

"Was the coke you stole hidden in a car?"

"An '82 Corolla wagon. You'd be surprised how many dopers buy Japanese."

"Why didn't they kill you when you gave it back?"

"You think I just drove up and handed it over? That would've been suicide. I parked it in an overnight lot and mailed the ticket and keys express. No way would I get close to those guys. That was two weeks ago, in L.A. I've lasted this long because I kept moving around, taking the bus. They never expect you to take the bus nowadays."

"Why did you steal it in the first place?"

"Because I got mad about something. Twenty-four hours later I got unmad, but it was too late by then. You can't undo a thing like that. The good news is, it's the kind of mistake you only make once."

Laughter wheezed from his chest.

"Would you like me to drive for a little while?"

"No thanks."

They passed along Main for the seventh time.

"What was it that got you so mad you stole their coke?"

"Nothing that matters now."

"But what was it?"

"Drop it, please. All I want to do is talk to Kevin and get out of here."

"Why not wait for them to catch up? If you really think there's someone after you and you'll never get away, why not get it over with?"

Autie felt she was being bravely provocative by asking this. It might make him admit he didn't want to die, and that would be the perfect cornerstone for planned flight and a new life far away with herself. But he just smiled. "When they kill me, it'll hurt. I want to postpone that part for as long as I can. Just a born coward, I guess."

"I think if you were really scared, you wouldn't make jokes about it."

"Yeah? You're pretty bright, but sometimes you don't know too much. You know what they did to one guy they found out was trying to make a deal with the feds? They cut his foot off with a chainsaw and let him bleed to death. Just one foot. Both feet would've killed him too fast."

"You're making it up."

He braked the car suddenly and turned to her, eyes bulging, the blue vein at his temple pulsing. The planes around his mouth were rigid with bitterness and contempt. His face demanded attention.

"Look at me and tell me again I'm making it up."

Traffic backed up behind them began honking. Milo set

the car in motion again, angry breath whistling through his nose. Autie believed him. Until this moment Milo's situation had seemed fanciful, a drug-induced magnification of some minor falling-out among dopers, the same kind of self-aggrandizement practiced by teenage hoods up in Billings; in short—no big deal. But the image of a chainsaw ripping into flesh made her skin crawl. Milo's belief became hers, and in the terrible new light of her belief it was imperative that Kevin be found quickly, so they could leave, run before the shadow approaching from who-knew-where. Her stomach began to knot with fear.

At one o'clock Autie thought she saw one of the Apprentices walking across a supermarket parking lot. Milo swerved off the street and they entered the building two minutes later, straining to see above the heads of the Saturday shopping legions. Down the nearest aisle they hurried, and up the next, searching among the stacked consumables for a being as alien as themselves. After ten minutes they gave up.

"Maybe it wasn't one of them. I'm sorry."

"Forget it."

On their way back toward the checkout, Milo paused in front of the seafood counter, where a dozen lobsters observed the world from a large tank, murderous pincers manacled by thick rubber bands, antennae snipped off short. They sat in darkly mottled ranks, immobile, neutralized, seemingly fascinated by the frantically bubbling column in their midst, dumb worshipers around an effigy of oxygen. The sign above them read: PICK THE ONE YOU LIKE AND TAKE HIM HOME FOR DINNER! The sign's cheery joke on Samaritanism, in contrast with the doleful inactivity of the intended dinner guests, appealed to Milo.

"Look at these guys, hypnotized by the bubble channel, can't even grab a can of beer and live it up till they get thrown in the pot."

"It's sad," agreed Autie.

"No," said Milo, "it's funny."

It was time to eat. They drove a few blocks and pulled in for a Sonic burger. Milo could only eat half of his. Autie couldn't tell if his poor appetite was due to drugs or depression. She laid the remnants of her own burger aside out of sympathy.

"What if we can't find him?"

"I'll give it till midnight, then I'm gone."

"Good. I'm getting scared."

Milo gave her a look that said, *To be scared, you have to be involved.* Autie clearly was still on shaky ground as putative partner. When the time came, she would simply insist on placing her suitcase beside his in the trunk.

More driving around. "I'm tired," said Milo, and they returned to the motel for some instant get-up-and-go.

A Cadillac was parked outside Room 22. Milo pulled up beside it, and only recognized Iris Kincheloe behind the wheel when he'd already opened his door to get out. It was too late for retreat. He watched her leave the car and approach him. This was Bernie Swenson's doing. He'd not only told her what Milo had told him about Sharon, he'd also handed over Milo's temporary address, the interfering shit.

"Hi," said Milo, prepared to be pleasant.

"Where is she?"

"I don't know, Mrs. Kincheloe."

"You must have some idea."

"No. We split up in L.A. and I haven't seen her since."

"Yesterday you told the police you lost contact with Sharon in Albuquerque, not Los Angeles."

"Right. Albuquerque."

"I haven't heard from her once since you took her away."

"I'm sorry."

"Are you? I don't believe you're sorry about anything." Milo's helpless shrug inflamed her disbelief even more. "I think you know but you don't want to tell, just for the fun of it, just because you think it's a big joke."

"I don't know where she is, and that's the truth," said

Milo, meaning Sharon could be buried just about anywhere.

"You do know! Tell me!"

"I don't know, Mrs. Kincheloe. I can't tell you anything,
honest."

"I'm going to have you arrested as an accessory to her
disappearance."

"I wasn't around when she disappeared. I don't know
where she is, and I didn't take her away. She went because
she wanted to. I'm sorry she didn't contact you, but that's
not my fault."

"Nothing ever is to people like you. You think you can do
anything at all and get away with it."

"Look, I can't tell you what I don't know."

"You don't even care, do you?"

"Of course I do, but there's nothing I can tell you. You
want me to lie? She married a millionaire and lives in
Hawaii, okay? There's no use in you getting mad at me,
Mrs. Kincheloe. It won't change a thing, not for you, or me,
or Sharon, believe me."

"Why should I believe you? Why should anyone believe
anything you say? Sharon believed you, and where is she
today?"

"I don't know where she is today, so please don't ask me
again. I'm going inside now, so goodbye."

He went to the door of Room 22, placed his key in the
lock and turned it. Iris Kincheloe pointed at Autie. "Are
you another one who believes what he says? Keep away
from him. He made my daughter disappear and doesn't
even have the guts to admit it to me, her mother. He killed
his own mother, did he tell you that yet? Don't go anywhere
with him, please. . . ."

Milo entered the room with Autie on his heels. He
slammed the door shut and leaned against it. Iris yelled at
him through the window, "When I find her she'll tell me
what really happened! The truth always comes out in the

end!" She rapped on the glass several times, then went back to her car and drove off. Milo sagged onto the bed and closed his eyes.

"I already knew about your mom," said Autie. "It wasn't Ray or Kevin. I got told at work."

"Uh-huh."

"Is it true?"

"It was an accident."

"That's what I was told. Nobody said you did it deliberately or anything."

"Fine, now can we please not talk about it?"

"Okay. I'm sorry. Do you want the curtains closed?"

"Please."

Autie darkened the room.

"Who's Sharon?"

"My ex-girlfriend from way back."

"Do you really not know where she is?"

"Sharon's dead."

"Oh."

"No, I didn't kill her, by throwing rocks or any other way."

"I didn't say you did. Why don't you tell her mother? She's got a right to know."

"It'd only open up a whole can of worms. I haven't got time."

"But if her daughter's dead, she has to be told, don't you think?"

"When I'm out of the picture you can go ahead and tell her, but right now I'd appreciate some peace and quiet."

Autie sat and watched him in the gloom, listened to his breathing and the air conditioner's steady hum. What had Milo's last words meant? Did "out of the picture" mean gone from Callisto, or gone from this world? Either way, Milo was not including her in his long-term plans. She had only ten hours left in which to change his mind. It was discouraging. Exactly how had Sharon died, and why

275

didn't Milo want to talk about it? His silence implied a disturbing complicity, despite his denial. He was a cold wind that had blown through town, passing from nowhere to nowhere, and she had been swept up in his wake like a fallen leaf; doubt the wind and she would drift again to the ground.

This notion of helpless involvement, of her riding Milo's heedless coattails, began to annoy her. Autie had prided herself on the way she'd handled her mother's death, and on her decision coolly to insert herself into the lives of the Kootzes. She'd been in command until now. If she truly was in charge of her life, why this entanglement with Milo, a doper convinced he was entering the final phase of his time on earth, a person with guilty secrets—no, she didn't believe he'd killed Sharon; it was something else, maybe not guilt, but definitely a secret of some kind—a person with no apparent interest in herself beyond a weary tolerance. What was in this for Autie Quist? Where were her strength and independence, the things she valued? Last night she'd been convinced it was love that drew her to the underweight figure on the bed, but now her old self had to be reconciled with the new, and the answer had to be— charity. She wanted to assist Milo out of sheer charity. He needed help, and Autie was the only one prepared to offer it. Assistance was her duty as a human being, a decent person. If it was flung back in her face, that was just too bad. She had chosen to do it, chosen of her own free will. The fallen leaf hadn't fallen at all, was green foliage offering shade to Milo, flimsy but honest shelter from the heat of his own despair.

Autie felt better now. If he left without her, he left; her commitment no longer hinged on acceptance in Milo's eyes. He was not the man of any smart girl's dreams, was an addict and former mule for a dope syndicate, a bum by anyone's definition, yet he cared enough about his half-brother to wait around, giving death a chance to find him that much faster, all to have a few words, offer a little

276

brotherly advice before departing, presumably forever. He was not worth loving, but all things considered, worth assisting. Autie would not look beyond midnight. The early hours of Sunday morning were dark and distant beyond imagining.

19

NINETY MINUTES' SLEEP and four lines of coke were enough to revive Milo. They cruised the streets again.

"What's happening in the park?"

"I don't know. Some kind of exhibition."

"Kevin might be hanging around. Let's take a look."

They parked and joined the crowd. Now Milo remembered; this was the annual festival for the promotion of local art. He'd attended one or two in the past, and it appeared that nothing had changed. Here were the same old wind spinners, plastic Pepsi bottles with sides split and splayed to catch the breeze while they hung by their necks; the same miniature windmills of sheet metal, gingham dolls, hand-painted duck decoys, string art, and Indian chiefs on black velvet; the same tepid watercolor landscapes and clumsy pottery; the same displays of wheat weaving, the embroidered homilies and clocks set in irregular slabs of overpolished wood; the same renditions of owl-eyed weeping children; the same mincing portraits of Jesus, lips primly pursed, eyes moist with compassion, a Technicolor heart leaping from his breast. Milo wondered if his favorite crap was represented this year, and it was, a whole eight-by-fifteen-foot pegboard display. He steered

Autie toward it. There they were, the pinnacle of native art in Kansas—the painted saw blades.

"Pretty neat, huh? Really grabs you by the throat."

Mountain waterfalls and picturesque farms were represented sparingly; the eternal theme of blade painting is the desert sunset. Lurid skies screamed over impossible Arizonas, flagrantly afire, threatening to scorch the tips of Gumby-green cacti, each of which had two arms, not more, not less. Purple mesas battlemented perspectiveless horizons, and above them hung the black flying M of the vulture, flanked by two or three lower-case cousins. The whitened skulls of longhorn steers littered these fantastic scenes, eye sockets disgorging a rattlesnake or lizard, broken teeth literally biting the dust. Milo couldn't picture western heroes riding off into these sunsets of bloodiest red; only Death could stay in the saddle here, a leering skeleton on a pale horse of bones. Whether on eight-foot whipsaws, traditional carpenter's blade, or circular buzz saw, the scene was the same, the desert dreamings of a disturbed child. Focal point for the entire display was a buzz-saw disk three feet across, the glare from its sinking sun splashed from the central peg to the backswept serrations of its circumference in orange and yellow, purple and red, a porthole view of nightfall in hell, framed by wicked cutting edges.

The creator of these objects sat in a canvas chair beside them, two hundred and twenty sweating pounds in a tank top and Bermuda shorts, one meaty fist hiding a can of non-diet Slice. He looked at Milo and Autie through sunglasses of deepest black.

"You can twang 'em, too," he said, "the long ones, anyway."

"I bet," said Milo, and they walked on. It had cheered him to experience a little jolt of recognition as he examined the blades. To know that something as awful as this was still being presented to the public, as it had been when he was small, granted an absurd sense of continuity to his return home. The blades would be here when he was gone, their appeal to tastelessness undiminished by any change in the public's appreciation of fine things. Garbage is forever, thought Milo.

"There's one of them!"

Autie was pointing across the crowds. Milo saw a dread-locked boy disappear behind the band rotunda. They caught up with him as he paused to watch a five-minute-portrait artist at work.

"Hi. I'm looking for my brother, Kevin Kootz."

The boy turned. His T-shirt declared EVERYTHING SUX. Milo was inclined to agree. "Huh?" said the boy.

"I'm looking for Kevin. You know where he is? It's important."

"Kevin who?"

"Is this guy one of them or not?"

"Yes," said Autie. "He came into the Seven-Eleven one time."

"Are you Michael, by any chance?"

"Yeah, so what."

"So don't be a dickhead, Michael. Where's Kevin? I have to talk to him."

"How the fuck should I know?"

"Do me a favor and go find him. You know the places he hangs out. Tell him Milo wants to see him. Tell him it's urgent. I'm at the same motel, same room as before. Got that?"

"Fuck off."

Milo smacked him lightly across the face. Michael yelped with alarm. Several people turned to watch, and for their benefit Milo said, "Don't use bad language. It's disgusting in a kid your age." In a softer voice he added, "Tell him he can have the thing he wanted yesterday. He'll know what I mean. Got it this time, Michael, huh?"

Milo sent him on his way with a shove. "Little prick," he said to Autie. "Are they all like that?"

"That's the first time I heard one talk."

They were being stared at.

"Let's go. I've had all the art I can handle for one day."

They watched TV in Milo's room until dusk. Milo looked constantly at his watch and made many trips to the bathroom, sometimes for bodily elimination. "Tension gets me in the kidneys." He paced back and forth. "I'm not waiting around after twelve, I mean it. Switch channels, will you? I can't stand this shit."

Beyond the drawn curtains, light began to lessen by degrees. The yammering inanities of the TV were reduced by Milo to silent mouthings. His suitcase was already packed. The waiting was unendurable. "Where the fuck is he!" Milo peeked out at the parking lot from time to time. The moon was full; he could see almost as clearly as in daylight. He was in the bathroom snorting lines when the knock finally came. "Go let him in!" Autie opened the door. Iris Kincheloe stood outside.

"Is Milo here?"

"No."

Autie surprised herself with the lie's fleetness from brain to mouth.

"I thought I heard him just now. He is here, isn't he?"

"No."

She began closing the door. Iris slapped a hand against the paneling to keep it open. "He's here and I want to talk to him!" Woman and girl pushed from opposite sides, equally matched. "Milo . . ." pleaded Autie, and he came sprinting from the bathroom, energy and purpose radiating from his nose, and slammed into the door with his shoulder. The lock clicked. Milo was sliding the chain home to ensure there could be no further intrusion when the first of the shots blew splinters from the door at hip height. He backed away fast, then danced sideways as five more shots blasted through the wood and plowed into the carpet and rear wall. Iris Kincheloe had a .357 Magnum out there. Autie was behind the bed.

"You okay?"

"Yes."

While Iris reloaded (if that was what the silence outside denoted), Milo tried to think what he might do if she managed to get inside the room. He could think of nothing, hoped the motel manager had dialed 911 already. There were no further shots through the door, but Milo and Autie stayed in hiding till a siren could be heard approaching; then Milo hid his depleted bag of cocaine between the bedsheets. Red and blue light flashed across the curtains. Car doors slammed and the siren died away to a plaintive moan, then stopped. A knock at the door.

"You folks okay in there?"

Milo opened it. "Yeah." The cops were as young as himself. He looked around for Iris, saw her standing beside her Cadillac, sobbing. Other guests were coming out of their rooms, reassured by the arrival of the cruiser. He pointed. "That's her. She's crazy." One cop knelt to pick up a handgun from the doorway (a .357; Milo had been right) while his partner approached its owner. The gun dangled by its trigger guard from the cop's finger. It had customized pearl grips; a lady's Magnum. "She was loaded for bear," said the cop. "She doesn't like me," explained Milo, but it clearly was not enough.

"This is getting to be a little ridiculous, don't you think?"

"True."

Milo and Bernie stared at each other once again across a desk at the station.

"Let's hear your side of it."

Milo's story lasted less than a minute.

"Wait here."

He waited alone for almost half an hour, then Bernie returned.

"You want to press charges against her?"

"No, just keep her away from me."

"She's not in the building. Left five minutes ago with her attorney."

"Rich people don't stay in jail cells overnight, huh?"

"Generally speaking. If she had've plugged you, it'd be different, but she only killed the door."

Bernie knew that Iris Kincheloe was a close friend of Judge Braddock's, in addition to which she retained the services of the county's sharpest lawyer. Two phone calls had been all it took to free her on bail. Bernie called it country club law.

"Can I go, too?"

"In a minute. You recall me giving you some advice about Autie?"

"What about it?"

"If she hadn't been with you, she wouldn't have been in danger of getting shot, know what I mean?"

"She came over to see me. I didn't invite her."

"She'd go away if you told her."

"Why should I tell her?"

"Because I'm telling you."

"I think there's something in the Constitution or some-place about freedom of association in this country. I think I'm right about that."

"And there's an unwritten law that says kids who aren't already screwed up by associating with the wrong people have a better chance of staying that way if they don't start. This is personal advice I'm giving you. Autie's already been sent back to the T-bird in a black-and-white. You leave her there, and if she comes around visiting again, you tell her to beat it. I don't want her mixing with you, Milo. You're bad for things that are good."

"Can I go now?"

"With pleasure."

When Milo walked out, Bernie was left wondering how much of his own behavior was dictated by guilt over having slept with Milo's mother, and how much by resentment and jealousy from wishing to sleep with Milo's girlfriend, if that's what Autie Quist was. Life would be simpler without Milo in town. Bernie probably wouldn't get anywhere with Autie, probably wouldn't even try, but at least he still had Milo's nifty Beretta, no mean prize.

Milo hadn't been offered a cruiser to return him to the motel, so he caught a cab. When he arrived, he found Autie waiting by the bullet-scarred door.

"I thought they gave you an escort home to Ray."

"They did, but as soon as I got out of the car they drove away, didn't even wait to see if I went inside, so I didn't."

"I just love cops, don't you?"

Autie smiled. Milo seemed in a good mood, considering. They went inside and saw the note that had been pushed under the door. "Uh-oh. Bet the management wants me to change rooms while they patch up the bullet holes." He unfolded the paper. "Balfour Tower. Kevin." There was nothing else.

"What's Balfour Tower?"

"An apartment block that got burned out a bunch of years back. I guess they still haven't torn it down. Four stories high. Some tower. Weird place for a meeting."

He retrieved his coke from the bed, picked up his suit-case, and waited for Autie to pick up hers. "It's a liberated age, lady. You tote your own bags nowadays."

"I can come with you?"

"Sure you can," said Milo. He felt reckless. Fuck Bernie Swenson.

They stowed their baggage in the Firebird's trunk and drove away from the Prairie Moon. Milo felt more than recklessness inside himself; he felt elation ripple through him like a flash flood. Unaccountably, his spirits were fly-ing, and he hadn't snorted powder in over an hour. Where had this turnaround come from—and when, precisely, had it begun? Milo backtracked carefully to the moment he could first recall feeling good—the moment he saw Autie waiting by his door. It was simple; it was obvious. All day he'd treated her like shit, but his nerves must've been stretched tight as rubber bands during the search for Kevin. Now that Kevin was within reaching distance, he felt relaxed. The close shave with Iris Kincheloe's Magnum had sent a healthy burst of adrenaline through his system, too. That was it, a threefold kick in the pants that had shaken him from spiritual torpor—Kevin, Kincheloe, and Autie Quist. He felt fucking great! He would defy Bernie and take Autie away. Ray would hate him for doing that, too; another incentive. Fuck them both; no one told Milo Ginty what to do. And the forces he'd been fleeing? They wouldn't catch him now. It had been two weeks already, and an old trail is a cold trail. They'd lost him, or he them, whichever, and provided he was careful the situation could be maintained indefinitely. Suddenly the night air was thick with the scent of freedom, the tires humming a highway song. Milo knew everything was going to be okay.

He turned to Autie. "Thank you."

"For what?"

"For staying around. I'm okay now. I can't describe it, I just know I'm okay."

"Because you found Kevin."

"That and some other stuff. Listen, I want to tell you something. You deserve to know. I already told you Sharon's dead, but the thing is, it's connected in a screwy kind of way with me ripping off the dope. I saw how she died. I wasn't there, but I saw it happen in a snuff movie. You know what that is? That's a movie where real people get killed real dead in front of the cameras. It's supposed to be a big thrill for certain kinds of sicko perverts to watch a movie like that. They get hold of people no one's going to miss, addicts, illegals, whatever, and tell them they can be a star in a sex flick, but after the cameras get rolling they start torturing them instead of screwing them, and then they kill them. They get the whole thing on film. That's how Sharon died, in a snuff movie. They put a cattle prod up her and electrocuted her to death from inside. They all laughed. I was down the back of the room where they were showing this flick on the VCR. I'd just collected a big shipment and was heading for the door, then I looked at the TV and recognized Sharon. I hadn't seen her in a year, eighteen months. She was into heroin when we split up. She looked bad, but it was her. They weren't torturing her yet, just doing things that were supposed to be sexy. You could tell she was stoned in the closeups. She didn't know what was happening. Then they started in with the cattle prod. It took maybe five minutes to kill her. Everyone in the room was laughing their head off, because when they put the electricity through her she jumped around like she was enjoying it. It was just the sickest thing. I felt like throwing up. Everyone in that room thought it was the funniest show since *Mork and Mindy*. And I worked for them. I worked for assholes who thought watching someone die on TV was funny. That's why I stole the dope, to punish them for laughing. Then I chickened out and gave it back. Some hero, huh? I blew the whole thing. Those guys still don't know why I did it. They wouldn't understand even if I spelled it out for them. That's what happened. That's what this whole thing is about."

"You must have loved her to do that."

"No. Believe it or not, all I ever did was like her, and not even for very long. That's what makes what I did kind of crazy, even to me. Anyway, I wanted to tell you. You should know where I'm coming from. Anyone who's capable of fucking things up that bad is capable of doing it again someday. You think about everything I've said, and the fact that there's cocaine in this car and I like it, really *like* that stuff. You think about it and let me know if you want me to drop you off someplace."

Autie thought about it.

"Promise me one thing?"

"What thing?"

"Promise me you'll write Sharon's mother and tell her. It's better to find out someone you love is dead than not to know anything at all, ever."

"Okay."

She couldn't believe he'd turned himself around so fast. He was utterly different, almost flip. Milo's sudden acceptance of her was more startling than the story he told. He'd revealed to her what no one else in the world knew. It was nothing less than absolute trust, and if that was how he felt, then maybe it would be worthwhile letting herself love him again, but cautiously this time. The golden smile flashing in the dashboard light was almost too beguiling.

"Where are we going to go?"

"Who cares. We'll talk to Kevin, then hit the road."

Should she request a stop-off at the Thunderbird to thank Ray for his hospitality? It might interrupt Milo's newfound flow of confidence. Milo was on a roll, and Autie didn't want to be the one who fouled it up—not now, when the thing she'd been wanting was so tantalizingly close. The last two days had been without precedent in her life, and the cause of it all was right beside her, stiff-arming the wheel like a getaway driver, trying hard not to exceed the speed limit. It had been crazy all along, out of control. Milo's mission of atonement had gone haywire from the start, and Autie held only faint hopes that the meeting with Kevin would resolve anything, but at least he could leave Callisto with one good thing—herself.

"Almost there. How about that little turkey, slipping a note under the door like Tom Sawyer. I'm surprised he didn't tell us to show up at midnight—the witching hour, I bet he'd call it. You okay?"

"Yes."

"Good."

The smile again. Autie returned it. Everything would work out fine.

"There it is, Balfour Tower."

He parked at the end of an unlighted street. The building's concrete flanks were washed ghostly gray by moonlight, every empty window seeming to release a black flame, frozen as it licked upward. The front façade had fallen away completely, left room-sized pigeonholes of deep shadow. They left the car and climbed broad steps of chipped concrete to a high wire fence long since snipped and rolled aside to allow access. Further steps led to what once had been an entrance. They passed through this to the charred remnants of a lobby, designed for spaciousness and light, filled with rubble and darkness. A staircase of concrete angled up and back to the floor above. The blackened walls rose to deeper blackness, the rear wall beyond the reach of moonbeams. Autie was sure she could smell shit.

"Kevin!"

"I don't like this place."

"Me either. Kevin! Get out here where I can see you or I'm gone! I mean it!"

"Up the stairs!" came a faint cry from above.

"No way! Get your ass down here with a light! Right now, Kevin, or I'm outa here! I'm counting down now. Ten! . . . Nine! . . . Eight! . . . ."

"Okay! Okay!"

There was considerable scuffling, then pallid lamplight began inching down the stairwell, accompanied by echoing footsteps, hesitantly placed.

"Move it, Kevin! I'm not waiting forever!"

"I'm coming! It's not easy!"

The lamplight turned a corner, became brighter, and the sounds of descent lost their eerie resonance. Shadows lurched along walls streaked by fire. Now the lamp was being carried down the first flight of stairs, and Autie could see her surroundings properly. The whole place was nothing but scorched surfaces of concrete, a wasted shell. A figure turned the angle in the staircase, flashlight in hand, came slowly down the final steps and stood before them.

"Hi, Kevin. Do we get invited up for cocktails?"

"Go where I go. Stay away from the edge."

"What's wrong with right here?"

"I've got something to show you. It's up there."

He preceded them up three flights. The stairs were open, the handrails and banisters destroyed. A careless step could lead swiftly to the stairwell's concrete floor thirty feet below. No one spoke during the ascent. Kevin's flashlight revealed glimpses of graffiti on every smoke-blackened wall, sprayed in yellow and orange for contrast; monstrous horned heads, cabalistic symbols, indecipherable slogans, and the number 666.

A short walk along a corridor brought them to a room laid waste by flame, shielded from the street. A camper's lamp burned brightly on the floor. Three more boys stood waiting. The scrawlings outside were here brought to poisonous flower. Murals of calculated crudity were spread across the walls. Gigantic cocks and screaming mouths collided with urgent frenzy; staring eyes with the slit pupils of demons oversaw an arsenal of edged weapons biting into human flesh; blood in abundance showered crooked pentacles and inverted crosses. Empty spray cans littered the corners like spent shell casings, the detritus of whatever battle the Apprentices imagined they were fighting.

"Aaah," said Milo, "the bridal suite. We'll take it."

Autie could have hugged him for his cool. This place was awful not just because of its deliberate ugliness, but because it was the chosen playpen of young boys. They stood mute and unfriendly, barbaric hair leaping from their heads in the frigid gaslight.

"Okay, where's the thing you wanted to show me?"

"First, where's the gun? Mikey said you'd give it to me."

"Ask Bernie Swenson. He took it."

"Bull."

"No bull, also no gun. We need to talk. I'm getting out of

here for good and I want to talk before I go, just you and me."

"You said you'd give me the gun."

"You don't need a gun, Kevin. I don't need one either. Nobody needs guns. I don't have it. Are you gonna talk to me anyway?"

"You said you'd give it to me."

"Is that a tape loop in your mouth or something? You don't need a fucking gun, but you for sure need some good advice, and you other guys need an earful, too. All this," he indicated the walls, the room, "is shit. You feed yourselves shit and you talk shit and do shitty things because your brains are shit. Nobody's listening to you, not in this world or the next or anyplace in between. Forget it. Show me the devil and I'll eat my shoes. Get serious for fuck's sake."

"If you don't give it to me, you'll be sorry."

"Do what? Listen, shithead, I'm taking a chance just hanging around to pass on a few words of wisdom here. Maybe you didn't notice those bullet holes in my door. There are people out to get me, little brother, and the more time I spend talking to you, the closer they get, so listen up!"

"You did it yourself. You've still got the gun and you said I could have it!"

"I don't have time for any more crap. Are you gonna listen, huh?"

"Fuck you."

"Hey, fuck you, too, and that goes for the rest of you broomstick boys. I feel sorry for you, I really do. Comic books and movies, that's all you know, so you don't know shit. You're garbageheads, all of you. Wake up!"

"Show it to him," said one of the Apprentices. "Let him see it."

Kevin took something from inside his jacket and held it toward Milo—a Ken doll, plastic face smiling, plastic hair immaculate, slim body dressed in a tuxedo, the closest approximation Kevin could find to the dark suit and white shirt Milo wore. Ken was Milo, and through Ken's heart was a nail long enough to exit below his left shoulder blade. Milo stared at the doll, allowed its significance slowly to penetrate his thoughts. Autie watched his face. All the aggression, all the anger left it; his expression became blank, then turned to sadness as Milo saw his time had been wasted. Kevin was lost, would never let himself be called home. The lure of the unreal had been too strong, the burden of the past too great. Kevin had surrendered himself to the myth of the omnipotent Other, the dark persona whispering promises through a jack-o'-lantern grin.

Milo grabbed the doll, took hold of his blandly smiling counterpart and held it close, saw the thing through Kevin's eyes, as talisman of urban witchcraft, a toy transformed from anemic clotheshorse to voodoo simulacrum. Kevin had backed away when Milo snatched it from him, now shared one side of the room with his fellow Apprentices.

"Very interesting, Kevin," said Milo. "Very pathetic. Got anything else to show me before I go?"

Kevin said nothing. Milo tossed the doll over his shoulder, consigned it to darkness. "So you want me dead. Why use a doll? Why not do the job right and stick with what you know. Why not use a *stone*. You're good at that."

"Fuck you."

Milo held out his hand. "Flashlight," he said. Kevin threw it to him. "Goodbye, Kevin." No answer. To Autie he said, "Come on," and they left the room, followed the corridor, made their way carefully down the gaping stairwell to the ground floor. Milo left the flashlight there, its beam washing the ceiling, and they walked to the car.

He drove slowly away. Autie waited for confirmation of what she'd guessed; the clue had been straightforward enough. But Milo sat hunched over the wheel and said nothing. Ten minutes' driving brought them to the edge of the Callisto High football field. The car was steered to the curb and parked. Milo rolled his window all the way down for air, then leaned back in his seat, eyes closed.

"Did Kevin kill your mom?"

"Yes."

He hadn't meant to say it, hadn't meant the truth to slip out so easily. The fact that it had done so told Milo he'd wanted to be rid of it all along, and if there was one person he could tell, it was Autie.

"I covered for him. He was only eleven. Maybe there are people who do good deeds and don't want any reward, but I'm not one of them. I wanted Kevin to think I'm terrific for what I did, and what's he do instead? Puts a nail through my heart. Maybe I deserve it for expecting a reward. I fucked him up. He's not Kevin any more and never will be again. It's like ripping off the dope. Nothing works out the way I wanted. That's the part that really gets me; it's my fault. My version of hell is having to slap my face forever and say, 'You goofed. You goofed. You goofed. . . .' "

He was slapping himself. Autie put out her hand to stop him, and Milo's face creased with grief. He began to cry. He couldn't stop; his whole body shook. He held the wheel to steady himself. Autie kept her hand on his arm, relieved that she allowed it. She wanted to do more, hold all of him, but didn't dare for fear of upsetting whatever impulses and balances were wrestling for supremacy within him. This was something between Milo and Milo, and no assistance would alter the outcome. A hand on his arm would have to be enough. He felt like a straw man, insubstantial, held together by string, a Kansas scarecrow, and when at last he laid his head on the wheel and ceased to shake, she was unable to tell if his calm represented victory or defeat.

Eventually, he raised his head, branded above the eyes with the wheel's imprint. "I need to walk," he said, voice congested with the residue of extreme emotion. "Want to come?" It was a plea as much as an invitation. They left the car and wandered onto the football field. Milo had never attended a game. The field was smooth with summer neglect, the grass parched, unmarked by cleats. They walked by mutual consent to the very center, and there stopped. Every wooden bench around the field was clearly delineated by moonlight, edges ruler-straight, a four-sided stack of unpopulated horizontal lines. Light pylons at the corners of the field stood blackly latticed against the sky. Autie could hear dogs barking in the near distance.

"I have to start all over," said Milo flatly. "Everything has to start from scratch. All the old stuff has to go." He wasn't looking at Autie, was talking to the moon. His tilted profile was not noble, but its vulnerability suggested to Autie a kind of wan doggedness. Milo was a reed beaten down by rain, summoning the strength to rise again. Here where the Callisto Cougars fought for supremacy over out-of-towners, Milo found heart, drew it down from the moon and from deep inside himself, and from the girl two steps away. In the forty-eight hours of their unusual acquaintance, they'd barely touched, but the new Milo wanted to feel, to sense, to understand through his skin the true nature of his kinship with Autie, and so he took those two steps and held her, and from there it was a brief descent to the ground and hasty, uncomfortable immersion in each other.

Autie Quist had been penetrated by two boys in Montana, and in both instances felt herself unchanged. Her coupling with Milo, while not achieving any significant sexual arousal, at least granted her a sense of accomplishment; this was what she had wanted, and Milo finally had wanted it, too. Lying between her thighs, his body surprisingly weightless, Milo was at peace, both donor and recipient of the great gift. Their bodies were still secured by the flimsiest anchor of flesh as they lay unmoving and breathed the odor of dying grass.

The dogs were closer now; Autie heard them through the steady breathing of the man on her chest. His exhalations were warm against her neck, and she imagined a glowing spot there, pulsing redly in the region of the jugular. The pressure of his body was no more than could comfortably be borne, and she left him as he was, warming his neck with her own breath. Autie was sufficiently exhausted to ignore the prickling of turf beneath her buttocks, but not so relaxed she could continue to ignore the dogs. They were definitely nearer, their yelpings a staccato chorus, but it was not until Autie heard the panting from their throats and the scrabbling of paws that she realized how very close they were.

"Jesus!" yelled Milo as the first, a Labrador, leapt clean over his back and continued running. The pack's leader had been audacious; the lesser mutts divided and ran either side of the bodies on the grass. There were at least a dozen, most with collars, but each had been liberated from ownership by the moon and their raffish leader. Canines in delirium, they ran down invisible game, tongues lolling for the kill, for uncanned flesh, hot and bloody. Milo and Autie stood and watched them reach the field's north side, turn in a wide arc and come racing back toward them.

"What are they doing?"

"They're nuts, I think."

The Labrador ran full pelt at them, panting hoarsely, legs stretched like a Greyhound's, name tag jingling, and the pack came hurtling in its wake. Naked below the waist, Milo and Autie felt their skin creep in anticipation of ripping fangs. Milo in particular experienced a sense of vulnerability bordering on panic; he could either shield his genitals and hope the dogs ran on by, or raise his arms to frighten them off and expose himself even more. In the few seconds left in which to decide, he placed himself in front of Autie.

"Haaaaaaaaaaaaaaaaaaaaahhhhh!!!"

His arms flew out like switchblades. Unnerved, the Labrador leaned sideways and flew past without slowing, pulled the rest as if by gravitation in a curved path around the howling apparition that moments before hád been lying passively on the ground. A boxer, a mongrel, and lastly a Pomeranian on ludicrously short legs, then they were gone.

"They must've got moon madness or something. You ever see anything like it before?"

"No."

They looked at each other. Milo, still with his tie and socks on, was a figure from a bedroom farce. Autie began laughing. Milo looked down and pulled a wry face. "These legs do not belong on the fifty-yard line." Autie's laugh became a howl, and she lowered herself to her knees. Milo laughed a little, then stopped; did Autie really think it was so funny, or was her laughter walking the line between merriment and hysteria? Now she'd fallen onto her side, laughing still. Her face, clearly visible by moonlight, was unrecognizable, and Milo realized she had, in the two days he'd known her, been somber most of the time. He who had been its cause now had banished it, with the aid of some leashless dogs. It was a modest breakthrough for them both. He helped her to her feet.

"You know what we should do now?"

"No, what?"

"We should put our pants on and get out of here."

The option of saying goodbye to Ray was raised again by Autie, and again rejected. It would only complicate things. She'd write him from somewhere else, thanking him for the temporary home he'd provided, wishing him well for the future. She could write it when Milo wrote to Sharon's mother, and they could mail them together, their last act of obligation to anyone in Callisto. It was all planned out in Autie's head. They would find a hideaway somewhere across the plains, the mountains, the deserts, the wide open warren of bolt holes that is America.

"We need some eats."

"Okay."

They stopped at the All-Nite Convenience Store on Walnut, bought snacks and Pepsis and returned to the car. Milo got behind the wheel. Autie was just about to get in, then stopped.

"Did you pick up the Hershey bars?"

"I thought you did."

"Back in a minute."

Milo drummed the wheel. A black pickup was parked a few spaces down. It hadn't been there when they arrived. He could see two men inside the cab. One of them lit a cigarette. The lighter's flame was too small to illuminate much beyond a pursed mouth and thick mustache, but before the first cloud of smoke spilled from the open window Milo knew the men had followed him here, were waiting till he drove away before making their move. Milo's car and the pickup were the only vehicles in the lot. Why would they park in front of a store and not go inside? They were waiting, he knew it just by looking. The nearest man, the smoker, was looking at Milo, too, Milo could tell by his silhouette. These were the guys, the ones he'd crammed way back in his head these last few hours, the ones sent to kill him. Their black pickup had a V-8 engine under the hood; plenty of horses. Could the Firebird outrun them?

His stomach lurched with raw fear. His death was close now, and its inevitability made him want to vomit. Why had he thought for even a minute he could possibly get away? It must've been Autie who messed up his mind, innocent Autie, who would never understand. She couldn't be involved with this, couldn't share his dying, was not a part of his transgression, now would never be part of his redemption, hope for which had come too late. Milo's life these past two weeks had been a downward curve with one joyous blip in its tail end before the inexorable descent resumed. Keep a tight asshole, he advised himself, and turned the key.

When Autie came out, the parking lot was bare. She stood there until the chocolate began melting in her hand.

20

IT HAD BEEN REGISTERED in Ray's name, so the Firebird's destruction was reported to him early Sunday morning. A Santa Fe Railroad freight had plowed into it at a level crossing west of town at a little after eleven, Saturday night. The body inside was mangled beyond immediate recognition. Two suitcases were found in the trunk, plus a small quantity of cocaine. An autopsy revealed the driver's blood contained substantial traces of the drug. The Santa Fe engineers swore they hadn't seen the car until they were almost on top of it; the Firebird had been parked across the tracks with its headlights off. The car had been dragged more than a mile, and its trunk and cabin had to be opened with acetylene torches. Ray went upstairs to tell Autie, who had drifted home at around twelve. She'd refused to speak to him, had locked herself in her room and cried. Now she would listen, and maybe talk.

Milo was buried a short distance from Lowell and Judith and Holly. They were Kootzes; Milo remained a lone Ginty. Bernie received permission from Ray to attend the funeral, and he noticed, in his cop's way, that Autie wouldn't talk to Kevin, wouldn't even stand near him. Kevin himself appeared stunned. All his sneering cockiness had gone. Autie was like a twanging wire, Ray like a man who has seen his predictions come true and can't help but look smug about it. Two days after Milo's death, Autie had come to Bernie and asked if there were bullets in his body. He told her no, then asked why there should be. She told him everything she knew, excluding Kevin's responsibility for his mother's death. That secret was for the big tepee. Autie had wondered if Milo was running from her, or from the men he was convinced were hunting him. There was no proof either way, but Milo's car had been facing Callisto, not turned away from it, when the train hit. Maybe he'd been chased beyond the railroad tracks, killed, then brought back and left in the freight's path to destroy any indications of murder. Bernie confirmed that included on the long list of Milo's injuries was a broken neck. It could have happened that way. She would never know for sure. When she was gone, Bernie wondered if Milo's confiscated Beretta might have saved him.

Was it the doll that killed Milo? Kevin had pondered the question with the Apprentices, but the more they insisted it had, the less he was inclined to believe it. The question nagged him, wouldn't let go. Milo crowded his thoughts until it seemed his head would burst like a dropped pumpkin. Last night Kevin had seen the Apprentices again, and one of them suggested they use a doll "to off your old man so the motel's yours. We could turn it into a freaky camp for initiates, you know? It'd be wild! Use a doll." Kevin said, "No," and the Apprentice had said, "Why the fuck not? It worked on your brother, didn't it?" Kevin had punched him without warning to the boy or to himself, then walked away. He didn't think he'd be seeing much more of the Apprentices.

Now the coffin was gone, lost to sight. It was over.

One week after the funeral Kevin had his head shaved, left his dreadlocks on the barbershop floor. He left feeling naked, diminished. Breezes played across his scalp as he examined himself in a storefront window. His head had the sex appeal of a plucked chicken. He was satisfyingly ugly.

Kevin went home, took one of Ray's bottles from its hiding place, and shut himself away to get drunk. Some things could not be faced sober—Autie Quist, for example. The looks she gave him, when she bothered looking in his direction at all, were filled with scorn. She knew the truth, wanted him to wash Milo clean with a confession, and Kevin wanted to, he really did, but it had been so long since that day by the lake, so long a time spent denying his memory of what happened, how could he turn around now and tell the truth? Couldn't they see how he felt about Milo? Didn't his baldness say everything that needed to be said? Autie hadn't even commented on it, and all Ray did when he saw the exposed scalp was shake his head in weary disbelief. They hadn't figured out that his hair had hidden the truth, and now that it was gone the facts were there to be seen by anyone, like they were tattooed ear to ear. It hadn't worked, so now he'd have to get drunk and confess the way Autie wanted him to.

He drank through the late afternoon and early evening. No one came looking for him. Why should they? Why should anyone give a shit about a coward and a liar? He deserved what he got—namely, nothing. His black room screamed at him from base to apex, the paraphernalia of devil worship about as potent as a novelty shop rubber mask. It was pathetic. How could he have believed any of that crap? Milo had tried to steer him toward the light, and Kevin had put a nail through a voodoo doll to freak him out, and Milo had died before midnight. There was no connection, Kevin knew that, but the sequence of events left a powerful impression of culpability. Tomorrow he would begin painting his room white, but that wouldn't be enough. A moral cleansing was required. His mouth must speak the words that would set him free. But Kevin couldn't do it alone, and so he pulled at the bottle.

When had he last been happy, really happy? He tried to remember, ran his life backward, week by month by year, until he came to the time of the partial eclipse. That had been a magical day. No one else had seen the scattering of little shapes on the ground beneath the trees, and no one could explain them to him. Milo had been the only one who believed his story. The precise sensation of wonder that had filled Kevin as he stared at the sun patterns had become blurred by time and succeeding layers of memory, but with effort he was able to locate and replay the moment. It made him want to cry, seeing those little golden shapes dancing on the insides of his eyelids. Crescents, he'd called them then, but really they were scimitars, cruel blades that fell invisibly through the air every hour and minute and second to flay the flesh from liars' bones, to cut and cut and cut down to the marrow, down to where the truth is held, eternally pink and new, inviolate and unchanging. The air around him was thick with them, reducing his body to component atoms in pursuit of the true thing Kevin had made a lie.

It was a slow night at the desk. Tuesdays usually were. Ray went to the kitchen for a drink. He found Kevin there, nose inches away from the erasable Things To Remember board on the wall, brow creased with concentration, fingers working the stub of grease pencil. Ray sat and waited for him to finish, preferring not to drink in front of his son, but Kevin seemed to be taking forever. Ray watched the back of his neck, noticed how vulnerable the exposed cords were, how thin and white, how pathetically egglike the cranium above. Kevin hadn't turned or spoken since Ray walked in, but Ray was used to being ignored. Soon Kevin would finish whatever list he was making and leave, and Ray could have his drink.

The pencil fell and swung on its string. Kevin was all through writing but didn't move, just stood there staring at what he'd written. Ray thought maybe he was on drugs. "What's the problem?" he asked, but Kevin neither moved nor spoke, kept his back to his father, face to the board. "What's wrong, you paralyzed or something?" Kevin's forehead touched the board. He leaned against it and his shoulders began to jerk. What was he laughing about? Ray felt the irritation he always felt when Kevin did something unpredictable or puzzling. "What's the matter with you anyway? What's the big joke?" Kevin wouldn't turn around or quit, and that brought Ray to his feet. He was sick and tired of being mocked in his own tepee. He went to Kevin and shoved his face at the boy's leaning profile. Kevin was crying. Ray could smell booze on his breath; had Kevin been invading his private stash? "What the hell's the matter with you, huh?" Kevin spun away from him, went and stood in the kitchen corner with his back to the room like an overgrown naughty boy. Ray read what he'd written on the board.

I KILLED MOM. MILO DIDN'T.
I'M VERY VERY VERY VERY VERY
VERY VERY VERY VERY VERY VERY
VERY SORRY.

Ray read it several times. "Is this true?" Kevin nodded his bald head. Ray didn't know what to do. He wandered out of the kitchen, went to the office and turned on the NO VACANCY sign, then locked the door. How could it be true? How could it? He went back to the kitchen just as Autie came downstairs. She saw his face and followed him through. Ray pointed to the board. "Look at that." Autie read it. "I know," she said. "Milo told me." They both looked at Kevin's back. Ray was furious. "Why didn't someone tell *me!*" No one had an answer.

Autie put her hand on Kevin's shoulder, and the impression of solidarity between them infuriated Ray even more. He'd been locked out, as always. Why the big secret? He'd

been made a fool of. All these years he'd hated Milo unnec-
essarily. All the heartache and resentment he'd suffered
since Holly's death had been misdirected. It was all a big
mistake, because he'd been kept in the dark. Why? Milo
had gone to his grave unjustifiably laden with Ray's hatred,
and Kevin had let it happen. And Ray just bet that trying to
cope with the lie was what had turned Kevin from golden
boy to demon child. Milo had told Autie, but Autie hadn't
told Ray. What did Autie have against him? Only his rejec-
tion of Milo. The wheel of requital and consequence had
spun madly out of control, and it wasn't Ray's fault! He
couldn't be blamed for any of it. He hadn't known the facts.
But now that he did, Ray was helpless, unmanned. What
did it all mean? He had to talk with someone who could
help him figure out the tangle of misconceptions and mangled truth. Autie and Kevin were talking softly together,
excluding him still. He went to the phone and dialed.

"Bernie? It's Ray."

They met at Frankie's Pizza Place. Frankie's was licensed.
With a beer apiece, they sat at one of the many empty
tables. Tuesday was a slow night here, too. Every table was
covered by blowups under glass from Frankie's graduation
yearbook for 1967. There they were, all the smiling faces,
unmarked by eighteen years of unlife, the girls crowned
with bell-shaped hairdos, most of the boys still sporting
brushbacks from the fifties, occasional bold souls daring to
wear a Beatle cut.

"Look at this," said Bernie. "Margie Roszak. Remember
her?"

"No."

"I had it bad for Margie. I think she married some guy
from Missouri. Jesus, here's Mickey Roper. Him you've got
to remember, skinny guy with skinny teeth? Ed Madden,
yeah. Jeannie Bruce, I remember her. This one I can't
place. Who's on your side?"

Ray looked down. Unbelievably, his own features stared

back, unsmiling, wary, a less handsome version of Kevin. How had he been able to see through those bangs, and was that a zit on his nose? The portraits surrounding his own were barely glanced at. That one there, that was him, Ray Kootz, eighteen years old when the shutter clicked. Ellie Quist was already pregnant with Autie. Judith was still alive. Holly was married to her Chicago Irishman, and Milo was three years old. None of it was reflected in those hair-curtained eyes. Ray hadn't known shit. Where had this kid gone? He stared at himself for half a minute, while Bernie watched.

"So what is it you had to tell me?"

Ray cranked his eyes up. Bernie's picture must be on one of the other tables. Maybe they'd look for it later. "Milo didn't do it. Kevin did."

"Do what?"

"Kill Holly."

"Says who?"

"Kevin."

Bernie chose his words carefully.

"Not much you can do about it now. Spilt milk, you know?"

"There has to be something."

"I don't think so. You'll just have to live with it, but don't let it screw you up. You've got responsibilities, Ray. Milo can't hear you say you're sorry. When something's too late, it's too late forever. You have to move on, know what I mean?"

"I fucked up my life."

"Join the club. Cry in your beer, why don't you."

"Is that supposed to be sympathy, or what?"

"I give you good advice and all you can do is sit there telling me your life's fucked. Is that supposed to be coping, or what?"

"Fuck you, pal."

"Back to you, bozo."

"Okay, my life isn't fucked, just very messed up."

"So's my canary's cage. What you do, you take the old shitted-on newspaper out and slide a new sheet in. Works every time."

"Newspaper."

"New. Fresh. Why don't you get married again?"

"Why don't you?"

"As a matter of fact, I'm thinking about it. Been dating a certain lady, a real nice person, works in real estate."

"Anybody's wife?"

"No."

"Should be a new approach for you, then."

"I'm not gonna fight with you, Ray. You can say what you like."

"Forget it."

"Good idea."

They drank half their beers. Ray set his down first.

"You ever get the feeling that nothing is the way we get told it is? Like there's really no difference between right and wrong, good and bad, it's just how you look at it, you know?"

"I'm looking at this beer, tasting it . . . and it's definitely wrong. This is a bad beer. Must be imported."

"I'm serious. Name me one solid thing that's positively true and righteous and can't ever be screwed up. Don't say marriage and don't say love; they can go bad and there's always two sides. Don't say democracy and freedom and being a patriot and all; I don't need to tell you about the war and those lying assholes in the White House. And don't say God; no one even knows his address. Don't say family, either; a family's an accident waiting to happen six different ways. Name me one rock-solid thing that's true no matter how you turn it around or stand it on its head or whatever. I'd like to know about it, I really would."

"One true thing?"

"Right."

Bernie stared at his glass, frowning.

"You're trying to turn me into a barroom philosopher. How should I know what's true? I'm a cop, not fucking Plato. You want another bad beer?"

"I think it's good beer. I'll take one."

"Be right back."

Ray stared again at his portrait. He knew no more now than he had known then, was simply older. Maybe when he was older still, he'd know nothing more than he knew today. Older than that, he'd quit worrying about it and concentrate on his rheumatism, probably die as ignorant as the boy beneath his nose. He almost didn't care about anything any more, but Bernie was right; he had responsibilities. Kevin and Autie weren't too impressed with him as a father, for reasons related to his shortcomings as a mere man, fallible, crippled by lack of wisdom. They were still his if he wanted them, if he would let them see he needed them. That's what he would do. What else was there? A foaming glass slid across the black-and-white image of himself, erased the young man there.

"What you were saying about nothing being solid, Ray, I know what you mean. I saw something one time in Khe Sanh, this dead VC sitting propped up on his AK-47, the top of his head sliced clean off by shrapnel, I guess, but he's still sitting up with his gun propped against his chest, still with his face on, just the top of his head missing, and it rains all the time out there, you know, and the inside of his head was filled with water, no kidding, maybe the brain got lifted out by the impact, I don't know, or vaporized maybe, but it's full of water, and in the water there's this bird, a little green bird splashing around having the greatest time in the birdbath in this VC's head. You see something like that, you know it's a crazy world all right. I never forgot it, never told anyone about it till now."

"A birdbrain."

"Exactly. A birdbrain. Drink your good-bad beer."

They drank several more, then left, said goodbye in the

parking lot. When Bernie had driven off, Ray began walking. He needed time to think, and so decided to take the long way home. It would lead him around many corners, along darkened avenues, and across his own faltering path. It would lead him by and by to his children.